THE MAGE'S DESTINY

ALENA JAMES

CRIMSON DOVE PRESS

Published in Australia by Crimson Dove Press

Edited by Krystal Nichol

Cover design by MiblArt

Alena James

The Mage's Destiny

ISBN: 978-0-6457158-4-2

A catalogue record for this book is available from the National Library of Australia

THE MAGE'S DESTINY

ALENA JAMES

CRIMSON DOVE PRESS

CONTENT WARNING

Blood, violence, gaslighting/mind control, toxic relationships, self-harm, implied sexual assault, mental illness, physical assault, BDSM themes, claustrophobia, graphic scenes, adult content, mentions of drug use, coarse language.

PROLOGUE

Candles perched themselves atop the floorboards of the room like dozens of curious owls. In the middle of the shimmering flock stood a woman in a white dress, tall and still, hair streaked with veins of gold. A smile lifted her delicate features as she gazed upon the Sorcerer before her. He loomed, a full head taller than her, cloaked in darkness. Black outfit, black hair, deep midnight eyes. He breathed out as if he didn't expect her to be there.

"I'm so glad to see you, darling," his words echoed around the bare walls, amplifying, splitting into a thousand coos.

She lowered her head, acknowledging him. "It's good to be here. Thank you."

The Sorcerer took a few steps forward, transfixed by the pedestal behind her shoulder. She turned to join his eyes upon the sight. Protected by a circle of salt, in the centre of a chalk pentagram, was a cast-iron pedestal and velvet box. The velvet held a gold claw, which itself cradled the most magnificent stone she had ever seen. A sapphire of a depth so rare one could lose their mind staring into it. Adrift in a network of reflections that go deeper into the brilliant blue, darker and darker, until the power of the stone imprisoned their soul. On the verge of her hearing, a name rustled like autumn leaves in the wind.

She nodded. Her lips moved: "Caerulus."

"Yes, darling. I got it for you." The Sorcerer approached the pedestal, breaking the protection of the salt, the chalk, with precise movements. As he took the gold claw in his hand, careful not to touch the stone with bare skin, she chuckled.

Too much power. It can turn anyone into ashes.

The Sorcerer whispered a simple spell. The ring on his index finger flashed green, and a solid gold chain flowed off his hand, encircling the gem in an intricate cage.

"It is all yours now, darling. You'll never be powerless again." He returned to her side, holding the artefact in his open hand.

"*He*. Not *it*," she corrected, itching to grab the stone off him. She had to be patient, though. Play nice and be compliant. Let him think he was in control. She frowned, straining her memory to remember his name—Corbin, her Master. Of course.

A shadow of annoyance crossed his face but he quickly regained a calm demeanour. "You're right. Does he...talk to you?"

She didn't respond as Corbin wrapped the chain around her neck and locked it in place. His hands were gentle, pulling her hair through to settle it back on her shoulders. A fleeting touch lingered on her skin longer than his hands were on her. She allowed herself a small smile. Yes, she could feel his desire from the moment she opened her eyes. The Sorcerer was still careful, letting her adjust, but this wouldn't last for long. Her gaze shifted down to the precious stone that settled in the crease between her breasts. Caerulus warmed his gold cage, radiating power in waves as if he was breathing, aligning his rhythm with her pulse. She let out a satisfied breath. The stone's presence was comforting. This was home. This was where she belonged. Wherever she went, he would follow. Or would *she* be following him instead?

It didn't take long for Corbin to clean up all traces of their presence. She chuckled again, listening to him talk about this place. A once sacred ground, where magic ran so strong he could use it without an artefact. The place he'd been looking for once he'd found that Caerulus, the stone of legend, was able to achieve what he wanted.

Your heart's desire. Oh, you don't have to explain, I feel it in my bones.

She kept her silence as he threw one last glance at the area.

Everything needed to be back to normal to make sure the Guards he'd put under a sleeping spell didn't get upset.

Flames were snuffed out of existence, the owls giving one last wink. "It's all over now, darling. We can go home."

She smoothed the invisible folds on her dress and smiled at him, this time with a purpose. Caerulus was now perfectly synced with her body. Confidence became her. Eager to stay alone so she could explore her new friend, she took Corbin's hand.

"Of course. As you wish."

The gem sparked, colouring her vision a gentle shade of azure. She had him in her mind now, and the whisper was becoming clearer. It wouldn't be too long before she could hear him properly. Before she could navigate his network of reflections.

PART ONE

CHAPTER 1. AYLA

The body of a young girl hovered above an altar, as if suspended in the liquid of an invisible jar, foetal in the way she curled into herself. A tall man with a face obscured by shadows unsheathed a dagger and presented a sacrificial chalice. The snaking gold pattern that adorned the chalice stood out in the darkness. The man placed his dagger against the girl's throat. Ayla watched calmly as the cup filled with liquid, red droplets escaping the rim. A lifeless thud fell on deaf ears as the young girl's body finally met the altar.

"You need sustenance. This will help while I'm working on another solution." The man handed Ayla the chalice.

Reluctantly, Ayla accepted it. The blood warmed up the cool metal and she wondered if there was magic involved.

Of course, there is magic. Everything he does for me is magic. Every word, every action. Killing these girls to help me stay alive. Looking for an answer in his old books. He'll do anything for me. Love made him weak. How pathetic.

Ayla startled at the strange, cold words in her mind. She never believed love made people weak. She never had thoughts like that in her life. Calculated, soulless, cruel. It was as if someone else was whispering them in her ears, and she didn't like it. Yet, part of her was responding to them against her will. The part that took the chalice and pressed it against her lips. The part that smiled at the warmth from the drink which tasted like mulled wine.

Her own body reacted in a strange way. His gaze was penetrating even though she couldn't see his eyes. Her pulse quickened. Joy filled her existence. She was weightless and free. Just a little more, and she would be able to reach her magic. A few more drinks like that, and there would be nothing to stop her.

***

Ayla delivered one last stroke of her brush and studied her painting. The canvas was dominated by greys, black blooms and monochromatic lichens disfiguring the white undercoat. Like all others in her collection, the picture was misshapen and abstract, though she knew the truth was far from it. Within the fumes of the paint was a safe space that gave her solace after those nightmares of blood-filled chalices. A beautiful world of never-ending fog—ugly to an untrained eye, but gorgeous in its ability to let you be imperfect—that she saw in her dreams. Not quite dreams, to be exact. The twilight state when she was neither asleep nor awake. Regardless of what it was, she felt good whenever she was able to bring it onto the canvas. Who cared how many she'd already used? The enchanted house provided an infinite supply of anything she needed, and she took advantage of that.

Soaking her brushes in warm water, Ayla ignored the strange whispers in her head that reminded her of the latest visions. Every time, there was a different girl sacrificed, but the feeling of odd satisfaction was the same. Each of them was a little too bright, a little too vivid. Too much red. She needed to grey it out of her mind, and the canvas always came to the rescue.

It's not real. It wasn't me. I would have never thought this way about anything. Wouldn't I remember if this actually happened?

Ayla's stomach churned as she thought about all the gaps in her memory. It pained to bring up the time, just before she left her old Master, of the strange sickness that consumed her. How that man promised he was going to help her heal. How desperate she was to relieve the pain that claimed her seemingly longer and longer each day. Wouldn't she have agreed to do whatever it took?

Wouldn't her conscience give her mercy by denying those painful memories?

"Wow, you really like your greys," a melodic voice pierced her dark thoughts.

Ayla turned around, a rushed smile on her lips. "It's nothing." She hurried to turn the easel around as if it was something to be ashamed of. "Hey, Lyssa."

"Hey," her new friend replied. The concern on her tanned face stirred up a mild agony. Silence hung long enough that she began to fidget with the ends of her glossy, chocolate hair. "When did you get up?"

"Not too long ago," Ayla gulped, chasing away memories of the dread that woke her in the wee hours of the morning, long before the sun came up. Lyssa didn't need to know this; the night terrors were Ayla's own demons to fight.

"I think you should see someone about these early mornings and your..." Lyssa pointed at the stack of canvases stashed in the corner. She hesitated, as if the paint would send rootlets to spread in the dampness of the air, before finishing her sentence. "Paintings."

Ayla bit her lip, cursing herself for not hiding her latest works with the others. There was no need for Lyssa to find out how tall the actual stack was. "I'm okay, really. Just getting used to my new life is all."

Lyssa shook her head but didn't push it. They'd had this conversation a few times before, with the same outcome every time.

A delightful aroma of skilfully brewed coffee broke through the awkward pause. It floated around the house, announcing the arrival of another beautiful day. The house that predicted her every need, enchanted to grant her every wish before she even knew it herself. The home straight from a dream. Here at Whitestone, things were different, but after her misadventures in the world of the Sorcerers, she was wary of trusting anything blindly.

Lyssa's face lit up when they walked into the open living area. Breakfast for two was already set up. A plate full of waffles, two bowls with generous scoops of vanilla ice-cream, and the ever-present cappuccinos with a smiling sun pattern in the froth. Perfect as always. Chilly breeze touched the light curtains, bringing in the fragrance of spring flowers. The smell of new beginnings. Nothing could compare to this.

"What a glorious morning!" Lyssa sighed in content, sipping at her drink.

Ayla chewed her lip, lost in thoughts about her immediate future. Holidays couldn't last forever, and the last term of school was about to start, though she only arrived to Whitestone a few short weeks ago. She didn't think the school's board would allow her to skip months of studies so she could start a new year with the beginners. Her name was already on the list of students. From the lengthy chats with her new friend, she knew a fair bit about local laws. Once a student was in Whitestone, they had to join the others, though passing the exams wasn't as harsh as at the Sorcerers' Academy. As always, thinking about that place delivered a blow of fear to her stomach. Ayla did her best to ignore it, serving herself a waffle. No need to stress over this now. She was safe. That part of her life was over.

Apart from lessons, there were other students to meet. Everyone was too busy with exams during her first week, and then spring called the students home to visit their families out of town. Lyssa stayed back to help her adjust, but they never saw anyone else from their class. Only the town's folk were out in the tidy streets. Friendly and accepting, they reminded Ayla of her old home. The little town where she'd spent her childhood, that she was forced to leave so unexpectedly.

"When do the classes begin?"

Lyssa threw back her hair and gently squeezed Ayla's hand. "In a couple of days. Everyone is coming back from the Equinox vacation today. Of course, you'll get to take it easy—after all, you've only been here for three weeks. Nobody expects you to know all the things that we've studied all year. You won't have to sit the exams. This term is about you getting comfortable with your new life, that's all." Her face brightened up with another idea. "Oh, some of the students are coming to meet you today! Not everyone at once, cause Bla…uh, we were asked to give you some space to adjust."

Ayla's eyes were fixed on the froth of her coffee. She preferred not to think about Blaze, though he was the person who brought her there in the first place. Something about this white-haired man didn't sit right with her. Maybe it was due to the strange shyness she felt in his presence, so much that she couldn't speak to him directly. This was something that had never happened to her, and it made her nervous.

"It's okay, Lyssa. I know Blaze left the instructions."

Yet another awkward silence hung in the air as Lyssa focused on her meal. The sound of her cutlery rattled about the space between them. Ayla picked up a fork and twisted it between her fingers. She knew that Blaze would have given her new friend some information about her past. However, there was no way of knowing how much of it he was aware of himself. Lyssa didn't ask any questions, as if Ayla's sudden appearance in the only enchanted house in town was a completely normal event. Her eyes betrayed her, though. It seemed like the young woman wanted to know so much more than she was told, yet she always restrained herself.

Ayla picked up her coffee and froze. The froth was now gone; only the whitened drink was left in the cup. Coffee with milk, sweetened with fine sugar. Exactly the way she liked it. Exactly the way Corbin ordered it to be served to her in his house. His way of apologising for the things he'd done. Terrible things that still haunted her through the haze that somehow remained in her mind. Her hands shook as she dropped the cup on the table. The brown liquid spread over the white wood like wildfire in a dry forest. Another trigger. Another memory. Gasping for air, Ayla imagined it like her own blood gushing from an open wound. The knife of a hooded Apprentice and his sinister words. *Devil's spawn. An abomination, out of this world.* His empty eyes and a veil of darkness that engulfed his figure. Then, the circle of candles and Corbin's ritual where he offered his life to save hers. How he never told her what price he took from her to pay her end of the bargain.

Ayla grabbed onto the edge of the table, steadying herself. Intrusive thoughts didn't stop. She ached for a faraway home, stuck behind the walls of the magic town of Whitestone that remained hidden from the rest of the world. The only ways out were portals that only higher-level students or Mages could open. She couldn't run back to the sleepy little town she grew up in. Where she knew every friendly face. Every street. Where she was happy.

Where her father, Darren, was brutally murdered, his death setting off a chain of dreadful events.

Heart beating violently in her chest, she gasped for air as memories of last year overwhelmed her mind. She could hardly register Lyssa's presence as if it was a distant picture of a futile attempt at comfort. The scenes of her failures and humiliation flew before her, one worse than the other. Blood on the white carpet of her living room back home. The terrifying auction where she was sold like a piece of meat. The bullies at the Academy. The terror she experienced every time her Master showed interest in her. The gaps in her memories she couldn't fill no matter how hard she tried. The awful nightmares and never-ending migraines.

Mint and camomile. The sweet smell filled her lungs and she finally breathed out, calming down. Somehow, she ended up in her bed again, a warm blanket tucked around her. The soothing scent came from a diffuser on her night table. She steadied her chest, silently thanking the house. It was good to feel cared for.

Someone's voice was coming from the hallway, pricking Ayla's ears.

"Don't worry, you made the right call," a pleasant male voice reassured. "I told you, Lyssa, these episodes are bound to happen but will hopefully lose their intensity as she settles."

"I know, Blaze. It's just so awful that there's nothing I can do when it happens. I don't even know what triggered it! I was so careful, just like you told me. It's heart-breaking. What happened to her back there?"

There was a small pause before the man spoke again. "It's not my story to tell. If Ayla feels like sharing, she'll do it when she's ready. If not, please respect her privacy."

"Of course. Kindness and patience," Lyssa replied. "I sometimes feel that I may not be the best choice for her, you know? Maybe someone like Saree would have been better. An Empath would be able to take her pain away."

"No," the man's voice was firm. "I won't risk a quick fix. The only way to properly heal is by learning to deal with difficult things. And you are a perfect fit. You're doing a great job, and I think your personalities are a good match. There's no need to doubt yourself."

"Thank you, Blaze, this means a lot. I just wish I could help more."

Ayla slid her feet from the embrace of the blanket and carefully lowered them on the polished oak floor. Thoughts floated in her mind like driftwood on the calm waters after a storm. She wondered if she really heard Blaze's voice or if this was an aftermath of her "episode". He didn't sound scary at all; maybe if she didn't see him, she could work up the courage to talk.

"You're doing plenty. I think she's awake now, so I'd better leave." His voice trailed off and a barely perceptible sound announced a closing door.

When Ayla stepped out of the bedroom, Lyssa was in the hallway alone. She spun around with a ready smile, flicking her hair behind her back.

"How are you feeling?" Lyssa's sweet voice held a small strain.

"Much better now, thank you." Ayla wondered if she should ask her friend about Blaze's visit but decided to keep it to herself. If there had been nobody there, Lyssa might think she was losing her mind.

The day went on as normal. After a cup of herbal tea, the girls went out for another walk around Whitestone. The changes were dramatic now that the students were back. The streets were busier, with groups of young people chatting here and there. The smell of freshly brewed coffee and hot pastries teased like a siren's call. Most students waved to Lyssa and came up to say hello, but their faces and names quickly blurred together in Ayla's mind.

"We're going to have a few people pop in later," Lyssa reminded once they returned to the house.

Ayla drew in a breath as anxiety crept closer. "I'm a little nervous," she admitted, tugging at a stray strand of her hair. Pain was a welcome distraction that always helped her re-focus; it didn't let her down this time, either.

"Hey, it's okay. There won't be too many, or so I hope. Just some of my friends who would love to meet you, maybe some more students who are curious. We can kick them out if it gets too much. Oh, oh, I hope my friend Carla is coming—she handcrafts marionettes, sews delicate little buttons for eyes, and has the most beautiful red hair you'll ever lay eyes on. I haven't seen her in a while, but she's one of those people who whips wind in your presence and hollows you out when she leaves. Much like I feel you could." Lyssa winked, threading her fingers through her long locks. "All my friends are dying to know you. You'll love it here, I promise!"

CHAPTER 2. AYLA

S he hardly had a chance to finish her sentence when the first visitor knocked on the door. A friendly face of a younger girl with impossibly violet eyes and neat blond braids swam into focus. A tray of cookies cut in the shape of stars sat in her hands. "Hi, Ayla. I'm Saree, one of your classmates. These are for you. I hope you like ginger!"

Ayla accepted the gift, wondering how this new girl knew her name. She corrected herself. After all, she was probably the only one starting in the last term of the year. All other students likely knew each other, though she hadn't been able to gauge the size of the school yet. Everyone would be curious, even more so when they found out about her origins. There were bound to be questions. She had to brace herself and keep it together.

Saree was already in the kitchen, removing the plastic from the cookie tray. Lyssa exchanged a few words with her and the girls giggled. Ayla tensed as she wondered if she would fit in with the new circle, if Lyssa would stick to her side when her other existing friends showed up. If they would accept Ayla as one of their own or if she would be ostracised here, just like at the Sorcerers' Academy.

The door opened again, this time bringing in a young man who held a large bottle of fruit wine in his hands. Another girl came in, then a young couple. Ayla smiled automatically, accepting gifts and thanking her visitors. With so many things happening at once, she didn't feel stable. The living room filled up with voices saying hello and catching up on the latest news after the break.

Her claustrophobia raised its ugly head as the house seemed too small to contain the crowd. Ayla excused herself and stepped out onto the front porch. Filling her lungs with fresh afternoon air, she counted to ten and back. All those people were there to meet her. They all had questions that she had to answer. She could take a little time for a breather, but she couldn't leave her guests unattended for too long.

Gentle breeze coaxed her eyes to open. At first, she didn't register the abnormality. It was physically impossible for a large animal to creep up so close to her without making a sound. Especially for an animal with hooves.

A snow white unicorn stared at her with its dark eyes carrying all the wisdom and love in the world. Its glowing coat, the flowing silky mane, the sparkling horn suddenly filled Ayla's whole universe. She stood still, marvelling at the beast's beauty. Didn't the old books say a unicorn would only show itself to those pure of heart? A mythical creature from the fairy tales, the symbol of purity and white magic itself. Ayla blinked back tears of happiness. This was incredible. Encountering a real unicorn was the highest honour imaginable. The most impossible thing of all.

Ayla sniffled, thinking about the odds of meeting something this wonderful on the very night she met other students. Something wasn't quite right. The unicorn's mane fluttered, yet there was no more wind. Ayla frowned and studied it closer. The horn had a tiny spark on it which didn't flicker; it looked more like a tin star glued on top. The body was covered with beautiful fur, yet no defined muscles rolled under the skin as one would expect from an active animal. Ayla shook her head, and the phantom unicorn dissipated into thin air.

Someone's clapping completely broke the spell. Ayla turned around to see a whole audience. A few young men and women, including Lyssa, stood on the doorstep, admiration in their eyes.

"Good job, newbie!" grinned a tall young man with ginger hair and a freckled face. "Only a couple new recruits so far have managed to pass my Unicorn test!"

Lyssa took Ayla's hand. "Rowan is our genius in illusions," she declared, casting a flirty glance at him. "He's been doing this prank for ages, and most of the time our newest members believe it's a real creature and try to touch it. How did you know it was an illusion?"

"Um, I didn't," Ayla mumbled, but nobody was listening.

The students pooled out of the house, their chatter filling the air. No long, red hair floated among the heads—Carla wasn't here or she'd know it. Absent-mindedly, Ayla registered that most of them were wearing a comfortable *gi* which seemed to be a uniform here, and considered changing from her summer dress before starting her lessons. Their outfit looked much more appropriate for the location.

"Were you born into a Sorcerers' family?" Saree's voice broke through her thoughts and everyone went quiet.

Ayla looked up into the sky, reminiscing. She didn't have to share her life story; a few details should be enough to tame people's curiosity. If she was careful, she could avoid the painful subjects.

"A Sorcerer named Darren found me when I was a child. I still don't remember anything about my earlier years or who my parents were. Darren raised me as his own daughter and then...um, things happened." She looked away, gulping down bitter tears. It wasn't until Blaze took her to Whitestone that she had a chance to properly grieve Darren's death at the hand of a murderer. She spent hours upon hours thinking about the motive, never arriving at anything worthy. Yes, she knew that she was the original target, but there was no explanation for their reasoning. The group of people who were hunting her remained a mystery. Good thing that at least, no one tried to kill her at Whitestone.

"He taught you how to use Sorcerer magic?" Saree asked, wide-eyed. Whispers rose in the air like tentacles of the morning fog.

"No. I didn't know anything about magic until another Sorcerer took me in." She closed her eyes, reliving her time with Corbin. It all started so well! There was no way she could have known where that path would have taken her. "Besides, I don't think a Mage can use Sorcerer magic anyway."

"That's right! They use artefacts and incantations encrypted in ancient runes. This is not like our pure, natural magic," Rowan stated with a confident smile. Following a flick on his hand, a falcon materialised on his shoulder and took off with a triumphant cry. "See? I can make things appear out of nothing. No need for tricks."

"Illusions *are* a trick." Lyssa nudged him.

Giggles infected the crowd as Rowan scrambled for a defence. Ayla watched them, smiling. The light-hearted banter was something she needed in her life after last year's troubles.

"What was it like? The world of the Sorcerers?"

The question startled her. Ayla caught the gaze of a tall blond girl who was standing in the back of the crowd. The girl was smiling, but there was no warmth in her pale blue eyes. Ayla took in her stance, wondering how this visitor slipped in without introductions. She was sure everyone else came to say hello, even though she didn't remember half the names. The faces, though, were her forte. She was confident she hadn't met this girl.

"I didn't see much of it. My Master kept me locked up most of the time in one house or another. The only other thing I knew was the Sorcerers' Academy, which was the worst experience in my life." She bit the inside of her cheek as she thought back to her time at the dreaded place. The bullies and cruel punishments. The humiliation and degradation. The cold treatment at home where she was starved and isolated from the rest of the world.

"Yeah, my first year at Whitestone was pretty rough, too. I kept getting in trouble for being a pest once I started learning about illusions," Rowan chuckled and stopped when Ayla cast a burning glance at him. "Um, probably not as rough as yours though."

"Hey, it's not a competition." Lyssa gestured for him to be quiet.

"It wasn't all that bad," Ayla uttered, deciding to lighten up the topic. "Despite being one of the Sorcerers, my adoptive father Darren was kind to me. I guess my other Master, Corbin, tried his best in his own way, too." She ignored the voice of protest in her head, brushing off the dread she now felt every time she thought about him. "Besides, you get used to how things are and it just becomes a norm."

"There's nothing of that sort at Whitestone. We're all here for each other," Saree declared, a solemn expression on her face.

Ayla studied the approving nods around her. People seemed compassionate and accepting, but there was no way of knowing if this was another ruse to trap her. She drew a deep breath and counted to ten. No, she had to stop thinking like that. An open mind for a new community would do her good. She thought about Blaze, the person who brought her there for a chance at a new beginning. Even though it had been some time since she'd seen him, he would show up eventually. She had to work up the courage to speak to him and thank him for this opportunity.

"So, Ayla, how come you've only arrived here now?" The blond girl's voice slashed her ears like a dagger. Arms crossed on her chest, eyes stone cold behind the impossibly long eyelashes. No trust, no mercy. Ayla wondered if this was her normal behaviour or if she herself had somehow done something wrong.

"I guess, it just happened," she managed a response, hoping this would be enough. The girl seemed a few years older than her; in fact, older than anyone in the room. Perhaps, she was one of the teachers or an assistant of sorts. *No way. A teacher wouldn't be wearing clothes like that*, Ayla thought to herself, contemplating the girl's mini-dress with a deep V-neck that accentuated her large breasts. The girl chuckled, delicately covering her mouth with her long fingers.

"Oh, do tell us! Everyone here wants to know all about you. After all, we don't always get recruits from the Sorcerers!"

With a deep breath, Ayla closed her eyes to collect her thoughts. She knew this was bound to happen. In the three weeks she spent here with Lyssa, she learned a great deal about Whitestone and its students. It was good to put faces to the names of Lyssa's friends. Saree the Empath who could feel other people's emotions. Rowan the illusion-maker. Jason the plant-whisperer. Cheeky Levi the mind-reader. They all seemed like wonderful, understanding people. She wasn't so sure about all others.

There was no way to back out. If she didn't tell them herself, they would make assumptions. There were many more other students in the house, apart from Lyssa's friends. It was a blessing in disguise. At least she'd tell them all at once and won't have to deal with Chinese whispers later.

With a deep breath, she opened her eyes and turned to the crowd. "I got very sick, and my Master tried to find a way to help me recover. Blaze told me that coming here would help, and it did. That's all I know."

The blond girl scoffed. "Is that it? How did Blaze find you? Did he tell you that you were a Mage?"

Ayla's forehead crawled with sweat. "He just...brought me here. I don't remember much about that night."

Lyssa cleared her throat behind Ayla's back. "Cake is served, everyone! Come grab a piece before it's gone!"

The excited crowd shifted towards the kitchen, interrupting the interrogation. The blonde held a long gaze at Ayla and a strange grin crossed her lips.

Ayla picked up a napkin and wiped the sweat off her forehead. Lyssa's warm hand squeezed hers. "Are you okay? Do you need a break?"

"It's alright. Thank you though." Ayla looked at her with gratitude. She picked up a glass of cold water and took a few long sips. When she looked around again, the blonde was nowhere to be found. Maybe she imagined her. She wouldn't be surprised if her mind played tricks. Maybe Lyssa was right and she needed a break after all.

A young man with ruffled brown hair caught her eye with his dazzling smile, the brightest in the whole room. Ayla froze, feeling his gaze roll over her like an avalanche. He must have been a few years older than her, with tiny wrinkles starting to settle in the smile lines. He was of a stocky build, and wouldn't be much taller than her. Ayla's thoughts automatically went to their height comparison. He seemed to be perfect to go dancing with. He wouldn't have to slouch, and his hand would rest easily on her waist. Excellent alignment.

She pressed her cold palms to her flushed cheeks and scorned herself for these thoughts. It was her first time meeting everyone and she needed to make a good impression. Not blush like a schoolgirl at the sight of a handsome stranger.

"How are you finding it here at Whitestone?" the young man asked, approaching her. Ayla relaxed as she dived into the shallow river of small talk about the weather, food and local delights that Lyssa had told her about. The conversation flowed smoothly from there on. She felt an unfriendly eye on her every now and then, but whenever she turned to its source, she couldn't find it.

The evening rolled in before long, and her guests started to take their leave. The young man was one of the last visitors to say goodbye. "It's very brave what you've done, Ayla. Leaving your whole life behind and taking a leap of faith coming here. You should be really proud of yourself. Just thought I'd tell you, in case you needed to hear it today."

Stunned, she blinked at him. "Oh. Thank you, uh..."

"Mace," he replied, lighting up with a smile again. "Let me know if you need anything. I know Lyssa's got you covered," he winked at Lyssa who playfully swatted at him with a tea towel. "But if you need help, or want to talk, or anything...I'm here."

He slightly bowed to her and left. Ayla turned back to the kitchen and nearly walked into the blonde.

"Be careful, sweetie. Just a piece of friendly advice." The blonde's voice was smooth yet venomous like a snake in the grass. "You probably don't know but Mace is dating my friend Ingrid. I don't think you want any trouble, do you?"

"What? No, I didn't..."

"Good girl. I knew you'd understand. Bye-bye for now!" The blonde turned her back and her heels clicked on the wooden floor.

"Wow. Okay." Ayla blinked when the blonde's back disappeared behind the door. Her condescending tone wasn't something Ayla was used to, nor did she expect to hear it in a circle of friends. Luckily, the blonde was the last visitor and their exchange remained private from the rest of the classmates. Lyssa stayed back to help tidy up, and now she was filling up the basin with some hot water to do the dishes. She flicked her long hair back before turning to Ayla.

"I'm sorry, Ayla. Sherice seems to be having a hard time accepting new people in her environment. Especially pretty girls who appear out of nowhere!" She giggled, waving a soapy finger at Ayla. Her naïve attempt to distract negative thoughts of the evening didn't work. Ayla still frowned, thinking about the short time she saw the new people, but chose not to pursue the sensitive topic until she'd had a chance to ponder it on her own.

"How do I go about the school? Do I need to sign any paperwork? Are the classes formed by the age of the students?"

"Don't worry, we don't have any kids here. It's called a school, but it's more like a university. You don't need to do anything. Blaze had settled all formalities before he brought you here." Lyssa paused, watching her reaction. "Is something wrong?"

There was no way to describe it. Ever since she set foot in this new house, Ayla felt his presence, though she didn't see him. Blaze was a mystery. A man who supposedly fixed her life by bringing her to the right community. She didn't belong with the Sorcerers, that much was true. Somehow, her old Master, Corbin, let her leave, though she didn't know how the two men came to the agreement. She couldn't speak to Blaze thanks to the strange shyness she felt in his presence. It was too bizarre.

"I just struggle with understanding it all," she confessed. "I'm grateful to be here, don't get me wrong. But Blaze...I don't know where I stand with him. My old Master allowed me to leave, so does it mean that Blaze...owns me now?"

Lyssa dropped a soapy mug on the floor. Dozens of shards flew in all directions, sharp pieces coated in soft white foam like cotton candy full of daggers. Ayla rushed to grab paper towels, and for a moment both girls were quiet, sweeping up. Once the floor was safe again, Lyssa replied.

"Nobody owns anyone in this community, it's something that the Sorcerers do. Not us. Here, women are equal to men. You'll be treated just like any other person."

"So, he's not going to do anything to me?"

Eyes full of concern, Lyssa dried her hands with the towel and sat Ayla on the couch. "Oh, Ayla. What happened to you there?" She didn't need an answer, though.

Ayla shook her head, trying to chase away the memories of Corbin. All the time she spent locked up in one room or another. When he got into her mind without asking, keeping her under a will-binding spell. She shuddered, a sudden chill crawling up her spine.

No, it's over. It can't happen again. I can't take it. Please, let it be over.

"Hey, it's okay. Nobody's going to force you to do anything here. Blaze, of all people, will never hurt you. He brought you here to help you have a good life in a supporting community, not drown you in trouble." Lyssa took Ayla's cold hands in hers, warming them up. Despite her near panic, Ayla smiled in gratitude. Her new friend was amazing, she knew it. From the recent conversation, she also knew that Blaze was the one who assigned her. Some day she was going to ask Lyssa directly. When she was sure she wasn't breaking any unspoken rules.

"I'm okay," she tried to sound convincing. Blaze's image bothered her as it always did whenever she thought about him. For some reason, she didn't want to discuss it with Lyssa, as if her inner turmoil was something to be ashamed of.

Taking the cue, Lyssa stood up. "It looks like you might have had enough for one night. One of the Healers will drop by tomorrow morning to have a quick check-up, so you'll need to have plenty of sleep before then."

"Why would a Healer want to check me up? I'm not sick, at least not anymore," Ayla protested. A bad feeling curled in her chest like a snake.

Almost at the doorstep, Lyssa glanced at her again. "It's just a formality. They'll assess your health, both physical and mental. This is done to make sure you are in the best shape for the lessons, and so that the teachers know your limits. It's not scary at all, Ayla. We all had a check-up before starting the year."

Ayla sighed, knowing that she would have to comply. There would be nothing out of the ordinary if everyone had to do it. It would be a regular procedure. Then why couldn't she shake off the bad feeling?

She said goodnight to her friend and closed the door. She had no reason to worry. The town was safe, and there were no mind games or tricks or lies here. In her three weeks at Whitestone, she only saw a regular life of regular people, in a regular little town.

The chilly breeze lifted the lightweight curtains in her bedroom, reminding her that there were still a few weeks to go before summer. The window needed to be closed for the night, lest she'd catch a cold. Her hand touched the wooden frame and froze.

A silhouette of a large white tiger flashed before her eyes. She blinked, calling to her senses, bringing to mind the way she saw through Rowan's illusion unicorn. She thought about the slow realisation that it was fake, as if she watched a performer at a puppet theatre. Her focus shifted to the shape of the tiger, its mane a brilliant white under the light of the waxing moon. The animal turned its head and for a moment their eyes met. Ayla held its strangely intelligent gaze for a few long seconds before looking away. She was confident this was not an illusion. A large predator in her front yard just sat there studying her. Nothing in its demeanour showed any carnal interest. On the contrary, the tiger watched her like a curiosity. The moment didn't last long. The animal lowered his head as if bowing, then turned its back and leaped over the fence.

Hands now shaking, Ayla slammed the window shut and bolted the frame. Her heart raced as if she'd just run a sprint. Maybe having wild animals roam the streets was a normality here, though she hadn't noticed any so far—maybe she hadn't paid attention. Or perhaps, the perfect new town wasn't as safe as it seemed.

CHAPTER 3. AYLA

The Healer turned out to be a sweet lady in her mid-sixties. Her faded cotton dress and comfortable leather shoes that have seen better days betrayed her as someone who didn't care much about looks. Ayla squeezed out an uneasy smile to welcome the newcomer as she showed up on her doorstep first thing the next morning.

"My name is Rhonda, I'm one of the Healers here. I'm just checking in to see how you're adjusting to the new life and if there's anything you need."

Ayla nodded in acknowledgement. She wasn't sure if she liked the constant attention, but this was a great chance for her to speak to someone other than Lyssa. Even though her friend was chatty and open about most things, there were some areas she avoided.

"I like it here. The people seem lovely." She gulped, remembering Sherice's attitude the night before. "Mostly. This house is straight out of dreams, and I have a great friend who welcomed me here and told me a little about this new life. I understand Lyssa was assigned to help me, right?" Ayla studied the Healer's face, alert to any changes that might betray any emotion. There was none of the ordinary, though.

Rhonda put her hands on the table between them and smiled. "Yes. It's not very common for students to start in the last term. Of course, we wanted to make sure you were comfortable here before you transitioned into studies. Lyssa volunteered as soon as Blaze made the announcement, though your story captivated a lot of other students. I believe you'll have a lot of friends here."

"Does everyone here know my story?" Ayla shifted her weight uncomfortably. She never was a spotlight-loving person. Going into a new school of magic was a stressful event. There was no way of knowing if she would succeed this time or fail miserably, as she did at the Sorcerers' Academy. At least at the Academy, she had Corbin as back-up. Here, she had no one. After all, Lyssa herself was just another student.

"Only the basics," Rhonda soothed as she looked at her with her kind blue eyes. "That you came from the Sorcerers' side and that you will be starting slowly. Blaze will be your Mentor for the time being, as he is the one who brought you here and knows more about you than any of us."

Ayla thought back to the strange night when she left her Master's house to follow the white-haired Mage into the unknown.

"What does a Mentor do?" she inquired, eyes on the Healer's face.

"A Mentor will guide you while you're finding your feet. Blaze is a great candidate for you. He's been bringing recruits to study at Whitestone for years now. This time is special, considering your history, so he'll stick around for a while. He's going to do something he's never done before." Rhonda beckoned her with a wrinkly finger, and Ayla leaned forward. "He'll be teaching combat training as an optional course. It's currently full, but I'm sure he'll make room for you if you wish to join."

Ayla pushed her half-empty drink away, her mood suddenly sour. "If the course is optional, I don't have to take it, right?"

Rhonda nodded, a strange concern in her eyes. "That's right. Don't you want to?"

"No. I feel really uncomfortable in his presence." She gulped, wondering how often she'd have to see him. "Is it possible to get someone else as a Mentor?"

The older woman shook her head, a sad expression now clear on her face. "No, dear. Not in your case."

Ayla's heart dropped. "Rhonda, please. I don't know what he did to me the night he brought me here. I felt compelled to follow him, so I did. But the truth is, I can't say a word when he's around. He terrifies me." She drew a breath, finally putting a label on her feelings. Yes, that was it. She was just scared of him. "Is it some kind of a spell?"

Rhonda's eyes widened. "A spell? Of course not. He's a Mage, Ayla. We don't cast spells, it's what the Sorcerers do. We don't need the help of an enchanted object. Magic is already in you. All you have to do is learn how to channel and control it. And Blaze would never make you do something you're not comfortable with. That's not who he is."

Ayla sighed, digesting the information. There was no other way to know about her Mentor than by spending time with him, whether she liked it or not.

"I just don't feel comfortable when he's around, that's all. I don't know how to explain this. Maybe it's his scars or the way he looks at me, like he's expecting something I can't provide." She wished she could drop the unease the way she dropped her words. With a bit of effort, a bit of thought, but once out, they were gone with nothing but a faint echo in their wake.

"What scars, honey?" Rhonda asked softly. Ayla blinked in astonishment. How could Rhonda not have noticed them?

"On his face. They are pretty obvious," Ayla clarified, slightly annoyed that she had to explain such an apparent thing. She noticed them right away during their original encounter. Two deep lines crossing his left cheek from the temple down, stopping mere millimetres from the corner of his lips. She shook her head, clearing her mind from the vivid image. That was too much detail to remember from the night she could hardly recollect.

"He has no scars, Ayla. It must be your fear getting the best of you...unless you can see something the others can't." Rhonda spoke slowly, weighing each word. "There's one more thing. I'm not sure if someone's already told you but one of the vital aspects to life as a Mage is being able to control and direct your emotions so you can channel your power in the most efficient way. Every day we face challenges, both internal and external, that may cause us great elation or heavy distress. Both of them need to be controlled so we don't get careless. This is why we put a lot of effort into daily meditations. I have been assigned to be your Meditation Guide to get you started before you proceed to any actual magic lessons. Would you be comfortable with that?"

Ayla breathed out her relief. Daily meditations with Rhonda meant she didn't have to do them with Blaze. That was a good thing. Maybe, if she could get other lessons to fill up her time, she wouldn't have to see him that much. The thought brought her solace. She was sure she could figure it out with time.

"That would be wonderful. Thank you." She smiled at the old Healer who beamed in response.

"Perfect! That's settled then. Before we begin, may I perform a quick check-up?"

"I'm not sick," Ayla protested weakly, already knowing she'd have to do it. Lyssa did warn her about the check-up. Despite her dislike for the idea, she reminded herself of the rules. If everyone had to do it, she did, too. For once, she didn't want to be an exemption. Every time she found herself excused from something, trouble ensued. It was better to go with the flow.

"It's a simple Healer's procedure, just to see if you're doing alright," the older woman soothed.

Ayla settled on the cosy lounge chair in her living room, with Rhonda taking a comfy poof in front of her. "Give me your hands, dear. I'll need you to relax and take a deep breath, hold it for four seconds...then release slowly."

Following the instructions of the Healer, Ayla relaxed as Rhonda's hands rested on her open palms. With every breath she opened up a little more, letting Rhonda into her mind.

She felt a light touch of the Healer's presence, gently brushing past her old traumas. This was nothing like the sessions with Corbin. He used to go inside her mind as if it was his domain, each time pushing a little further. Rhonda was gentle and inquisitive. She didn't pull up the images the way Corbin did; instead, she probed at some of the things that brought Ayla pain without causing it.

Suddenly, an electric shock ran through Ayla's body, forcing a scream out of her lungs. A foreign presence she never registered before lashed out at the Healer and threw her out of Ayla's mind. Eyes wide open, Ayla jerked her hands away from Rhonda, wrapping her arms around her body to stop the sudden shiver. The strange presence calmed and coiled at the back of her mind like a sleeping snake, but now Ayla was aware of it. Careful not to disturb it, she listened to her instincts. Her suspicion was right. This was not something she ever remembered having.

Rhonda's expression was stunned, mirroring hers. "I'm so sorry, Ayla. There is something strange there, some form of dark magic that seems to be feeding off your life force. I just tried to touch it, and it charged at me. Are you alright?"

"Not really." Ayla attempted to keep her voice even, but it still broke down to a whimper. "Can we stop, please? I need a break."

"It looks like some kind of a parasite," Rhonda mused, scratching her nose. "We can try and remove it, but I'll need to know a little more before we touch it. I don't want you to get hurt."

A cup of steamy camomile tea was already waiting on the small coffee table. Ayla gratefully picked it up and took a sip. As she expected, the temperature of the drink was perfect. There was no need to wait for it to cool down. The enchanted house served her well.

"Um, I nearly died last year. My Master performed a rare life ritual to help me recover. Maybe this is what it is," she mumbled, averting her eyes.

"How bizarre. A life ritual? I haven't heard of anyone using them, not in our century at least. Something this old would undoubtedly have side effects I wouldn't be familiar with." The Healer put her hand on Ayla's shoulder and gently squeezed it. "I'm sorry, dear. I won't try to touch that again."

Ayla nodded her gratitude and focused on her drink. Rhonda switched to the same small-talk Ayla usually indulged in with Lyssa, and soon her anxiety released her from its clammy grip. The hint of honey in her drink made Ayla's thoughts circle back to her teenage years. She used to have these mid-weekend kitchen chats about everything and nothing in the company of her adoptive father, Darren. Those were the blissful days before he got murdered and she was kidnapped.

The drink in her mouth lost its flavour. Would she indeed find a better life here?

She put the cup back on the table, no longer thirsty. The old Healer stood up, and Ayla followed suit.

"I think we can leave it for now. Let's try meditation, shall we?"

Without a word, Ayla followed her to the secluded garden at the back of the house. Guarded by a wall of green bushes, it was a perfect hiding place for anyone who wanted to spend some time outside but remain invisible to the eyes of others. There was a small gate leading out, but it was so well-masked that Ayla would have never thought it was there until she had stumbled upon it during her explorations with Lyssa. They both found it as a great getaway point for when things went wrong—as if anything could ever go wrong in a house that protected its dweller.

Rhonda directed her to settle on the grass that sprang like a pillow under her weight. "Close your eyes and focus on your breathing. Imagine that the whole world is slowing down; there is only you, the garden and the beat of your heart. Take a breath in and listen to the rustle in the leaves and the birds chirping in the trees. Hold it and picture the flowers in bloom, their colours bright like the wings of exotic butterflies. Breathe out and let go of the tension and insecurity. You are safe and calm as you go to your happy place. Imagine it in all the detail as if you're there now. Breathe in...hold...breathe out."

Ayla relaxed, allowing the gentle instructions to guide her thoughts. The sweet smell of blooming flowers in her garden teased her nostrils. The grass felt soft and fresh. Cheerful birdsong filled her ears. As Ayla deepened her focus, she could separate each voice, each flutter of the wings. The gentle breeze caressed her skin and stirred lighter strands of her hair that had escaped the embrace of a ribbon on her ponytail. Her breaths slowed down as she held the pauses. Inhale...hold...exhale...

The familiar fog slithered around her ankles. Ayla looked around at the vast plain of grey. Nothing else moved around her; nothing mattered in this strange twilight world which gave her solace in her most vulnerable times. It was peaceful and quiet. The fog stopped when she stopped, and followed her when she walked. Ayla inhaled the bland nothingness and slowly opened her eyes.

"What did your safe place look like?" Rhonda's face was calm and kind.

"It looks like a fog. A never-ending plain filled with nothing but grey. It's beautiful."

"How bizarre. Going into the Mist from the first attempt?" Rhonda's voice was calm, but a sparkle in her eyes gave away her excitement.

"The Mist?" Ayla rubbed her eyes, gaining back the sense of reality. It slowly dawned on her that the sun was already high up in the sky. Her stomach rumbled, reminding her to head to the kitchen and see what the house prepared for her. This place surprised her every time, and she was keen to know what it had in store whenever she came back.

"Yes. The Mist is a place between worlds. Some say it's the twilight zone between dreams and reality, some think this is where the soul travels after a person's death. Not everyone can access it, mind you. Only the strongest Mages or those with a particular talent can send their astral form there. Meditation can help you focus enough to access it, but I didn't expect you to get there from the first attempt. This is incredible!"

Ayla held the door to the house, letting the older woman go first. A thousand thoughts were dancing in her mind. Was it her power all along? "I've always thought it was just my self-defence mechanism, like dissociation. This was the place where I'd go when I felt overwhelmed. I'd just end up there somehow."

Rhonda glanced at her, a quizzical expression on her face. For a moment, it looked as if she was going to say something, but decided against it. "What do you have planned for the rest of the day?" she asked politely instead.

"Not too sure. I think Lyssa was coming over," she uttered, itching to grab her paints and brushes again. An odd mix of anxiety and excitement danced in her chest, eager to get free. Yes, the moment the Healer set foot outside her door, a canvas was coming out and she was going to indulge in another painting.

Rhonda said a warm goodbye and took her leave. Ayla remained by the door, gaze fixed on a spot of darkness within a shadow on her wall. Tree branches and leaves swayed on the white painted surface, but that one spot seemed out of place. A fragment of her imagination, nothing more. Ayla stared at it until it became nothing but a blur, then shrugged and turned away. She had more important things to do than stare at a spot in a shadow.

The easel came out of the corner with hardly any effort on her part. A fresh canvas didn't stay blank for much longer. Large, confident strikes quickly greyed out the white. Her brush lingered over the black paint before she made a choice. Without a second thought, she drew line after line, deepening the effect of the grey, creating shadows and undertones that were never there on her earlier paintings. Focused on one area at a time, she lost herself in the moment until she ran out of space. Only then did she step back to look at the full picture.

Much darker than before, the fog slithered and twirled, with deep shadows within. Eyes wide, Ayla stared at the black blooms in the background that were more prominent now. Sinister and bizarre, they were still only abstract. *It's only a picture. This doesn't mean anything.* Ayla glanced at it again, wondering if she should take Lyssa's advice and show her paintings to someone who can help interpret them. Would the same person be able to interpret her strange visions?

No. I'll figure it out on my own. The house gives me this chance to sort myself out, and I'll take it. Nobody needs to know about this.

She faced the easel away from the door and cleaned up the space. A late lunch was served on the table, and she dug into it. Enjoying her light yet nourishing garden salad, Ayla once again asked herself what she had done to deserve this. Her thoughts went to Blaze and she wondered how he came upon this task to retrieve her from the Sorcerers. It was almost as if he knew she was suffering and came just in time to get her out of the hell her life had become.

Once the dishes were done, Ayla decided to return to the backyard. With Lyssa still not around, there is nothing else Ayla wanted to do. She decided to save the walks along the streets of Whitestone for later and to enjoy the beauty of her private space. The serenity of this spot enveloped her, and for a moment she closed her eyes, giving in to the sensation of soft grass under her bare feet, the refreshing smell of greenery and flowers, the gentle rays of sun on her skin.

Suddenly, an acute feeling of someone's presence yanked her out of the trance. She opened her eyes wide only to see the white-haired man enter the garden. He stopped a few steps away and looked straight at her. Ayla's breath caught up in her lungs. Captured on the spot like a rabbit in a trap, she couldn't make herself look away from the steady gaze of his bright emerald eyes. Even though he wasn't a big man, he seemed to be taking up a lot of space. Ayla startled as her own words came to her mind. Fear, that was the feeling she had for him. Was it an animal's bloodlust she saw in his eyes, or was it something more terrifying than that?

She gulped nervously as he made a couple of steps towards her.

It's not like he's going to attack me. If he wanted to do something bad, he would have done it when he brought me here. Why bother keeping me alive otherwise? I'm just tired and overwhelmed. It's all in my head, this fear. I have no reason to be afraid of him.

"I'm not going to hurt you." Blaze slowly turned the palms of his hands to her, as if showing he had no weapons. The sound of his voice was pleasant, yet she couldn't shake off the tension. His gaze had her pinned on the spot. "It's okay to feel a little afraid. After all, you hardly know me," he observed. "Take your time to adjust, I'm not in a rush. I just wanted to drop by and see how you were doing. The lessons are starting tomorrow, but we'll take it slow. No need to stress."

Her lips refused to move, though a myriad thoughts raced through her head. Blaze waited politely, his expression as friendly as ever. When the pause grew awkward, he broke eye contact, and she could finally breathe. Twilight had already descended, dulling the colours of the garden. His hair changed from white to silver, the shades of the upcoming night giving it more texture. Smooth and slightly wavy, it held an alluring shine that promised a luxurious touch. Ayla scorned herself for the intrusive thoughts. Someone else's hair, no matter how gorgeous it looked, was the least of her concerns.

Ignoring her silence, Blaze spoke again, "I'll let you have some alone time. When you get to know me, I'm sure you'll feel more comfortable having me around. For now, just rest and don't think too much of it. I'll see you tomorrow."

Almost without a trace, he disappeared through the hidden gate in the lush green wall. Ayla let out a relieved breath. Now that Blaze was gone, she felt terrible about her behaviour. How rude of her not to even thank him for everything he'd done! Angry with herself for the stupor she felt in his presence, Ayla locked the back door behind her and leaned against the wall. The fireplace was lit up, sending waves of warmth throughout the house, and a delicious smell of roast chicken floated out of the kitchen. On the dining table, a full meal was served, and as always, with just enough on her plate. A couple of candles lit up the space for a romantic atmosphere, and a glass of chardonnay sparkled near her plate. Ayla picked it up pensively.

"A drink is exactly what I need right now," she decided, taking a couple of sips. The flames from the fireplace cast a warm glow onto the soft textured leather of the furniture. Delighted by the feeling of being at home, Ayla gave in to the relaxing atmosphere. Things were going to work themselves out. They had to.

CHAPTER 4. AYLA

The girl's hair was a golden red so vibrant it nearly glowed. Ayla admired the colour, wondering if it was dyed or natural. The same question people often asked her about her highlights. She smiled, thinking that they would have something to talk about. There was magic in the air, so thick she could almost touch it. The magic she had felt before.

Dark magic.

Ayla blinked as reality hit. The ginger-haired girl was on the same stone altar as the others before her. Her eyes were closed, her body immobile as the hot liquid pulsed out of the open wound on her neck. Straight into the sacrificial chalice held by the hand of the Sorcerer she knew so well.

He only used the first blood, leaving the rest to waste on the floor. Ayla's hands felt the weight of the gold warming up in her hands, and her lips took a sip of the drink. Her body rejoiced, demanding more. One sip after another, until the chalice was empty and she felt light-headed yet strong. The magic of the stone on her chest fuelled her up, taking her inhibitions. No more pathetic attempts at pleasing everyone. No more fear. She was the chosen one and her time was nigh. Very soon, she will be the one to command. The one to hold the whip. The one to be feared.

In horror, Ayla stared at the stone, pulsing and heaving on the heavy chain around her neck. Something gazed into her eyes from its depths. An evil so ancient it physically hurt to hold its deadly stare. A force that knew she was nothing but a vessel for its own gains. The magic it gave her was only borrowed until it was fully sated. And then, it would destroy everything in its way.

Destroy *her*.

The stone pulsed one more time, consuming the world around her. Ayla squeezed her eyes shut, distancing herself from the sapphire's mind. The attempt didn't go unnoticed. Like a snake, the stone collected its power and charged at her, burning the skin upon its touch. All the way through, as if reaching to snatch the little that remained of her soul.

***

Ayla splashed cold water in her face, chasing away another realistic dream. She didn't expect her memories to come back so quickly, and certainly didn't enjoy reliving them when she was supposed to be resting. Was this how Corbin helped her heal? Or was he still doing it when she was asleep? After all, she did get much better since she'd left his mansion.

The skin on her chest stung. She studied the pink spot between her breasts, where the sapphire had touched her. It was strange to see something so vividly, to feel its rhythm aligning with hers. Yet, she had never seen it in her life. Not until these visions started to haunt her.

She shuddered, thinking about drinking the blood of those victims—if they were real, of course. One could never be certain with Corbin. This could have all been a ruse, another one of his mind spells. A sleep spell, perhaps? Ayla didn't know if he could visit her here. She knew that Whitestone was closed off to Sorcerers, which would explain why she hadn't seen him.

The only person who knew was Blaze. Lyssa had little bits of information, but she wasn't the one who took care of all the arrangements. *He* was. Maybe it was time they had a chat.

Thoughts swarmed in her head as her hands stripped the easel of the painting and stretched a fresh canvas over it. The paints lost their lids and a thick brush found its way to her hand. Focused on her breath, Ayla listened to the sound of her heartbeat in her ears, trying to slow it down. Everything was going to be okay. Dreams were only dreams. No doubt, it was just her subconscious settling in the new place that she still thought was too good to be true.

Deep breath in. Hold. Slow release. One stroke at a time. One bit at a time. No need to rush. Things would happen in due time. For now, she could relax and heal.

Dark blobs looked bigger now. Ayla studied them closely, looking for resemblance with anything she knew. There had to be some sort of significance to them. She listened to her inner voice, wondering if this was something she should be concerned about. As always, only silence answered her call. Maybe it was nothing after all. Only then she realised that she'd pulled a clump of hair from her left brow.

Turning the easel away from the door, she picked up the frothy cappuccino that was already waiting for her on the small table, just in time to meet the first shy rays of the sun. Mint and vanilla. An unusual combination, but it somehow tasted good.

Lyssa didn't take long to show up. "Hey girl, how are we doing this glorious morning?" Her tone was nonchalant, but there was a trace of concern in her brown eyes. She tucked a strand of her chocolate hair behind her ear and studied Ayla's face. Immediately, she set about filling in her eyebrows for her. "You've been up drawing again, haven't you?"

"Yeah, just had some weird dreams and couldn't go back to sleep," Ayla confessed, watching her friend. There was something off in her aura today, and she needed to know what. "Did something happen?" Before answering, Lyssa picked up a mug of latte that appeared before her. She inhaled the sweet bitterness of the skilfully prepared brew with the relaxed demeanour of someone taking their time. Ayla waited patiently, fighting the desire to start tapping her fingers on the polished wood of the coffee table.

"One of the girls from our grade has gone missing. You know my friend, Carla? She'd stayed behind after the break with some personal stuff, so you haven't met her. She wasn't the best student, but she was one of us," Lyssa sniffled, putting her drink down. "It's different when you hear news of those disappearances coming from all other parts of the world, but you really feel it when it happens to someone you know. Her beautiful hair was the envy of the whole school. Sun-kissed ginger, we called it."

She drew in a sharp breath and closed her eyes for a moment. Ayla stared at her, refusing to believe her ears. Someone went missing in this perfect world. A girl from the same school as her, one that left a hollow in her wake.

Shocked, Ayla thought back to her nightmare. The young woman had ginger hair. Was it a coincidence? "When did she go missing?" she probed, hoping that Lyssa would be comfortable to share.

"Not that long ago, maybe a couple of days? It was the same abduction as all the others. No signs of struggle, but a very unusual disappearance. Carla's a happy girl. Never had any history with running away or anything like that. No recent break-ups, no trouble at school or with family. Her life was perfect, and she looked forward to coming back here." Lyssa hesitated before speaking again. "Good thing we're safe here at Whitestone. I'm glad you're not out there on your own."

"Yeah, me too." Ayla resisted the temptation to scratch the sensitive pink spot that seemed scorched after the touch of Caerulus. What kind of game was Corbin playing? She shivered, thinking about the last sacrifice. So, the timeline was right. If this girl, Carla, went missing two days ago, it would make sense that she was killed last night, just as Ayla saw it. This meant these visions weren't memories. Corbin somehow made way into her dreams and was working some magic there. She considered her strange thoughts and the way she felt there. No, it wasn't possible. She was not the kind of person to do this.

This is so messed up. I wish there was someone I could talk to.

"I was wondering," Ayla tried in her sweetest voice. "Is there a way I can speak with my Master? I haven't seen him since Blaze brought me here. Makes me wonder if there's a reason for that." There, she said it. Even with her memory patchy as it was and the dread she felt whenever she thought of their life together, he was the only person who could give answers to her questions. He was always happy to share deep knowledge about things most people wouldn't have even heard of. He would be the best choice to help her clear this fog. As long as she could keep him from intruding her mind, of course.

Lyssa picked up both their cups and took them to the sink. She busied herself with the washing, taking her time again. Ayla silently counted to ten, then backwards. So, her friend did know more than she showed, but for some reason didn't want to share.

Just as Ayla opened her mouth to remind her about the question, Lyssa turned off the tap and looked at her again. "I'm sorry, Ayla. I don't think you'll be able to see him again. Something bad happened to you there, which was why Blaze had to intervene. Your...Master...hurt you, but I don't know the details. It's all very complicated."

"I want to know the whole truth, Lyssa, you don't need to protect me," Ayla demanded. "Tell me what happened. Please!"

A delicate knock on the door interrupted them. "It must be Rhonda, for your meditation session," Lyssa swept up her bag and threw one last glance at her friend. "Look, Ayla, I only know so much. Blaze has all the information you need. And he's your Mentor, so he'll tell you. You'll just have to ask him. All I know is that your Master is not allowed to see you anymore. Some kind of arrangement they have." She opened the door and let Rhonda in.

"Good morning!" The older woman shone a dazzling smile, chasing away the bad thoughts clouding Ayla's mind. Despite herself, she smiled back.

"I'll see you later," Lyssa waved and disappeared in the street.

Ayla welcomed the new visitor and offered her a coffee. Rhonda seemed in high spirits. Maybe she would shine some light on her questions.

The session showed steady progress. Rhonda stuck to the plan, and Ayla followed her instructions with the obedience of a star pupil. She detached her attention from the surroundings, focused on her breathing, and let things go. It was much easier today, and Rhonda expressed her surprise at the progress. "You are doing so well," she proclaimed as they left the welcoming back garden. "Connecting with your power should come easy, as long as you keep practising this."

Ayla lowered her head in gratitude. It had been a while since anyone praised her for success. All the way back to her days at the old university, when she was a top student in her grade. How long ago was that!

"Here's your schedule for this week," Rhonda handed her a small envelope. "The red ones are recommended classes—they are obligatory for other students, but they're just there for you to get a taste of what it's like. The green ones are optional. Make yourself comfortable, no need to rush. I'll see you tomorrow."

Following the old Healer's advice, Ayla took her time after the meditation to collect her thoughts. She stood on her front porch, sipping on pink lemonade as she absorbed the blissful rays of the sun. Everything seemed to be in perfect harmony with her being. Ayla smiled, reminiscing about the last time she felt happy. These moments no longer caused her soul-crushing distress. Finally, she was coming to peace with the past.

She glided her hand along the engraved letters of her name on the envelope. How good it felt to have something addressed to her personally! To be able to walk outside the house and go somewhere, anywhere, without fear of being locked up. Here at Whitestone, she didn't have to be afraid of her father's murderers. They would never find her.

The envelope revealed a small piece of paper with her schedule that was put together in bright, happy circles. Ayla caressed it with her fingers, a dreamy smile on her face. Finally, a place she belonged. A place that she could make her own. She revelled in the thought of something good happening to her again. How majestic would it be to become a star student again! After all, didn't Rhonda praise her for her success at meditation?

It took her a moment to register the date on the schedule.

It's today! And the first class is...introduction to magic. With Blaze. At noon.

Ayla's gaze darted to the wall clock. It was already twelve! She was going to be late for her very first lesson, and with Blaze, of all people. He did tell her about this lesson the night before, how could she forget? With a quick glance in the mirror, she ran out whispering the address under her breath.

The Healer's Hub was only a couple of blocks away from her house. Ayla rushed through the vaulted gates past the multiple wooden doors, hoping despite all odds to be there on time. Memories about the Sorcerers' Academy intruded her mind. She squeezed her hands into balls as her thoughts went back to the long list of punishments students faced there, one more terrifying than the other. Rhonda's soothing words completely left her mind. She couldn't let her new Mentor down, no matter how uneasy she felt around him.

Ayla stormed into the garden and halted in surprise. There were no students around. Frowning, she checked the address. The garden beyond the Healers' Hub. There it was, and there she was. With no other soul in sight.

She breathed out, heart pounding in her chest. Now what? If the lesson had already begun, the students must have gone somewhere. Wouldn't be too far—after all, she was only a few minutes late.

A delicate cough alarmed her. Ayla spun around and found herself face to face with her Mentor. Blaze took a few slow steps towards her and she instinctively walked back to restore the distance between them. Her eyes searched the area for other students.

Blaze greeted her with a smile, as if she was acting normal. "Sorry I gave you a fright. You were running late and I wasn't sure if you were coming at all."

"I'm so sorry, I didn't mean to," Ayla wanted to say, but the words stuck in her throat. Like the night before, his composed, powerful demeanour felt intimidating. She shifted her weight from one foot to the other nervously as he cocked his head to one side, studying her.

"It's okay. I know you're still finding your feet around here. You're not in trouble." Blaze's eyes were kind and understanding, with a hint of a smile in them. The scars on his left cheek were a stark contrast to his friendly demeanour; it seemed impossible for someone like him to be getting into fights. He was just a Mentor who wanted to share his knowledge and teach her something new. A person who dared to come to Corbin's house and take her away. He wasn't dangerous at all.

Lyssa said he won't hurt me. He won't make me do anything I don't want to do. I shouldn't be afraid.

Ayla struggled to reply again. An invisible force kept her in place; despite her attempts to reassure herself, she still felt terrified. After all, Corbin was nice at first, too.

"It's okay to be a little overwhelmed. We need to start our training, but like I said yesterday, there's no rush." Blaze followed her glance around the garden and smiled.

"There are no other students in this class, Ayla. You're beginning very late in the year, and the others have already had their introduction to magic. I'll be teaching you privately until you're comfortable to join the others."

Ayla's eyes widened as she processed the meaning of his words. She was stuck with these lessons until she was ready, whenever this may be. Alone with this man for who knew how long. She itched to turn and run, though there was nowhere to go. The walls of Whitestone wouldn't let her out, not until she became a full Mage.

Blaze held a pause, giving her space to talk. Ayla tried again, but no words came out of her mouth. She cursed herself for feeling so helpless in his presence. What was it with this man that made her feel this way? She tried to distract herself with the beauty of their surroundings. The apple blooms everywhere, with delicate petals already starting to fall and cover the ground with a thin layer of snowy white. Their sweet smell filling the spring air with joy. The breeze on her skin, as gentle as a feather's touch. The gentle chirping of the birds busy with their daily routine.

"We'll begin with the basics and see how it goes." He directed her to sit down on the lawn and settled opposite her. Thankful for her choice to start wearing a *gi*, Ayla crossed her legs, mirroring him. Blaze didn't react to her silence. He continued with instructions as if her behaviour was completely normal.

"Think about your meditation sessions. This is very similar. Clear your mind of all that's in the way. Look inside yourself and let go of anything holding you back. Put your hand on your chest like this," he placed his own hand just above his solar plexus. Ayla automatically traced it, taking note of the smooth skin on his neck and down his collarbone. His *gi* didn't reveal much below that, but she could tell the outline of the muscles under it. For an instant, she wondered what they would look like exposed, and immediately scorned herself for the thought.

Blaze's face remained composed, although she caught a glimpse of amusement in his eyes. "Your power will manifest as a white flame. It's in your core; always has been, always will be. It will come to you when you're ready."

With her eyes closed, Ayla found it much easier to concentrate. His voice softly guided her, pleasant and soothing. The further she distanced herself from the noises of the blooming garden, the clearer his voice became, as if he were whispering straight into her ear. Which wasn't true, of course. She would have felt his breath on her skin if he had his lips so close to her. She would have felt the warmth of his body next to her. He would've felt her goosebumps. This was just an illusion.

Her breathing slowed down until all she could hear was Blaze and the sound of her own heartbeat. There was nothing she could see beyond the veil of darkness. Nothing moved in this spot frozen in time. Only the steady rhythm of her pulse gave away the minutes that were ticking by.

A faint glow lit up the blackness around her. Ayla straightened her back, alert. Her head snapped to her left, then to her right, searching for the flame Blaze had told her about. Her pulse quickened as her excitement rose. The flame was so close, she just had to focus!

The glow disappeared as quickly as it emerged, and Ayla opened her eyes, annoyed. After her success at the meditation, she expected more of herself.

"That was a good attempt," her Mentor praised her.

Ayla tensed up, fighting the dominance of his gaze. Once again she asked herself what it was about the man that made her feel uneasy. She wondered if it was the way he looked at her with that kind understanding demeanour, or his scars, or his low, gentle voice when he spoke to her as if she was a skittish doe ready to run away. There was nothing else that she could think of. She had never felt this stupor to be unable to speak in someone's presence before, and it was annoying.

Blaze got up, brushing the white petals off his *gi*, and Ayla mirrored him. "You've done great! Even if you think it's nothing, remember that it takes some Mages years to get to the point you are at today. You have a gift, Ayla. With patience and time, you'll be able to reach the flame and use its power." A hint of sadness crossed his eyes when she didn't respond. "I'll see you tomorrow at noon, here in the garden. Have a good rest of the day."

Ayla waited for his back to disappear behind the columns of the Hub before she allowed herself to relax. The session felt intense, yet not draining. She reminded herself that he never stayed to teach at Whitestone before, that the only reason he was still there was to help her. He spent his own valuable time on these lessons. Being unable to talk to him was unnerving. She wondered if he thought she was rude or if he just dismissed it as initial shyness. Regardless of what it was, she needed to fix it if she was stuck with him.

CHAPTER 5. AYLA

B ack at home, Ayla jumped into a hot shower, scrubbing off the uneasiness of the first face to face meeting with her Mentor. Water pelted her skin. The temperature was scorching hot, but she hardly noticed it. She soaped up a soft sponge with enough gel to cleanse half a dozen people, and violently rubbed her skin as if trying to remove it completely.

"I hate this! What the hell is wrong with me?" she yelled at her reflection in the steamed-up mirror. The reflection didn't reply. Ayla seethed at her own helplessness, looking for a way to relieve the anger. Her hands slid over her body, skin the shade of angry red from the near-boiling water. She wondered if she would get blisters if she were to turn up the heat. Pain didn't help her this time. Maybe she needed to divert her effort into something else. At least she was washed and clean.

Her mind jumped from one object to another as she contemplated the things she saw in the kitchen. There were knives there, and there were candles she could light up. Cuts or burns, which would be a better distraction from her distress?

She held her breath for a few long moments, counting to ten, then breathed out on ten. There was no reason for her to go back to the old ways. She was done with hurting herself. There was no danger for her in Whitestone. The door was open for her to come and go as she pleased. No one was forcing her to do anything she didn't want. Yes, she had to have those sessions with Blaze, but that was the only thing agitating her. She could figure out a way to deal with it. She had to.

The fluffy towel and the cosy bathrobe enveloped her body in an aura of relaxation and warmth. Despite her perturbed mood, she gradually succumbed to the feeling of security the house provided her. The house that Blaze gave her.

Getting out of the bathroom with a towel turban on her hair, she was startled to see a formally dressed Lyssa in her living room.

"Hey, what happened to knocking?" she protested, glancing at the closed door to the cupboard that held stacks of paintings. Her friend wouldn't be digging around the house, of course, but if Ayla herself didn't close it, Lyssa could have caught a glimpse.

"You wouldn't open the door, but it was unlocked so I let myself in. Damn girl, you sure take long showers," Lyssa teased.

Ayla rolled her eyes. "It's been a stressful day," she confessed. "I had my first session with Blaze today."

A wide smile graced Lyssa's delicate features. "I'm so glad! Did you like it?"

Ayla collected her thoughts before answering. "Um, no. It was terrible. I couldn't talk to him and it was really awkward. Is there anyone else I can train with?" she asked, recalling the way she felt in the blooming garden.

"Why couldn't you talk to him? I didn't think he was the chatty kind who wouldn't let someone cut in." Lyssa winked. At any other time, this would have made Ayla smile.

"No, it's just me. I feel strange around him. I want to say something, but words aren't coming out. I'm just frozen."

"Lips are sealed, huh?" Lyssa chuckled, but stopped at Ayla's burning glare. "Sorry, I couldn't help myself. But wow, that's really odd. Sorry to hear you're having trouble."

Ayla shook her wet hair out of the turban and carefully patted it dry. "I don't know what to do. Honestly, I have no idea how I'm going to have any progress studying with him if I can't even give him feedback on what's going on. I act like such an idiot when he's around, I can't stand it."

"Most of the girls here would gladly take your place," Lyssa observed. "I checked out the schedules and it looks like you're the only one who gets one-on-one training with him! It might help if you take a good look at him when he's not paying attention," she winked. "Maybe you're just shy because he's handsome and confident. Or maybe you need to focus on the things he's trying to teach you instead of checking him out, though I don't blame you," she added dreamily. "Thinking about him purely as a Mentor might help you get over your...defiance."

Ayla stared at her. "Are you joking?" she hissed. "I can hardly breathe when he's around, and you're telling me I'm defiant?"

"Hey, calm down, girl, I'm only teasing." Lyssa raised her palms up in a gesture of peace.

Ayla counted to ten again, forcing her breathing to slow down. *Get yourself together. She is only joking. It's just banter. No need to get all defensive as if it means anything, because it doesn't.*

"I've actually come to invite you to a party that Mace is throwing to celebrate the last term of the year, and of course everyone is welcome."

"Sounds great!" Ayla beamed, grateful for the change of subject. A real-life party, with students from a kind and accepting community! Nothing seemed better in her whole life! Back at university, she was always a bookworm and an A-student who was so focused on studies the whole world went past unnoticed. But here, at Whitestone, was her chance to catch up. She had to take it.

Ayla's face dropped as she thought about the unfriendly blonde from her first encounter with other students. "Oh, there's something I've been meaning to ask you. There's this girl, Sherice. She seems to be the only person who seriously dislikes me here. Any idea why that might be?"

Lyssa puffed her cheeks, staring at the wall clock behind Ayla's back. "Not a great topic, babe, but you would have found out one way or another. Remember how I told you some of us have very specific talents? Well, Sherice hasn't been at Whitestone for years after her graduation. The only thing that brought her back here was finding out that Blaze was coming."

"So what if he was coming? From what I understand, he brings new recruits here all the time."

Lyssa took a deep breath before continuing, "This time is different because he's staying. Sherice is a Breeder. They are known for producing perfect babies whose powers are identical to their fathers. Breeders play a huge role in our society, considering that the Mage race is on the decline. So far Sherice has had three children, and all of them were exact copies of her partners. She's always had a thing for Blaze, considering his power and I bet it was his looks, too!" She giggled again. "Anyway, The Council thought it was a good idea to pair them up, as the Mage community could use a bit of a boost in power. The problem is, Blaze isn't interested and he doesn't really care what the Council says. Of course, Sherice was convinced she could get what she wanted if she got a chance. Too bad that Blaze only gives group lessons in combat and the only one-on-one sessions he has are with you. This drives her crazy."

"I knew this was too good to be true." Ayla shook her head. "Something always goes wrong whenever I think life is getting better."

Checking out her perfect makeup in the mirror, Lyssa interjected. "Sherice might be a tough one to play, but Blaze has been taking really good care of you. You had to start the lessons sooner or later. The Council doesn't like students doing nothing. They're cutting you so much slack only due to Blaze's request, otherwise you would be stuck in the classes with the rest of the students, ready or not. I'm sure your situation with him will get better. Perhaps, you just need a bit of time to get used to him."

"Right. So what time is the party?" Ayla ignored the mild panic in her mind. There seemed to be politics everywhere she went. Now she had to deal with this woman who was obsessed with her Mentor. What else was she going to discover in this peaceful school? Her thoughts turned dark as she remembered Lyssa's remark about a girl from their class gone missing. Maybe having a jealous woman on her tail wasn't as bad, after all.

"In about an hour's time. Sorry, I forgot to tell you yesterday. Let's see what you've got for the occasion." She nudged Ayla towards the bedroom. Ayla couldn't hold back a smile. She never had a friend like this before. Someone giving her advice, supporting her in difficult situations. Someone she didn't mind having in her own bedroom checking out the contents of every piece of furniture until she found something she liked.

The wardrobe boasted all colours of the rainbow, and all kinds of formalwear. The pastels, the bright colours, the shimmering fabrics and noble silks mixed with boho dresses and futuristic neon attires. Anything her heart desired was there for the picking.

After a few outfits Ayla finally stopped on a short strapless dress in classic black with a lace-up back, and a pair of black stilettos. Lyssa dug into one of the drawers and produced a matching strapless two-piece bikini.

"This is for later. Put it on under your dress," she winked mischievously. "Mace's house has a hot tub, so this might come in handy."

Lyssa helped Ayla do her hair and makeup. The mirror brought Ayla a completely different version of herself. Finally out of her training clothes, the woman looking back at her was undeniably attractive, with a wave of dark brown hair revealing golden strands here and there. The skin-tight dress flattered her slim figure and perfectly cupped her breasts, while the stilettos made her visually taller.

"It's going to be a great night," Lyssa promised with a playful glint in her eyes. "You'll love it!"

As they headed out, Ayla threw one last glance at the house. The windows went dark the moment she left the last step, covering the rooms under a blanket of darkness. She knew that the lights would turn on as soon as she returned. It was strange to be out after sundown, but this was a life she'd never known before. Something she had only read about, now offered to her on a silver platter. A chance she couldn't miss.

She could sense the party from afar. Ayla immediately got into a festive mood at the sight of fireworks, sophisticated decorations seemingly made from hundreds of candles floating in the air, young Mages playfully throwing phantom fireballs at each other. A glowing ghost of a man in knight's armour floated in front of her and bowed, and Lyssa dismissed it with a sweep of her hand. Captivated with everything around her, Ayla looked around, trying to take it all in.

Light dance music pulsed through the air, the bass setting itself deep within Ayla's heel. The two friends approached the house, front doors leaking with smoke. Lyssa was confident in her steps as she led the way. At the entrance stood a small table with welcome drinks, either beckoning or luring her into a very friendly dragon's maw. Lyssa picked up a drink. Following her friend's example, Ayla picked one up, too.

The flavour was so light and delightful that it made her head spin for a second. She was surprised at how smoothly it went down, and finished the glass in just a few sips. Lyssa set her own empty glass on a tray next to the drinks and grinned.

"That's Levi's handy work. He sure knows how to have a good time!"

"Um, is there something in this drink?" Ayla eyed the empty glasses, regretting her choice.

Lyssa burst out laughing. "Like drugs? Of course not! He just makes the best cocktails in town. The only danger here is how much you drink!"

The girls walked in, spotting a group of young Mages that surrounded a middle-aged man in a plain blue shirt and black fitted jeans. Ayla smiled, noticing Mace's friendly face as one of the people in the group. He beamed, beckoning them to come closer.

"That's the Scholar of Elementals," Lyssa whispered to Ayla. "He's one of the teachers at higher levels."

The Scholar raised his eyes at her and smiled as the two girls made their way towards his group. "You must be our newest recruit. Come on over, no need to be shy," he encouraged, and Ayla grinned, taking an immediate liking to him. The group continued their happy chitchat, and Ayla quickly found herself immersed into the light-hearted conversation.

"So how are you finding it here? Have you signed up for many lessons?" inquired the friendly Scholar.

"Not yet. I'm still finding my feet," Ayla replied cautiously.

Mace smiled at her. "You'll do great. Just see what other students in your class are doing and try everything. Best way to learn!"

"Exactly! Take me, for instance. I've been here for two years now and haven't progressed a whole lot." Lyssa nodded to strengthen her argument. "I haven't uncovered my special gift yet. Just trying everything and going with the flow until I find out."

"You're connected with your power, though. That makes things easier when you study." The friendly Scholar gave her an encouraging smile.

"That definitely helps, though it's a bit random." Lyssa turned her right palm up and breathed out. A small white flower bloomed in her hand, its petals gently shifting and dancing as if made from pure flame. It was different, yet familiar. Ayla leaned towards it, her heart fluttering in anticipation. This was the most beautiful thing she had ever seen. The power of Mages, so close for others yet so far for herself. She sighed quietly, wondering how long it would take for her to connect with hers. "It took me a few months to find even a shadow of this flame." Lyssa's eyes were fixed on her.

Ayla averted her gaze, realising her thoughts must have been plastered all over her face.

"A flame doesn't cast a shadow." Mace poked his tongue at her.

"Oh hush, you! I'm trying to be evocative here!" Lyssa frowned, but her serious face quickly burst into a laugh.

"Oh no! 'Evocative' is a big word for a pretty girl!" Someone's ruffled hair swam into Ayla's line of vision. A new student who squeezed into the little circle was carrying a drink in each hand.

"This ratbag here is Levi." Lyssa gestured at him, and Levi gave her a playful bow.

"At your service. Though I wouldn't call myself a ratbag. That was totally unnecessary, Lyssa!"

Ayla stared at the newcomer wide-eyed. Even though he seemed like the youngest student here, there was something about him that gave away a vibe of a more experienced Mage. The fashionable fitted shirt and ripped jeans, hair styled in spikes to reflect the latest trend and his playful tone seemed to be nothing but a cover-up.

"Nice to meet you," she uttered.

Levi pushed a cocktail in her hand. Ayla was astonished to see it was *Sex on the Beach*, her favourite. She got a taste of it during a short cocktail making course she took for fun when she was at university. It was the most daring thing she had done back then.

Levi flashed a snow white grin. "I'm so glad to finally meet you! Lyssa told me a little about you, but I don't need much anyway."

So this was the mind reader. Ayla pensively took a sip of the drink. It tasted exactly like her most successful creation. The perfect combination of sweet and sour, with the bitterness of liquor barely noticeable. She thanked him, wondering about the extent of his power. He was in his second year if she remembered correctly. She wondered how much control he had over other people's thoughts and if there was a code of conduct to keep him out of her mind.

He smiled as if knowing what she was thinking. Ayla shivered. He probably did. Or maybe it was obvious because that was how everyone reacted upon meeting him.

"I can't actually read your thoughts," he confided, gently touching her shoulder in reassurance. "To do that, I'll need way more practice. My power is knowing—or having a good guess—of a person's desires or fears, whatever they are experiencing. The stronger the thought or feeling, the easier it is to read it. I knew you wanted a drink, and I saw the one you were after clear as day. All the ingredients and the way you liked it made. It was too easy! Actually made me wonder if you knew I was here and did it on purpose."

"Uh, no, I didn't," Ayla held an awkward pause. "So, how do you handle it? Is there a way you can stay out of people's heads?"

Levi scratched his head. "Well, yeah. There are some techniques that help. Some people are naturally resistant to my powers. For instance, Blaze, your Mentor? Impossible to get into his head—believe me, I tried. That was so embarrassing. He knew right away. I can tell you, this was the worst. The girls were around, too. They had a blast laughing at me. Can't blame them, though. It doesn't always happen that someone reads the mind of a mind reader."

"Can *he* read minds?" Ayla asked, battling a slight panic.

Levi chuckled. "That's what people say. But no, I don't think so. He's just really good at guessing. Basic psychology."

"It must be hard, living with a talent like yours." Ayla studied his fox-like features.

He raised his hand to check that all the spikes on his head were still perfect. "I'm used to it. I live in the house furthest from anyone else's, a bit like you. Mine isn't enchanted, though." He winked at a pretty brunette who was carrying a golden tray full of fruity drinks. "Soon, very soon, my darling." He blew her a kiss before turning back to Ayla. "See? Makes it easier to communicate."

"I guess it does make a relationship...interesting," Ayla responded, looking at the brunette's slender back disappearing in the crowd.

Levi choked and bent down for a few moments, nearly spilling his drink. When he was done, he stared at her with disbelief in his brown eyes. "Girl, are you crazy? Relationships are hell with a gift like mine. Imagine the time after the honeymoon period is over. When your partner starts having questions or some bad thoughts you'd rather not know. It's awful! So, I tried it and after a few failed attempts one straight after another I decided to stick to the surface. Easy, shallow, no strings attached. At least, for now, until I learn how to switch my powers off."

"Makes sense," Ayla took another sip of the cocktail. Something white flashed in the corner of her eye but when she turned her head, it was gone. There was nobody with snow white hair in the room. She didn't need to worry. Why would she?

"Well, I better get going. I'm one of Mace's waiters for the evening and I can sense trouble. Slacking while others are working isn't great, you know?" He grinned at her. "I'll see you soon, babe."

Lyssa grabbed her by the hand and guided her towards the large living room. All the furniture had been pushed to the walls to clear an open space for a dancefloor. An upbeat tune kept the spirits high, and Ayla followed her friend into the busiest part of the area.

"Don't mind him, he has zero idea of what's appropriate. He calls everyone 'babe' and can get a little too friendly," Lyssa explained. She nodded her gratitude at the student who moved aside to let them into their dancing circle.

"I feel like everyone's watching me," Ayla confessed, pulling the hem of her mini-dress down.

"Well, you're new and also really pretty! This dress looks amazing on you, by the way. Careful not to pull that hem down too much though, or the top will slide off! Unless that's what you're aiming for." Lyssa winked with a coy smile.

Blushing, Ayla dragged the top up. "Um, that's definitely not something I was after."

"Hey, this is a no-judgement zone! Do what you like." Lyssa squeezed her hand. Her eyes focused on something behind Ayla's back. "Oh, look! I think the hot tub is ready. Let's grab a spot before it's full!" She jerked her head towards the back door.

The two followed the excited chatter out onto the wooden veranda. Ayla's eyes widened. The backyard held two long tables, twelve spots at each already taken. The few students who didn't fit were standing nearby chatting, chilled drinks in their hands. Atmospheric lights dotted the wooden floor, framing the edges, whilst round floating lanterns provided illumination throughout the area. Further away, the place got darker. As the two girls walked past the cheering crowd, lights became more sparse until there were none left. The hot tub had lighting of its own, reminding Ayla of her time in Hong Kong. Back then, the tub was the only thing she had to herself. Here, she would have to share with a dozen others.

"Jump in!" Lyssa already disrobed, her lean body contoured by a deep blue swimsuit. Ayla wrapped her hands around her shoulders, suddenly shy. Her dress revealed more than she was used to as it was and removing even that felt strange. Other students in the hot tub were busy chatting, with hardly anyone looking at her here. She had nothing to be ashamed of.

Lyssa helped unzip her dress. "You look beautiful. No need to be nervous—look, everyone's wearing the same. You'll feel better when you're in."

Lowering her feet into the warmth, Ayla settled on the edge of the tub while she got used to the new sensation. It was her first time being so close to strangers in the water, and wearing very little didn't help. She needed to get over her inhibitions before she could truly relax. Which wasn't easy—it felt like everybody was judging her.

It's all in my head. Everyone is having fun, and no one is even looking. I don't need to stress about it. Maybe if I have another drink, it will help me relax.

She settled on the bench near Lyssa, submerging her body into the water to her shoulders. The tub lights changed colours, going from brights to pastels, painting faces of her peers. Lyssa giggled and said something, someone responded. An atmosphere of light-hearted chatter reigned over this place, and it welcomed her friend and her into it. Ayla rested her back against the warm texture of the tiles and closed her eyes. In her mind, she distanced herself from the crowd and focused on her breathing, slowing it down until the anxiety released her, but kept her eyes closed for a little longer.

A wave of heat brushed her skin like a feather. Almost unnoticeable, so subtle she couldn't be sure it was real.

The heat from the water was a different sensation. No, this wasn't it. Maybe it was a trick that someone created, or an innocent prank just to see who would notice. Ayla opened her eyes, an idyllic smile on her lips, prepared to react to the fun that was undoubtedly planned for the group. What she saw made her freeze.

Two bright green eyes took over her world, pinning her down. Blaze's gaze was that of a predator. Triumphant over trapping his prey. Ready to pounce, yet holding a pause to torture her with fear and fruitless hopes of escape. But she knew it was nothing like that. *It's all in my head. He's not intimidating at all. I have nothing to be nervous about.*

Despite her own reassurance, the arguments she told herself felt weak. There was nothing she could do to stop the tension she felt in Blaze's presence. She wondered why he was at this party and then cut herself short. This was for everyone; after all, one of the first people she met here was a Scholar of Elementals, a permanent teacher. There was no rule saying that Blaze couldn't come. There was no rule saying he couldn't approach the tub. And there was no rule prohibiting him from looking the way he did.

She ordered her eyes to look elsewhere but they ignored her when Blaze took off his *gi*, revealing his muscular torso. With an enormous effort, she forced herself to look away. It wasn't proper of her to stare. Ayla scorned herself, checking the reaction of others. Most girls didn't bother hiding their appreciative glances. He was probably used to it, though. He was undoubtedly aware of the effect that a man's bare chest, strong arms and toned physique could have on a woman.

A gentle touch on her hand startled her. Lyssa cleared her throat, nearly making Ayla jump. Following her friend's gaze, Ayla realised what it was about. Blaze was getting in the water, and the only free space was right opposite Ayla. In the small quiet nook. Very, very small nook. Ayla gulped nervously, pulling her legs up to her chest as he slid into the water. The ripple created by Blaze's body reached Ayla, and she pressed her back into the tiles. Heart in her throat, she was frantically looking for an excuse to leave. She felt almost naked as her imagination pictured her swimsuit going transparent. The idea of getting out right in front of him was terrifying. Her cheeks felt the tormenting heat of shame, although she had nothing to be ashamed of.

Willingly or not, he cornered me here. Why? He could have waited until I left. He knows I'm not comfortable in his presence and has kept his distance so far. Why change now?

An eerie silence alerted her. All eyes were on her, expecting something. Ayla glanced at Lyssa for help, but it was Blaze who spoke. "I asked what you were drinking." He pointed at the fruity cocktail that somehow appeared next to her. Ayla noticed Levi's mischievous face among those still dressed. He winked at her, and she felt the blush nearly burn through her skin.

He knows. He knows exactly what I feel like. I've never been more embarrassed in my life!

She shook her head at Levi, hoping he would understand. Surely enough, the young Mage pressed his index finger to his lips, a grin on his face. With that problem under control, she turned to her major challenge. Whatever she did, she could not let the whole crowd see her weakness. This was nothing out of the ordinary. Just one guest asking another about her drink. Easy question.

Except it was her favourite cocktail. That was the trap, and she walked straight into it.

The pause grew awkward. Thankfully, Lyssa rushed to the so-called rescue. "It's *Sex on the Beach*. Ayla really likes it." Lyssa slapped her lips, eyes wide in horror. "I meant the cocktail. She likes the cocktail."

Blaze chuckled. "I see. What else does she like?"

Eager not to waste time, Ayla took a large sip of her drink and immediately regretted it. Levi made it much stronger than before, and her head spun. Terrified, she put it back, but the damage was done. She thought about the drinks she'd already had and about the last time she had alcohol, more than a year ago. This was enough to knock the sense out of her. She should have been more careful.

Blaze raised his hand to pull his long hair from the water and rest it on the edge of the tub. His simple gesture went unnoticed by the rest of the crowd, but Ayla's eyes caught on it. A familiar knot formed in her chest, blocking the airways. The half-blurred memory stood in front of her, taking over her vision. Another man raising his hand at her. His cruel dark eyes without a hint of sympathy. The helpless wait of the imminent strike. Ayla flinched, trapped in this tight corner without a way out. Despite the warm water, goosebumps crawled under her skin. Dark spots danced in her vision, mocking her.

Did you think you could escape? No, darling. One man or another, there's no difference. You'll end up exactly where you started. Where you belong. There will be no happy ending, not for you.

Corbin's face emerged before her eyes, an evil grin on his face.

It's not real. He's not here. I'm safe.

"Ayla. Ayla! Are you okay?" someone's voice demanded her attention. Through a veil of fear, she saw Blaze's hand reach for her. With the last crumbs of self-control she had left, Ayla held back a whimper. Instead, she pressed her back further into the tiles to escape his touch. The soft texture turned into sharp daggers, biting into her skin. Eyes wide, she shivered at her prospects. There was no way out. In a fraction of a second, he was going to touch her. No, to hit her. And then, when she could handle no more pain, he would tell her it was all in her head, and she would be stuck questioning her sanity. Anything was better than this. She couldn't allow him to touch her, not in a million years.

Shallow breaths invited a familiar sense of dizziness. Ayla panted, struggling to process her thoughts. The black spots dancing in her vision mocked her, covering the picture in front of her. Fear confined the voice of reason to the back of her mind. Only a faint whisper told her that Blaze wasn't Corbin, that things were different. That she wasn't owned property here and could do what she wanted, no longer restrained to her room.

"Get Saree," Blaze ordered one of the students, pulling away from her. Someone rushed out of the hot tub, and Ayla's Mentor took over her vision again. He wasn't looking at her, though; his concerned expression was directed at someone next to her. "Lyssa. Help her out, please."

Someone dragged her rigid body out of the water and wrapped a long fluffy towel around her shoulders that covered her to her toes. A strong arm led her out of the backyard and into the house, away from the noise, into a large powder room.

"Come on, honey, it's okay, you're safe," Lyssa cooed, rubbing Ayla's shoulders through the towel. Despite her effort, Ayla was freezing.

Shivering all over, Ayla couldn't stop thinking of terrible pictures that took over her mind. A hand raised in the air, striking her with a force enough to send her flying across the room. The feeling of hot blood soaking her shirt within seconds. Her own reflection in the mirror, with circles under her eyes, a fractured lip and a haunted expression. Corbin's face distorted in a grimace of anger, and herself cowering before him. The feeling of helplessness, knowing she belonged to him to do with as he pleased. She remembered it all now.

"He's just like Corbin," she sobbed, curling into a ball. "He told me I was safe, that he would protect me. And all he did was hurt me again and again. Now Blaze is going to do the same. This is exactly how it starts."

"No, Ayla, he won't hurt you. He didn't even touch you tonight when he saw you were uncomfortable. He won't do anything to you, I promise." Lyssa sat on the floor next to her, arm wrapped around her shoulder, squeezing it gently. "You *are* safe here."

Her words were just another sound in the cacophony that surrounded Ayla. Everything was too much. Her own thoughts betrayed her, sending a dark panic through all fibres in her body. "I'll never be safe, Lyssa. He terrifies me, don't you understand? He's just like Corbin. I *know* he'll hurt me, that's what he wants. They're exactly the same. I can't take it. I can't..."

She rocked back and forth, arms wrapped tight around her knees. Someone else rushed into the room, lowering on the floor in front of her.

"No, don't touch me!" Ayla screamed, curling tighter into herself. That was it. He came for her and she couldn't escape.

A warm hand brushed her cheek. Ayla raised her head and met a calm gaze of violet eyes. "It's me, Saree. I'm here to help, if you let me." The Empath caressed her face, speaking words of comfort. Ayla breathed out as her fear and pain gradually faded away. Listening to Saree's soft voice, Ayla reluctantly let go of her knees. Her breathing normalised and she felt the pressure slowly lifting off her.

"Thank you, Saree," she whispered, light-headed. The feeling of relief helped with the panic, but didn't stop the aftermath of drinking over her limit. With a strenuous effort, Ayla raised herself off the floor and lunged towards the toilet, only making it in time to empty the contents of her stomach into it.

Lyssa rushed to hold her hair, gently patting her on the back. "It's all good, Ayla. You're okay. We'll take you home now, and you can get a nice sleep. Tomorrow will be a new day."

Exhausted, Ayla allowed her friends to take her by the arms and lead her out. "That was so embarrassing," she confessed, taking a regretful look at the house. The party went on without her, but she knew everyone would remember her shame. She managed to embarrass herself in public.

"Things happen. People are very understanding and supportive here," Lyssa soothed, helping her out of the gate. Luckily, Ayla's house was only a short walk away. Neither of her friends said anything about the episode, which was a blessing. Her own scrutiny wasn't as merciful, though. Ayla shivered as she thought that she was seeing Blaze for their lesson tomorrow. And then again on many, many occasions until she connected to her power. The idea of remaining calm and pretending that nothing happened was a pain of its own.

CHAPTER 6. AYLA

Rhonda took her hands off Ayla's head and gave her a reassuring smile. "It's going to be okay. Are you feeling better?"

"Much. Thank you." Ayla looked around the room, gracing every Healer with a grateful smile. There were three of them in the Hub that morning. After the traumatic events the night before, Rhonda brought her there as soon as the sun came up.

"Thank you for letting us help. You've been very brave." A middle-aged Healer, similar to Rhonda in the way she moved about, threw a kind glance her way. She put away the wet towels they had used to cool Ayla's burning forehead.

Ayla sat up awkwardly, her head still spinning.

"Take it slow," Rhonda warned, offering her arm.

Ayla leaned on it and waited for a few seconds. The dark spots still danced in her vision. The procedure did make her feel better, though. She was grateful for the Healer's intervention, even though she protested at first when Rhonda ushered her to the Hub. They didn't do the now-routine meditation either.

"You're in a bad space right now," she told Ayla then. "With your ability to jump straight into the Mist during meditation, you can end up somewhere you might not have wanted to be."

Absent-minded, Ayla agreed, and didn't regret the choice. Rhonda was right. After a humiliating experience at Mace's party followed by another night full of terrors, it was good to feel surrounded by the people who cared.

Out in the garden, the apple blossoms were all gone, their petals swept away by the cleaners. Instead, green leaves sprouted from every bud, covering the trees in their fresh summer outfits. The sun was out in the sky, warming up the stone walls of the graceful old building.

Ayla sat down on the stone steps, wrapping her arms around her shoulders. This was a good morning to be alive. Her mind was at peace, though she knew it was temporary. The trauma of her past was going to keep coming back until she learned to deal with it. Or until time dulled it down. Regardless, she had a lot of work to do. The road ahead was rocky and she had to be strong enough to follow it. Maybe discovering her abilities would help.

Nobody followed her out, and she was grateful for the Healers' discretion. No one pushed her to discuss the events of the night before. It was good to be on her own for a little while. Enjoying the fresh spring air, she took a slow, leisurely walk through the garden. Her skin absorbed the rays of the sun that already reached the mid-morning point. A gentle tug in her stomach reminded her she hadn't had breakfast yet. It was time to head back to the house.

"Hey," a greeting touched her ears.

Ayla stopped. The worst thing right now would be to have a run-in with Blaze. She tensed up, even though it wasn't his velvet baritone. This voice belonged to someone completely different. Someone she had spoken to not too long ago.

"Hi, Mace," she replied, feeling the heat spread on her cheeks. Last night was his party and he probably witnessed her disgrace. Despite Lyssa's reassurance, Ayla felt ashamed of herself.

Mace stopped opposite her. "How are you doing? We were pretty worried yesterday when you felt unwell. I'm so sorry, Ayla. I didn't know you survived assault before and probably don't want to have any men around you. Just wanted to let you know we'll be more careful in the future." An expression of concern took over his cleanly shaven face.

"Who told you that?"

Mace shrugged. "No one. We kind of assumed. You acted like someone with that kind of trauma, that's all. A friend of mine behaved somewhat like you after a triggering event."

"Sorry about your friend." Ayla looked him in the eye, unblinking. "I just don't usually drink much, and yesterday I went above the limit. That's all."

His eyes were full of sympathy. "Oh. That's good then."

An awkward pause ensued. Ayla tried to think of a way to change the topic, but nothing came to mind.

Mace cleared his throat. "I was heading down to the botanicals class. Would you like to join me?"

"Sure!" This was a relief. She did want to check out the classes, but wasn't confident enough to go yet. After all, she was told that they weren't compulsory for her. "Is it okay if I just show up?"

He chuckled. "Of course! We won't even be in the garden today. This one would be checking our dried herbs from last month. The sun was lovely in the past few weeks, so the herbs should be ready now."

Matching his pace, Ayla couldn't help but wonder. "Can you tell me more about it?"

Mace smiled. "Absolutely! I'm sure the Scholar will tell you way more than I can, though. You're going to love her."

"Why's that?"

"Meera is the quiet one among all of us loudmouths. She graduated more than three decades ago but decided to stick around to teach the new generations. Classes used to be much fuller than now." He held a pause.

"What happened?" Ayla watched his expression turn from joy to sadness. There was still so much to learn about this world, even though Lyssa never shied away from her questions. Sometimes, Ayla wondered if she would ever be able to learn it all. To fit into this society the way she was never able to during her time with the Sorcerers.

"Well, our population is on a decline. With a lot of Mages settling with non-magic users, our bloodlines became diluted. Magic is slowly disappearing. This is why the Council introduced the new laws to keep it going. Destined couples are encouraged to have as many babies as possible. Breeders get assigned to any decent Mage. Meera still remembers the old days, when everyone had freedom of choice." He glanced at her worried face and gently touched her shoulder. "Don't worry, Ayla. It's not that bad."

She wanted to ask more questions, but Mace went quiet as they approached the tall door of another building. A simple wooden shed that was big enough to fit a couple dozen people only had a few students gathered around a rectangular table. An older woman greeted them warmly.

"Come on through, Mace, we're just about to start. And you must be Ayla, our newest addition. I'm Meera, the Scholar of Nature Studies. Lovely to finally meet you! Please, take a seat anywhere you like. I'll just do a quick recap of our previous work here so you're all caught up." She dragged a large box from under the table and placed it between the students. "This is our herbarium. At the end of last term, we picked up these herbs from our winter garden. Primrose, nightbloom and lovehaze are our major focus this time. Let's see how they came out."

The box produced a series of flat glass plates that trapped dried-out plants. Mace placed his next to Ayla. "I'll share mine until you get your own."

"Thanks," she whispered, looking around the room. For some reason, she believed that Lyssa would be everywhere she went herself, but there was no sign of her.

Tracing her gaze, Mace chuckled. "Looking for Lyssa? She took this class last year, but I'm sure she'll be around somewhere."

Feeling caught on her thoughts, Ayla nodded and focused on Meera's words.

"Primrose qualities are mainly to increase one's physical appearance. As some of you may already know, bathing in primrose-infused water is bound to increase your beauty. It's not for internal consumption, though; drinking its pure essence would give you a sore stomach. Tea or essence diluted in water would be acceptable, though." Meera unlocked her glass plate, and the students followed with theirs. As she held the fragile flower in her thin fingers, the aroma floated all over the space. Delicate and sweet, it resonated with Ayla as one of the usual bases of her chosen perfumes. Beauty indeed.

"This one is going home with you." Meera swept her hand around the table as the students carefully placed their dried stems into velvet pouches, stacking the glass plates in the middle of the chair. "You can use it in your bath tonight and tell me about the results at tomorrow's lesson."

"Here, take mine." Mace handed her the flower and pushed the burgundy pouch towards her. Ayla reluctantly took it, gently pressing the herb into the darkness.

"Won't you need it for yourself?"

"Oh, I've done this course as well. I'm only here to catch up on some knowledge I might have missed before. Nature studies play an important role in my talent. So, in order to keep the flow, I'll need to focus on the basics while I play around with higher level stuff."

Meera waited until everyone was done and continued, "Our next ones are nightbloom and lovehaze. Now, we'll only briefly touch on the first one. Its major uses are in mixtures to help you sleep, and in small doses can even be used with babies. You have to be careful with it, though. Too much, and you can end up in a coma-like state. Lovehaze, however, is completely different. As you can tell by the name, its qualities capture the most mysterious power of all—the power of love." She held a pause, taking time to look into each face until her gaze stopped on Ayla. Somehow, this felt directed at her.

It's all in my head. I overthink too much. It's not like she meant anything in particular. Besides, there's no love in my life, and probably never will be.

"Who can tell me about potential uses of lovehaze?" Meera asked the group. A few hands shot in the air, competing for attention. "Saree."

The violet-eyed Empath flashed a dazzling smile. "You can make a herbal brew using the pure plant itself. Blossoms hold the strongest power for creating a feeling of lust, while young stems and leaves are for a deeper attraction. Brewed together with nightbloom petals, they can create a feeling of relaxation, which is a life-saver after a long day. The stems can help connect with one's personality, if they struggle finding their core."

"Excellent. I'll just add that lovehaze essence has long been used in love potions. The abuse of its power made this beautiful plant banned from quite a few communities. However, it's still a great little herb. If used properly, it can be a wonderful tool in your collection. It's all about what you mix it with."

"I'll show you where all our herbs grow," Mace told her after the lesson was over and everyone was dismissed. He gestured to the back of the room, letting her go first. She walked through the weathered white door, with paint peeling off here and there. The place seemed old, yet there were signs of someone trying to keep it tidy. The floor was clean, the tall windows crystal clear. Rows upon rows of herbs illuminated the greenhouse, raising their leaves towards the skylight.

"It's beautiful." Ayla looked around in awe. She had never been to a greenhouse before. The emerald hues coloured the air around her. Herbal essences filled her nostrils with a perfect combination of sweet and bitter, refreshing and head-spinning, sour and spicy.

Mace led her to one of the rows which featured pale yellow flowers that reminded her of camomile. Sturdy stems carried juicy leaves, almost covering the delicate buds. "Here, have one for your own experiments." He picked a small stem and handed it to her.

"Are we allowed to pick the flowers here?" Ayla breathed in the strange aroma of lovehaze. It had a much deeper smell than primrose, heavier, more...primal. Her eyes widened as she thought of Meera's words of the plant being banned from some communities. It would be easy to use it for all the wrong reasons. She imagined all the people suffering from unreciprocated love, desperate to make their sweethearts love them back. Wouldn't it be something a person would do, if they had the power?

"Meera made an exception for you." Mace looked her straight in the eye. "They're all very supportive here, Ayla. You don't need to worry about a thing. And even if you don't pass from the first attempt, you can always try again next year. There's no pressure."

As they walked out of the greenhouse, the study room was already empty. Ayla took one last look around before following Mace out in the sunny street. So this was what studying here looked like. She didn't have to be stressed about being the best. There were no expectations, and it felt like a bliss.

A shadow crossed the path, followed by a pair of pedicured feet in elegant gladiator sandals. Ayla raised her eyes to the woman who stopped right in her way. For someone of an age similar to her own, the newcomer seemed much more confident.

"Hey, Mace," she sang in a high-pitched voice, wrapping her hand around his neck. She stood on tippy toes to reach his face, and planted a gentle kiss on his lips. Ayla looked away. So this was the girl Mace was dating. She completely forgot about her.

"This is Ayla, our newest student." Mace carefully pulled away and took the girl's hand in his. "Ayla, this is Ingrid."

"I'm his girlfriend," Ingrid stated, her blue eyes stern. Her features were much sharper than Sherice's, which made Ayla wonder who was the leader in their dynamic.

"Nice to meet you, Ingrid." Ayla tried to sound nonchalant, but the trick didn't work.

It looked like Ingrid was another person who disliked her the second she met her. She touched her large hoop earrings before choosing an answer, as if deciding if Ayla deserved one. Finally, she decided to speak, but not to Ayla. "Mace. I've been looking all over for you, babe. We've got somewhere to be, remember?" She shot a killer look at Ayla, deliberately slowly gliding her gaze on Ayla's body from top to bottom and back. Ayla frowned.

"Oh, of course!" Mace offered his elbow to Ingrid and she readily hooked her arm through it. "We're going to the combat lesson. Would you like to join us?" He caught himself short, gauging Ayla's reaction. When she gave none, he continued, "You don't have to come along, of course. Only if you want to. This class is non-compulsory, so you can just watch if it's more comfortable."

Ingrid pulled him forward. Mace threw an apologetic look at Ayla, mouthing a silent "sorry". Ayla shrugged, pretending she was focused on the path ahead. So what if someone had a cute boyfriend? She didn't care. It wasn't like it had been forever since she had someone embrace her like that.

Lost in thought, she didn't pay attention to the road until Mace spoke again. "We're here," he announced, gesturing to the pathway between two buildings. Ingrid walked first, dragging him by the hand. Ayla followed them through. The lane ended in an open yard. A few students were already there, warming up in their *gis*. Ayla wondered what attracted them to this class. Self-defence was a great skill to have, but combat lessons were a completely different thing.

Ayla took one of the benches propped on top of one of the staircases, unsure about joining the rest of students. Mace and Ingrid went ahead. She looked around, noticing she was the only spectator there. The chatter below grew in tonality, announcing someone's arrival. The mane of brilliant white swam into the line of her vision. Of course, how could she forget? This was the class Blaze taught, and she walked right into it. The only way out of this courtyard was back through the narrow passageway, straight past her Mentor. It wasn't like she could stomach the thought of looking him in the eye again. Not after her incident last night.

"Good morning," Blaze's voice echoed in the stone well, and the choir of students eagerly responded. "Let's get started with a little warm-up."

Someone rushed through the passageway, ruffled hair flying in the wind. Lyssa and Rowan ran through as if chased by wild cats. With a quick peck on the cheek, the young man joined the rest of the group. Lyssa looked around first. She immediately spotted Ayla and waved at her.

"May I sit this one out?" she asked Blaze.

He didn't object. Lyssa rushed up the stairs, with Blaze's emerald eyes tracing her. He looked directly at Ayla, sending her adrenaline through the roof. She sat still, focused on her breathing. There was no menace in him, no trace of the primal predator she saw the night before. Or *thought* she saw. He was just an ordinary man.

In mere seconds, Lyssa plopped on the bench next to Ayla. "Hey, girl, I've been looking all over for you. Where did you go?"

"Rhonda took me to the Healers and then I bumped into Mace and we went to the Nature Studies class. I actually thought you'd be there." She held a pause, collecting her thoughts. "Then we had a chat and everything was okay until Ingrid showed up with a gross display of affection right in my face. It's not like I was going to do anything, I know he's taken. He was just being nice, that's all. Anyway, she dragged him to this class and he invited me to come along. I completely forgot it was Blaze's." She sighed and pressed her cold fingertips to her eyes. "I'm such a mess."

Lyssa chewed her lip. "Ingrid was at the party last night and saw your reaction. She might have tricked you into coming here."

"But I haven't done anything wrong." Ayla glanced down at the yard. Students were still doing their warm-up exercises. Blaze split the class in two, and one half was stretching while the other was running laps. Thankfully, he wasn't looking at her, so she could study him a little better. Until now, she didn't get a proper chance to do it.

"She's just jealous. Mace showed interest in you, even though he was only trying to help. She saw it as a challenge to their relationship. It has been a little rocky lately." Lyssa patted Ayla's hand, reassuring her.

"How come you were late?"

Lyssa chuckled, covering her mouth. "Um, let's just say I got a little...caught up with Rowan."

Following her gaze, Ayla looked down at her friend's companion. "Are you two dating?" Ayla asked absent-mindedly.

Lyssa grinned. "Well, dating is too big of a word for what we do. We just hang out, if you know what I mean."

"Oh." Ayla went quiet. It was the second time someone mentioned a superficial relationship, making her wonder if that was such a bad thing. If this was a norm here, why not try it? "It's a bit of a new concept to me, but I haven't...hung out with anyone for some time. How do you go about it? Starting out, I mean?"

Lyssa widened her eyes. "Ah, it's a bit difficult in your situation, I'm afraid."

"Why's that?" Ayla frowned, wondering if she was special in the wrong way again.

"Well, you weren't brought up with this concept. It would take some getting used to." Lyssa shifted in her seat, hiding her eyes.

Ayla shook her head. "You're not telling me the full story. What's up with the secrets?" She glanced down at the yard again. The warm-up was over, and students were split into pairs, practising. Blaze walked from one pair to another, giving brief feedback or showing a correct position. One of the students tumbled just as he was passing by, and he caught her. Ayla wrinkled her nose, recognising Sherice. A wave of dislike and anger shot straight for Ayla's head.

Her friend traced her gaze. "Are you okay?"

Ayla clenched her teeth, fighting through the red fog in her head. "All good. I think I've had enough for now. Can we leave?"

"Of course," Lyssa replied, an expression of concern on her tanned face.

Ayla forced a smile, following Lyssa's slender back down the stairs. She shouldn't care if Sherice flirted with her Mentor. He was his own person and it was his own life. If he wanted to date someone, it was his business, not Ayla's. Her nostrils flared as she pictured him and Sherice together. Her stomach churned as if she were about to puke. Thankfully, a sharp pinch distracted her. Ayla looked down at the palms of her hands, both covered in marks. She wondered how long she'd been digging her nails into them and dismissed the thought. It didn't matter as long as it worked. As they made their way past the arena, Blaze glanced at her, but she pretended not to notice.

Focus on the path ahead. He can't stop me from leaving. I don't have to talk to him and he can't make me. Next time, I won't be caught like this. I'll never come to his class ever again.

CHAPTER 7. BLAZE

"How is that shoulder?" Rhonda threw some herbs into the mortar and reached for a small emerald bottle on the top shelf.

"It's been acting up lately," Blaze confessed, watching her swift movements.

"I'll make you a fresh batch of the healing serum. Can't believe it's still bothering you after all these years."

"The knife was enchanted to deliver a deadly hit even if it was a scratch. I only made it due to my shifter nature. Looks like the pain is here to stay."

"Is it constant?"

"Thankfully not. It just flares up every now and then, especially in stressful times."

She met his gaze. "I'm so sorry. How is she doing?"

"Not great." Blaze averted his eyes, as always pained to discuss the sensitive topic. "Ayla can be difficult to read sometimes. I know what's going on for the most part, but her deeper thoughts are in the dark. This is very concerning."

Rhonda added more liquid into the mortar and reached for some seeds in small pouches. "Is she coping?"

"She's doing her best." Blaze sighed. There was no one else he could talk to about this. "I am very worried about her. My visions haven't stopped, you know? I still see bits of her past, and the more I know, the more concerned I get."

"What do you mean?"

Blaze drew in a sharp breath. "The Sorcerer, Corbin. I saw what he did to her." When Rhonda didn't respond, her eyes alert, he continued, "He didn't just take her memories. But I saw her right there in his grip, how he held her down and forced her to do his bidding. How he beat her up till she wasn't able to move. He didn't even gag her, Rhonda! He threatened with something worse if she wasn't quiet, and when she could no longer contain the screams, he would put a will-binding spell on her and continue with his entertainment until he was satisfied."

"This is terrible. I'm so sorry, Blaze."

He shook his head. "She was under one spell or another for the most part of those last few months before I took her away. Every time after the torture he would hold her in his arms and tell her he loved her. Then, he would take away her memory of the night and tuck her in to sleep with a quiet apology, only to repeat the torture again once her bruises healed. Every time, Rhonda! Every time after his cruel entertainment he said words of love, and now I'll never be able to say them to her myself. After everything he's done, I am certain this will be a trigger. And if all those memories come back to her..." he paused, focusing on his breath. Those painful thoughts never left his head. He hoped that talking about them with someone else would help him process them. "She tried to take her own life before. If she remembers everything, I'm afraid she'll try again. It terrifies me to even think that a trigger can happen any time and I may not be there to help her."

Rhonda didn't reply, studying his face. Her hands stopped for a moment, then continued mixing the serum. A soothing concoction of mint and spices rose in the air, dulling the tension just enough to keep him talking.

"I can't even do anything to the son of a bitch," Blaze confessed bitterly. "He bound her to him with the life ritual, and now any pain or torture that happens to him will affect her, too. I wish there was a way to undo it. You have no idea how much it hurt to see her in his dungeon on the night I took her away. She was terrified, shaking all over, and so thin I was afraid a gust of wind would carry her off. A ghost of her present self."

"Yes, I remember my first check-up with her. Never in my life have I seen anyone in this condition," Rhonda admitted. She added a pinch of salt and a couple of lingonberries to the mortar and crushed them with the rest of the mixture.

Blaze's hands closed into fists. "I had to be civil with him. To keep my temper under control and not give in to his provocation. His whole existence is a slap in my face, a challenge I'll never be able to accept. I told him to stay away from her as part of our agreement, but I can't do anything if he breaks it. We both know it."

"This is frustrating," Rhonda replied. One of the drawers produced a tiny vial with a deep red liquid that she put on the table in front of him. "Look, Blaze. I understand this is hard. She shouldn't be fighting the pull."

"She only resists because Corbin severed her connection to me and damaged her so much. I don't know if she'll ever be able to trust a man again." He closed his eyes, calming his breath. Ayla's condition was a raw wound in his heart that wouldn't heal. There was nothing he could do but to remain patient and keep trying.

Rhonda pushed the vial towards him. "Have you considered nectar of passion rose?"

Blaze's eyes snapped open. "Absolutely not."

"Hear me out. It will only take one drop, no more. She'll be able to relax and connect with her true feelings. Everything else will come naturally."

"They call it a date rape potion for a reason." Blaze shook his head, staring at the old Healer. "I can't do this to her. She can make her own choice and I won't push her. And if she can't trust me, it's okay, too. I won't trick her into doing something she wouldn't do herself."

The old Healer sighed, glancing at the vial. "It's here if you change your mind. Now," she scooped up the serum from the mortar and rubbed it in her hands, before applying it to his shoulder, "this is going to sting a little."

Blaze startled as the cold bite crept through his skin all the way down to the bone. It was better than the pain he felt whenever the old wound reminded him of one of the worst mistakes in his life. When he was careless enough to turn his back on a Sorcerer and got stabbed with an enchanted blade. Never again did he trust them.

Rhonda handed him the serum. "I'm sorry I can't help Ayla more. When I saw that dark magic inside her, I knew it was an integral part of her. The suffering will never stop, but that abominable blood bond keeps her alive. That poor girl."

Shifting his shoulder to check for any remaining pain, Blaze glanced at the Healer again. She pushed the vial with the nectar of passion rose into the palm of his hand and folded his fingers around it. "Take it. You never know when you might need it."

"I won't." He shook his head and turned to leave. "Thank you for the serum, Rhonda. I feel much better now." His thoughts switched to Ayla and the ways he could help her. Absent-minded, he put both vials into a pocket of his jacket. The nectar of passion rose escaped his attention as he focused on more pressing matters. Only when he got back home in the end of the day did he remember about it. It was too late to take it back then. Blaze promised himself that he would return it first thing next morning. However, fate had other plans.

CHAPTER 8. AYLA

The small table in Ayla's dining area produced two sparkly glasses filled with chardonnay. Lyssa swished the wine in hers, staring at rays of afternoon sun through the liquid gold. "This is life," she sighed before raising her glass to Ayla's. "Cheers! To happy times."

Ayla clinked the glass with hers. The girls simultaneously took a small sip before placing the drinks down on the table. "I hope happy times show up soon."

Lyssa patted her hand. "Is this about the lessons again? Oh, Ayla. I told you things will come in due course."

"Well, it's been weeks and I haven't progressed at all." Ayla took a longer sip of her wine. "Can I try with another Mentor, literally anyone else?"

"Come on, babe. You know you can't just change your Mentor. Besides, some of us have been at Whitestone way longer than you. It took me a whole semester to finally get a tiny spark of magic. Look at you though! The Mist called you during your very first meditation. Magic will come soon, too. Have some patience!"

"No, I'm telling you, Lys! This man drives me crazy. You know, he only lets me try once or twice, and then the lesson is over. Who does that?"

"Come on, Ayla! You get so worked up over it. He probably doesn't want to upset you, so he only does the bare minimum and leaves you be. Isn't this what you want?"

When Ayla didn't respond, eyes fixed on the stem of her glass, Lyssa continued, "Look. You're angry when he spends time with you, and you're angry when he cuts the lessons short. What do you want him to do?"

"Ugh, I don't know! Why doesn't he leave me alone?" Ayla jumped off the chair and rushed to the bathroom, angry tears rolling down her cheeks. Her strange emotions were getting stronger, and it was becoming more difficult to control them. She understood that Blaze saw her discomfort and kept his distance. She knew he had to teach her, as he was her Mentor, and she needed his lessons before she could progress to others. Everything apart from Nature Studies and his combat classes required use of magic in one way or another. She avoided seeing him as much as she could. Somehow, it made things worse when they met for their one-on-one sessions. Blaze allowed her to try but didn't push. Each session only lasted a few minutes.

"Are you okay?" Lyssa's delicate knock on the door brought her back to reality.

Sniffling, Ayla patted her face with a fluffy towel and opened the door. "Yeah, all good. Sorry, it must be that time of the month coming. I've been very emotional lately," she apologised, hoping her friend believed her.

"It's okay." Lyssa put her hand on her shoulder, giving it a gentle squeeze. "I had an idea. Why don't we go out tonight? A real outing in the city?"

"The city? You mean downtown?"

"No, babe. The actual city. Twintown is not too far from here. A few other students are going, and we can come along."

Ayla wavered on her spot, unsure about this. "How do we get there? I thought Whitestone was hidden away from the rest of the world?"

Lyssa laughed. "It is! But higher-level students can open portals. Lucky for us, Mace is coming along." She winked at Ayla. "Ingrid and he broke up last night, and he needs a distraction. So, we'll also have Saree with Jason, Levi, myself and you! Rowan is busy with his studies, so he won't be coming this time."

Despite herself, Ayla couldn't hold a smile back. "Let's do it!"

The bar, which couldn't decide if it was a cosy diner or local pub, was bustling with activity at peak hour. An electric fireplace brought a flash of modernity against exposed brick walls and vintage photographs. Waitresses glided through the crowd, balancing trays of drinks in their hands. Under the dim lighting of a sleek corner booth, the group exchanged relaxed chatter. A bright-coloured cocktail with a flirty umbrella and a slice of pineapple appeared in front of Ayla. She glanced up at Mace. "I didn't order it."

"My treat." He flashed a dazzling smile.

Ayla couldn't help but smile back. She had some pocket money of her own that was provided by the school as a stipend. Being careful about her spending, she was able to save a little. The gesture of good will was a pleasant surprise, though. She rolled the straw between her fingers. "Thank you."

He raised his glass and held her gaze. "Cheers!"

"Cheers!" the group echoed as everyone picked up their drinks.

For a moment, everyone was busy and Ayla had a chance to study Mace's cleanly shaven face. She wasn't sure how she felt about him. Yes, he was charming and clearly liked her. However, every time they met, he acted like they were only friends. He was a gentleman, opening the doors for her, giving her a hand to support her when she faltered. That was it, though. Ayla wondered if he only kept his distance because of Ingrid. Now that the obstacle was gone, she hoped he would finally make a move. Being out in the city where nobody knew them, in a dimly lit bar would be the best place to find out.

"Why is it called Twintown?" Ayla looked around at the faces of happy customers enjoying their drinks and food.

"The people who live here have no clue and just take it as a given. However, the town was built as a twin to Whitestone, though they developed differently after. Twintown, as you can see, is now much bigger and busier, which serves the purpose. If anyone was to look for a town here, they would find one. Going to Whitestone takes a Mage to let someone through the wall of protection around it," Lyssa explained.

A pretty waitress in a fitted uniform swiftly covered the table with plates full of classic pub food. Ayla's mouth watered at the view of loaded fries, salads of all varieties and charcuterie. "Wow, that's a lot of food," she noted, trying to act nonchalant, though her stomach grumbled.

"Well, we're all really hungry and this is the only bar that serves decent meals! Dig in, babe!" Levi declared as he passed her a plate with fries. "Ladies first."

"Thank you." She accepted it and held herself back, only taking a few.

"My pleasure," he purred, taking the plate back.

Lyssa rolled her eyes. "You have to stop flirting with every living soul, Levi. Not everyone likes your familiarity. One of these days you'll get yourself in trouble. Again."

"No need to be jealous, babe, I was going to serve you next." Levi offered the plate to her, and Lyssa snorted. "What? I can't help being likeable."

"You can't help being arrogant, that's what. Thank you though." She placed a few fries off the shared plate onto hers and whispered to Ayla, "This boy is crazy. Don't take him seriously."

"I heard that!" Levi raised his voice, throwing his hands in the air. "That was offensive! I am really upset now!"

"Have a drink and chill out," Jason pushed a beer towards him.

Levi grabbed the drink and made a few exaggerated gulps. "Yeah, okay. I'm better now. You are forgiven, Lyssa."

"Thank you, Your Majesty." Lyssa bowed and the group laughed. So, this was what being part of a community was like. A beautiful, warm place where everyone felt safe and accepted for who they were. A dream come true.

Before she had a chance to speak, a loud thud announced a spilled drink. "Oops," Levi giggled, wiping the table with the sleeve of his trendy shirt.

"Sheesh, man. There are napkins right here!" Lyssa pushed a caddy with cutlery and a generous bunch of paper napkins that were skilfully folded to resemble petals of a flower. "Must you be gross?"

"Shocking. Absolutely shocking. A total disgrace," Levi responded. "It's not necessary when you just want to have fun. Besides, who cares when you have magic?"

Ayla watched his sleeve dry within a matter of seconds. "How did you do that?"

"Simple. I want it gone, it's gone." Levi shrugged. "It's really easy. You'll know it once you connect to your magic. You might just want to use it for everything!"

"Yeah, like you do? And risk a burnout?" Saree shook her head. "You have to be more careful, Levi."

"I'm in total control, babe. Don't you worry your pretty head."

"Well, you nearly burned out before, my man," Saree noted, taking a sip of her amber-hued lager. Like her boyfriend, she seemed to prefer beer. "Remember Mr Frog?"

"Pfft, that was nothing!" Levi dismissed her as the group started giggling.

"Who's Mr Frog?" Ayla asked. A sense of belonging evaporated as she thought about their lives before. They had history together; their friendship was strong. She was still an outsider who had to make her way in this new world.

The group laughed. "Oh, you won't believe! This dufus here," Mace pointed at Levi who immediately pouted, "wanted to trick a pretty girl. So he transformed himself into a frog and chased her everywhere she went. That was just after they studied the origins of the folk tales, I think there was one with the frog prince?"

"Yeah! That was one of the dumbest things I've ever seen!" Jason laughed, wrapping his arm around Saree. "Well, go on!"

"I refuse to engage," Levi turned his head away, but a half-hidden smile gave away his amusement.

"So, she took him and put him into a terrarium filled with delicious worms and juicy flies. Yum yum!" Mace served himself a few pieces of ham and cheese off the platter. "Thankfully, the girl wasn't cruel, so she only kept him there for a few minutes and then let him out. Lesson learnt, I hope!"

"But you're not a shapeshifter, are you?" Ayla picked up her cocktail. She hadn't heard enough about them to be sure about the way their magic worked. This was her chance to learn more.

"Of course not! Shifters normally choose one shape and stick to it. I used transformation, which allowed me to change my physical shape for a little while. You can't do it for long, though. Takes a lot of power and concentration to keep it. I lasted a few minutes, so it's a good thing she let me out so quickly. Otherwise, I would have gone back to my normal shape and could have hurt myself with the shards of glass from the damn terrarium."

"Classic Levi." Saree smiled, moving a plate of salad in his direction. "Here, have some vegetables. Might make you smarter for next time you decide to make a fool of yourself."

Jason opened his mouth, then hesitated. He glanced at Saree and then darted his eyes away. "That girl was Carla, wasn't it?"

"It sure was. The prettiest girl in my grade with the most beautiful red hair I've ever seen. She started in Lyssa's class last year," Levi said quietly. "I hope she's okay."

Ayla averted her eyes, thinking about her vision of the red-haired girl on the altar.

"How about you, Ayla? What's the funniest thing you remember from school?" Jason raised his eyebrows, shifting the group's attention to her.

Ayla blushed, embarrassed. "Um...I didn't really have anything funny at school. I just studied." She shrugged to switch their attention to something else. Anything would be better than having to think about her past.

"Studied all the time?" Levi stared at her in disbelief.

Ayla shied away from his gaze. "Yes. I'm sure you can see it in my thoughts."

"Unfair! You promised not to pry, you little mischief," Lyssa wagged her finger at him. "Careful now, or I'll kick you out of here!"

"No, you won't. You guys love me too much!" Levi poked her tongue out at her.

Ayla took a breath as the group continued on with jokes and Levi retorting with witty remarks. She was glad they changed the topic, but the bitter aftertaste still lingered in her mind. Pretending like nothing happened at the Sorcerers' Academy was silly. Her past would remain with her no matter what she told herself. She had to learn how to embrace it and move on with her life. For starters, secure her friendships. And then, maybe even find a deeper relationship.

"So, Mace, what's your family background?" Ayla asked, noticing his eyes on her.

He leaned forward across the table so she could hear him through the noise. "I grew up in a foster family. When I turned sixteen, my powers were unlocked and a recruiter brought me over to Whitestone, just like you. Can't believe it's been almost 10 years! Hopefully, I'll be ready to get out of there soon."

"Were you born to non-Mage parents?"

"No, silly. I was adopted when I was just a baby, and my powers were locked at the Nursery. When I was sixteen, they manifested and I became one of the students."

"Sorry about your parents," Ayla uttered, hoping her question didn't hurt his feelings.

Mace smiled. "Oh, my parents didn't die. I was born to a Breeder. See, my biological father wanted to settle with a regular human. According to the law, the only way he could do that was if he conceived a baby with a Breeder and then he would be sterilised. This is how you keep the magic going through bloodlines. When I was born, the Breeder handed me over to the Nursery. This is a facility where children of Mages get assessed and their magic is locked until they are old enough to control it. But because children need love, I was placed with a family who looked after me. Being an adopted child isn't as bad as they say."

Ayla startled as if he read her thoughts. "I was adopted, too, but I never knew my biological parents. My father, Darren, raised me as his own." Tears welled in her eyes as her thoughts circled back to the happy memories of her childhood, up to her gruesome discovery. Darren was murdered because of her, she was sure of it. The guilt had always been in her heart since.

"Hey, it's okay."

Lyssa's hand warmed the skin on the shoulder. Ayla sneaked a peek around the table. Saree and Jason were exchanging quiet remarks over their drinks. The only people who paid attention were Mace himself and Lyssa. Ayla pulled herself together.

"Yeah. It's just...a difficult subject."

"I'm sorry." Lyssa's gaze traced the figure of a waitress walking back to the bar. "Oh look! They are about to start!"

"Start what?" Ayla looked in the direction her friend was pointing to. A couple of energetic waitresses climbed on top of the bar. An upbeat tune sounded through the speakers, its volume amplified against the previous songs. The waitresses started dancing, attracting cheering comments from the gathering crowd.

"Come on." Lyssa grabbed her hand. "Have you ever danced on the table?"

"Uh...no." Ayla hesitated. This was her chance to do something crazy. Something she never thought she could do but had always wanted to try.

"This might help." Levi's face with a devilish grin swam into her focus. He pushed a shot glass with a layered drink into her hand. "Liquid courage, babe. One gulp and you're good to go."

"What's this?" She turned the glass in her hand, still unsure.

"You don't want to know. Let me just say that it's going to help you have a great time." Levi winked and pointed to the bar. "Come on! There won't be any spots left if you wait too long!"

"What the heck." Ayla shrugged and finished the drink in one go. The fiery liquid went down her throat, instantly warming her up. Her head grew light and she carefully shook it. Already regretting that she accepted the drink that was much stronger than what she was used to, she still made her way to the bar. Lyssa was already on it, squealing with delight.

"Yeah, you go, girl! Get up here, I've saved you a spot!"

Ayla looked around for a chair to serve as a step. The crowd cheered, but there was no free furniture. Someone's hands wrapped around her waist.

"I'll give you a boost." Mace's voice sounded deep and sensual in her ear.

"Thanks," Ayla replied as he lifted her on the bar next to Lyssa. Her friend had another shot in her hand that she readily offered her. Ayla exhaled and downed that, too. Her head spun with delight as she took in the faces below. Her previous inhibitions slowly released their grip as she enjoyed her new position. The support from the crowd below was overwhelming. The whole room was dancing, charging the atmosphere with freedom she'd never experienced before. Smiling ear to ear, she twisted and turned to the beat, basking in the attention, her mind fuzzy and light. Now she understood why people did this and regretted not having done it sooner.

A mass yell of approval made her turn her head. To her horror, one of the girls on the other side of the bar removed her top and threw it down. Another one followed suit, making the crowd bellow. Ayla's eyes darted to Lyssa who handed her another shot.

"I'm not taking off my clothes." Ayla had to raise her voice to cover the blaring music. She looked at the glass in her hand, then at Lyssa's encouraging gestures. "Okay, last one and then I'm done." Ignoring the tiny voice of reason in her mind, she finished the drink and bent to put it down on the bar for the bartenders to sweep away. Big mistake. Her head spun and she squeezed her eyes shut to regain her balance. It didn't help. Horrified, she realised she was about to trample over and down on the floor that suddenly seemed too far away.

Mace's hands helped her once again. "Are you okay?" His deep eyes looked at her with concern.

"Yeah. I normally don't drink this much," she confessed, shooting a glance at Lyssa's swaying hips above.

Levi's cunning grin appeared next to her. "Nonsense! If you want to have fun, why not go all the way? This is what you've always wanted but were too scared to try. This is the time, babe. You're safe among friends and Mace here is our sober companion, so he'll take us back to Whitestone when we're partied out." He pointed at the array of shots covering the table next to him. "Drink with me. Go crazy. Let it go. See what a taste of freedom brings you."

Ayla looked at his face that seemed too friendly to refuse. Maybe he was right. She was too scared to try anything like this, but she already mustered the courage to dance on the bar. Who knew what else she could do if she relaxed and gave up control? She picked up one of the glasses and clinked it to Levi's. "Cheers."

Lyssa climbed down, fixing up her top. "Oh, drinks! Thanks, boys." She finished another shot and grinned at Levi who shot a meaningful look her way.

Mace poured some water in the glasses and offered it to the girls. "Drink responsibly." He frowned at the silent exchange between Lyssa and Levi. "Don't even think about it, you two. I won't be able to collect the lot of you if you start smoking again. Remember last time?"

Levi scoffed and rolled his eyes. Curious about the unsaid words, Ayla stared at him. It was Lyssa who spoke, though.

"Levi makes a mean joint," she explained. "It's so much fun, you won't believe it. This is something you have to try yourself. And it's completely safe! No hangover or anything like that." She looked at Mace's disapproving face. "It's not for everyone, of course. No pressure to try something if you're not ready."

Ayla shifted her weight but underestimated her ability to remain on her feet. Her ankle twisted and she stumbled over. Thankfully, Mace was there to catch her. She smiled at him, enjoying the warmth of his hand on her waist. This was what she needed. A reliable shoulder by her side.

Her gaze slid behind his back and her elated mood evaporated when she saw a new person walking through the crowd. "What the hell does *she* want?"

"Good evening," Sherice's greeting was meant to sound sweet, yet it felt like sandpaper to Ayla's ears. "Fancy seeing you all here. Date night?" She glared at Mace whose face reddened.

"Of course not. We're just out as friends, that's all," he hurried.

Sherice nodded, an expression of distrust on her face. "Sure, sure. Careful who you hang out with, Mace. Her kind can get you in trouble." She shot a glance in Ayla's direction.

"Excuse me?" Ayla returned her stare.

Sherice chuckled, her expression indignant. "People like you can get decent folks in trouble. Sorry, I didn't realise you were a bit deaf. Or are you having trouble understanding things? Too drunk, are we?"

Ayla stepped away from her seat, fists clenched into tight balls. Red anger seethed inside her, cutting through the alcohol-induced haze. "Do you have a problem with me, Sherice? What's your deal?"

Lyssa rushed to her aid, with Mace stepping in, too. The rest of the group kept silent, watching them wide-eyed.

"Break it up, ladies." Lyssa waved her hand between Ayla and Sherice, demanding their attention. Neither of the opponents took the chance to back away.

Sherice chuckled, holding a pause. Her eyes, two perilous lakes.

"What's my deal? Are you really that dumb?" Sherice threw a condescending look at her, shaking her head. "Wow. That's even worse than I imagined. I feel sorry for you."

"Stop it," Ayla spat through clenched teeth. Her opponent leaned forward to be on the same level as her.

"Or you'll do what?"

Ayla raised her hands, but Lyssa intercepted her. Keeping her arms to her side, her friend ushered her away. "Don't fall for it, Ayla. She's just mad about you and Blaze."

"What about me and Blaze?" Ayla grunted, knowing that her friend was trying to help. "What is it that she's losing her mind over?"

"Girl, you need to take a breather and calm down a little. Maybe it was a bad idea to keep you drinking. Do you want to go wash up and maybe have a few minutes to yourself?" She pointed to the bathroom sign at the back of the bar.

Ayla glanced at it, admitting that Lyssa was right. It would be better for her to have a break. Who knew, Sherice might be gone by then. After all, she blatantly attacked her in front of witnesses. They wouldn't let her stay after that.

Ayla pushed the door with a bad depiction of a woman's shape on it. The bathroom air was cold, infused with a citrus essence, without any sounds marking another person's presence. Ayla leaned on the marble vanity, looking at her reflection. This wasn't the face of the happy person she was supposed to be. Surrounded by new friends, safe in a new community, accepted for who she was. No, this was the reflection of a woman in pain that provoked that anger. The anger that she couldn't explain herself.

The air was still, with only a hum of the air conditioner getting through the heavy door. It felt surreal to know that on the other side of it the place was full of noise. Laughter and chatter of dozens of people, clanking of drinks, shuffling of feet. Cars flying past out in the street. Not a sound here, though. How bizarre.

Goosebumps covered her arms as a sudden chill cooled her skin, sobering her up. Something was wrong. It was too quiet, even considering the soundproof door. The citrus smell masked something else. Ayla looked around, her senses on high alert. Ayla made one cautious step further, then another. There it was, a cabin with its door slightly ajar. It was the thing causing a disturbance—or rather, lack of disturbance. Ayla finally understood what bothered her. Everything around her was in motion, except this one spot that was unnaturally quiet.

She pushed the door open and froze on the spot. A young woman lay on the back, eyes glassed over, staring at the ceiling. Her throat was slit, with blood pooling all around her. No more movement in her body, no more laughter, no more pain. She was dead.

The heavy door gave in as someone walked through. The girl behind her stopped, the sound of a dropped handbag startling Ayla. A shrill scream. It echoed on the bare stone walls so much her ears nearly popped. The door swung open again, bringing in the sounds of the bar. Someone grabbed Ayla's hand, dragging her away from the scene.

"Oh no, Ayla." Lyssa's sweet voice sounded in her ear, but there was fear in it. "We need to get you out of here. Come."

She pulled her along, but Ayla couldn't move. Her body went rigid, her mind numb. There was a dead body in front of her. A dead body she found. Alone. And now there was a witness who saw her standing over it. Paralysed with terror, she stared at the dead woman's eyes, wondering about the last thing they saw. Her own visions came to mind. Corbin slicing throats of young women just like that. Where did he put the bodies?

She stared and stared, vaguely aware of the fuss going on around her. People were talking all at once, their words slurred into one. Echoing in her mind, ringing in her ears. *Murder.*

"I didn't do it", she protested weakly. Nobody heard her. The cacophony in the background was nothing but a hum; then, everything went quiet. Footsteps approached her, and she startled when a hand touched her shoulder. Through the fabric of her shirt, it felt warm and comforting. The touch was a fleeting one, as if the person only wanted to get her attention but not impose. Ayla slowly turned towards the source.

Blaze studied her face, an expression of concern in his emerald eyes. "Are you okay, Ayla? Are you hurt?"

She shook her head, wondering if she would ever be able to forget the gruesome scene. Yet another one to add to her previous experience. More dead bodies on her way. She briefly thought about the reading she got at a fortune-teller's tent a lifetime ago. *Your father's curse will destroy everyone around you.* Maybe this was true, after all.

"Come on, we need to get you out of here," Blaze urged, gently pushing her between shoulder blades. Like a marionette on the string, she nodded and made one rigid step towards the exit, then another. His voice was very different when he spoke again. "Mace and Levi, stay here and secure the space until the Enforcers arrive. Lyssa, collect the others outside. I want everyone to be ready to leave as soon as possible."

Following his instructions, the group quickly broke apart. Through the wall of greyness, Ayla watched people moving around, everyone's eyes wide but actions precise. Mace and Levi produced a yellow tape that they stuck around the cabin with the body. Mace stayed inside to watch, while Levi followed her out and stood by the entrance, telling the ladies that the toilets were out of order.

Blaze led her to a back alley, where the rest of the group were already waiting. With a practised move, he let a ball of spinning white energy float from his hand into the middle of the passageway. The light pulsed, expanding, until it became the size of a door. A door that opened to another place.

"Stay with me," Blaze whispered to Ayla. She stood still by his side, watching the others go through the portal. Blaze made sure everyone went through until the only one left was Sherice. She gave him a gracious smile.

"Thanks for your help, Blaze. The kids are getting out of control, aren't they?" She shot a sharp look at Ayla, though it immediately disappeared. Blaze gestured for her to go through the portal.

"After you." Once she was gone, he turned to Ayla. "It's your turn."

She stepped through the glowing light. A thought in the back of her mind wondered how different the portals were here. Nothing like the cold darkness of the Sorcerers. Maybe it was due to the different way magic was used, or maybe the sensation depended on the person opening them. Regardless, this time it didn't frighten her, and she was glad.

Blaze was the last to come through. Ayla looked around, surprised to see that they were in front of her house. The group of others was waiting nervously. Everyone was still there, even Sherice, waiting for his instructions.

"Okay, everyone. You can go home now and try to get some sleep. Please stay inside until you've been notified it's safe to come out. Whitestone's walls have stood strong so far, but I want to make a few checks to make sure they're still secure. Are there any questions?"

"No, sir," students muttered, hiding their eyes.

"Good. You're free to go," he dismissed them. Rapid steps announced multiple departures, and in a matter of seconds Ayla was the only one standing beside him. Too late she realised that his words were addressed to everyone, and made a move to go to her house. His voice stopped her. "Ayla, wait."

She stopped, frozen to the spot. She knew it! He didn't truly believe she was innocent. A wave of terror washed over her like an icy blast. She was in so much trouble!

"You're not in trouble," he spoke in a soft, soothing voice. "It was very traumatic to see what you saw tonight. You've been very brave, though. Are you sure you're not hurt?"

She shook her head as the chilly breeze of the night wrapped around her. Shivers came first, sending tiny ripples of cold through her body. First on the surface, going deeper under her skin. Blaze looked into her eyes. "I know you didn't do it. Somehow, you just ended up in the wrong spot at the wrong time. For now, I need you to go home and get some rest, okay? There will be some mint and camomile tea waiting, but you'll need a bit more to help you fall asleep tonight. Take this and put two drops into your tea." He placed a tiny vial into her hand, careful not to touch her skin. She automatically took it, wondering what it was. As always, her tongue didn't move in his presence and she was silent. "It's just a bit of herbal essence. Part nightbloom, part primrose, with a little bit of spiced apple. It will help you relax and take away the fear. I need to go back and help the boys, but you'll be safe as long as you stay inside."

Ayla nodded, hardly registering his words. With the vial in her hand, she walked up the steps and closed the door behind her. She had a lot to process after the night's events.

One thing she knew, though, was the most important one. Blaze didn't blame her for the murder. He was going to find out who did it, and he was going to protect her. She was finally safe.

There was no sound to announce his departure, but somehow she knew he was no longer there.

CHAPTER 9. AYLA

"I've put these together for the term's project." Ayla produced her glass plate with three delicate stems that were now dry. Primrose, nightbloom and lovehaze. She had picked them up herself once she became more confident at the greenhouse, and was keen to catch up with others. Even if there was only one subject she could do without actively using her magic, it was better than nothing.

Meera nodded in approval. "You've selected very fine specimens. See how the lovehaze branch here has a full bloom and a couple of buds? They can be used in different tinctures with a slight difference in their properties. Can you tell me what they are?"

Ayla beamed with a ready smile. Finally, there was something she was good at! Learning had always been her strongest suit. "Full blooms are predominantly used to make lovehaze essence that people use as an aphrodisiac. Buds are good for warming tea to help chase away sadness and boost love to oneself."

"Very good! You're catching up so fast!" Meera turned to the class, announcing the next task. Her words blurred together as Ayla tried to contain her excitement. How good was it to finally get praise for something that she'd done! Students took notes, studying the new plant Meera was showing them.

Lyssa sat by her side, mostly to keep her company. After the events of the fateful night, Mace was nowhere to be seen. "He got in trouble for taking everyone to town," she whispered to Ayla when Meera started talking to another student.

"He hasn't done anything wrong. None of us knew something like this could have happened." Ayla shifted her eyes on her notes, though her focus remained with the conversation. "Did they find out who killed that girl?"

"It's tricky. She was no ordinary girl, but one of the students from higher levels here. The Enforcers are looking into it, but for now nobody's allowed to leave Whitestone. Except some male Mages, because the killer seems to favour females." She shrugged, staring at Ayla's herbal display. "I don't know, girl. We have to be careful. I wouldn't want to be in her place."

"Me neither." There was nothing left to say. The lesson was over, with Meera giving them an assignment to read a few chapters on the uses of nightbloom and lovehaze combinations for next time. "I need to go to the library.

This class had the Introduction to Nature Studies in the first semester, so I want to try and catch up on everything."

"Go girl!" Lyssa's bright smile lit up her face, lifting Ayla's mood. "It's at the Council building. Remember how to get there?"

"Aren't you coming with me?" Ayla's voice dropped. She was so used to her friend's company it seemed odd to go somewhere without her.

"I need to see Rowan," Lyssa mumbled apologetically. "But I'll see you back at your place for afternoon tea, how about that?"

The two parted, following the small group out of the classroom. Ayla sighed, thinking about Lyssa's relationship. Rowan seemed to be a great influence on her, though they were spending increasingly more time together now. Ayla was happy for her friend, but a slither of sadness crept in every now and then, reminding her she was still alone.

The library was at the back of the beautiful Council building. Ayla marched through the front reception along the corridor with arched ceilings. There would be a small passageway in the back that would lead her where she needed to go.

One of the doors on her way was ajar. Despite her effort to keep moving, Ayla stopped. There were hardly any visitors or gatherings in this building, and hearing voices was not something she expected. Curious, she crept closer. The door led to a small antechamber to one of the halls.

The voices were much clearer here, as if they were talking right next to her. Throwing a quick glance back, Ayla stepped closer. She wasn't going to linger too much. Just to find out what was happening and leave straight after.

"I really don't think this is much of our concern," a young male voice came through first. Ayla peeked in the keyhole, hoping one of the speakers would cross her line of vision. "If your girls are disappearing, maybe you should look into your own ranks first before throwing around accusations. You know where this can lead, Councillor Jasper."

"We understand, don't get us wrong, Your Highness. There are a few investigations underway now to figure out the way this murderer works. So far we see that only younger Mage women are targeted, either students or fresh graduates. This has been happening all over the world, and now that it's so close to Whitestone, we have to take this as a serious threat."

"What Prince Drake is trying to say is they don't care if we're all dead, as long as the Sorcerers are safe," someone's steely voice cut through.

"Hey, break it up. Reeves. Blaze, can you tell us your thoughts, please?"

Ayla shifted in her spot, uncomfortable. One thing was to eavesdrop on an anonymous conversation, even if it did include the Sorcerers' Prince. A completely different thing was spying on her Mentor. She needed to leave. Yet, her body didn't obey her, leaving her at the spot to find out more.

"The disappearances are quite concerning, especially now that we found a body so close to Whitestone," Blaze's voice was smooth as ever, though the tonality was very different from the way he normally spoke to her. "The Enforcers sent a unit to investigate, and I'll work closely with them. As soon as we get more details, I'll let you know."

"The disappearances started shortly after you brought your protégée to Whitestone. She was spotted next to the latest victim." This voice was cold and sharp.

"I am aware. One of the students alerted me of the unauthorised gathering outside of Whitestone and I arrived shortly after the body was found. I'm confident this was nothing but a coincidence."

"How can you be so sure, Blaze? A girl with unknown powers, showing up out of nowhere, in the midst of uncertain times. Getting caught red-handed with the latest victim's body. That's one hell of a coincidence." The sharp voice sounded unconvinced.

"She didn't just show up, Councillor, I've been looking for her for years. It's not Ayla's fault that her magic hasn't manifested yet, and she's trying her best. It will happen eventually. Have some patience."

Jasper cleared his throat. "Which brings us to the next question. If you're so sure she's not faking, why is it taking so long for you to unlock her power? These are uncertain times indeed; we need to get our students on training as hard as they can, learning how to protect themselves in case of an attack. Your protégée is the only one with unknown powers, which is suspicious as hell already. You have to push her."

"I agree," the Prince spoke again.

Blaze sounded annoyed. "Do not assume that you can tell me what to do, Sorcerer. I will keep the peace, but nobody will meddle in my own affairs. The poor girl is confused and scared; if you knew what's been done to her, you wouldn't be suggesting pushing her. Maybe you should investigate one of your own who damaged her so badly I'm not even sure I can ever heal her completely."

"I'm sorry, Blaze. I wish we had more time to let her recover, but we simply don't." Jasper's voice echoed against the walls. "If she possesses great power, she can be a valuable asset. If she doesn't and if you refuse to cooperate, she might well become the next victim. You have to push her, it's the only way. Force her if you have to."

"No." Blaze's voice was cold as ice. "I'll never make her do anything against her will. If or when she's ready, she will come to me on her own. I took the responsibility for her and I will protect her."

A strange silence fell upon the room. Ayla hugged her shoulders, thoughts racing in her mind. There was a lot to ponder, and she needed to get out of there unnoticed. She snuck out of the room, changing her mind. She could go to the library later. Now she needed to have some time on her own.

***

The living room was full of people again. Ayla smiled, looking from one face to another. All her friends showed up to give their support and reassure her nobody believed the fateful event of the past week was her fault. Lyssa was the first one, of course. She was the one who brought the news.

"The school Board ordered all the students to stay within the limits of the city, and any travels outside need to be reported and approved prior. Poor Mace is still in trouble, but it shouldn't take much longer. After all, he had the best intentions in heart."

"Nobody expected to find what you found," Rowan stepped in, scratching his unshaven chin. Lyssa giggled when he planted a kiss on her cheek, tickling her.

"Exactly," Levi chimed in. "After you all left, Mace and I kept watch until Blaze and the Enforcers came along. There was nothing to report, though. This girl, Darlene, went missing a couple of days ago, but since it was something she used to do, nobody was looking. They confirmed that she'd been dead for hours before her body ended up in that bathroom. The place was clear of any signs, so they believe it was a portal. The whole thing reeks of dark magic, and you know what I've always said."

"Dark magic means Sorcerers," Lyssa finished, her eyes serious. "It couldn't possibly be one of us. Only Sorcerers can get so corrupt they'd consider murder as something to obtain their goals. After all, they used to enchant their artefacts with the blood of Mages."

"What? I didn't know that." Ayla drew in a sharp breath. Things suddenly made a lot more sense. She knew the Sorcerers needed an artefact to use magic, but never knew how magic was collected there in the first place.

"Yes. Magic lives inside us, but it is finite. If you use all of it, you won't have any left. With Sorcerers, they don't have any of their own but they possess the ability to steal it from others. That was the major cause of the ancient wars. Power. It wasn't until all the Mage communities joined forces and fought back so hard they really pressed the damn Sorcerers against the wall. They signed the Treaty, and now each society sticks to their own rules. At least, they used to until recently." Rowan stared at Ayla, as if considering whether to tell her more.

Lyssa slapped him on the arm. "This is nonsense." She turned to Ayla, a sympathetic expression on her face. "Nobody blames you, of course."

"Why would someone blame me?" A chilling realisation started making its way in Ayla's consciousness. So there *was* an undertow in this peaceful sea. And there she was, thinking this was a perfect world.

Lyssa sighed, throwing a burning look at Rowan. "Like I said, this is nonsense. Some people believe that the chain of events started with your arrival to Whitestone, as if Blaze disrupted the normal way of things by taking you away from a Sorcerer. But it was the right thing to do. You didn't belong in their world. Your old Master was either using you for his twisted entertainment or secretly draining your power for himself. Either way, this is unacceptable. Those ways are long gone, and doing it is illegal. Mages are allowed to claim their own, especially if there is cause to believe a Sorcerer was stealing your magic."

"Yes, but it hasn't happened for centuries," Rowan intervened again. "It could be pure coincidence, but the disappearances started shortly after you came here."

"Right, as if Ayla could travel all the way up North within a couple of hours to kill someone. When she can't even open a portal to get outside Whitestone yet," Lyssa remarked in a sarcastic voice.

"Are you guys fighting?" Saree's sweet voice cut through the escalating tones.

Ayla didn't notice her and Jason joining them until they were in her direct line of vision. Jason had his arm around his sweetheart, and despite the heat of the discussion, Ayla couldn't help but marvel at the harmony of their union. The plant whisperer was a perfect fit for Saree's Empath abilities. Both quiet and mostly keeping to themselves, they seemed to be a couple that was meant to be.

"They're not destined, if that's what you're thinking," someone's playful voice whispered just beside her. Ayla startled, turning towards the source of the sound. Surely enough, Levi's sly grin told her he knew all about her thoughts again.

"Can you stay out of my mind, please?" she hissed, trying to clear her head. Knowing that someone could just browse her thoughts was unnerving, and she had already had her fill with Corbin.

Levi's grin became wider. "Your thoughts are plastered all over your face." He stepped closer to make sure only she could hear him. "It's actually not that easy to read you, honey. Your mind is like fog. I only know about your most prominent ones, or your deepest desires," he smirked, making Ayla think about the scene at the hot tub and its strange beginning.

"Okay," she replied, uneasy. Whatever he meant, she wasn't comfortable discussing it further.

Levi nodded and stepped back. "Think about it. We could have had a great little fling, you and I, if it wasn't for your special circumstances." With a wink, he disappeared behind the kitchen breakfast bar, busying himself with fruit punch. Ayla stared at his back. Special circumstances?

Turning back to the main discussion, she realised the conversation changed direction. The friends were discussing something she had no idea about. After a few moments of listening, she gave up. "What's *journeying*?" she dared. The group went quiet.

"Uh, it's when someone can travel a distance while they're in the Mist," Jason responded, averting his eyes. "You don't...sleep-walk, do you?"

"Of course not, that's silly," Lyssa intervened, brushing off his comment. "They're trying to find out if your success with the Mist has something to do with your special powers. Those of us who are lucky to ever see the Mist, can only astral-project there. There was only one person in the history of Mages who could *journey* there in his physical form, but we prefer not to talk about it."

The group muttered a short phrase and simultaneously knocked on wood.

"Have you seen the Mist yourselves?" she asked, glancing at one face after another. A wave of headshakes was her answer.

"I think Blaze can go in, but I don't know of any students or other teachers who can. Maybe some of the Healers, but they are great at keeping their secrets."

"Not so great at keeping mine," Ayla mentioned bitterly. "How come my ability is now public knowledge?"

The sound of an opening door interrupted the conversation. Irritated, Ayla turned to see the newcomer. The wide grin on the beautiful face was the last thing she wanted to see.

"Hello, Sherice," she hissed through clenched teeth. "Fancy seeing you here, among all my friends who came to support me. Shall I take this as a compliment?"

Sherice snorted, looking around the house as if she was searching for someone. When she didn't find what she was looking for, she relaxed and graced Ayla with an answer. "Not really. Just wanted to see if you were still in your cute little house and not locked up in jail yet."

"I didn't do anything wrong!"

Lyssa stepped in. "Sherice, it was really not cool of you to rat her out to Blaze. We know it was you. You'll have no friends left if you keep this up."

Sherice let out a bitter laugh, eyes sharp on Ayla. "Why would I want to be her friend, of all people? Just because Blaze told you to be nice to her doesn't mean everyone has to."

"What's your problem?" Encouraged by the presence of her friends, Ayla felt confident to step up for herself. She had enough of bullies in her life. If she had to confront the blonde about it, so be it.

Sherice turned around with a theatrical look. "Look at you, guys. All gathered here to support a suspected murderer. Someone who could potentially target any of you next. Are you seriously going to stand by her side?"

"Take it easy," Rowan stepped in with a note of warning in his voice. The crowd went quiet, watching the conflict in front of them.

Ayla drew in a deep breath, battling her anger. She reminded herself of slow, deep breaths, about counting to ten and back, about happy thoughts. Anything would do to help her clear the veil of red rapidly clouding her vision.

Sherice watched her effort with a mocking grin on her face. "Why's that? Because I might hurt her feelings?" she asked, throwing a condescending look at Ayla. "The poor damsel in distress who comes and gets everything she wants, without ever having to work for it like the rest of us. You should enquire, Lyssa, see how cushioned her life was with the Sorcerer. Who, might I add, is pretty powerful and quite good-looking too! See any similarity there?"

Unable to contain her fury, Ayla stepped forward and raised her hand to slap her. Lyssa intercepted her wrist. "Stop, Ayla! It's a provocation, can't you see?"

Struggling to breathe, Ayla peered at her opponent with burning eyes. Rowan stepped between her and Sherice, keeping the distance between them. Sherice chuckled. "You're a coward, Ayla. This is why you killed all those girls. To show them you're superior, when in reality you're nothing but an empty shell. All the blood in the world can't help you."

Rowan grabbed Sherice by the arm and nudged her towards the exit. Exasperated, Ayla stayed still. Once the blonde was out the door, Lyssa let go of her.

"I'm going to kick her arse," she muttered through clenched teeth, digging her nails into the tender flesh of her palms.

Lyssa turned her around to face her. "Come on now, Ayla, calm down. You know she's more experienced and she'll most likely kick yours. That's exactly what she wants, can't you see? But the last thing you want right now is the school Board investigating a cat fight in your house. Come on, let's get some air."

Lyssa half-dragged her out on the back porch, leaving the silent group behind. The sharp chill of the air cooled Ayla's cheeks, though the rage in her heart was burning strong.

"You can't let it get to you," Lyssa soothed.

Ayla shivered. "I know. It's too soon after she made me angry last week, and now people probably think I have issues. I don't know what to do."

"It's going to be okay." Lyssa hugged her, and for a while neither uttered a word. It was a quiet time of the night. Too quiet to be disrupted by a fight.

CHAPTER 10. AYLA

Corbin traced the outline of her face with his fingers, the flame in the fireplace dancing in his eyes. She smiled, grateful for his presence. This moment had been building up between them, and even though he was getting closer to her every day, it was never close enough. The blood of the sacrifices gave her strength, but also a high that she couldn't explain. Corbin was the one providing it to her, and she lusted after it—something she had never felt before. To get more, she was ready to do whatever he wanted. If this was what he desired, she was prepared to give it to him.

"How are you feeling?" His smooth voice rolled over her like a sheet of silk.

"Much better, thank you."

He moved a little closer, pushing her into the wall. "I was hoping we could do something different tonight."

"Anything you want," she tried not to blink when he peered into her eyes. Ayla knew he could see inside her mind. Somehow, since the sacrifices began, he seemed to have lost the ability. She could tell blatant lies and he never noticed. Maybe it was the presence of Caerulus. Her new friend long became part of her. There were whispers in the middle of the night in a language she didn't understand that somehow sounded familiar. Shadows hiding in the corners that slithered after her. None of that bothered her. Not anymore, at least.

He lifted her chin, locking her in place. Not a muscle moved on her face as he lowered his head and pulled in a deep breath of her fragrance. "I love the way you smell, even though you're not afraid of me anymore. Those pheromones can't be compared to anything in the world. I don't care, though. As long as you are alive and well, nothing else matters."

The tickle of his breath travelled along her cheekbones towards the sensitive skin under her ear. His hand rested on her throat, with his thumb ever so slightly pressing on her artery. Reminding her who was in control. She stayed still, heart racing. It was okay. He couldn't hurt her, not when she was under the protection of Caerulus.

The stone sent a warm impulse through her body, all the way from her chest, to settle low in her belly. That was a betrayal she didn't expect. Corbin gently nipped at her ear, making her gasp. "Will you be gentle?" she moaned, losing control of her body.

He pulled away, looking into her eyes, a wicked smile on his lips. "When was I ever gentle, darling? I don't do gentle. You'd best remember it."

She shivered when he increased his grip on her throat. A sudden yelp escaped her lips when he sank his teeth into the tender skin on her neck. There would be a bad bruise tomorrow, she knew it! He held the bite in place, tugging at her skin, bruising it more with every instant. Ayla suppressed another scream. It was horrible... but pleasant.

She squirmed and tried to push him away, but he was much stronger. "No fighting, remember? Stay still and it won't hurt as much," he grunted, unclenching his jaws. Ayla let out a rushed breath, struggling to process the new sensations. The side of her neck burned after the bite, but the warmth in her belly grew to heat now. Caerulus pulsed on her chest as if mocking her. Traitor.

Corbin twisted her around, quickly binding her hands behind her back. She didn't have time to realise that he got the rope somewhere, that he grabbed her by the arm and dragged her to his bed. Those black sheets that frightened her when she first saw them now made her excited. She wanted to know what he would do, and it was terrifying and thrilling at the same time.

He redid the binding, cuffing her hands one to each side of the bed. A silk band covered her eyes before she had a chance to protest. "Please, Corbin. I want to see," she pleaded. Only a chuckle was her answer.

"No, darling. You'll do what you're told to please me. And it pleases me today to see you blindfolded and cuffed, just like that. You agreed to it, remember? It's time to pay it off."

Hating herself and her treacherous body, Ayla arched her back to meet his touch. No matter what he was going to do, she was eager for it. The great sapphire clouded her mind, and all that remained was the strange lust for blood. And whatever it was Corbin wanted to do.

***

That night Ayla struggled to fall asleep. Turning from one side to another, she played the past events in her mind over and over. At the pub, it was Sherice who provoked her, but she stomped off into the bathroom on her own accord. Anyone could see she was in a bad mental space and could have done something rash. By accident or by choice, it didn't matter. If Blaze wanted to cover up for her, he'd have to work hard on making her look innocent.

She didn't kill that girl. It was Corbin, she was sure of it. The ugly wound on her neck matched the ones she saw on the sacrifices. She managed to drift off to sleep, only to see one of the haunted dreams again. Herself under the influence of the sapphire, writhing and squirming in Corbin's arms to gain his favour. Ayla was disgusted with herself.

The way she felt in that dream, the way she acted, the thoughts that went through her mind...It was atrocious.

Unable to go back to sleep, she got up and turned on the water in the shower. Standing under the scorching hot stream, she rubbed the soft foam all over to cleanse herself. No matter how hard she rubbed, the revolting feeling remained on her skin like a sticky film. The mirror didn't show any bruising that should have been there after the things Corbin had done. Her hand slid down her body, feeling all the spots he had tainted. There was nothing there. Not a single mark. No way of telling someone even touched her.

Yawning, she stumbled into the kitchen. The jug of water was on the kitchen bench in its usual spot. Ayla picked up a glass, wondering if she was thirsty or not. The house would normally serve her a drink already poured when she needed it. Why not now?

Pop. A strange noise came from the door. Ayla stood still, clutching her glass. What was that?

A wave of light followed it, with the sound of an explosion muffled as if it was far away. She ran towards the windows and peeked outside. There was nobody in the street; it was an ordinary night, like any other. Something had shifted in the air, though. Unsure what to do, Ayla put the glass down. Everything seemed normal, as if the strange explosion didn't just rip through the night. There was an abnormality though. An anomaly that hadn't been there before.

She had to find out what it was.

Without a second thought, Ayla rushed out of the house. The peaceful street was immersed in pure darkness, with the only source of light being the lantern on her porch and the rare stars that peeked through the rips in heavy storm clouds. Static electricity was in the air, the messenger of a storm coming. Ayla ran towards downtown, hoping she'd find the answer there. As she approached the Healers' Hub, she could hear a fight. That was it, the anomaly. A fight in the safe, peaceful streets of Whitestone.

A sticky fog pulled at her ankles. Ayla glanced down, frowning. This substance was nothing like the delicate touch of the Mist that she was used to. This fog seemed to be made out of storm clouds, grazing along her skin like the teeth of a predator getting ready to strike. She stepped back, but the fog thickened, its tentacles rising higher by the moment. Its pull intensified, shifting her away from safety. The sounds dissolved into a background hum, confusing her sense of direction. There was no way of knowing where she was headed or where she came from. Panic gripped her heart in its steel fingers, pushing her to run away somewhere, anywhere, to escape the fear.

Ayla took a deep breath and started walking, picking up her pace with every step. She couldn't tell how far she'd gone nor if she had moved at all. All that was left to do was to keep walking until she got somewhere.

The atmosphere grew darker and the air breathed an icy chill on her skin. Ayla's gaze caught on the walls trapping her from both sides in a narrow alley that hadn't been there before. It smelled damp and rotten, a stark contrast to anything she had encountered in the safe streets of White-stone.

She could have sworn this was something new. Walks downtown had been a daily routine for her and Lyssa, and they'd never seen this little nook just off the main street. The houses on it made no sense; it was all stone walls without windows or doors in sight. Ayla made another attempt to leave, already realising the fog brought her there for a reason. Something else was coming; this was only the beginning.

Someone grabbed her by the arm and dragged her into a corner that came out of nowhere. The man's figure seemed vaguely familiar, but she couldn't remember when she could have seen him. Ayla squinted, straining her mind. This memory was just out of reach. She had seen this figure before, this exact one. The way he moved, the way the tentacles of darkness around him danced in the invisible wind and reached for her. She knew this person. This was the one who tried to kill her.

The figure pushed the hood back, revealing the un-shaven face of a man in his mid-twenties. The mocking expression in his dark eyes matched his crooked smile. "Well, well, well. We meet again."

"Kendall?" she fished his name out of her memory. That was the Apprentice of a Sorcerer who trapped her after Darren's murder. The same man who attacked her last year and left her to bleed out on a cold winter road. She would have been dead if it weren't for Corbin's intervention.

He grinned. "Oh, you remember my name! I was worried you'd have forgotten all about me." He stepped closer, a ring on his index finger sparkling to life. The graduation ring from the Sorcerers' Academy. The symbol of his privileged status.

Ayla traced it with her eyes. "Congratulations on your graduation," she said flatly, thinking of a way to keep him talking.

Kendall chuckled. "Thank you, that's lovely of you to say. I'm glad to be out of that hellhole. Looks like we have something to talk about, though. I see that you managed to survive our last encounter."

The stone wall behind her was cold. Kendall held her in place with just one hand, so close she could feel the heat coming off his body. "I did. Sorry about the disappointment."

"Not at all, not at all. Glad to see you again. I've been looking for you." He produced a knife and put it against her throat. Almost gently, the cold blade caressed her skin as her assailant smiled at his triumph. Ayla kept very still, holding her breath. She cursed herself for running out of the house. It was clearly the safest place in town. What was she thinking?

"I can only guess how you survived," Kendall's voice turned to an intimate whisper. "If only you bled out like you were supposed to, none of this would have happened. By staying alive you've put all your friends in danger. Your father died because of you. Your Master and your little Academy boyfriend were under constant threat as long as they were with you. And now your presence is putting this whole town at risk. How can you be so selfish, Ayla? Can't you see how much damage you're causing?"

Ayla's eyes filled with tears as she thought back to that fateful afternoon when she discovered her father dead. She was sure it was Kendall and his accomplices who murdered him trying to get to her. But nobody explained why they hated her so much. And she couldn't think of a reason why someone would turn her life to hell and threaten all the people who cared about her.

There was nowhere to run, nothing she could do. Any careless move, and he would cut her throat. It would take the slightest pressure, and that would be the end.

"That's right, be a good girl and stay quiet. It won't be long now," he whispered as his iron fingers dug into her shoulder. Ayla winced and closed her eyes. Time seemed to stand still. She thought about her sessions with Blaze and slowly let out a breath. It was important to stay calm if she wanted to succeed.

The power should manifest as a white flame.

Blaze's words echoed in her mind. If she was indeed worth something, now was the time to prove it. Slowly, carefully Ayla tried to picture the flame in her mind. It should be within reach, just on her fingertips...

A faint flicker appeared in the darkness of her mind, and a relieved smile flitted her lips. There it was, exactly as Blaze told her. He knew she could do it, and now she finally did!

Kendall shoved her harder against the wall, and she clenched her teeth. Her head burst with pain from the impact, and the weak glow disappeared as her focus shifted.

"Think you're so clever, don't you?" There was anger in his voice now. Ayla whimpered as the cold steel pressed against her neck, leaving a trickle of hot liquid in its wake. Eyes full of tears, she could hardly see his face in front of her.

"Why?" Her voice broke as she struggled to keep each breath as shallow as possible.

Kendall chuckled, pulling the knife away from her neck.

"It's your father, sweetheart. Your *real* father, not Darren. Our group was tasked to protect the world from him and his heritage."

"But I didn't do anything wrong. You seem to know more about my family than I do. Why not tell me then, if you're going to kill me anyway?"

Kendall smirked. "It doesn't matter anymore. I have a new Master now who has a use for you."

The knife went into the sheath with a quiet clink. Ayla stared at him in disbelief, struggling to understand what this meant. Kendall's grip on her shoulder tightened. "You're coming with me."

"No!"

Her scream only seemed to amuse him. Dragging her along, he made a step back into the fog, then another. Ayla struggled to breathe as panic clouded her mind. How in the whole town of Mages was there nobody to hear her?

The iron grip loosened and Kendall suddenly let go of her. Clutching on to her sore shoulder, Ayla leaped as far away from him as possible. Whatever the distraction was, she didn't have the luxury to wait. Her back found the cold stone wall again and she nearly groaned at the prospect of being stuck right behind her assailant and nowhere to run.

The fog grew lighter. Ayla rubbed her eyes and when she opened them again, it was almost gone. Only a few centimetres from the ground were still covered with dark, sticky greyness, giving way to clear night air. And then, there was something else. *Someone* else.

The glowing white fur of a majestic tiger seemed to fill the alley with light. His expression determined, the tiger let out a growl that shook Ayla top to bottom. It was a sound of danger that outweighed anything Kendall had shown so far, yet she somehow knew that was no threat to her. The tiger came to chase away the darkness. To get her out of the fog and back to safety.

The following action flew by in a blur. Ayla hardly managed to see the blows that were exchanged between the figures of dark and light. Kendall struck at the tiger with his knife, still stained with Ayla's blood. This only made his opponent more aggressive. The white animal threw himself at the dark Sorcerer with the fierce force of a parent protecting their young. The sheer energy coming from him was enough to break any spell, any ritual designed to cause harm.

Ayla gasped when the tiger's next attack drew blood from the black robe of his opponent. The quiet rip of the cloth bounced off the stone walls and the tiger turned his head to check on her. This second was enough for Kendall to flick his uninjured hand with a ring that now sparkled a crimson red. A circle of darkness opened up in front of him and he hurriedly stepped into it. In an instant, the dark spot in the air disappeared with a quiet pop.

Tense from the events of the night and unsure of what to do about the tiger, Ayla wrapped her arms around her shoulders. There was nowhere for her to run, and besides, the animal that so easily scared off the man who killed Darren wouldn't even break a sweat chasing her if he wanted to. Shivering in the cold breeze, she stood rooted to the spot, waiting for his next move.

The tiger made a couple of steps towards her and stopped, gauging her reaction. His emerald eyes were calm, without any shadow of imminent attack that she was afraid to see.

"Tigers don't have green eyes," she whispered. His careful yet steady approach reminded Ayla of her Mentor. He acted the same way, as if cautious of driving her away. She wondered if he could be Blaze's Familiar, or a spirit of ancestors that came to protect her. Ideas of the tiger's possible origin filled her head, one crazier than another.

A gust of wind brought about a few drops of cold rain. Ayla realised that in the rush she had left the house in her lightweight chemise. The adrenaline of the night didn't let her feel the cold before, but it was catching up. Shaking but too scared to move past the tiger to get out of the alley, she squeezed her eyes shut. Maybe if she pretended like she wasn't there, he would go away and then she'd be able to run back home, lock the door and try to forget about everything that happened here.

Something warm gently wrapped around her shoulders. With a start, Ayla opened her eyes. Her Mentor was standing in front of her, his hands keeping a leather jacket from sliding off her body. Before she could control herself, she glanced down. After all the stories that she'd heard about werewolves and various changelings, she half-expected him to be naked. Luckily, this wasn't the case. He was wearing a loose cotton shirt with long sleeves and a pair of jeans, as if he had to leave a social outing to come to her rescue.

Blaze's mouth slightly twitched in amusement as he caught her glance.

"No, I don't lose my clothes when I shift, Ayla. I'm not a werewolf."

She startled at the sound of his voice. Having him stand so close to her was unnerving yet somehow comforting. After all, he saved her from Kendall. He was the only one who came to help, the only one who had been protecting her since she had left Corbin's mansion. Her breathing shallow, Ayla closed her eyes again as another wave of panic hit her hard.

Blaze's hands took her by the shoulders and gently pulled her towards him. Ayla's whole being protested against it, yet her body did nothing to resist. Limp and obedient, she allowed him to wrap her in a warm embrace, safe from anything the world could throw at her. His shirt smelled like fresh lavender, mixed with a sweet undertone of bergamot and citrus. The best combination of fragrances she had ever encountered. Teasing and alluring, it was a secret siren calling her to give in and come closer to its source.

With her head buried in his chest, Ayla shuddered, letting go of the stress of the night. She was much shorter in stature and barely reached up to his shoulders, which allowed her to hide her tears. Cursing her weakness, she couldn't hold back her terror of what would have happened if Blaze hadn't appeared when he did.

"Shhh, it's okay, Ayla. I'm here now, you're safe," he whispered, gently patting her on the back. Gradually, slowly she calmed down, acknowledging his control of the situation. Ayla closed her eyes, relaxing against him. His steady heartbeat resonated with her whole body, making her own heart beat a little faster. She wasn't afraid of him anymore; things felt different somehow.

A strange feeling stirred inside her chest. Something uncoiling, awakening, wanting to be free. In mere seconds, it intensified, overwhelming her thoughts. Blaze let her out of his embrace and stepped back. Ayla gasped, trying to contain the new sensation. She looked into his eyes, seeking an answer.

Blaze gently took her hand and turned it palm up between them. The touch of his skin sent a longing across her body, but it didn't stop the strange feeling in her chest. On the contrary, it seemed to make it stronger.

"It's okay, Ayla. Let it come. Channel it here, in the centre of your palm." His velvet voice was a welcome comfort as his hand was holding hers steady. "Don't be afraid. Let it go. I'm right here to keep you safe."

What is he talking about? She drew in a shaky breath and tried to relax, focusing the strange sensation on the palm of her hand. At first, nothing happened. The force wavered as if deciding whether to follow her order. Slowly, almost invisible at first, sparks of white whirled over her hand. More and more showed up, relieving the pressure off her chest. Enchanted, Ayla watched them grow and merge into one another until they formed a solid form. A tiny white flame. Flickering in the dark, it seemed to be changing shapes. Its core was a small ball of pure white, while the aura was ever-shifting, hinting at the possibility to grow. Despite the rain, the show of her power stayed alight, and there was no mistake that she finally cracked the code. She did have magic; she just needed to find the right way to bring it up.

"This is it, Ayla. Your magic." Blaze's soft yet clear whisper rolled over her ears. Ayla chuckled, watching the dancing flame. The power of finally discovering her gift was intoxicating. She wasn't a *null*, and she was going to learn and grow, and prove everyone wrong.

The flame wavered and lost some of its volume. Ayla realised that Blaze didn't keep contact with her skin. He must have removed his hand when the flame appeared. She frowned, heartbeat accelerating again. She couldn't lose it, not when she just found it!

Panic rising, she tried to find the same source of power in her chest. There was nothing but the red void of fear. The flame danced over her hand, now only a fraction bigger than a nail on her pinkie finger. Tears of helplessness clouded Ayla's vision. Was that it? Was her magic nothing but a little burst that lasted mere seconds?

Blaze's hand slid under hers and a surge of energy over-whelmed her for a moment. She shook her head, making sense of it. Sharing of power was something she had only read about, and trying it herself was completely different. It only took a few seconds for her to understand what he was doing. With another deep breath, she let his magic join hers and the blossom of white grew bigger and brighter than before. Ayla breathed out, relieved. Even though it didn't feel quite like her own effort, it was better than anything she had done so far. Her eyes met Blaze's gaze, kind and warm like the touch of his hand on hers. The words of thanks wavered on her lips, but not a sound came out. The strange barrier kept her silent, so she tried to express her gratitude in her eyes.

"You're doing great. The flame disappears when you lose focus. That's why we have meditation sessions to learn how to control our emotions. You are very talented, Ayla. It won't take you long now."

Somehow, his gaze wasn't intimidating anymore. The euphoria of finally finding her magic overshadowed any reservations she'd had before. This was the person who be-lieved in her, whose endless patience and constant encour-agement helped her discover her hidden talent. The wave of gratitude came upon her as she held his gaze, smiling, thankful for his presence in her life and everything he had done.

The scars on his face didn't seem as terrifying as before. Those two ugly marks going from his left eye down to the corner of his mouth looked like they could have been left by a claw of a large animal. She studied his chiselled cheekbones and strong jaw, lingering on his lips that seemed luxuriously soft. Almost imperceptibly, she swayed towards him. This man was not intimidating. He was the one who could protect her. Take care of her in uncertain times. Cherish and nurture her the way no one else could. The white flame burned bright, feeding on his power that came to her through the warmth of his hand.

"Ayla?"

She jolted.

The familiar voice dissipated the captivating moment. Ayla blushed, turning from Blaze as if she was caught doing something immoral. The magical light went out in a quiet pop as soon as she changed her focus. Heart pounding in her chest, Ayla turned her face to Corbin. His unexpected visit was a mystery. Hot shame flowed to her cheeks as she remembered her strange dreams about him. The visions she wasn't sure were real. She wondered if they meant that he had another kind of claim on her and why he hadn't come to see her until now. Then, she remembered the pain he had put her through last year and her heart stopped in dread.

The two men exchanged hard looks.

"Hello, Corbin. What brings you to our parts at this time of night?" The ice in Blaze's voice could have frozen a whole town.

"I felt that Ayla was in danger and came to help her as soon as I figured out where to open the portal to," Corbin growled through clenched teeth. A soft rustle of his black robe announced a few leisurely steps towards Ayla.

She fought the urge to curl into a ball, trying to reassure herself she was safe.

"Great timing. As you can probably see, she's not in danger now," Blaze pointed out in a steely voice.

Corbin ignored him, all his attention focused on Ayla. She shivered in the cold rain, her eyes fixed on him. Something was very different about his demeanour. He looked much older than she remembered, with shadows settled deep under his dark eyes. His jet-black hair was starting to show grey, his face hardened as if he'd had a lot of grief since she last saw him. An expression of pain in his gaze struck her with a pang of guilt as if any of it was her fault.

"I'm sorry I didn't arrive sooner," he said in his deep voice, looking straight at her. Pulled towards him by an invisible cord, she opened her mind to him. The impenetrable darkness in his eyes was a familiar comfort which promised solace and safety. It was impossible to resist it. All her troubles would be forgotten if she had given in, just like she had in the past.

"You know I never meant to hurt you," he uttered so quietly she could barely hear it. His low voice dragged her deeper into oblivion. There was nothing else in the world except the two pools of stark blackness in front of her.

Ayla could feel his presence in her thoughts, searching, going through most recent memories. Someone was calling her from far away but it wasn't important anymore. She flinched.

Something strange emerged from his pursuit. A glimpse of his own thoughts, or perhaps a memory made its way into her vision. Ayla spotted the majestic sapphire encased in a gold mould, sitting on a pedestal that was surrounded by a chalk-drawn circle. The stone radiated power, the dark magic she was now too familiar with. She saw herself standing next to it, her hand extended towards the gem to absorb its energy.

The image escaped as quickly as it appeared, as if it was an accident. The excruciating migraine struck her hard, almost making her fall down on her knees. Everything hit her at once. Memories of suffering and pain she experienced in the last weeks of her stay with Corbin. The nightmares, the episodes of lost time, the apathy that seemed to always be there no matter what she did. Until Corbin would come and comfort her with that gaze of his dark eyes, making things better for a while.

"Stop it, Corbin! You're hurting her!" Someone's voice echoed far away, beyond the darkness. Ayla gasped as her legs nearly gave in, but strong hands held her up. The veil of pain slowly thinned as her forced connection with Corbin faded. As she blinked to adjust to reality, Blaze lifted her chin with his finger and gently turned her face towards him.

"It's okay, Ayla, you're safe," he soothed, gently caressing her cheek. "You're not his slave anymore. I won't let him hurt you again."

She let go of the tension, surprised at how easily it happened. Blaze's presence was a different kind of comfort. There was no intrusion into her mind, and the pain dissolved once she allowed herself to trust his power again. A sigh of relief escaped her lips as she blessed her lucky stars for his intervention. There was no need to ponder why he was able to snap her out of misery. She was just glad that he did.

"You put her in danger, Blaze," she heard Corbin's voice, low yet threatening like a snake in the grass. "This is not what you promised."

Shaking his head, Blaze scoffed. "You're unbelievable. If you're so keen, I can speak with you later. Right now, I have to take Ayla home. She's had enough suffering for the night." His voice was a drastic change when he spoke to her. "Come on, sweetheart, I'll take you home."

Ayla hardly remembered the walk back. Blaze's hand on her waist was keeping her up, but even with his support she nearly tripped over a couple of times. She didn't notice how they made it to her house and how Blaze gave her a cup of hot tea that smelled like camomile, mint and honey. There was something else in it, a calming and sweet undertone that cleared her mind of the leftover pain and shock. Smiling as she drifted off to sleep, she snuggled into the jacket that Blaze wrapped her in before he left. The smell of curated leather mixed with warm wood and a hint of citrus blended well with his own scent, enveloping her in a soothing embrace. Ayla clung onto his jacket as it could protect her from the world's troubles. This time, there were no visions to disturb her.

CHAPTER 11. BLAZE

Ayla was a quivering mess. The encounter with her former Master didn't go well, and Blaze saw clearly that his primary instinct to keep them apart was right. He had never witnessed the mind spells in action himself, but knew enough to understand that it wasn't a good idea to try and physically break eye contact between the victim and the perpetrator. This could severely damage the victim and leave her stranded in the darkness with little chance of survival.

He hardly kept it together when he saw the outcome. Ayla was pale like a ghost, shivering all over. There was not a hint of the intimacy for him that she displayed earlier. The Sorcerer took it all. Now Blaze had to start over, and who knew if it would be more difficult this time.

Good thing Lyssa was around to lend a helping hand. Blaze didn't want to take Ayla all the way into her bedroom, and Lyssa was very understanding. She took over with a promise to stay with Ayla until she fell asleep, and to stop by first thing in the morning. Blaze silently thanked his lucky stars. She was the best fit for Ayla. He chose well.

When he returned to the alley, the Sorcerer was still there. Waiting, watching, like a predator ready to pounce. Blaze rolled his shoulders, automatically doing a quick check of his power. As always, it was right there, on his fingertips.

Corbin's midnight eyes stared at him with indifference, but there was an undertow of something deeper. A darkness so profound it made Blaze's skin crawl with goosebumps. Whatever this Sorcerer was, whatever he had become since their last meeting, was a drastic change to the person he'd been before. Blaze had to keep him away from Ayla at all costs.

"Well. Tell me what you want, Corbin. What is so important you chose to break your word to stay away from her? I thought we had an agreement."

The Sorcerer held a pause that Blaze knew so well. The mastery of those breaks in the conversation was one of the tactics to annoy the opponent and trick them into making rash decisions. Blaze waited patiently, determined not to fall for it.

"Ayla and I share a blood bond that you won't be able to comprehend," Corbin responded, an expression of superiority plastered all over his face. "I can feel when she is in danger. Thanks to the bond, I can find her anywhere.

It took me a while to figure out a way to get through the defences here, but I made it."

"You were too late. If it weren't for my intervention, that maniac would have killed her," Blaze retorted. He took a brief breath, trying to calm his emotions. It wasn't easy; the damn Sorcerer got between him and Ayla once again.

"He didn't want to kill her," Corbin responded, an expression of sadness crossing his face. "This is not what it was about at all."

Blaze looked at him quizzically. "What do you mean?"

"Never mind." Corbin shook his head, restoring his smug demeanour. "You were supposed to keep her safe, Blaze. Not try to get into her pants."

Even though Blaze knew it was a provocation, he couldn't keep quiet this time. "It's not like you refrained from it yourself. Unlike me, you did it without her consent. If it wasn't for that blood bond you forced upon her, I swear I would have challenged you."

Anger boiled inside him, ready to burst any minute. Magic filled up his lungs, only waiting for his command to charge. Its presence cooled his temper. *I can't use my power on a hot head. It's a recipe for disaster. Calm down, Blaze. It's not worth it. You have to stay calm for Ayla's sake.*

Corbin's face changed. For a moment, he seemed stunned. "I never slept with her, Blaze. You'd know if I did." He closed his eyes and held another pause. When he spoke again, the smugness restored its reign in his voice.

"There is so much more to pleasure than simple sex. You're a primal though, so I don't expect you to understand."

Blaze clenched his fists. Direct insults didn't sit well with him, but this wasn't high school. He didn't have to react to everything. "Can't believe I'm having a sex talk with you, of all people. Thanks for educating me."

It looked like Corbin didn't expect this answer. He chuckled, slowly measuring his opponent with his dark eyes. "Now that I think about it, though, I should have used my power more. Less mental, more physical. Something like you would do yourself."

Easy, now. I'm calm, very calm. He won't provoke me no matter what he says.

Magic tingled on Blaze's fingertips, a reflection of the flame of anger in his heart. Air caught in his lungs, making it hard to breathe. There was nothing but a red veil covering his eyes, colouring his opponent a sinister crimson. *From hell he came, and back to hell shall I throw him.*

"Too bad the moment is gone, isn't it?" Blaze managed through clenched teeth. "Good thing I'm not like you."

Corbin stepped closer with a mischievous smile on his lips. "Oh, but you are. We are very similar, you and I, whether you realise it or not. Your animal side knows exactly what I mean. Tell me you don't feel the overwhelming desire to hurt her whenever she's around. To take what's yours, without asking permission. To do what you want, throwing away the shallow layer of civilization. Go ahead, Blaze. Tell me the truth."

Shaking his head, Blaze stepped back. How did Corbin know? *He's a sick bastard, that's how. He believes everyone is as twisted as he is. But I'm better than this. I won't give in to this madness.*

"My animal side has no say in how I live my life." The conversation was draining. Blaze needed to finish it before he did something stupid. He shifted his weight to another foot and stared straight into the Sorcerer's eyes. "You said you came here to protect Ayla. It appears that she didn't need your protection. Perhaps, you should go."

Corbin chuckled, a shadow of sadness in his eyes. "Of course. You need to understand, Blaze, that something's wrong with this girl. I know you feel exactly what I said earlier. She is a lure for any predator. It's a curse she carries everywhere she goes, and death follows her close. Maybe this is something you can think about in your free time. Have a good night."

With a smooth gesture, he opened a dark portal and stepped in. The rip in the fabric of space whooshed closed behind him. The sounds of the night came back in their full glory. Nightingales sang their songs, bats flapped their wings, a cat's claws patted along the paved street. Everything was back to normal.

Blaze wiped his forehead. Despite the cool air, there was sweat on his skin. He sighed, finally allowing himself to relax. The worst of it was over, at least for now. He needed to release the tension as soon as possible before the animal side took over. Blaze breathed out and welcomed the primal in. Ayla was safe in the house. He didn't need to worry about a thing when he went on a hunt tonight.

CHAPTER 12. AYLA

"He turns into a *tiger*, Lyssa. Like a werewolf, but a tiger." Ayla placed her coffee on the table in front of her, staring at her friend. She slept in this morning and was pleasantly surprised that nobody came to wake her at sunrise. Lyssa only showed up after breakfast.

Rolling her mug by the handle in front of her, Lyssa studied the ripples in the drink as if it was the most interesting thing in the world. "You told me that a few times now, love. Did this traumatise you the most out of everything that's happened?"

Ayla pouted. "As a matter of fact, yes! I didn't expect anything like that. And somehow, I feel like someone should have told me about his ability to turn into a huge killing machine. I nearly wet my pants! One guy already tried to kill me, then another guy showed up as a giant tiger. What the hell is happening in this town? How many other things am I not aware of?" She realised she was panting and stopped.

Lyssa's eyes were fixed on the froth of her cappuccino. "I'm sorry, Ayla. I thought you knew he was a shifter."

"How would I know? Nobody told me!" Ayla thrashed her fingers through her hair. It wasn't Lyssa's fault, of course. She was just angry that everyone seemed to simply know the things she needed to learn every time. It was their birth right, and she still had so much to catch up on.

A coy smile crossed Lyssa's lips when she looked at Ayla again. "Well, the good thing is that shifters don't lose their clothes during transformation like werewolves do."

"Yeah, he told me that much." Ayla tried to keep a still face, but it was impossible to stay mad at Lyssa.

"I'm just glad you're safe and were able to come home in one piece. Have you had your meditation session today?"

"Not yet. Rhonda never showed up, so I thought something was wrong. I was just going to check at the Healers' Hub after breakfast. Maybe she was hurt during the attack last night and I need to organise the session with someone else. Do you know how many people were affected?"

"Most students are okay. I think some people from town got hurt, as there were a few rogue Sorcerers roaming the streets. Something was wrong with them, you know? It's like they were under the influence of a drug. Once captured, they immediately denied remembering anything. The Council kept one of them in custody and released the others to the Sorcerer authorities."

"Do you mean there is a Sorcerer here at Whitestone? One of the psycho bastards who attacked the town?" Ayla's heart set off in a violet beat.

"Oh, he's kept in the vault under the Council's building. Don't worry, Ayla, it's one of the most secure places in the world."

"*Whitestone* was supposed to be one of the most secure places in the world," Ayla interrupted. "How did those Sorcerers even get here?"

Lyssa held a pause, chewing her lip. "I'm not sure. Blaze is on it, though. I hear he's been at the emergency Council meeting this morning. They're brainstorming ways to secure the town even more, and trying to figure out where the breach came from. You know, you can only get to Whitestone when you know exactly where to go. For a Sorcerer or another being to get here, they'd need a direct channel open from our side. Someone must have opened a portal to lead them here."

"Sherice," Ayla said immediately.

Lyssa held up her hands. "Woah, I know she's no angel, okay? But this is a serious accusation. She has no motive to introduce a bunch of murderers into the place she lives at herself. She could have been killed, too."

Ayla puffed her cheeks, blowing a stubborn strand of hair off her face. She knew that her friend was right. There was no way Sherice could be convicted of letting the Sorcerers in without solid evidence. Besides, after her incidents with the blonde, Ayla herself was just as much of a suspect.

A sharp knock on the door startled her. Lyssa jumped off the chair. "This must be Rhonda! She'll be able to tell us the news." Her voice dropped as the new visitor stepped over the threshold.

Ayla looked up to check the interruption. It was completely normal, she told herself as she took in the outline of the muscular male figure against the light of the mid-morning sun. His brilliant white mane was almost blinding in this light. He wore a *gi*, and it wouldn't seem like anything out of the ordinary if he was anyone else but himself. The source of Ayla's bewilderment and torment. The subject of her hidden thoughts and fears. Her reserved, daunting Mentor who single-handedly took total control of her life and she accepted it as a new norm.

Following a welcoming gesture from Lyssa's hand, he walked inside.

"Good morning, Blaze," she greeted him, throwing a quick glance Ayla's way. The atmosphere changed straight away. Unsure whether she was supposed to get up, Ayla stayed rooted to her chair, cold coffee in front of her. Getting a visit from him wasn't something she expected.

Blaze returned Lyssa's salutation before turning to Ayla. "Are you feeling better today?"

She opened her mouth, but unsurprisingly, no sound came out of it. Irked with herself for the reaction, she nodded, hoping this would be enough. After all, Blaze never insisted on her talking. If this was anything like their usual meetings, he would tell her a couple of things and then leave. It wouldn't take more than a few minutes, she was sure of it. Nothing to stress about at all.

Lyssa exchanged a strange look with Blaze before turning to her again. "Um, I actually need to run. Got to see Rowan before lessons today. I'll catch you later, okay?" She gave Ayla a quick hug before saying goodbye to Blaze. Within seconds, her slender shape was out of the room. Silence fell as Ayla tried to think of a way to get out of the situation. Surely, Blaze understood how tormenting it was for her.

"Rhonda is taking care of the wounded at the Hub," he explained in his smooth voice. "I'll help you with your meditation today."

Stunned, Ayla sat there, staring at him. She was glad he didn't mention anything about the scene from the night before. The way she felt before Corbin's intervention was inexplicable, but that night changed something. Her dreams featured the elegant outline of a white tiger leaping out of the shadows to protect her. Ayla averted her eyes from his as he lowered himself onto a chair next to her and spoke to her about the morning developments. She hardly registered his words through her own turmoil. The thought of his leather jacket still in her bed bothered her. It was rude of her not to return it to its owner, but for some reason, she was secretly hoping he'd forget all about it so she could keep it. That jacket brought her peace for the first time in what seemed like forever. For a brief moment, she imagined herself in Blaze's embrace, safe from anything life could throw at her. She was sure something else would have happened if it weren't for Corbin's intervention. Or perhaps, she imagined things thanks to the stress of the night and a dire need to feel safe.

"Is that okay?"

Ayla blinked, realising that she missed everything he told her. Cheeks burning, she nodded, hoping for the better. Blaze directed her to follow him out of the house and down the streets towards the town's central square. Thanks to her daily walks with Lyssa, Ayla easily matched his pace. A slight bounce in her step brought out a smile on her face. She grew much stronger and fitter since moving to Whitestone. At some point, she would get through the invisible barrier and thank Blaze for what he'd done.

Her Mentor led her to the garden by the Healers' Hub, towards the same spot they usually occupied during their magic lessons. Ayla took in her surroundings, calming her nerves. She realised that she associated this spot with him and it was peaceful. There was no need to think about Blaze's jacket, or about the warmth of his hand boosting her emerging power. Nothing in his actions indicated that he wanted to hold her accountable for being vulnerable with him the night before. As always, he remained calm and respectful. This time though, she wished the session would never end.

Ayla settled on the grass and crossed her legs. Deep breaths in and out, she pushed the shame of her strange feelings out of her mind. It was not proper of her to even entertain the idea of anything other than their existing arrangement. She just needed to focus on the lesson and not him as a person. Easy.

"Make yourself comfortable and close your eyes. Listen to the sound of my voice and let go. Imagine your mind like a sphere of colourful splashes. They are all your impressions and emotions. One by one, we need to disentangle them. Your mind needs to be clear before we proceed to the next step."

Unlike all the times with Rhonda, Ayla struggled to clear her mind. Her thoughts kept going back to the night before and the way she felt with Blaze. Unknowingly, she reached for her power to produce a warm ball of light like she did then. It levitated above her hand and she breathed out a smile, calming her mind and watching her troubles burn in the steady flame.

Ayla didn't hear the rest of his sentence as her consciousness slipped straight into the grey limbo. The fog swirled up at her presence. She let out a content sigh, letting it slither over her skin. This was her safe place. Nothing could happen to her here; the fog was there to keep her secure from all the trouble from outside. There was just her, only her, and nothing else.

A sudden wave of darkness swallowed the grey, sending shivers down her spine. Ayla spun around, unsure of what happened. This wasn't something she had ever experienced before, and she didn't like it.

An image popped in front of her, so clear she recognised it immediately. Her old bedroom at Corbin's mansion. Neutral colours of the walls and furnishings. The faint lavender smell of fresh linens. Candle flames dancing in the corners. And herself, wearing a white summer dress. Holding the gold chain in her outstretched hand. Watching the ancient sapphire turn around the axis. Its power filled the room, so thick it almost replaced the air itself. Ayla stared at her own figure, unable to move. If this was her past, there was no use in warnings. What happened had already happened. All she could do was remain a silent observer.

This stone is not your friend. Its power is immense, but it's foolish to think anyone could harness it. Caerulus will give you a taste of magic for a price. Each time he will give you less and demand more until there's nothing left. Stay away from it.

Ayla willed herself to move away, but her body remained rooted to the spot. She tensed up, thoughts racing. Maybe she was under the spell of the gem. She knew how powerful it was, felt its force pulsing through her body when it ordered her to take sacrifices, to drink the warm blood, to allow Corbin to do whatever he wanted as her body betrayed her.

With an enormous effort, she summoned the white flame of her magic. To her surprise, it sprouted to life from the first attempt. Its joyful bright petals shifted in the invisible wind, rising up and down, a small but fierce force between her and the image of herself holding Caerulus.

Then something strange happened.

Ayla watched the figure turn her face towards her, eyes cold and calculating. It was a bizarre feeling, as if seeing her own reflection suddenly obtain a mind of its own. The reflection pierced her with a deep glare, and a crooked smile crossed her face. She put the sapphire back on her neck, her face a triumph when the stone sparkled as if coming to life.

Ayla instinctively poured more power into the white flame. Wide-eyed, she stared at her reflection touch the sapphire. The feeling of danger intensified and she braced herself for an attack, as absurd as it felt to have her own self going against her. The flame danced above her palm as she stared at the pulsing gem. Whatever it was doing, it wasn't good. Ayla had no idea if she had a chance to stand against this challenge, in this strange place that was far away from the safety of the Mist.

A sharp sting jolted her back to reality. Ayla looked down and saw a burn on her hand as the faint glow slowly disappeared above it. She grimaced in pain and lifted her eyes to Blaze's preoccupied face. He changed as soon as he noticed her gaze, regaining his composed expression. He took a small vial out of an external pocket and poured a few drops on her injured hand, soothing the pain.

"It's best to avoid using magic while you're meditating," he said gently and Ayla blushed in embarrassment. She was aware of it, of course; Rhonda told her of great tragedies that happened to Mages who tried to do it. Ayla was engulfed by shame that it was Blaze of all people who caught her doing such a silly thing. She should really know better, considering how well she'd been performing at her meditation. And now that she had a chance to prove it to him in person, she failed miserably. In her defence though, she didn't just use magic, and she wasn't just meditating. She tried to protect herself from a strange attack of her subconscious, or whatever that was. Ayla wished she could talk to someone about it. Blaze would know, of course. If only she could start speaking!

Blaze's soft voice took her out of the pit of self-pity. "Are you hungry?"

Listening to her rumbling stomach, Ayla realised it was indeed time to eat. Suddenly aware of her surroundings, she blinked, adjusting her eyesight. It was already twilight; once again, she somehow lost so much time. Cheeks still burning, she nodded, cursing herself for the shyness. Never, never in her life had this happened to her. Maybe this was to do with his shifter nature that she hadn't fully understood. Maybe it was something else. Regardless of the reason, she just needed to start talking. That was all she wanted. At least, that was what she told herself.

"I'll treat you to dinner. Come," Blaze got off the grass and she followed his lead, wondering. He knew that her house would have food ready, so she wouldn't have to cook. There must have been a reason why he would invite her to come with him instead. Blaze looked at her sideways. "It's been a rough couple of days, and I understand something strange happened during your meditation just now. I just want to make sure you're okay before taking you back home."

Ayla blushed again, thinking that all her reservations must have been obvious on her face. She shuddered, remembering the wicked expression in her reflection's eyes. That was the gaze of a killer. The person who took all those sacrifices. The one who drank the blood and—she saw it now—drained them of their power. How could she have done it? And most importantly, where was Caerulus now?

Preoccupied with her thoughts, she didn't notice they had reached their destination.

"We're here," Blaze announced.

She stopped in her tracks, reality finally hitting her. It was evening, and she was about to go into Blaze's house. Alone.

CHAPTER 13. AYLA

S lated roof, plain exterior, minimalist patio—it was one of the most standard houses she had ever seen. Inside, the entrance led straight into the dining and kitchen area, and a small hallway with doors. Ayla threw a quick glance along, guessing where they went. One would open to the bathroom, one to the laundry. One would go to the bedroom. She looked around, dissecting her impressions. It seemed that Blaze either liked minimalist style, or didn't spend much time in the house. All the furnishings were basic, without any decorations. The dining area she walked in only had the shared breakfast bar with the kitchen, a plain round table for two, and two simple yet comfortable chairs. Ayla absorbed every detail. This seemed like a house of a bachelor, without a single detail hinting at a loving partner being around. She knew that Sherice came to Whitestone for Blaze; however, she never asked her friends if Blaze was seeing someone. Maybe it wasn't public knowledge. He had the right to his privacy, like anyone else. It was none of her business. She shouldn't care.

Her nose caught the mouth-watering smell of a warm meal. Slow-cooked lamb with rosemary and vegetables, with a wealth of spices she couldn't distinguish. Ayla turned her head, realising she didn't notice Blaze walk in, carrying a slow cooker. He opened the lid, letting out the aroma, and gestured towards one of the chairs. "Make yourself at home. Would you like a drink?"

She nodded, starting to feel awkward again. This was going to be a one-sided conversation. By accepting his invitation, she agreed to spend more than a mere couple of minutes in his company. She trapped herself. Or maybe it was he who trapped her.

Ayla lowered herself on the chair, gingerly putting her wrists on the table. Aware of his eyes on her, she looked at the cracks between wooden planks on the floor. The paint on them was starting to peel, but it wasn't obvious yet. Focusing on them, Ayla convinced her mind that counting the cracks was the most important thing. She'd figure out the rest once she knew exactly how many there were on the stretch from the kitchen bar to the window on the opposite wall.

Blaze placed a crystal wine glass full of clear liquid to her right and a simple, short glass with water to her left.

"I know you're struggling, Ayla. The past few days have been an enormous stress. I understand that you're still cautious of me, I really do, but I need you to start talking to me." His emerald eyes were kind and soft, without a trace of the primal that she noticed at their first meeting. Blaze pointed at the drinks in front of her. "This is light fruit wine with a drop of primrose and lovehaze. You've studied their properties at Nature's Studies, right? The effect will be gentle but noticeable. It will give you a boost of confidence and help you relax. I'm telling you this so you are aware of exactly what I'm giving you." He sighed, lowering his eyes to the other drink. "The wine might help you feel more comfortable, but it's your choice. If you prefer not to have it, I will respect that. The second glass has plain chilled water if you decide you'd like it instead. There is no pressure either way."

Ayla stared at the wine glass in front of her, processing the information. She was wrong about him; he was not like Corbin at all. Her old Master would have just forced her to drink it if that was what he wanted. Blaze was offering her a choice. Wavering on the edge of the decision, she stalled, studying the condensation on the sides of the wine glass. She wondered if he meant what he said or if it was a test. There was no way of knowing if he would get angry if she refused the wine. If he would stop their sessions altogether and choose another student to mentor. If he would take back his jacket and never speak to her again.

Or maybe it was her trauma talking. Blaze hadn't shown any signs that this would be something he would do. Maybe he did mean that she had a choice.

I do need to talk to him, she persuaded herself. *What's a bit of wine going to do? He told me exactly what it is and what effect it will have. He's not drugging me or anything. I'll be okay.*

She picked up the glass and took a tiny sip. Beautifully chilled, the drink tasted light and pleasant. Like diluted berry and apple juice with a mix of something sweet. Orange blossoms, perhaps? Ayla wondered if that was what lovehaze tasted like, or if this was primrose. She looked at it again and took a proper sip before placing the glass back on the table.

Blaze brought two plates and cutlery and offered her to serve herself first. Still unsure of her situation, Ayla took a spoonful of the risotto. Even as she scooped the decadent rice, she knew it was going to be a sensational dish. The way it crumbled on the serving spoon, the delightful aroma of spices, the scatter of vegetables and meat throughout made her mouth water. It had been such a long time since someone had cooked for her.

The taste didn't disappoint. Ayla stretched out her portion, taking tiny bites and savouring each of them. She silently wished she could devour the whole plate in one setting and get another helping without seeming rude.

Granted, it was the first time she had a meal in his company, but this was so delicious!

Blaze raised his glass with a similar liquid and took a sip.

"What are you drinking?" she asked.

"The same thing as you."

"Why would you need a boost of confidence?"

"I don't. I just like the taste."

He smiled at her, and Ayla finally realised—she was talking to him! And it wasn't as terrifying as she imagined. Her thoughts must have been plastered all over her face.

Blaze put his glass down. "I'm glad you made this choice. Thank you for agreeing to have dinner with me."

The meal was finished before she realised it. Blaze picked up the plates and took them back to the kitchen. Watching his back, Ayla realised that the pleasantries were over. He brought her to his house for a reason. Whatever he wanted to talk to her about was going to happen in the next couple of minutes. A snake of terror coiled around her throat. A tight knot curled in her stomach. Her thoughts jumped around in her mind. Restless. Panicked. Dark. What if he did suspect her of the murders and this was his way to interrogate her? Ayla pressed the palms of her cold hands against the polished wood of the table to stop them from shaking.

Through the veil of darkness, Blaze's green eyes swam into her vision.

"It's okay, Ayla, you're not in trouble. I'm not going to hurt you, we're just here to talk. If you don't want to, it's okay, too. I won't force you to do anything you don't want to do."

She listened to his smooth voice, letting it work its way through her darkness. Blaze pulled the chair to sit opposite her, but he didn't take her hands in his as she thought he would. Instead, all he did was speak to her softly, directing her to focus on her breathing. To clear her mind and let go of the tension. No magic. Just pure human compassion. A calm, balanced presence that she so desperately needed but didn't realise until now. Slowly, very slowly she restored some control of her body. Blaze soothed her a little more and moved back to his spot once she started breathing normally.

Ayla stared at her now-empty glass and he filled it by one-fourth. She uttered an awkward thanks and took a hurried sip. The drink relaxed her so quickly that she wondered if her panic attack mere moments ago was real. There was nothing for her to worry about. She shouldn't be scared of her Mentor. He was there to help, that was his job. Nothing more.

"We need to talk about your meditation today. You used magic as if you were trying to protect yourself. Can you tell me what happened?"

Before responding, Ayla took another sip of her wine. He was someone who knew the most about her, and someone who knew about the Mist. Choosing her words carefully, she told him about the attack from her own reflection. Blaze listened without interrupting. Encouraged, she spoke about her previous experience in the Mist, only omitting the visions of sacrifices and her strange encounters with Corbin. When she was done, she caught her breath and chased it with the last of what was left in her glass. It was so much easier to talk to him now. She reached for the bottle, glancing at him for permission, and poured a full glass once he nodded.

"Has anyone ever attacked you in the Mist before?"

"No. I didn't know it was possible. Every time I'm there, it feels like I'm the only thing that's real. I thought this was a memory of mine, or a nightmare. That place was not in the Mist itself. Instead, it felt like the Mist somehow took me there."

"I must ask, Ayla...Have you ever seen yourself do any other things like that? Did that stone look familiar?"

There it was, the trap. He knew what to ask, and she had to tell him the truth. If she lied, he'd get the wrong information. Ayla pulled herself together. If she told him everything, he'd know how to protect her. He'd know what to do.

With a sigh, she told him about blood sacrifices. Every sentence was torture, and Blaze's face darkened as she progressed with her story. There was no way of stopping now, though; she couldn't tell anyone else about this. If the

Healers couldn't keep her secret, she wasn't sure if Lyssa would. But Blaze hadn't betrayed her trust before. He needed the full story. Except for the parts with Corbin. She wanted to keep those to herself until she figured them out.

When she was done, he kept quiet for a few moments. Ayla finished her glass, surprised at how quickly the wine evaporated. There was still some left in the bottle, but something told her he wouldn't approve if she tried to have more. Ayla scolded herself. She shouldn't be drinking so much, at least not in his presence.

"I'll need some time to think about this. Thank you for sharing with me, I know it must have been hard." He leaned on the table, his gaze soft and kind. "You've been through so much in such a short time, but have kept it together. I'm very proud of you." Ayla glanced at his hands that lay on the table so close to hers, and a strange desire to touch them flooded her mind.

Skin to skin, just the way it was supposed to be. She imagined them tracing her jawline, cupping her cheeks, brushing her hair back and gently gliding over her shoulders before pulling her close in a tight embrace. She glanced at his lips, wondering how soft they were. What his kisses would feel like. Whether he was gentle or rough. Whether his touch on her body would warm her or burn. Whether he would resist if she offered herself to him right here, right now.

Ayla breathed out, heart racing. Her mind was inundated with strange images, one more tormenting than the other. She forced herself to focus on her surroundings, but these intrusive thoughts didn't disappear.

Blaze's emerald eyes seemed to shine in the descending darkness. There were a few candles burning around them that hadn't been there before. Ayla shivered, deciphering his expression. The primal lust in his gaze that had scared her before was back. This time, it felt different. Fire found a reflection in her own body. Longing pulled her closer to him. A feeling that the last shred of her self-control was about to disappear, pressed against her stomach. She couldn't keep her eyes off his face, wondering what it would feel like to trace his scars with her fingers. Whether he would allow her to come closer. Whether he truly wanted her or if it was nothing but a trick her mind played with her.

I'm just drunk, she realised. *How many glasses have I already had? Didn't Meera say that lovehaze in larger quantities can induce an illusion of physical attraction? That must be it. Besides, I haven't been with anyone for months, and seeing all my friends having sexy fun is hard. That's all there is to it. I'm just lying to myself.*

"Are you okay?" his voice purred so close she startled. No, he was still in his seat yet it felt like he was right next to her. His breath was warm on her neck, teasing her with a promise of what was to come. So close, yet out of reach.

Ayla tried to distract herself with the cracks on the wooden floor, but it was fruitless this time. He was like a siren, pulling her deeper under his influence.

Her pleading eyes focused on his face. Surely, he could understand her body language, her desperate expression. With his ability to read people, there would be no way he'd miss it. Ayla scorned herself for her thoughts, but they didn't stop. A myriad of questions flooded her mind as she hung on to the slipping time. Dinner was over, and so was their conversation. It was the perfect time to move on to something else. She wondered if she had to make the first step and tell him about her feelings. Her heartbeat accelerated, and she reasoned with herself that it was improper to flirt with her Mentor. Ignoring the faint voice that pleaded with her to control herself, she leaned forward to shorten the distance between her and Blaze. Her lips parted as she focused her gaze on him. She couldn't understand how she could ever fight such a clear attraction to him. Yes, she needed to tell him. Sooner rather than later.

The sound of a moving chair brought her back to reality. Startled, Ayla traced his masculine figure getting up.

"It's getting late. Come, I'll take you home."

Careful not to stumble, she got up, too. Blaze opened the door and she walked out of his house, too shocked to say a word. Her racing thoughts slowed down in a limbo of insecurity. She was so sure of her perception! It pained her to realise she was wrong. She misread him. There was no attraction from his side. All he did was make sure she was okay and take her out of the situation before she embarrassed herself.

As they walked down the dark, empty streets, Blaze's expression was neutral, his gaze scanning the way ahead to spot any potential dangers. It was easy to match his leisurely pace, though Ayla wanted to slow down, to extend this short walk and to figure out what happened. The feeling of rejection hurt, and she blinked away the bitter tears of disappointment.

I'm such an idiot for thinking he wants me. A man like this would never want anything to do with me. He's just here to teach me, and once I've learned, he'll leave me all alone to find my way in this world. What was I thinking, making a fool of myself?

Immersed in negative thoughts, Ayla didn't notice that their journey was over. Blaze walked her up the steps to her front porch and stopped. She turned around to face him, desperate for an explanation and dreading it at the same time. He smiled at her gently, but it wasn't the kind of smile that would encourage any provocative actions. This was just a polite "have a good night" smile. Nothing more.

His hands lay on the railing of the stairs, only a couple of paces away. The tension was back now, filling her body with longing. If he didn't want her, that explained why he never made a move. Any indication of what he wanted. A true gentleman, he didn't give her any false hopes, and she should appreciate it. But letting it go just now was impossible. She thought of the warmth of his hand supporting her flame on the night of the attack again, of the way he made her feel safe. It was unbearable to realise he was never going to touch her. That he didn't reciprocate her feelings and that everything she felt that night was nothing but a sweet delirium brought to her by lovehaze wine.

"I'll be away tomorrow, but we can resume the lessons as normal once I'm back."

He was just going to leave her like that, tormented with uncertainty.

Ayla's foot slipped on the steps. Terrifying thoughts invaded her mind, one worse than another. *He's going to think I did this on purpose. He'll see I'm too drunk to stay on my feet and he'll despise me forever.*

To her surprise, it wasn't as bad as she convinced herself it was. Her balance wasn't thrown off and she quickly steadied herself. The only problem was that she accidentally grabbed his hand on the railing. An electric shock ran through her body, making her shiver. The only thing she could compare this to was when she just learned to pleasure herself. A simple touch wasn't meant to be so intense. It was simply not possible—yet, there it was.

Blaze froze on the spot, looking as shaken as she was, but his face regained its composure in a matter of seconds. Ayla made a rushed step back, conscious of how she breached his personal space. As if her behaviour that night wasn't enough, she needed to disgrace herself even further!

"I'm sorry," she muttered, hoping the apology sounded sincere. In the dead quiet of the night her breath was too loud and she cursed herself a thousand times for forgetting her place. She should have never been drinking at his house, what was she thinking?

He nodded in acknowledgement, his green eyes alert. Ayla wondered if he ever relaxed. It always seemed like he was ready for anything life had to throw at him, always checking his surroundings, always making sure it was safe. He was the person she wanted to be with, but it seemed that she ruined her chances.

"Thank you for the lovely evening," she managed, trying to sound as civil and nonchalant as possible.

The corners of his mouth lifted in acknowledgement. "You're welcome. And thank you for telling me about your visions. I hope you feel better tomorrow."

She lingered on the steps, weighing her options. He would walk away any second and she would never find out the answer to her burning question. It had to be now. This was her only chance.

"Wait! Have I...done anything wrong? Did I upset you?" she whispered, her heart in her throat.

Blaze's expression changed; for a moment she thought he was going to take her hand in his.

"Of course not. Why would you think that?"

"Um, it's just the gist I got," she croaked, a merciless blush burning on her cheeks.

He sighed and stepped closer. "Ayla, you didn't do anything wrong. You've had a rough couple of days, and tonight you finally let go of some of that tension. It's okay to feel overwhelmed and out of your zone. Remember what I said, though. The drink gave you confidence, but it might have altered your perception a little. After all, you've had quite a bit."

Ayla's cheeks were scorching hot. She cursed herself for drinking so much. He probably thought she was an alcoholic. Her carelessness was going to cost her her new reputation.

Blaze's hand hovered over hers as if he was about to touch it again. He quickly changed his mind, choosing to place it on the railing a few tormenting centimetres away. "I don't want you to do something you might regret, Ayla." His whisper sounded clear in the silence of the night. "Come to peace with your thoughts and stop fighting your feelings; then we can talk again."

He lifted his hand to her face, but the touch never came. She felt his warmth just over her skin, tracing her cheek down to her chin. The craving to be closer burst in her belly, its burn so intense she nearly gave in to the urge to lean into his hand.

Torn with her inner conflict, she hardly noticed Blaze step off the porch. "Good night, Ayla," he said gently.

His back disappeared into the night, but she stood there, eyes fixed on the darkness in front of her. She touched her cheek where Blaze's fingers lingered just moments ago, savouring the memory. Maybe it was all in her head. Maybe tomorrow she would feel like it was just a dream. Regardless of what was to come, tonight was her night. With the fruity wine still rendering her light-headed, she giggled, considering her circumstances. She could have been blamed for the murders of all of those Mage girls, but she didn't care.

She knew Blaze would protect her. This was the one thing she was sure about.

CHAPTER 14. AYLA

It was that time of the day, the gate between worlds, as Darren used to say. Twilight—the thin line between day and night, light and dark. The grey area in all beginnings. Nobody's time, and everybody's time.

The last rays of the setting sun silvered the calm water of the sea as the gentle waves licked the land. Hardly a thing moved in the stillness; perfect weather for candles.

Ayla looked around, wondering why there was no fog or darkness around her. Maybe this was an actual dream at last. She was so used to having bizarre visions of herself that seeing something different struck her as odd.

The pastels around her were soothing yet vivid. Testing her theory, Ayla took off her shoes. The sand was still warm after the hot day, and the air smelled like salt and iodine. It felt so real as if she was there in the flesh; yet, there was no way she could have been. It was just a dream.

A line of candles to her right distracted her wandering mind. Their flames flickered tame and bright, giving off more light as it got darker around. Curious, she walked towards them. Any dream that provided intrigue in one way or another was a good dream.

Cool silver air caressed her skin like a lover's touch. Ayla took a deep breath, enjoying the peaceful evening. Only a distant cry of a seagull broke the otherwise silent time. The candles were getting closer until she realised it was a circle rather than a line. A man's figure sat cross-legged in the middle of it. Ayla slowed her pace and stopped a few steps away as she recognised him.

Blaze's face was calm, eyes closed, as if he was immersed in some sort of trance. Sitting perfectly still, he was like a statue. The only thing that betrayed life inside him was the barely noticeable movement of his chest, rising and falling with his relaxed breathing. Ayla stood on the spot, staring. There would be a reason why the dream brought her to this spot and she had to find out.

She inched closer. If this was indeed a dream, now was her excuse to study him properly. He looked exactly the way he did in reality, with the exception of scars. His cleanly shaven face had no sign of them. Blaze's whole image gave off a feeling of serenity and peace, making her wonder if he would be able to see her if he woke up.

He's not going to wake up. It's my dream, possibly influenced by the events of the day. I need security, and somehow think he's someone who will give it to me. This is why I'm here, and this is why he's in a trance. So that I don't feel awkward to stare at him.

The little spiel gave her the confidence to step closer. Nothing changed in the stillness surrounding her; the waves kept lapping at the sand just a few metres away. Ayla wondered if anything special would happen if she crossed the line between the candles. A hurricane in the open sea, or thunder and lightning. Or maybe nothing at all. Unsure about the consequences, she sat down on the warm sand just outside the circle. Looking up at her Mentor's face, she allowed her breathing to slow down.

"I don't know what to do, Blaze. The emotions are overwhelming, and it terrifies me. There are only so many things I can discuss with Lyssa. I know that you'd be able to tell me everything, but how do I learn to speak to you? We can't rely on drinks all the time. I am so sure now that I've overstepped the boundaries tonight." She sighed, carefully checking his face for a reaction. Not a muscle moved under his smooth skin; he was oblivious to her presence. Ayla continued, "I saw something when you came to take me from Corbin's mansion. A strange expression in your eyes that scared me so much I lost my ability to speak. I thought that you were just like Corbin, that you would start with a promise of safety and lead me down the path of pain and destruction. Do you truly want to keep me safe or is it another ruse? Maybe I'm struggling to comprehend that I can ever be safe. Will I be able to speak with you tomorrow? Or are we going back to where we started?"

She let out another sigh, staring at the sea behind his back. Darkness had fallen, with the first shy stars sparkling on the velvet of the sky. Ayla wondered when the dream would end. She had a chance to speak her thoughts out, and even though he didn't hear her, it was good to have let them out. She smiled, looking at him. Someone was going to be lucky to have a man like him, unless he already had a partner. He probably did. Maybe more than one. Ayla was still learning about this new world and its customs. What did it feel like to live like Levi, a butterfly between relationships?

A quiet pop startled her. Eyes wide, she stared at the circle of candles, no longer surrounding her Mentor's figure. He disappeared as if he never existed. The wind gusted from the sea, blowing off the candles one by one. Ayla jumped, rushing towards them. "Blaze, wait! Where did you go?"

Nobody answered as the wind grew wilder, tugging at her hair. Ayla grabbed the long hem of her dress and crossed the line between candles.

Suddenly, all the flames came back to life, roaring towards the dark sky. Ayla stopped in the middle of the circle, heart drumming in her chest. She looked around at each of the tiny lights, now burning at full strength. A strange force kept her in place as she tried to cross back to the beach. Before she had a chance to ask herself any questions, the wind lifted her like a feather and whirled round and round until she felt dizzy. Ayla tried to connect to her magic, but it was no use when she couldn't focus. The wild air roared in her ears so loudly they nearly popped, until suddenly, all senses were gone. Ayla squeezed her eyes shut, hoping to restore her eyesight. When she opened them again, the scenery had completely changed.

The fog swirled around her legs like a pet, happy to see its owner. Ayla relaxed, threading her fingers through it. "It's so good to be here. You have no idea what I've just seen. Such a bizarre dream!"

She walked through the soft substance, speaking softly as if a loud voice would make the Mist go away. Someone was talking in the distance, though; those voices were not quiet at all. There was no place for elevated speeches here, not in the Mist! Ayla directed her steps towards the sound. Unsure of how, but she needed to restore the peace and quiet. The Mist was a safe space, a silent space. Anyone who disturbed it needed to be kicked out!

As she approached the source, the fog lifted, showing her the new scene. Those voices were familiar—too familiar, in fact. Corbin and Blaze, arguing about something. As she crept closer, she realised they weren't actually in the Mist; rather, it was an opening of sorts that showed her their conversation as if she were looking through a window. Something felt familiar about this, though her memories were elusive again. They slipped out of her focus as they sometimes did. She had to just take this as a given and reflect on it later.

Ayla strained her ears to catch the bits of their conversation.

"What the hell, Blaze? What did you give her, nectar of passion rose?" Corbin's voice had never sounded so scary. Ayla shivered, cowering in the fog, as if he could get her.

It's okay, he can't see me here. He can't hurt me. I'm safe.

Blaze's chin lifted in defiance as he spoke in a controlled tone. "I was pretty sure I made myself clear before. We had an agreement, and you've already broken it once. Are you stalking her now?"

"Ayla and I share a blood bond. You gave her so much nectar I could feel it in my bones! This can be very dangerous, Blaze, you have no idea what it can trigger. She's so fragile now, after everything…"

"Yes, after everything you've done, Corbin. Say things the way they are, no need to cover them up. *You* damaged her, not me. And I would have never given her anything as potent as passion rose. It was a weak solution of primrose and lovehaze, diluted with light wine. Ayla has been studying their properties herself, and she knew very well what I gave her. It was an educated, consensual decision. Not that you'd know what it is anyway."

Corbin clenched his jaw and didn't respond. After a few moments of silence, Blaze spoke again. "Look, I wouldn't do anything to harm her if that makes you feel better.

However, she's still so skittish when I'm around I can't be sure she's going to stay or run for the hills the next second. It doesn't help that the first time she truly connected with her magic was following a traumatic event where she nearly got killed. We'll have to tread very carefully now as she progresses, to make sure she doesn't sway towards the darkness. Something happened during her meditation today and she got hurt. I needed to know what it was so I could keep her safe. I needed her to *tell* me, Corbin. This poor girl couldn't master a single word in my presence ever since I brought her here. There was no other way to help her speak, I tried all other methods without much luck. Again, she knew exactly what was happening."

"Lovehaze would have driven her up the wall with lust if she ingested as much as she did."

Blaze sighed. "That's the side effect, yes. But Ayla is a big girl now, Corbin. She can make her own decisions. When I saw she wasn't fully in control anymore, I took her back home. Don't worry, nothing else happened."

Corbin rubbed his temples, his expression stressed. "Look, Blaze. I just...miss her. Wouldn't you feel the same way if you lost her the way I did? I can feel everything that's going on with her, and it's heartbreaking. I never wanted to hurt her. I never wanted it to get to this. The only thing I ever wanted was for her to be safe and happy."

"Well, you had a strange way of showing it. It's been weeks now and she's still cautious of me. It looks like the damage is too deep. We have another threat that might very well target her as the next victim. Ayla needs her powers to be activated so she can protect herself if I'm not around. I'm not going to force her, but we need to start somewhere. She needs the training, and every day she's not using her power in full is a day lost."

Corbin cringed as if he heard something blasphemous. "Spare me the details. I still can't believe that she needs *you* to get to her magic. I thought I tried everything, but all she needed was a Mage and a prophesied connection. Fuck you, Blaze."

"No need for insults," Blaze shook the invisible dust off his shoulder and changed his stance. "I hope you got the answers you wanted now and can have some peace. Like I said before, I don't mind if you need to ask, but please stay away from her. I'll tell you what you need to know myself."

A gentle tug made Ayla look down. The tiny swirl of the fog pulled at her ankles, leading her away. When she looked up again, the men were gone. A soft wall of greyness surrounded her in a safe cloud, making her wonder if she imagined the conversation between her old Master and her new Mentor.

CHAPTER 15. AYLA

"Did something happen? You're not yourself today."

Ayla glanced at Lyssa's concerned face and forced a smile. "I'm just a little tired, that's all. It will pass."

Her friend's expression remained puzzled as they made their way down the streets of Whitestone. The days got hotter as they headed into summer, so they made a few changes in the schedule. Now the two friends met up before sunrise and had a quick light breakfast before going out for their morning walk. It was a wonderful feeling to see the world awaken around them; besides, at this early hour, there were no other people around. The perfect set-up.

She started feeling off after her dinner with Blaze. Something shifted in the sleepy little town. Now she was hearing whispers and caught strange glances cast her way. Nobody said anything directly to her, but the atmosphere was tense. Only Lyssa remained a loyal friend, keeping her happy-go-lucky demeanour. Her friends tried to stay positive as well, though every now and then Ayla noticed a shadow of doubt cross their faces.

Warm rays of the sun coloured the roofs a shade of gold by the time the two friends made a full circle of downtown. Ayla stopped by the small town café that opened early. They always marked the end of their walks with a reward. A nice hot brew. Today, something was different.

The girl at the counter was in her early teens. It wasn't abnormal for Whitestone—some families had children help out with the business as soon as they learned how to count. This girl stared at Ayla wide-eyed as if she didn't understand a word. Ayla glanced at her friend, unsure of what was going on. Lyssa stepped in. "Two lattes, please. One with skim milk, one regular. Both medium size."

The girl continued to glare. Lyssa cleared her throat when someone's steps announced another presence. A middle-aged man appeared from the back room, wiping his hands on the apron. An expression of welcome on his face quickly changed. Frowning, Ayla watched him gesture for the young girl to leave. Once she was gone, he turned to Ayla. "I'm sorry, but we can't serve you here. You should go."

"What? Why?" Ayla stared back at him, stunned by the sudden change. She didn't realise how far the suspicions had spread around the city, and this was the first time she was confronted directly. Her feet refused to move as a mocking voice in the back of her head told her she was insane.

Lyssa pulled her arm. "It's okay, we'll leave. I hope you have a great day," she muttered through clenched teeth.

Ayla followed her out into the street but her friend didn't stop there. Lyssa pulled her further along and only once they were on their way back to Ayla's house, did she speak again. "Those kidnappings and murders are making everyone jumpy these days."

"I have nothing to do with them. Why is the whole town blaming them on me?"

This made sense now that she said it out loud. If Sherice was trying to frame her, she would spread the rumours. Who knew what people thought now? Maybe the current news showed her standing over a body with a knife covered in warm blood. Or someone walking in on her finishing the kill. Ayla shuddered, considering her position. The guilty look on Lyssa's face told her that her suspicions were correct.

"It's just a misunderstanding," her friend finally managed. "There's nothing else to talk about, and people being people just need to put a face to the crime. Which we know you didn't do! I don't believe it for a second, and neither do our friends. Blaze doesn't, either."

"Do they really think I'm a murderer?" Ayla gestured towards the coffee shop. "That I'm going to kill the people who serve the best coffee in town?"

"I know, this sucks." Lyssa looked her in the eye. "Some people don't have anything else to do with their lives other than make things up. You shouldn't take this to heart, Ayla. This is all words, and they can't hurt you. Once Blaze sorts it out, it will be back to normal."

Thinking about Blaze hurt. Ever since their dinner almost two weeks ago, she hadn't seen him or heard anything. She only knew he wasn't in town, as the combat classes were put on hold "until further notice" as someone told her. That was at the beginning of everyone ignoring her. Things got more difficult every day. Sometimes, she wondered if he left permanently, unwilling to deal with her. She second-guessed herself, playing the events of their last night together in her head over and over again. Even though she knew it was important for her to tell him about the attack during her meditation, she couldn't stop blaming herself for everything that went wrong. Maybe talking to him wasn't a good idea. Maybe he felt that her actions threatened the peaceful community, too, and didn't want anything to do with her. Or maybe she overstepped the boundaries and now he was never coming back to help. Regardless of what it was, she felt like there was nothing but gloom left for her.

"Hey, it's going to be okay," Lyssa gently squeezed her hand, bringing Ayla back to reality. "Things will work out, I promise. Blaze will take care of you."

"He's not here now, is he? Why did he leave?" Ayla's words felt heavy and bitter in her mouth. "I thought he was going to protect me, but he just disappeared. I don't know what to think...It's all my fault." She sat down on the steps of her front porch and covered her face with her hands.

Lyssa settled next to her, wrapping her arm around her friend's shoulders. "No, Ayla, none of this is your fault. People are scared and they blame you because these murders started happening after you came here. But that makes no sense, right? You've never opened a portal in your life, and you only just discovered your magic."

Ayla sighed. The feeling of emptiness and despair was overwhelming. Lyssa was a helping hand in times of turmoil. Her only true friend. Drawing a sharp breath, Ayla told her everything about her visions, about the attack during meditation, about the dinner with Blaze. Lyssa's eyes got wider and wider as the story went along until an expression of shock was all that was left. Exhaling as she spoke the last word, Ayla glanced at her. The glassy eyes of her friend made her regret sharing, but it was too late now. The cat was out of the bag.

"Please don't tell anyone," she pleaded, searching for sympathy in Lyssa's eyes. Ayla suddenly realised that her fate was now in this girl's hands. She'd be in huge trouble if Lyssa spilled the beans to someone. Anyone, at this stage. With the whole town turning against her, it was not a pleasant perspective. Her words could turn the remaining friends into enemies or it could be proof that would allow the Enforcers to put her into jail. Ayla shook her head in a desperate attempt to clear her mind from intrusive thoughts about the things that could happen to people in a local jail, especially those convicted of serial murders. Her imagination painted scenes one more gruesome than another. It was too much.

"Of course, I won't," Lyssa snapped out of shock and stood up. "This explains a lot, though. Come on, let's get you inside and have a nice cup of tea. We need to think of something to make it better until Blaze comes back."

"He's one of the Enforcers, right? Like the police?" Ayla feared the answer.

"He used to work with them and I believe he might still have connections. Don't worry, Ayla, I told you he'll help."

"Not after that dinner," Ayla confessed bitterly. "I was acting like such a fool. You can't imagine the thoughts that went through my head. He even said to me that he didn't want me to do something I might regret, that's his exact words! A nice way of saying that I had too much to drink and needed to sober up and think about my behaviour."

Lyssa smirked. "Look, you're not the first one to have those thoughts about him, okay? I don't think you've done anything to damage your relationship. He was a gentleman, that's all. But think about this. He's already done so much for you. All those things you might not have noticed. Do you have any idea how much he risked by going to one of the most powerful Sorcerers to take away his Apprentice? I didn't think it was possible, especially considering how much your old Master tried to hide you from everyone. Blaze spent months tracking you down all around the world. He pulled so many strings just for permission to bring you straight here and enrol you without a test for abilities, unlike all other students. To get you into classes when the year was almost over, and to get an exemption from exams. To arrange for you to live in the best house in town and not in a dorm like most other students. To get permission to teach you one on one to spare you from the trauma of seeing others succeed when you were only starting out yourself. He organised everything for you. And thinking that now he'd leave you over a bit of mischief at dinner is silly. He wouldn't abandon you, Ayla. You have to believe it."

Ayla was silent, digesting the information. Maybe Lyssa was right. After all, she had no idea how much Blaze had done until her friend put it together for her. Why would he bother, though? This made no sense. Putting so much effort into something would mean an ulterior motive. She had to figure it out.

"Why would he do it?"

Lyssa shook her head, showing that the time of confessions was over. "You'll have to ask him yourself. Maybe in the meantime, you can focus on building up your confidence so that you can talk to him once he comes back."

CHAPTER 16. BLAZE

It wasn't until the sun was well and truly on the way down that Blaze made his way back. The past weeks had been exhausting, but he knew he had to stay persistent in his search. The Enforcers were stuck in the corner with only one suspect left. He couldn't let them have her. She was innocent, he knew it. No matter what, he had to protect her from trial.

He passed Ayla's house on the way. The only way to check on her without going in was to allow the primal part into his mind. Not fully, but just enough to let it see the auras. A quick scan revealed two presences—Ayla's and Lyssa's. Sadness flooded his mind as he watched Ayla's aura gradually shift colour from disturbed orange towards panicky red. Things had changed a lot since he last saw her. While Lyssa was still in, he had a bit of time.

Blaze allowed himself a quick wind-down to collect his thoughts after the long trip. Possible scenarios kept playing in his mind as he had a contrast shower, followed up by a quick sandwich. Everything he could think of required her compliance. If she trusted him, that wouldn't be a problem. But if there was still fear...Blaze sighed. Fear was a strong moving force that acted in the most unpredictable ways. It could work well as a stimulant, but in most cases, it would backfire. In their unstable relationship, he was sure it would be a bad idea to rely on it.

And whatever he did, he could not let his primal out. Not for one second. If Ayla saw even a shade of it in his eyes, all her inhibitions would come back.

The sun almost disappeared beyond the horizon when he made up his mind. He couldn't stall anymore; going into her house at night would put her reputation at risk. Besides, in her distressed state, Ayla might work herself up even more if she found out he had returned to town and didn't visit her.

The short walk never felt so tormenting. Eyes fixed on the road ahead, breath controlled, head clear. His girl was close to panic. He had to be the one in control to help her calm down. It wouldn't be easy, but there was no other choice.

She opened the door right away. Blaze's smile froze on his face when he saw her haunted expression. Ayla stood rooted to the spot, with such dread in her eyes as if she saw the scariest thing in her life. He halted, unsure of what to do. Something must have happened in his absence, and he had to find out as soon as possible.

"It's just me, Ayla. Can I come in?" he asked softly. She moved to the side, eyes wide on her pale face, but didn't say a word. Blaze nodded, closing the door behind him. He kept his expression calm not to distress her any further, though strange thoughts were whirling in his head. She made a painful step forward before his departure, and now something threw her a few steps back. It was even worse than their first encounter at Corbin's mansion. If she was scared then, now she was paralysed with fear. There had to be an explanation. He was going to find out, even if she couldn't speak to him again.

He gestured for her to sit down on the sofa, and she immediately obeyed, maintaining eye contact as if he would attack if she broke it. *It's okay, I'll be patient. She showed me that she can overcome her fear before. She can do it again. I won't push.*

"I just wanted to check on you, that's all," he soothed, sitting down on the chair opposite her. Ayla remained still, and only her shallow breathing betrayed her anxiety. "What happened to you? Did something scare you here?" She shook her head. Blaze tried again. "Did someone...do something to you?" Another negative. Blaze stifled the urge to take her hands in his. "Something clearly happened. Are you afraid that *I* can hurt you?"

A small shiver ran through her body. It would have been easily missed if he wasn't paying attention. *That's a yes.* "Why do you think I'd want to do that? I took you in under my protection. Nothing has changed. I'm still here to keep you safe. I'm on your side." The shivers grew stronger. Ayla's tense pose changed as she wrapped her arms around her shoulders. Blaze weighed all possibilities. He'd left her feeling guilty but tried to let her off easy. He told her he was coming back, so she shouldn't have felt threatened that he'd abandon her. His trip took him much longer than he expected, though. Maybe she doubted him, after all.

There had to be something else. He studied her, wishing he could see even a little inside her mind. She was at Whitestone the whole time, safe from any outside threats. Something must have happened here.

The murders. After the incident at the bar, there were probably some accusations floating about. He had hoped that Lyssa would help. However, if the whole town believed the rumours, it would have been a difficult time. That didn't explain why Ayla was terrified of him, though. She should have known by now that he wanted to protect her.

All thoughts evaporated from his head when he saw tears building up in her eyes. Ayla couldn't handle the tension too much longer. She was about to break.

"It's okay, Ayla," he cooed when those tears finally burst out of her eyes. Her whole body was trembling now, though he saw she was still trying to contain her emotions. There was no more reservation left. His girl was helpless, desperate for comfort. He promised to take care of her. Now was the time to do it.

She protested weakly when he pulled her close, but the attempt was almost non-existent as if she'd given up. Her body was tiny in his arms as she shook all over.

"You're safe, I'm here." He caressed her chestnut hair, inhaling her sweet scent—florals, with a fresh undertone of citrus, overwhelmed by the smell of fear. Her hair was silky soft under his hand as he glided it from her head down to her neck, holding himself back from lowering it past that point. She sobbed uncontrollably for what felt like hours. Blaze kept her close, reassuring her of safety again and again. Sooner or later she was going to calm down and he'd have to let her out of his embrace. Until then, he could enjoy her proximity, even though he'd have preferred different circumstances.

Sobs gradually became quieter until only sniffles remained. Blaze realised she was clutching on to his shirt as if it were a lifeline. Her tiny grip was barely noticeable. If it was enough to help her feel safe, it was enough for him. He wished she'd never let go.

Ayla went quiet, keeping her head buried in his chest. Blaze listened to himself, slowing down his breath. She needed to know he was calm. Not a single beat should betray his heart going faster in her presence. No, he was reserved and in control of himself. "It's okay, sweetheart," he repeated, fighting the urge to kiss the top of her head.

She shifted a little and lifted her face to his. "I thought you came to arrest me," her whisper was on the verge of hearing.

Stunned by the revelation and the fact she managed to speak, Blaze gathered his thoughts before responding. "You haven't done anything wrong. Everything that happened was a misunderstanding. I know you're innocent, Ayla. You're not a murderer." He kept her pleading eyes locked with his, choosing each word with care. "Besides, I'm not working for the Force anymore."

She didn't reply, still peering at him. Blaze raised his hand to caress her cheek but stopped himself before touching her skin. It wasn't the time to test the effects of physical touch between them again, not when she was like this. "I'll take care of you, Ayla, I promise. I'll do everything I can to keep you safe." He tried to sound convincing, hoping that she wouldn't notice the slight strain in his voice.

"I'm just so scared, I'm sorry," she muttered. Blaze gently squeezed her shoulder through the thin fabric of her shirt. At least she was talking again.

"I know, sweetheart. No need to apologise." He spotted a cup of steamy brew on the small coffee table by her side and nodded at it. "Have a drink. This should help."

Ayla obeyed, picking up the cup with her delicate hands and taking a sip. He carefully studied her. The girl lost some weight again as seemed to be the case whenever she was stressed. Her total compliance was concerning, though. Blaze wondered if she was going to do everything he told her without questioning it. Was it the side effect of Corbin's cruel "training"? Did she subconsciously feel like he owned her now? *Fucking Sorcerer. I hope he burns in hell*.

The drink put some distance between them. Ayla finished the cup and placed it back, turning to look at him again as if awaiting further instructions. Blaze sighed. He couldn't stall any longer, no matter how much he wanted to protect her feelings. He had to do what he had to do.

"I've got a little gift for you," he started cautiously, pulling the amulet out of his front pocket. Ayla looked at it, her expression quizzical. "I have to explain this a bit better. Some people think that you...*journey*. This means going into the Mist in your physical shape. It's an extremely rare ability. Only one Mage in history was ever able to do that. He called himself a Mistwalker. *Journeying* means you can use the Mist to go from one place to another without the need for a portal. The Mist works in mysterious ways that haven't been studied properly. Mostly because there aren't many people who can see it in the first place." He put his hands on her shoulders, looking into her eyes. "I don't believe this is the case; however, there are concerns that you might be doing it in your sleep without realising it. It's difficult to check since you live on your own, and I don't want people showing up at your house at night to check if you're still in your bed. I can't move anyone in here with you, as it will show that I believe those rumours. The only thing I can offer is this amulet." He opened the palm of his hand, letting her have a look at it.

Silver sparked in the dim candlelight, outlining the smooth lines of a tiger's silhouette. Ayla looked up at Blaze again, questions all over her face.

"This will keep your body tethered to reality whenever you go into the Mist again. If there is another kill while you're wearing it, this will be proof that you have nothing to do with it."

Her fingers hovered over the silver. She stared at it, thinking about something beyond him. Blaze wished once again he knew what was going on in her head.

"Can I...take it off myself?" she finally whispered.

That was when he understood. *You poor thing. How much healing we still need to go through until you are recovered.* "Of course! It's not a collar." He watched her reaction. The sharp change in her eyes told him his suspicion was right. The trauma of her past threw her back whenever she saw a trigger, anything that would remind her of the things that happened in the Sorcerers' world. "You have to promise me that you won't. There is no point in having an amulet that protects you if you're not going to wear it. Do you want to put it on yourself?"

She nodded and gingerly picked it up by the delicate chain. Blaze watched it settle on her neck just on the verge of her décolletée as she pulled her hair through. That was it. He told her what he needed to say, and she heard him. There was nothing left for him to do. It was time to leave before she felt awkward.

"Thank you."

Before he knew it, she covered the small distance between them and hugged him. Stunned, he placed his hands on her back, automatically caressing it. So she did feel the pull after all. It pained him to see that she needed to be terrified out of her mind to suppress her inhibitions and come closer.

"Can I show you something?" she whispered, taking a small step back.

Blaze dropped his hands, letting her go. His mind cheered at the thought of her sharing something with him on her own accord. A moment like this had to be cherished. "Of course. What is it?"

She paused on her spot, hesitating, before making a decision. Blaze followed her to a small door in the corridor. She drew a sharp breath and turned the handle.

The small room was full of square towers. Blaze flicked the light switch on and stared at stacks upon stacks of paintings. Ayla stood next to the doorway, hiding her eyes.

"May I?" he asked, stretching his arm towards one of the canvases. When she nodded, Blaze took the top painting off the stack closest to the door and studied it. The greys were unmistakable. "The Mist."

Ayla nodded again, pointing at the stacks. "There's more."

He picked up paintings from different stacks and compared them. Soon, he understood. Every picture held a slight difference. The ones closest to the door showed lighter shades and a lighter hand. As her skill developed, so did the details in the paintings. The small stack hidden in the depths of the room seemed to be the most recent work. Blaze held his breath as he studied the black shapes, half-hidden by the fog. An image so vivid it sent shivers down his spine.

"Did you see these...things when you went to the Mist?" he probed gently, though his mind was screaming danger.

She shook her head. "I don't think when I paint. It's like I'm in a trance. This is what happens, and it gets darker each time." She looked up at him, eyes wide. "I'm so scared, Blaze."

"Thank you for sharing with me." He held his hand to her and she accepted it right away. Trying to think about his next words, he pulled her towards him again. This time, she settled in his embrace without a fight. "This was so brave of you, Ayla. I'm very proud to see how far you've come, and I understand how hard it would be to share something so private with someone."

"Can you help me?" She shivered as he stroked her hair.

Blaze hesitated. Giving a promise he wasn't sure he could keep was not something he did. "I'll do my best to figure this out," he replied with caution.

She nodded and held on to his shirt. He gently settled on the floor, keeping her close as he enjoyed every moment, alert to any change in her pose that would signify that she wanted to pull away. Moments flew by but she stayed. Her breath slowed down and she relaxed against him. For another minute, he waited, but she didn't move anymore.

"Did you fall asleep?" he asked softly. There was no reply. She did! With all the tension she experienced during his short visit, it was no wonder her body needed a break. Blaze allowed himself a small smile. It was still a win, however small. She felt safe enough to fall asleep in his arms. There was hope for him yet.

Her body was light like a feather when he took her to bed. Tucking her in, he admired her delicate features once again. Ayla was indeed the most beautiful girl he'd ever laid his eyes on. It was a great honour to know she was meant for him. Even realising that it would take months if not years to nurse her back to health, it was worth the wait.

His smile evaporated as he thought about the task at hand. He didn't have months or years. Faces of the Enforcers and the judge at court floated in his memory. *If you don't find another lead in the next fortnight, we're taking her in for a trial.*

Ayla could be dead before the next full moon.

CHAPTER 17. AYLA

Ayla shook her head. "I don't want to."

"Come on, honey. It's been a while now. We need to resume your meditations. You need to learn to connect with yourself and stay in control of your emotions. We've talked about this," Rhonda cooed, pouring a cup of soothing mint tea. Glorious rays of rising sun marked the arrival of another warm day. The air was still at this early hour, with birds chirping their happy songs in the tall trees surrounding her little backyard. Everything was perfect. There was nothing to show her anything was wrong.

Except for her past experience. Ever since the attack of her subconscious that happened during her meditation with Blaze, Ayla couldn't shake off the foreboding feeling that it would happen again. The whole idea was terrifying. She wasn't sure if Rhonda would be able to bring her back. If Blaze couldn't do it, the old Healer wouldn't be able to, either. What if she got stuck in her own head without a way to return?

"It's going to help with your anxiety," Rhonda tried again. "You're starting your lessons with Blaze again, aren't you? You'll need to be in control to connect with your magic."

"No!" Ayla's voice broke as threw the cup into the bushes and plopped on the soft grass. Bitter tears burst out of her eyes, soaking her cheeks. The mood swings were getting worse. Her fear of meditation seeped into her visits to the Mist. This seemed to have destabilised her, and now there was nothing helping her unload the burden that seemed to be getting heavier every day. The murders. Being ostracised by most of the city. The concerned expression in her friends' eyes. Blaze disappearing for weeks when she thought things were getting somewhere. The attack of the Sorcerer. The fear of getting locked up for things she didn't do. Her subconscious rebelling against her. Strange visions of Corbin. The blood lust in her dreams and...the other kind. No, that was too much. There was no way meditation would help. Every time she closed her eyes, one terrifying thought replaced another in a dreadful dance that became so overwhelming she could barely keep it together. Angry outbursts happened every day now. She couldn't control them.

Rhonda was quiet, waiting for her to calm down. Once Ayla stopped crying and wiped her eyes with the sleeve of her plain green *gi*, the Healer spoke again. "We can try at the Healers' Hub if you like. Surrounded by others who can help soothe your mind. Maybe your friend Saree can help, too."

"Saree takes the pain of others and goes through it herself," Ayla retorted, thinking about the help she had already received from her Empath friend. "I can't do this to her." She looked up at Rhonda, a sudden realisation in her mind. "Wait. Is that Sorcerer still locked up in the Hub?"

The Healer chewed her lip as if deciding if revealing the information would help her cause or ruin any chances. "Yes. He's in a secure vault though, and he has none of his artefacts. He's completely harmless, Ayla. He can't hurt you."

Ayla caught her breath, counting down from ten. That was another fear factor, as if there weren't enough already. The dark figure in the night, saying his new Master had a use for her. "Has anyone interrogated him?"

"He wouldn't talk." Rhonda stood up and headed towards the bushes to get Ayla's cup.

Ayla jumped off her spot. "I'll get it. Sorry, Rhonda. I made the mess, I'll clean it up." She signed, staring at the wet spot on the ground. Her tea was only a herbal brew that wouldn't harm the environment. It was quite hot though, so a few roots would get burnt. *Something's wrong with me. I need help.*

"Blaze is there with the Enforcers this morning," the Healer suddenly voiced. "I'm sure we'll know more soon."

Ayla startled, freezing on the spot. She thought about her deep fears about him and wondered about the ways he could make people talk. Something told her he may not just use a few kind words and sweet fruit wine with a criminal.

She suppressed a shiver, chasing those thoughts away. It wasn't the time for guessing games. There was already too much on her mind to add to the load.

"Please, Ayla." Rhonda's kind eyes looked sad. "Just have a try. The other Healers will be around, you'll be safe. We can't hide from our fears forever."

Ayla glanced around her peaceful backyard. Nothing was threatening here, either, but maybe the Healer was right. It had been weeks now. Maybe she recovered enough from whatever it was that turned her own self against her and it wouldn't happen again. At least she had the reassurance of safety. A dubious one, but the one she chose to believe.

"Let's go," she decided.

Rhonda's face immediately relaxed. "Thank you, honey. You won't have to stay longer than you need."

Ayla ran down the front steps, setting a quick pace. She didn't worry about the old Healer keeping up; everyone she'd met so far had been in great physical shape. Somehow, she felt that if she walked fast, she wouldn't have time to second-guess herself. As they approached the Hub, she slowed down.

A small crowd had gathered around the building. Faces tense with anticipation. Chatter in the air. They went quiet as Ayla walked past. She tried not to heed any attention to the curious glances cast her way. *This has nothing to do with me. I'm just one of the students.*

Are you, though? A mocking voice from the back of her head didn't hold back. *Or are you the murderer they fear? The one who journeys in her sleep to accept those sacrifices Corbin gives you. To drink their warm blood and have those...encounters with him that leave you tainted for hours after waking up. The things he does to you that you hate but secretly enjoy. There's no need to lie to yourself, Ayla. You're the monster they think you are. And once you're caught, they won't show mercy.*

Ayla suppressed a scream. Anything to stop that voice, to mute those harsh words. True words. The words that made her hate herself, yet there was nothing she could do.

"Are you okay?" A familiar voice pulled her out of the pit of self-destruction. Ayla blinked, coming back to reality. The crowd didn't matter anymore. Blaze stood in front of her, deep concern in his emerald eyes. Ayla averted her gaze as if he could read her thoughts. This would be even worse.

"We're going to try meditation at the Hub today," Rhonda explained.

Blaze kept his eyes fixed on Ayla's face. "It's alright. I'll take her."

"If you're sure..." the Healer let the sentence hang in the air.

Blaze gently touched Ayla's shoulder. "Come on, Ayla. Follow me."

There was a small strain in his voice, and Ayla second-guessed herself once more. Pushing down a knot in her throat, she matched his pace as he walked out of the Hub's garden and into the streets of the city centre. He continued on towards the outskirts, making her wonder where he was taking her. The houses became more and more scarce until the road became a path in the woods. In the middle of pine undergrowth, Blaze turned off into the forest. After a short moment of hesitation, she followed him.

Ayla drew a sharp breath when he stopped at a peaceful glade surrounded by pines. Taking his invite, she settled down on the soft green grass. Blaze sat down opposite her and smiled. "Let's try here, shall we? Maybe a change of environment will work a little better."

She closed her eyes, fighting the urge to resist. His low baritone carried her on its smooth waves, guiding her to clear her mind and let the blissful emptiness fill her being. Slowly, she relaxed, allowing him to take over. He was going to take care of her if something went wrong, she knew it now. There was nothing for her to be afraid of.

In a moment, she saw herself standing in the middle of a meadow. Blinded by light, she blinked a few times before she could see her surroundings properly. It was all familiar somehow; however, she couldn't recall where she would have seen this before. Blaze was standing next to her, smiling.

"It's working," he uttered, pride in his emerald eyes.

Encouraged, she turned to fully face him. "Where are we?"

Blaze gestured around. "This is my happy place, Ayla. We met here once before, though it was a while ago." A small cloud of sadness crossed his face. "You probably don't remember it."

"I don't." She studied the tall grass with bright wildflowers scattered throughout. "How is this different from reality? And how are you here with me?"

Blaze smiled again. "I went in with you to keep you safe. Not the best option in case something happens outside, but this is all I can do right now. You need to start connecting with yourself again without the fears of what happened before. I'll stay by your side while you're healing, until you can do it on your own again."

Ayla processed this information. Now was the time for her to ask any burning questions. There were so many of them, yet nothing came to mind.

"You don't need to talk," he gestured around. "We can go for a little walk. I'll tell you about this place if you want."

"Of course I do!" she smiled back, her thoughts growing light like a feather. This was indeed a safe place. If this was for Blaze what the Mist was for her, she wanted to know. There were so many things she wanted to know about him, so many mysteries she wanted to unravel. This was her chance.

"This is the meadow I used to roam when I was a child. My parents owned a small house in the mountains, and we stayed there while I was growing up. This was the place I went to whenever I felt sad or overwhelmed. Nature always helped me connect with myself and understand my emotions. This is where I learned about the other part of me." He paused, glancing at her. Ayla kept his gaze, eager to know more. "I learned to shift here when I was a teenager. My father was a shifter, too, and he taught me about safety and control of my impulses. It gets tricky when a primal side tries to take over the human. Back then, it was overwhelming and scary. Luckily, I'm not a werewolf."

"What's the difference?" she heard herself ask. She tried not to stare at him too closely, as in this vision he had no trace of the scars she saw in reality. Here, he was probably the way he *wished* he was. Looking at herself, she realised that was her case, too. Her body felt different, and she felt much stronger, more flexible yet more fragile than she was in reality. Maybe this was how it worked.

"Shifters have magic while the werewolves don't. Another big difference is that weres don't have a choice. Come full moon, they have to change. There are special facilities around the world designated for them to go to when the time comes. Weres are dangerous as they cannot contain the animal inside. On the other hand, shifters can change shape as they wish. If I don't change for a long while, it feels uncomfortable, but it's not a must for me. I can wait until the time is right. It's also a great way to cope with stress or any other strong emotion, as shifting changes the whole perspective. Full moon, however, increases my magic ability."

"Is that why you came to take me from Corbin's house on the night of the full moon?" she suddenly asked. All the questions started coming to life. All the things she wanted to know yet was too afraid to ask. She didn't know how long they'd stay here and when the conversation would end. She had to hurry.

"Yes," Blaze paused for a moment as if choosing what to say next. "I wasn't sure if he would let you go, so I had to be prepared for anything, in case things went wrong."

"Can you tell me why you came looking for me? How did you know about my existence and that I needed help?"

Blaze stopped and looked her in the eye. "He really did erase all your memories." He sighed. "Let's say I just...knew you needed help, that you were ailing. It wasn't easy to find you, but once I did, I knew I had to protect you. This is what I've sworn to do, and I intend to keep my word."

No one had said this to her for a while. Ayla stepped closer and stopped, looking up at him. "Why do you care what happens to me?"

Instead of replying, he lifted his hand and ran his fingers along her jawline down to her chin. She lowered her gaze to his lips, the longing from their previous encounter settling in. Her chest tight, she carefully leaned into his touch and exhaled when his fingers lingered on her skin. It didn't feel as intense as when he touched her in reality, and maybe it was for the best.

Does he actually want me? Or is this whole situation a fruit of my imagination and things will be back to awkward when I come back?

Greedy girl, the mocking voice cut through her happy thoughts. *Sherice is right. You want them both, don't you? Maybe you deserve to be punished.*

Shut up, she ordered it. *Can I have a moment of peace? Something that I won't be ashamed of after?*

But you will be. How are you going to look him in the eye if you kiss him now? How are you going to act around him, after all the things Corbin does to you in those vivid dreams? Are you sure there's nothing to be ashamed of?

Ayla stumbled on her feet, overwhelmed with contradictions. The voice was right. She was a mess. There was no way she should be trying anything with Blaze until she sorted herself out.

All thoughts evaporated when Blaze caught her and pulled her close to him. "It's okay, Ayla," his whisper was clear as if the words echoed in her brain. "I understand. You're feeling the pull but you're still fighting it. Let it go, don't be afraid. There is nothing you can do to change my position with you."

She closed her eyes, heart beating violently in her chest. If only he knew what was going through her head!

"I'm scared," she muttered, feeling his warm breath on her skin. Blaze didn't respond, but his hands remained on her body. With a sigh, she leaned closer and touched his lips with hers.

An electric shock ran through her body. Startled, she pulled away. Before she had a chance to speak, the wildflowers twirled around her in a crazy dance. Blaze's face moved further away. Ayla tried to cover the distance between them, but it was no use. She remained in place, as if something kept her on the spot.

The Mist enveloped her in its grey embrace. Ayla exhaled, collecting her thoughts. It was good to be back here again, though being torn away from Blaze at such an intimate moment was overwhelming. This was her safe place, though. As always, there was nobody around. Ayla stepped forward, studying her surroundings. Each step was noiseless, with the fog absorbing every sound. There was no sign of Blaze around. The Mist was purely hers, and hers alone.

Touching the soft grey clouds, she wondered if she could lie on them. If they would lift her off the ground and carry her to a place she didn't know. After all, she'd never tested her limits before. Right now though she needed to go back. Blaze would be worried.

Startled, she listened to her inner voice. She didn't know how time worked in the Mist, if she had been there for a moment or an hour. She didn't know if Blaze would be able to bring her back if she were to get stuck. She turned in her spot, unsure of her further actions. The time in the Mist normally only lasted for so long and then she would wake up. However, she didn't get here in a dream this time. Where was the way?

A soft touch warmed the skin between her breasts. That was when she understood. The tiger amulet that Blaze had given her. The silver produced a faint glow, but it wasn't a pulsing light like Caerulus. Instead, it gently reminded her of its existence. Curious, Ayla placed her hand on it. A hardly noticeable pull came through her skin. Ayla closed her eyes, focusing on the feeling. An invisible thread went somewhere beyond the soft grey clouds...beyond the dark planes of her vivid visions that contained sparks of eerie blue and the black covers of Corbin's bedroom. Further away, where things went lighter and easier. Towards the surface, through a thin veil that separated the other side from reality.

She jolted awake to the sight of green pines framing the darkening sky. Blaze's concerned face swam into her line of sight. "Are you okay?"

Ayla nodded, taking his offered hand without a second thought. The moment her skin touched his, the feeling of longing hit with an overwhelming force. She saw a reflection of it in his green eyes when he helped her up but kept his distance. His touch lingered for a few more seconds before he let go. Ayla sighed, disappointed. Being so close to him was a torment she wasn't sure she could stand.

She didn't notice when Blaze's hand ended up on her waist. She didn't resist when he pulled her close and looked deep into her eyes. Her whole body trembled when he brushed her skin with a featherlike touch of his fingers going down her jawline, pausing on her chin. She leaned into him, unable to stay back any more. *I don't care anymore. I need this, I need him. Right now.*

It was clear now that he was holding back. Ayla inched forward and touched his lips with hers. The electric feeling was so sharp that she startled, but stayed put. No matter what, she wasn't going to let go.

"I'm sorry," she mumbled, trying to gather the crumbs of dignity she had left. There wasn't much to say; he didn't respond to the kiss. It was clearly a mistake. Just like on the night of their dinner, she made a fool of herself once again. Red shame scorched her cheeks when she thought about the consequences of her actions. What was she going to do now? He was going to despise her forever. Maybe it was time for her to run away. Hide somewhere far, far away, and hope nobody came looking.

Blaze cleared his throat. "You haven't had anything with primrose and lovehaze today, have you?" When Ayla shook her head, he continued, "That's good. I need to know you're making an educated decision, Ayla. Are you sure you want to go through with this?"

With a lump in her throat, Ayla nodded. She had never felt so uncomfortable. He was asking as if it was nothing out of the ordinary, yet she was hoping he felt the same agony. She stifled the burning need to jump on him, to let him carry her away and beg him to do whatever he wanted. Anything to stop the fire that seemed to be burning in her body. He was the cure to the strange disease that consumed her. Maybe being with him had been her destiny all along.

Realisation hit her. This was what she wanted. Ever since their first encounter, she had him on her mind, that was why she felt so awkward in his presence. That was why she avoided him. That was why she couldn't talk to him, or keep his gaze. She had always wanted him but resisted her feelings. It was that easy.

"Where would you like to go?" he asked, his smooth voice the most pleasant sound in the world.

Ayla looked up into his eyes again. "Wherever you take me," she replied, stunned by her bravery. An enormous weight lifted off her shoulders when she accepted her feelings.

Blaze took her hand, fuelling the fire inside her. "Very well."

This time, it didn't feel strange. She walked by his side, holding his hand and enjoying the warmth of his presence. There was no more fear, no more hesitation. For better or worse, she wanted to experience everything he gave her. She was finally ready.

CHAPTER 18. AYLA

The cottage looked exactly the same. Blaze let Ayla in, holding the door for her. Nothing had changed since the last time she'd been there. Only her feelings were different now. Casting a cautious glance around, Ayla struggled with a sudden rush of anxiety. She swallowed nervously, stopping in her tracks. Blaze handed her a glass of cold water.

"It's okay, Ayla," he said again, his voice rolling over her like a sheet of silk. "Remember that you don't have to do anything you don't want to do."

Throat dry, she gratefully took a couple of sips. "Thank you."

Blaze took the glass out of her cold fingers and lifted her face towards his again. "Are you having second thoughts?"

"No," she rushed. There was nothing else she could say; she only hoped he didn't ask for more. The glass clinked against the marble bench, the sound echoing in her ears. His warm hand took hers again. "I'm ready, Blaze," she replied much more confidently.

He smiled and gently tugged her along. "Come, I'll show you around."

Ayla gasped when he pushed the bedroom door open. Instead of the expected furniture, her gaze met a thin semi-transparent veil of glowing light. Holding onto Blaze's hand, Ayla stepped through it. A chill ran down her spine as she crossed the threshold.

The landscape in front of her was breathtaking. The last rays of sun rested on the surface of the calm sea, tiny waves lapping on the white sand under her feet. Ayla looked back to the door they came through, but there was no sign of it. Her clothes felt unusually light and upon inspection, she discovered that the pastel *gi* was replaced with a semi-transparent white beach dress. Surprised by the unexpected transformation, she glanced at Blaze.

His attire changed, too, but so did his looks. He was no longer the picture-perfect model. Here, the scars on his cheek were deep and raw. His hair was much longer, and his body seemed to be slightly changing as if he were in-between shapes. He was taller and more muscular, with sharp animal-like features cutting through the human image. His body was covered with fur that disappeared whenever she looked closely. *His two shapes*, she understood. *Human and animal. Two in one. Which one prevails here?*

Blaze waited for her reaction, one step away from her. When she raised her eyes to his face again, there was no more reservation. She knew he desired her; there was no doubt about that. He stayed on the spot, though, and only his gaze betrayed his true feelings. The same animal that scared her when they first met had a strong presence here.

Moments flew by as Ayla stood still, considering her options. She glanced back to the place the door was just moments ago. Insecurity gripped her again, a clot of anxiety blocking her throat. She couldn't allow herself to move forward and she couldn't move back. Her body wanted to go to him, but her mind wanted to resist. There seemed to be no right way.

She shifted her weight and looked at Blaze again. The ugly scars on his cheek. The doubling shape that confused her senses. She stepped closer, inhaling the sweet evening air. Twilight descended upon the beach, colouring everything silver. The gate between worlds. Not here, but not yet there. The in-between, when all the lines blur into one. Two in one, just like her Mentor.

Stop fighting it, a small voice said in her ear. *Whatever may be, may be. Trust yourself and take a proper look. Then you'll know what to do.*

"You look different. What is this place?" she finally managed.

Blaze's bewitching emerald eyes locked in with hers. "It's a pocket universe. I had it set up for you and me when the time came. This place has magic of its own. It strips all the outer layers, all the masks we wear, to show us in our true form. Don't be afraid."

Almost against her will, she lifted her hand and softly touched his. A tiny spark ran through her skin. Ayla shivered in joy, seeing him in the new light. Yes, the shifts between his two shapes were clear, but they no longer frightened her. Instead, it was thrilling. What would a closer touch be like? An embrace, skin to skin at last? A kiss?

"I'm not afraid," she whispered.

Blaze gently squeezed her hand, filling her with anticipation. "Good. Look over there."

Her eyes obediently followed his gesture, and a small gasp escaped her lips. A white-washed beach house was waiting for them, the path illuminated with a range of candles, their lights flickering in the gentle breeze.

The door was ajar, revealing a cosily set up room. The polished wooden floor cooled her feet, as the open windows let in the warm ocean breeze. A large bed took up most of the room, its crimson silk sheets a promise of what was to come. Next to it was a small table with a tastefully served light meal for two. Ayla glanced at it without getting into too much detail. Agitation took over her senses as she grew more impatient. Now she understood she made the right choice. Only Blaze could ease her struggles. And he was there, next to her, burning with the same desire that consumed her. Ayla bit her lower lip hard, hoping that the pain would clear her mind, but it didn't help.

Her breathing shallow, she turned to him, barely holding herself still.

Blaze pulled her close, relieving some of the pressure inside her. Ayla looked up at him in desperate craving, wishing for him to make the next step and anxious that it was taking so long. The soft touch of his fingertips against her cheek was the worst torment she could have ever imagined. They brushed her skin down her jawline, pausing under her chin, then moved ever so gently down her neck towards the collarbone. She leaned in, shivering with anticipation. Every touch ignited tiny sparks on her skin, sending waves of heat all through her body. An inexplicable force held her in place, stopping her from giving in to the rush. This was his area; she knew he was in control and she had to be patient. She gulped, restless, as he tucked a stray strand of hair behind her ear, leaning in until his breath warmed the sensitive skin just under her earlobe. Ayla arched her back, pushing herself towards him. Why did he have to torture her so?

"Please, Blaze...stop tormenting me," she begged, unable to contain the wild instincts that threatened to overcome what was left of her self-control.

She knew the difference between the intensity of a touch and a kiss straight away. When his lips pressed against the delicate skin on her neck, it was no longer a spark, but a full-blown fire. One after another, his kisses set her universe aflame until he finally touched her lips.

An electric shock ran through her body. Blaze stopped for a moment, a light shiver betraying his impatience, but soon continued by planting more tender kisses on her neck down to her shoulders, gently moving the light fabric of her dress out of the way. Ayla shuddered in anticipation; her body was so hot it felt like she was about to burst from this powerful sensation. Every touch of his hands and lips left a burning mark on her skin, and she arched her back to give him more. It felt just right as she found herself completely naked, lying on the feathery soft sheets, with Blaze's breath now warm on her stomach. His hair had a golden glow in the unsteady candlelight; Ayla took it in, letting out a quiet moan as he went down further.

A couple of centimetres past her belly button he stopped and pushed himself up to be level with her. His face was suddenly serious as he looked into her eyes.

"Are you sure you're ready, Ayla?" he inquired in his soft, deep voice. "There's no turning back if we go through with this."

Ayla's heart skipped a beat as she revelled at the sound of his voice saying her name. Then the realisation of his words hit her. Why would he even question it?

"Yes, Blaze...Please, don't make me beg," she answered, her voice hoarse. Her desire was so overwhelming she couldn't contain herself anymore. As he pulled his shirt over his head, she reached for the belt of his pants. Just before she touched it, Blaze deftly intercepted her move, grabbing her by the wrists and fixing them above her head as he lowered himself back down, pinning her to the bed.

"Patience, sweetheart. All good things to those who wait," he teased and she reddened. His hand gently brushed her inner thighs, taking its time sliding higher. Ayla wriggled down to meet his hand for a deeper touch, but his shrewd gaze fixed her on the spot, making her lie still.

Blaze inhaled and gave her another kiss, a passionate and deep one this time. As Ayla struggled to process its power, another sensation shook her body. She felt the full length of him as he finally entered. She gasped and opened her eyes wide, scared and aroused at the same time. It was clear now why he didn't want her to touch him too soon. Ayla tried to free her hands to push herself up off his shoulders to move away but it was too late. He had one hand holding her wrists and the other firmly keeping her hips in place as he slowly moved further. She tensed up and for the first time tonight felt pain.

Blaze let go of her wrists and tenderly caressed her face. She squirmed to look into his eyes again.

"Shh, it's okay, Ayla. Don't be afraid," he said again calmly, his voice soothing as ever. "I'll be very gentle, you just have to try and relax. Or do you want me to stop?"

She shook her head, too overwhelmed to speak. *I don't think I can take it all, but damn if I ever want him to stop.*

"It's going to hurt, I'm afraid, but just in the beginning. It will get easier soon, I promise. Breathe with me," Blaze whispered in her ear, planting sweet kisses on her neck.

Once again she gave in to his sensual touch, and as soon as she stopped fighting it, she was on fire again.

Blaze moved her hair out of the way and kissed her neck all the way down to her collarbone. Ayla forgot about the pain, moaning with desire, all her senses tuning to him. Blaze paused for an instant that felt like an eternity. When she nearly lost her mind with mad craving, he finally continued. This time, she barely noticed the pain. It wasn't long until she got used to him, and his movement started bringing her pure pleasure. Ayla's body was no longer hers; everything she ever was, everything she would ever be belonged to him alone. It was so clear that made her wonder how she didn't see it before. There was no more fear; only this sweet and agonising moment that trapped her forever like a butterfly in amber.

Blaze kissed her again, deeply, greedily, and she felt their breaths synchronise. Ayla writhed under him, eager to take more no matter what it cost. She knew he was holding back; if he felt the same way she did, there was no way he could be so reserved. Regardless, whatever he was giving her now was enough to tip her over the edge. She dug her fingernails into his back as the tight ball in her belly unravelled in a painfully slow instant.

Ayla struggled to catch her breath, blinking herself back to reality. Her lover paused to watch her, his hands gently tracing her cheeks while she recovered. Once she could see clearly again, his cheeky grin told her this was only the beginning.

Ayla lost track of time, immersed in what seemed like all the orgasms she'd ever had and more. As she grew hungrier, he got rougher. Gone were the gentle touches and sweet kisses; his primal side was showing more and more, driving her insane. This was what she wanted. The wild ride she suspected he could give her, the animal to satisfy her cravings. Close to another peak of pleasure, she bit his neck when he leaned in for a kiss, and he reciprocated. Encouraged, she did more and received more. It wasn't the time to think about consequences; she wanted him to mark her as his for the whole world to see.

Finally, she felt Blaze approaching his peak. She squeezed his hips with her legs, wanting to share his climax, but at the last moment, he broke contact with her body. Ayla's mood dropped. She hoped he'd let her have his seed.

Blaze gave her a long gentle kiss on the lips.

"Not yet, sweetheart," he whispered in her ear. "We have to be careful for now."

Still flushed, Ayla couldn't help but wonder. "I thought Mages were in control of their...uh, reproduction," she uttered.

Blaze propped himself up on the elbow, caressing her with his gaze. "Typically, yes, and under normal circumstances. Things are different during a Joining. No spells, no regular birth control, no alterations to our physique would work. This is still risky but it decreases your chances to get pregnant. I think it's time you learned that we are no ordinary couple, you and I. We are destined for each other."

Ayla studied his open face for a hint of a smile, but nothing told her it was a joke. He was dead serious. "I've never thought I could be destined to someone. I thought it was more of a myth from the little that I've heard."

"It's definitely not a myth, my sweetheart. Destiny is decided when a Mage is born, but it needs a series of events to trigger what is known as a 'pull'." His expression grew sad as he averted his eyes. "I had a rough past. One night, I had a vision of you in my dreams. I knew right away it was a sign that my destiny was out there. For years after, I searched for you, with those dreams luring me on. More than a decade passed, and I lost hope. I convinced myself it was a coping mechanism to deal with my guilt of the past—until the Prophet summoned your image. That's how I learned you were real, and you needed my help. That's why I came to take you away from Corbin as soon as I found where he kept you."

"How come I didn't feel the pull?"

Blaze sighed. "Your connection to me got blocked. I saw you in a particularly vivid dream once, and we even managed to speak. You were fully aware then. I was sure this was when you understood it, too, but there was no contact since. I continued seeing you, but things were going worse and worse. Something happened to you. I could no longer approach you or speak with you, but it seemed like you still felt my presence." He rolled on his back, inviting her to put her head on his chest. Once she settled, he caressed her dishevelled hair, gently untangling it.

"Why couldn't you find me earlier?"

Blaze wrapped his arm around her. "Corbin watched you like a hawk. I'm not sure if he knew I could see auras, but he definitely masked yours. By the end of my search, he had moved countries twice. I was just lucky that his Familiar wanted to get rid of you so desperately she decided to help me."

"His Familiar?" Ayla felt a knot forming in her chest. Blaze's embrace no longer comforted her. Thinking about Corbin ruined all the feelings of intimacy.

"Raven. Her human shape was a maid, I believe."

Ayla sat up, wrapping her arms around her. The temperature around her dropped, but she knew it was her own reaction.

"It's okay, sweetheart. We don't have to talk about this." Blaze sat up, too, but kept his distance.

Ayla closed her eyes, trying to chase away the memories she still had of Corbin's mansion. Some of them suddenly came to the surface of her mind. Corbin's face, distorted by anger, and his hand raised to strike her. Her own hand, covered in blood as she wiped it off her face. The feeling of desperation and hopelessness when she wanted to end it all.

And then, her more recent dreams. The things he did that made her despise herself, the pain he so freely inflicted on her that she hated but secretly craved.

"No," she whimpered, covering her face as if it would protect her from the tormenting images. "No, no, no. This couldn't have happened. It's all in my head." Gulping down the tightness in her throat, she struggled to breathe as if the air got sucked out of her lungs. Dark magic followed her everywhere she went. She was a fool to believe she could have peace.

A barely audible clink made her open her eyes. Blaze was up, holding a glass of chilled water in his hand. His expression concerned, he handed it to her, careful not to touch her skin like in those first days.

Taking a small sip, she squeezed out a smile. It wasn't his fault that someone hurt her in the past and that her mind was a mess. He was only trying to help, and he hadn't done anything wrong. Yes, she got scared of the primal in his eyes, but he never acted on it. He wasn't the man who damaged her, and it was unfair to treat him like one.

"Thank you, Blaze," she managed, her voice hoarse.

"Of course. We'll get there, sweetheart. Do you need to be alone for a bit?"

Ayla took a deep breath and silently counted to four, breathing out on six. "No. Please, stay with me." She thought about the way she finally felt safe on the night she connected with her magic, when Blaze helped her keep her flame alive. When he wrapped his jacket around her shoulders to keep her warm. That he was the one to take her away from Corbin's mansion and the abuse that was disguised as care. He was different. He would never hurt her.

She finished her water and gave the glass back to Blaze, touching his fingers. He understood right away. The glass clinked on the table, and Ayla pulled her lover back to bed. Snuggling into his chest, she listened to her body. Nothing alerted her of any hidden threats. Being in his arms was where she had always belonged, this was clear. Slowly at first, her hands travelled over his torso, caressing his muscular arms, running down his stomach. Ayla chuckled when she felt him shiver under her touch. She lifted herself on the elbows and slid her body on top of his. A deep, sensual kiss was as arousing as it was painful. She gasped, realising her lips must be over-sensitive from all the attention they got that night. Maybe this was what Blaze felt, too. This time, he allowed her to take charge and only supported her weight when she wiggled on top.

Sweet fatigue overcame her when she finally rolled back onto the silky sheets. She whispered, "I don't think I can move anymore."

Blaze gently pressed a chocolate-glazed strawberry against her lips. "I'm not expecting you to. Try this."

The sweetness of chocolate complemented the hint of sour in the crispy flesh of the berry. Ayla savoured it, eyes closed in delight. This was pure bliss. The moment she never thought she would experience. To be loved and cared for like this. To have her lover by her side, cherishing her and staying alert to all her needs. Someone she cared for just as deeply. What had she done to deserve this?

Ayla allowed herself to melt in his arms, nurturing her joy. Something at the back of her head kept nagging at her like a half-closed water tap.

No, darling. You didn't deserve this. There is no happy ending for you. All this euphoria is in your imagination.

It's all in your head.

CHAPTER 19. AYLA

A yla woke up with a start. It was dark outside the cabin but the beach was flooded with the brilliant glow of the moon. Immersed in deep sleep, Blaze was by her side, his arm keeping her securely next to him. Exhausted after the Joining, Ayla wondered what woke her. Her energy was low, and she knew she needed more sleep. Yet somehow she was wide awake, a strange urge pulling her out of bed.

She wiggled out of Blaze's embrace, checking that he was still asleep. He didn't even move. Quietly, she put on her dress and snuck outside. Back to the beach she went, with the light of the full moon resting on peaceful waves. The candles were gone, but the night celestial gave off plenty of light. White sand was coloured a cold silver, crumbly under her bare feet.

Ayla stopped where she thought the threshold was. She wasn't sure how it would work, but something was different about her now. A strange confidence filled her lungs as she spoke.

"Show me the door," she ordered in a clear voice that carried across the water. To her surprise, the portal appeared right away, opening into the familiar hallway of Blaze's house. Without hesitation, Ayla crossed over. The house was dark and lonely without its owner. Ayla paused, glancing back at the shimmering veil behind her. Was she right to leave? She didn't get a chance to ponder any longer. The urge felt stronger here, and she barely caught a breath before her legs carried her out of the house.

She ran down the dark streets, adrenaline pushing her body further. The sense of urgency only got stronger as she approached the small town square. Now into one of the alleys...

He was waiting for her just behind the ancient building of the Healers' Hub, deserted at this hour. In the deceitful glow of the moon, he looked almost like he did in the old days, his face smooth and handsome, his raven hair seemingly absorbing the light. His dark clothes were a perfect cover for the shadows, and only his pale skin betrayed his presence.

"Ayla," he breathed with relief. "Are you alright? I couldn't feel you through the bond, it's almost as if you disappeared." Corbin stepped closer and stretched his arms towards her for a hug. In the middle of the gesture, he stopped as if hitting an invisible wall.

Ayla felt a sharp sting from her silver tiger necklace.

A painful expression flashed in his eyes as he studied her close. Ayla blushed when she thought about the way she looked. Blaze didn't hold back in the end, so she was sure she'd have a few visible love bites on her neck and shoulders. Her lips felt overly sensitive from his demanding kisses, her hair was dishevelled. She lowered her eyes, hiding her shame. It didn't occur to her what would happen to the blood bond when she crossed the threshold into a pocket universe. No wonder Corbin was worried. She just wished he didn't find out about her new relationship this way.

"You belong to him now," Corbin said bitterly.

Ayla thought of the time he got furious when he found out about her school boyfriend back at the Academy, and stepped back. She suddenly realised it was a mistake to come here. Blaze was far away, immersed in a sleep so deep he didn't even move when she left. A faint fear crept into her mind. If something went wrong now, he wouldn't be able to help her. Ayla glanced around, her thoughts racing. She wondered if the Healers actually lived in this building or if they were stationed in the houses on the outskirts and there was nobody around to hear her if she needed help.

He won't hurt me. He only came here because he was worried. Now that he sees I'm okay, he'll leave and I'll go back to Blaze. Nothing's going to happen. I'm okay.

Corbin covered the distance between them, his stare breaking her defence.

"So you do have magic," he whispered, lifting her chin to look him in the eye. "You can't imagine how much danger you're in. Come with me, I can still save your life. When they come, Blaze won't be able to protect you."

"What are you talking about? Who's they?" Ayla jerked her head to break free from his cold finger under her chin. She hated when he did that but was too scared to push him away.

Corbin shook his head. "There are bigger things at stake now that you have found your magic. You don't have enough time to learn about your powers before they take you. I wish you'd stayed by my side, safe from it all. I never meant to hurt you, my sweet girl. You were innocent, but I didn't want to see it. I wanted to punish you and went too far."

"Tell me what's going on. Who is coming? Why am I in danger?" she demanded.

"Remember the people who killed Darren? They searched for you all over the world, but weren't too persistent, thinking you were a *null*. Blaze activated your power but you don't know what to do with it, and your time is running out fast. I can still help you, Ayla. Please, come with me. I'll hide you away until this is over."

"No, Corbin. My place is here now, I'm sorry," she softened her voice as much as she could.

"You don't understand. Maybe I'm asking too much." He pursed his lips into a thin line and held a small pause before continuing. "Look at yourself, Ayla. He marked you all over. I can feel his greedy paws all over your body, not an inch left untainted. He's an animal, a primal. All he thinks about is sex." Corbin's face turned into a grimace of disgust. "I've always been so soft with you, so cautious. It didn't work, and I see why. What you needed was some brute force to keep you grounded. This is what I should have done with you."

A small shiver crawled down her spine, reminding her that it was the middle of the night and she was alone with one of the most dangerous Sorcerers in the world. That Blaze didn't know she was gone. That there was nobody to help her if something went wrong. That Corbin had a short temper and didn't hold back when he got upset.

"No," she mumbled, already knowing this would escalate their confrontation.

"So it's okay for *him* to hurt you?" Without a warning, he grabbed her by the throat, digging his fingers into her tender flesh. Ayla yelped, pushing him away. Corbin's nostrils flared. "Look at yourself. Slut!" Fast as lightning, his hand let go, only to strike her hard, breaking the skin on her lips. The force of the hit sent her flying against the wall, her head hitting it with a loud thud. Unable to stay on her feet, she slid down on the cold stones of the street.

Ayla sat up and felt her head for a bump, wary of a potential concussion. Corbin grabbed her by the hair and pulled her up, rolling her head back. "I should have let you die," he hissed, each word dripping with venom. "After everything I've done for you, this is how you thank me. Ungrateful little bitch!" He slapped her again, then again, keeping hold of her hair. Too scared to fight, Ayla raised her hands to cover her face, but he didn't stop. Stinging strikes rained on her hands until all she felt was numbness.

"Please, Corbin, stop," she begged, sobbing. She knew there was no way to stop his fury. Her tears only seemed to have made him angrier.

"Isn't this what you like? Look at those marks on yourself! Are you going to tell me that didn't hurt? No, my darling, you loved it. This is what I should have done all along. You only respect force and pain, nothing else."

Her legs gave in. Corbin lowered his hand, letting her slide down. Ayla tried to push up on her elbow, but there was no more strength left in her. She slumped on the ground, peering at the clear sky scattered with stars. *He'll let off steam and won't hurt me anymore. I need to persevere just a little bit longer. It's not like he's going to kill me*, she told herself.

Corbin sat down by her side, his dark eyes full of pain. "You betrayed me, Ayla. I did everything I could to keep you safe, to give you everything you needed. Then you walked out on me, and now this." He sighed, wrapping his arms around her. His hand gently threaded her hair as he lowered his face to hers. Ayla flinched, expecting more hits, but they didn't come. Her stomach curled into a tight ball.

He didn't just get sweet because he forgave her. Whatever he was about to do was scarier than any beating.

"My beautiful, innocent girl. Why did you have to leave? None of these terrible things would have happened if you stayed." He caressed her bruised cheeks, his eyes sad. "I saved your life, my darling," he whispered softly and planted a kiss on her forehead. Her heart raced in approaching panic. She tried to crawl away, but her body didn't obey. "*I* gave it to you, not him. And now I'll take it back." His hands wrapped around her throat, gently at first, slowly tightening their grip.

Ayla writhed on the ground, now understanding his previous tenderness. He wasn't just being kind. It was his way of saying goodbye.

"Please, no," she rasped, clawing at his hands. There was nothing she could say in her defence; nothing she could do to make him change his mind. *This can't be the end, not now!*

"Shh, don't fight it. Trust me, it's for the best. I'll free you from suffering, just like you asked me before," he cooed as his fingers dug deeper into her flesh.

At the edge of losing consciousness, she desperately reached for her power. It sprouted at her command, no longer a delicate white flame, but a raging inferno. The wave of raw energy ripped through the thin veil of her control, going loose on her assailant. In an instant, Corbin was thrown across the small alley to the opposite wall. Ayla coughed, drawing a full breath—the best luxury in the world, having access to air again. Red spots danced before her eyes as she watched his stance change.

"Your power is stronger than I thought." A stunned expression crossed his face. Corbin rose to his feet and peered at her as if he'd seen her for the first time.

Magic danced on her fingertips, spreading all over her body. Ayla pushed her back to the wall, keeping an eye on her former Master. "Stay away from me!" she croaked, directing another wave at him. This one was more effective; the force didn't just go around her like an explosion, but was aimed at him alone.

Corbin's head hit the wall, making her smile. *That's right, get a taste of your own medicine, you son of a bitch.*

He raised his hands in front of him. "Calm down. Ayla, the power of Mages is different from the Sorcerers. You can't throw it around like this."

"Watch me!" she screamed, pushing another wave of blinding light towards him. *Make it hurt, really hurt. Burn his skin, poison his blood, rip his heart out. Everything he's ever done to me, let him taste it all himself. Tenfold.*

Corbin lifted his hand with the graduation ring on his index finger as if deciding whether to use it. There was no flash of green that she knew would follow if he used his magic. This made her more frustrated. Why wouldn't he defend himself?

Fight me, damn it! Make me angry, give me an excuse to kill you!

After everything he had done, he deserved to be punished. She kept sending one wave after another until the flame didn't come to her anymore. With a frown on her face, she stared at her hands which were hardly glowing now, as opposed to their brilliant shine mere minutes ago. Corbin rolled his shoulders and made a cautious step towards her. "Stop, Ayla. You need to calm down before you burn out."

"Don't touch me," she exhaled, frantically searching for the magic within herself. There had to be something left. She wanted to do so much more, she was only getting started! She was going to serve him justice no matter what it took.

Corbin stopped, turning open palms towards her. "I'm sorry, Ayla. I shouldn't have lost my temper like I did."

"You nearly killed me! What the hell is wrong with you? Thinking you can just say sorry and walk away?" Anger boiled in her blood. "*Sorry* doesn't cut it, Corbin. Isn't this what you told me when you beat me up for bad grades? Isn't 'sorry' the word you always said tucking me to sleep every time after your sick entertainment? I can't remember it all, but I sure remember some." Ayla scrambled on her feet, trying to ignore the cold that made her body crawl with goosebumps.

"You're shivering. Ayla, you used too much of your magic too quickly. Please, stop, before you lose what's left of it. I'll go, okay? You need to get to a safe place and rest now."

She screamed in frustration, hitting the wall with her fists. All she wanted was to keep pushing the limits, but the power was no longer responding to her call. The chills grew stronger as if the temperature dropped. She knew it couldn't be the case. It was too warm these days. Something was wrong with her.

"Stay away from me," she snapped, bitter tears rolling down her cheeks. "I never, ever want to see you again!"

Corbin looked at her, sadness and guilt set deep in his eyes. "I really am sorry. I shouldn't have attacked you." He sighed, circling his hand in the air. A dark portal opened next to him. Before stepping in, he turned his head to Ayla again. "I hope you can forgive me someday."

Without another sound, he walked through the frame of darkness. The gentle swoosh in his wake erased the dark outline from existence. Ayla was alone in the little alleyway, adrenaline wearing off as the cold crept under her skin, cutting down to the bone. She shivered, pulling the lightweight cotton on her shoulders as if it would protect her from the cold inside. It was time to go back. She knew Blaze could explain what happened to her. He'd be able to fix whatever damage she had done. She just needed to make it back to him.

Ayla took a step towards the alley's exit and wavered. Her body no longer obeyed her, too exhausted to move. She slumped on the ground, freezing. Something was wrong, and there was no one to help.

Light steps announced another presence. She lifted her head, and hope reignited in her chest. Someone was there after all. He was going to help her.

The figure pulled the hood off his head. A wicked grin illuminated his face as he sat down next to her. "Hello again, little Ayla."

"Kendall," she breathed out. "How did you get here?"

"It's not that hard when you know where you're going. And once the gate has been opened for the first time, the rest is easy."

Another presence made her look to her left. A dark hooded figure approached her with a deceitfully slow pace. "Hello, little princess. Took you long enough to leave the Mage's protection," the figure hissed in a low tone, taking the hood off.

Ayla shuddered, looking into the hollows of his eyes. She hadn't seen this one before, but she knew better than to nurture any hopes. "Are you the Sorcerer from the vault?"

The figure chuckled and exchanged a meaningful glance with Kendall. "Clever girl." He stepped closer and drew a deep breath. "Just had your gift uncovered, too. What a treat for the Master."

"I don't have a Master anymore." Ayla thought about her fear, hoping to call the adrenaline back. It would give her temporary strength to face whatever this was. The figures stood still, watching her with amusement.

"So cute. So helpless," the second figure grinned, exchanging a sinister look with Kendall. "You didn't tell me she was pretty."

"It's her pheromones, Les," Kendall responded, keeping his gaze on Ayla. "She's just had her first Joining, can't you tell? Still high on hormones like a bitch in heat."

Les chuckled, studying Ayla's face. "Yes, now I see what you mean. Such a sweet little girl though. So tiny, so scared. Exactly my type." He swiftly covered the distance between them and grabbed her hair, forcing her to look up.

"Careful. She has magic now and can sting," Kendall warned, but his eyes were laughing.

"She used it all up, you saw it. Going to take her a little while to have it back, and we'll be long gone by then." Les licked his lips, focussing on Ayla again. "I'm not surprised Master wants you. Maybe he'll let us have you once he's done. If there's anything left."

Kendall's chuckle made her body tremble. "Or maybe we can play with her a little before we deliver her to him. This one is so delicious to torture, you have no idea."

"It's okay, sweet girl, no need to be afraid," Les crooned, smiling at her horror. "Don't worry, we won't kill you. Just a little play, that's all. It won't be as elaborate as what

Master would do, but I can guarantee that you won't be bored."

With the last of her energy, Ayla tried to break free, but her attempt was crushed. "Blaze," she whispered, desperate for his presence. "If you can hear me...I need your help."

A swift strike on the face made her yelp. Les's merciless eyes swam into her vision. "Shut up, you little bitch! Nobody can help you now."

The feeling of being a victim she knew so well surfaced again. Ayla whimpered, looking for any hint of her magic. Just one more try. It would buy her a few seconds to scramble out of the alley. Hopefully, there would be other people on the main street. At least someone to hear her scream. If she could scream.

Corbin's voice sounded through the veil of haze in her head. That was what he'd tell her during those long nights filled with pain. *"Scream as much as you want, my darling,"* the voice crooned. *A firm hand pulled her hair further, jerking her head back.* "Nobody will come. I own you, remember? You're mine to enjoy as I see fit. You can only go when I say you can go."

Another slap jolted her back to the cruel reality. Exhausted and unable to defend herself, all she could do was try and curl into a ball to cover herself as much as possible. The maniac hit her again and again, eyes sparkling with excitement.

"Come on, Les, take it down a notch. We need to get her out of here. Master doesn't like to wait." Kendall caught the other man's hand before it delivered another hit. Almost blind from pain and the blood now flowing freely over her face, Ayla prayed for it to end. She didn't care when someone grabbed her by the arm and dragged her to her feet. Unable to stand on her own, she stumbled.

Please, Blaze. Please, help me.

The night was still and quiet. Moonlight filled the empty streets without a sound in the air. Only her heartbeat and the quiet steps of the two men who were hauling her somewhere away from safety. Her white flame was reduced to a tiny spark, barely feasible through the wall of pain. Ayla sobbed as Kendall circled his hand and opened a dark portal, almost identical to Corbin's.

I shouldn't have told Corbin to leave. At least I know him and the things he can do. With these two, I stand no chance.

"Who is your Master?" she squeaked, hoping that a question would slow them down.

Kendall grinned. "Oh, you know him very well. He's been trying to get his hands on you for quite some time. Shame that you disappeared from the Sorcerers' world, but he knew you wouldn't go far."

"Does he have a name?"

"Too eager, aren't you?" Les interjected. "We won't ruin the surprise. You'll see for yourself soon. Very soon, little Ayla. He won't keep you waiting for too long."

The stone pavement still reflected the light of the moon, but somehow, it grew dimmer. Ayla wondered if that was the proximity of the portal. Only a few more paces, and they would go through it. She squirmed in another desperate attempt to break free, already knowing she had no chance against the two of them.

A thin veil of fog crawled under her feet, so light it was almost unnoticeable. Ayla stared at it, her mind numb. The clear night was no place for fog. Or was it?

She plopped on the ground when her assailants simultaneously let go of her arms. A bright light flooded the alley, but it didn't come from the moon. Ayla squinted, trying to make out the shape that appeared between houses. Not a tiger this time, Blaze stood still at the mouth of the alley, studying his opponents.

She knew he was going to come.

CHAPTER 20. AYLA

Ayla glared at the thin tube supplying clear liquid to her arm, needle burrowed into her skin. *I hate goddamn needles.*

The young Healer rushed to clear the bedside table of get-well cards and bunches of half-wilted flowers. Her eyes were focused on work, though she threw a few curious glances at Ayla. "How are you feeling?"

"Much better," Ayla lied. The hospital environment was pressing on her like a pile of rubble after an earthquake. She felt trapped under it, leashed to her bed by the transparent tube. "Can I leave?"

"Not until the head Healers allow it, I'm afraid," the girl averted her eyes, wiping the small table with a pale blue cloth. "But Blaze will come and visit soon! Maybe he can persuade them to let him take you home."

Ayla's cheeks flushed. She wasn't sure how much the town folk knew about her new relationship with her Mentor. The last thing she remembered was the outline of his silhouette at the end of the dark alley before he charged at her assailants. There was nothing else in her blurred memory, apart from the healing greyness of the Mist that took her in its embrace the moment she closed her eyes.

The nurse placed a bouquet of fresh wildflowers next to her. Ayla stared at it in dismay. Those were the exact ones that Darren used to bring home when she was a child. This wasn't public knowledge; she didn't mention them even to Blaze. Nobody in this town should have known. Pure coincidence?

She didn't think so.

"Um, Kayla?"

The young Healer looked up, a ready smile on her face. "You remember my name!"

"Yes," Ayla frowned. "Where did these flowers come from? Is there a card?"

The girl ruffled through the bouquet. Ayla's fingers started tapping on the metal edge of the bed. In a few excruciating seconds, the Healer found the tiny envelope in pastel blue that was hardly noticeable among the cornflowers. Ayla nearly snatched it out of her hand. A feeling of foreboding blinded her senses. She paused, trying to shake it off.

A plain piece of white paper didn't look threatening at all. Until she read the words on it.

"Just four more that shall be bled,
Then, the target's on your head.

Tell yourself a million lies,
But only one of us survives."

Her heart stopped, gripped with terror. The young Healer glanced at her, a silent question in her eyes. Ayla shook her head, not willing to speak about it.

"It's okay," she croaked. "I'm just a little dizzy."

Clamping her hand around the tiny piece of paper, she lay back on the pillow. Blaze would have an explanation, she was sure of it. She shook her head at the tray with a modest breakfast on it that another Healer brought into the room, and curled up on her bed. Her eyes fixed on the wall, Ayla thought about the strange little rhyme and the flowers. It made no sense, yet there was a logic behind it. She just didn't want to see it.

A tiny creak of the door alerted her of another presence. Rhonda walked into the room, followed by two other Healers. All of them donning light grey robes and sombre faces. The last one to come in was Blaze, his expression serious. Ayla sat up on the bed, wondering if he would join her. His eyes were sad as they met hers. There was no answer to her burning questions. Ayla bit her tongue, determined to ask him later. Whatever this was, she was sure he was only distant to keep their status unknown.

Blaze took the chair next to the bed, but nowhere as close as she wished. The Healers settled down opposite her, their robes a soft rustle in the silence of the room.

"How are you feeling, Ayla?" Rhonda glanced at one of the other Healers who took out a notepad and a pencil.

Ayla looked at it, too. "Much better today, thank you," she responded cautiously.

The pencil made a few strikes on the paper.

"I think you need to tell her what's happening before you proceed any further." Blaze's voice was cold as he peered at the Healer with the notepad.

The woman sighed and put the pencil down. "Of course. My name is Karina, and my companion here is Kieran." She pointed at the other Healer, a tall man with greying hair. "I'll ask you a few questions, that's all. Kieran may assist me in case I forget about something. Rhonda will act as a witness. Blaze doesn't really need to be here." She threw a sharp glance in his direction. "However, as your Mentor, he has the right to defend you in the unlikely case something goes wrong."

"Why would something go wrong? What's this about?" Ayla's voice sounded nothing like her own. A bad feeling crept into her chest.

Karina picked up her pencil, no longer paying attention to Blaze's glare. "The Mage Council is currently investigating the kidnappings and murders of the Mage girls. The Enforcers are working hard to progress on this case, but the leads go nowhere. The Council is quite concerned, as you can imagine."

"I have nothing to do with it," Ayla responded a little too quickly. Her heartbeat accelerated as she thought of the meaning behind Karina's words.

Maybe it's nothing. They might just be worried that something can happen to me. I don't need to stress.

"Of course. Nobody is blaming you," Karina responded just as quickly, casting a glance at Blaze. "It's curious that these events started shortly after you arrived at Whitestone, though. Then, you went out to Twintown and found one of the bodies. It's probably nothing but a coincidence. However, there are certain rumours..."

"You're not basing your accusations on rumours, I hope," Blaze interjected. His voice was soft but with a steely undertone.

"Absolutely not. We're not accusing her of anything," Karina crooned, peering at Kieran.

He took the lead. "We hear about your overwhelming success with the Mist. Do you have any physical sensations when you're there? Feeling smells, hearing sounds? Does the Mist itself feel...special to you?"

Ayla's eyes widened when she understood what he was hinting at. "No," she lied, looking straight into his eyes.

The man shifted in his seat. "That's good. You are a very special girl, you know? We're just trying to make sense of the situation."

Karina put a dot in the notebook. "Let's talk about last night. Tell me, Ayla, what made you walk down the streets in the middle of the night? How did the Sorcerers get here?"

"I don't know," Ayla muttered, looking at Blaze again. She wished she could have had a few minutes alone with him before they showed up. There was no way of knowing if he revealed that they had Joined or if the Healers thought she woke up alone in her bed and decided to take a jolly walk downtown.

"I think you might want to ask why she was so brutally hurt. If it weren't for my intervention, who knows what could have happened? I hope you understand that she was a target. Ayla didn't do this to herself. Maybe the Sorcerers told her something to give us some clues." Blaze turned towards her. "Did they?"

"Just that their Master wants me to be delivered to him. They didn't mention a name or anything," Ayla mumbled, realising this wasn't enough. Her hand felt the crispy edge of the paper. Of course! This was the clue! "Actually, there is something. These flowers were delivered today," she pointed at the stand. The group politely glanced at them.

"Very pretty," Karina uttered, noting something down. "And?"

"Look at this note." Ayla handed the crumpled paper to Rhonda. With a quizzical look, the old Healer unwrapped it.

"What note, dear?"

It can't be.

Ayla snatched it back, staring at the blank page. Not a word, not a smudge of ink showed the presence of a message. She shook her head. "It was here just a few minutes ago! I read it before you walked in. There was a message!" Her throat closed down as she struggled to push the air into her lungs. The message had been there, she was sure of it! Trying to prove it showed her as unreliable.

I'm crazy. Is there anything that's real anymore? Or am I trapped in my own head, lost in a fake reality with no way out?

Hyperventilating, she rocked on the edge of the bed. All faces blurred into one, but nothing mattered. The voices swam around her as if she was hearing them underwater. No tones, no rhythm—just a blubbering mess that made no sense. She pushed her hands to her ears and squeezed her eyes shut.

It's not real. I'm not here.

Someone's hands lifted her over the muttering. Strong and safe, they held her close to a source of warmth. A steady drumbeat resonated in her ears. Ayla gripped onto something soft and stayed still. Her heartbeat slowed down, matching the rhythm of the drums. A subtle touch ran through her hair, flowing from the top to the nape of her neck. She breathed in a calming essence of lavender and citrus. Everything was okay.

"You're safe, sweetheart. I'm here."

Ayla lifted her face and met Blaze's emerald eyes. It felt good to be in his arms again, though she wasn't sure how long that would last. "Did they go?"

"Yes. I sent them away. It was a bad idea to start with. You still have a long way to recover, but the Council pressed for this 'chat' as they called it." His eyes were tainted with sadness. "I'm so sorry, Ayla. This is not how I pictured the beginning of our life together."

"Me either," she mumbled, feeling the muscles through the cotton of his shirt. It was good to finally be able to touch him, to talk to him. There was so much she wanted to say!

Her smile dropped as she thought about the disappearing message. "Blaze, the note..."

"It's okay," he soothed, picking up the crumbled paper off the bed. "It's here."

"There was a rhyme," Ayla repeated the message out loud.

With each word, Blaze's face darkened. "A threat," he said, staring at the paper as if it would bring the words back. "Four more to be bled?" He scratched his chin before looking at her again. "If this is about the Mage girls, the message is pretty clear. The body count is now up to eight. If four more girls are to be killed, it will total twelve. A symbolic number."

"Then, the target's on my head," Ayla recited. "The Sorcerers mentioned that their Master wants me. What for?"

"That is not a question I can answer." Blaze looked her straight in the eye. "I wonder, though. After our Joining, we both went into the Slumber that should have lasted a few days until we fully recovered. How come you woke up only a couple of hours after?"

The skin on Ayla's neck went taut. She wasn't prepared for questions from Blaze, and this one caught her unawares. "I just felt like I had to go, so I left. I didn't know I was supposed to stay there for a few days."

"It's something that happens to destined couples after their first Joining. Doesn't take that long any other time. The first Slumber is crucial as it synchronises our energies and shapes our future lives, as well as our enhanced abilities. However, no one has ever awakened so shortly after. What happened, Ayla? What made you leave my side and go straight into the clutches of danger?"

Ayla went quiet. She thought about the urge that forced her out of his embrace and sent her tired body running down the streets. A grimace of anger and disgust on Corbin's face. She didn't need to protect him anymore. He was gone from her life now, never to return. She could tell Blaze the truth. Running her fingers over her lips that nearly healed now, she thought about the hot blood gushing out of the split. Her terror when he tightened his grip around her neck. The sting on her hands and cheeks when he struck her again and again. Blaze needed to know about this. It was Corbin who did it. He deserved to be punished for his actions, for everything he had done to her.

She held her tongue. For some reason, the words didn't come.

"I don't know, Blaze." Frustrated with herself, she exhaled and focused on the little rhyme.

Blaze wrote it down on a piece of Karina's notepad that was left on the stand. Now he was rereading it, with a frown on his face. "Only one of us survives. What does that mean?"

"I don't know," Ayla repeated. This seemed to be her chosen phrase of the day. The inability to answer questions was starting to get on her nerves. "Can we go home?"

"I'll talk to them. For now, nobody knows about our Joining, so I'll have to take you back to your house. We'll stay apart for just a little longer. I'm not sure if our new relationship status is going to help or put you in greater danger." He touched her hand with his lips, sending a tiny electric spark up her arm. "I swear I'll do everything I can to find the true criminal and bring them to justice. Then, we can be together again."

Ayla nodded like a marionette on a string. It was too much for her to process. Excusing herself, she rushed to the bathroom. Nothing but bitter bile came up as she grabbed on to the white toilet seat. The little rhyme stood in front of her eyes. Neat, rounded letters. So easy to read. So familiar. The handwriting she would never confuse with anyone else's. Her own.

Ayla breathed out and stared at the mirror. Colourless cheeks, haunted eyes. Her hand trembled when she raised it to her face to trace the healing wound on her lip. Something was wrong.

Then, it hit her. She met the gaze of her reflection, as scared as her own. Hers, yet not completely. There was more to it behind the mask of fear. Behind the thin veil of reality, dark fires shifted in a sinister dance. Deeper still, there were voices telling her stories of ancient evils. Beyond them, a whisper she knew so well from her strange visions. And the eerie blue of the great sapphire with a majestic name. Caerulus.

Its light—*his* light—put a blue glow into her eyes. Her reflection became clearer as it lost traces of her haunted expression. The Ayla in the mirror was a completely different version of herself. She smiled, staring back at her.

"You can't hide from yourself, Ayla. The clock is ticking and shadows are closing in. Embrace the darkness—or die."

PART TWO

CHAPTER 21.
TENEBRIS

She stretched in her bed, kicking off the feathery soft sheets. The sun was already high up in the sky, but dark curtains blocked some of the light to protect her sleep. Sleep was precious, especially after an offering. Not that she was ever going to tell anybody. To the rest of the world, she had no flaws, no weaknesses. Let it stay this way.

Long chestnut locks fell on her back in a silky waterfall as she ran through them with an ivory comb. She checked out her body, still not quite used to having it. It was perfect; the only thing she hated was that it wasn't exactly hers. This would need to be changed as soon as she'd gotten what she wanted.

First, I'll cut the hair to about shoulder length, she mused to herself. *Then, I'll colour it something dramatic to get rid of those stupid highlights. Bright red or jet black, maybe. Have it straightened, too. Maybe leave the body shape as it is. Looks attractive enough to get most people to do my bidding. And definitely a change of wardrobe. The bitch has no taste whatsoever. Who even wears summer dresses past their teens? Disgusting. Leather would suit best.*

A confident knock on the door revealed a smug face of a tall man with a blond mane who walked straight into the room. She flicked her hand towards him, slamming the door behind him. "First you knock, then you wait for permission to enter. Not that hard to remember, is it?"

The visitor lowered his head, the grin still on his lips. She sighed, exasperated. This was what she had to deal with! With Corbin gone, she had to find her own place in the world. Luckily, this one came along, eager to assist, but still in need of some training. Rude, so rude.

She covered the pulsing stone on her neck as she gathered its magic. When she turned to the blond Sorcerer again, she was ready.

"Julian. I know it's hard for you to distinguish between me and my worthless original. That's fine. Your inner drama doesn't concern me, though. I promised you'll get your heart's desire once I've collected enough power, did I not?"

"You did," he nodded.

"So, what seems to be the problem? Bit of common courtesy wouldn't hurt, would it?"

Julian grinned again. "I am the Master they fear. And we are allies. I thought you knew how I work—sorry if that upsets you, but this is me."

She glanced at him as the stone radiated a brilliant blue. "We're not allies. You might be their Master, but don't forget it is me you serve. I can crush you with a simple thought." He met her glare with one of his own. She tilted her head, drawing on the gem's power. Julian's grin disappeared as his face lost some of its colour. *Serves you right, you bastard. Remember your place.*

"Okay, you made your point," he croaked and she loosened the invisible binding that strangled him. "I'm sorry, Tenebris."

"Good boy. Don't worry, it won't take too much longer before we part ways. I'll need four more offerings and then we'll be done."

"What about Ayla? I don't think I'll be able to get her, not with the resources we have."

Tenebris chuckled. "That's the easy bit. She'll come to us on her own." She studied Julian's face. "You don't want her magic, do you?"

"No, Tenebris, you can have it. I only want her," he licked his lips.

Tenebris resisted the urge to roll her eyes. What was it with Corbin and now Julian? Their obsession with this girl made no sense. At least Corbin was out of the way now. She bit her lip, chasing away the bittersweet memories of her time with him. She did hate him at first, but the things he did resonated with something deep inside her. Not having him around anymore was a blessing and a curse. He wasn't distracting her from her goal or restricting her life to the way it suited him. But she did miss his dominance. Julian's weak attempt at taking his place was crushed like a bug in the ground. A true Master turned out to be a rare find.

"Fantastic. Let's get the ball rolling, then. I wish to receive the next offering as soon as possible. Make it happen before breakfast for extra points."

Julian backed out with a slight bow and shut the door behind him. Turning back to the mirror, Tenebris allowed herself to relax. The shards of her other personality stung whenever she tried to do something on her own. Like reprimanding Julian. Or accepting a sacrifice. She could feel the resistance inside. Thankfully, Caerulus was there to crush it. The only thing she couldn't figure out until recently was the light presence in her thoughts. An echo of her counterpart's feelings. It took her a while to decipher the meaning behind it. Ayla and she were still connected. This bond was a daily reminder that she was but a mere copy. That the original still had the true magic, while she relied on the borrowed power of Caerulus. The power that needed to be fed.

Not for much longer, though.

Once she walked into the ceremonial chamber, her determination was back. There was nothing to stop her. She was going to collect all the power she needed to satisfy Caerulus, and once she drained her original, she would be whole. Free from Ayla's thoughts, free from everything that was holding her back. Free to do as she pleased.

The young woman on the bench turned her face to watch her. Eyes wide in recognition, she mumbled something against the gag. Tenebris scoffed, pulling it out of her mouth. "Good morning. Do you have something to say?"

"I knew something was wrong with you ever since we met. You don't have to kill me, Ayla. I'll never tell anyone it was you, I promise! You can have my boyfriend, anything you want. Please, don't do this!"

Tenebris shoved the gag back into the girl's mouth. "What's this now? One of her peers from Whitestone?" She didn't bother looking around, knowing that Julian would be nearby.

"I believe so. During the mind sweep, I found out this is an acquaintance of hers. There was a bit of tension there when this one's boyfriend showed some interest in helping Ayla."

"Perfect." Tenebris grinned, grabbing the young woman by the hair. "Excellent motive to get rid of a romantic rival." She stared into the girl's eyes, taking in the fear and mad hope of her next victim. *So sweet. Soon, very soon I'll be able to take them myself. Can't wait to get rid of this little weasel.*

Julian nodded, oblivious of her plans to kick him out of his own home. He set the chalice in the middle of the pentagram, next to the girl's head, and picked up the dagger. "Caerulus," he called. "Accept this humble sacrifice and feed the power of my lady Tenebris."

Darkness crawled from the corners, pushing out all traces of the morning sun. The ancient gem sparkled on Tenebris's chest, warm in his gold cage, his heat seeping through her skin. As always, his anticipation became hers. No matter what she did, keeping her master happy was paramount.

Not a master. I'm not his slave, she told herself. *An ally, perhaps? Or a benefactor. Yes, that would be more accurate. Damn Corbin and his twisted training. I have no masters and I never will.*

Julian switched to Latin, reciting passages from the ancient book that Corbin had left behind in his rush to leave. Each word was another step towards achieving her goal. The gem's power was overwhelming now. His hunger burned in her veins like a flow of scorching lava. It used to be an excruciating pain the first few times, and this was when she needed Corbin the most. Once she got used to it, though, she had no need for him. Besides, her little weasel was ready to jump at her command.

She smiled, looking at his solemn face. He was a product of her own making. Within mere weeks, she nurtured his influence in the Sorcerers' world, making him a fearsome Master whose identity was only known by some. A perfect puppet who did her bidding. Sure, sometimes he forgot his place and needed a gentle reminder. With his pride, it was a tough pill to swallow. She kept him in check with the promise of a better life, though. His heart's desire, that pathetic girl. *Do whatever you want with her after I've taken her power. I might actually enjoy watching how far your imagination leads you.*

CHAPTER 22. AYLA

Ayla wiped off the rest of the mirror and checked for smudge spots. The shiny surface was flawless, yet she dragged the soft cloth along the edge. All that mattered was making it as beautiful as ever.

Lyssa crossed her arms on her chest, watching her. "Come on, Ayla. You know that the house cleans itself. Shall we have some tea instead?"

Ayla stubbornly rubbed at the bottom corner. This menial work allowed her to focus on something else. Anything, as long as it didn't involve the stress of her situation.

"All done," she threw the cloth in the hamper and washed her hands.

Her friend's worried expression softened. "Good! There's a mint and chamomile brew, and also some chocolates from the coffee shop. The owner admitted he acted like a jerk and wanted to apologise."

With one last glance at the impeccable bathroom, Ayla followed her friend into the living area. She had been hard at work all morning, scrubbing and washing. The mirror was her last project, the biggest dare to overcome. Avoiding to look at it was not a good tactic. Once Ayla was over the initial shock of her discovery at the hospital, she had some time to think. Her reflection was right. It was impossible to run forever. If she was having hallucinations, she had to figure them out. She had enough of constant fear.

It didn't help that after that brief encounter Blaze left on another mission and she hadn't seen him for days.

Anger rose in her chest like a snake lifting its head, ready to strike. Ayla took a deep breath and counted to ten. Before leaving, Blaze gave her a vial with a mixture she had to take daily to suppress her magic.

"You're not trained enough to contain it," he told her then. "If someone sees you using it, they'll know immediately that you and I Joined and released your power. We need to keep this to ourselves for now until I've figured out a way out of this mess. I'll have to leave for a few days to help the investigation, and I can't take you with me. It's too dangerous. Please promise me you'll be patient."

She promised, of course. It was excruciating to watch him go when all she wanted was to be in his arms forever. There was nobody she could speak to about her feelings. Even Lyssa didn't know.

Ayla wondered how things would have been different if she were to finish the Slumber. Didn't Blaze say it normally lasted a few days? The town would have noticed their extended absence. Maybe, he had another plan which was ruined when she ran off so soon.

Watching the sun dance in the clear herbal tea, Ayla played the events of the past days in her head. There were still a few missing pieces to the puzzle. She was sure now that she was somehow connected to the murders. Those visions didn't lie.

A tingle in the tips of her fingers told her it was time to have her tincture. Magic was strong and cunning, playing up at times she least expected it. With a sneaky glance Lyssa's way, Ayla grabbed the tiny bottle with semi-transparent liquid out of her hidden pocket and put a couple of drops into her tea. Lyssa was busy arranging the chocolates on a plate and didn't see anything from the kitchen. Ayla gulped down the tea and poured herself another cup.

Much better, she thought, as the warm numbness subdued the tingle. One of the things the potion didn't do, however, was take away the torment of being separated from Blaze. It would have helped to at least know when he was coming back. Living in limbo was torture.

"Ingrid is still missing."

Ayla startled as Lyssa put the tray on the table and looked at her.

"Is this Mace's ex-girlfriend?" Cold, sticky fingers of fear brushed along her back. *Here's the motive.*

Lyssa nodded. "Yes. Don't worry, nobody suspects it was you anymore. She walked off on her own and just never came back. You were with the Healers, with a guard by your side any time of day and night. There was no way you could have done anything to lure her out, unless it was a form of a mind spell. Which is a Sorcerer thing," she added hurriedly.

A quiet knock on the door made Ayla's heart somersault. It was high time he came back! She rushed to open it, nearly dropping her tea. The desire to see her lover overpowered any inhibitions. Who cared if Lyssa saw it? Ayla could no longer hold it back.

Her face dropped at the sight of the visitor. "Hi, Rowan," she mumbled, trying to hide her disappointment.

"Is Lyssa here?" He looked past her shoulder into the small kitchen.

"Yes. Come on in."

Ayla stepped to the side, her thoughts dark. What was taking Blaze so long? Did he torment her on purpose?

Rowan scooped her friend in a tight embrace and for a few long moments there was nothing but the sound of kissing. Ayla stifled her frustration. *It's okay, I'm fine. They don't know.*

Does it make it acceptable to rub it in your face? A mocking voice at the back of her head whispered. *You're upset because deep down, you know he's not coming back. Just like Darren and Eric, he abandoned you. Only Corbin was a constant in your life, and you shunned him. No wonder you're completely alone.*

Ayla drew a deep breath and lowered herself on the sofa, ignoring the smooching in the background. *Blaze is coming back. I just miss him so much! I know he loves me. He wouldn't abandon me.*

Did he actually say he loves you? I don't recall that, the voice chuckled. *You are just desperate, Ayla. Being destined to someone doesn't mean you love them. It's just that fate leaves you no choice. He might have feelings for someone else, as he has the right to. What makes you think you're so special?*

"Shut up!" she screamed, covering her ears. Bright images popped up before her eyes, one more vivid than another. Beautiful women with seductive smiles and gorgeous bodies fluttering their eyelashes at her lover. Their fingers gliding through his long hair. Their delicate collarbones exposed as they laughed, throwing their heads back. And him, returning their attention.

She rolled her hands into fists, shaking. "It's not true. It's not true," she muttered, her breath shallow.

Lyssa's arm wrapped around her shoulders. "What's wrong, Ayla? Talk to me. What happened?"

"Tell us how we can help." Rowan lowered himself on the floor in front of her, his eyes concerned.

Ayla squeezed her eyes shut, but it only made things worse. The images in her mind weren't going anywhere.

On the contrary, they were growing stronger in intensity. "I need to talk to Blaze," she croaked, hoping it didn't sound too desperate.

"He hasn't returned yet," Lyssa stated cautiously. "When you say you need to talk to him...does it mean you *can* now?"

Another knock on the door spared Ayla the answer she wasn't ready to give. Eager for a change to distract her from the dark thoughts, she scrambled on her feet. Step by step, she made her way to the door, happy that Lyssa didn't insist. Maybe her friend could tell she needed this. Or maybe she wanted to stay with her boyfriend and steal a few more kisses while Ayla was at the door. Whichever it was, it worked fine.

Ayla's knees trembled when she saw the newcomer. The afternoon sun gave his brilliant white mane a warm tint of gold, blinding her for a moment. There was no time to process her emotions. Everything happened at once. The wall of self-control broke apart like a dam, letting her secret out.

She threw her arms around Blaze's neck, her whole being lost in an insatiable desire to be close to him. As close as she could get. To be safe in his tight embrace and feel his warm breath on her skin. To anticipate his kisses. To let him touch her anywhere, and to reciprocate. Nothing mattered, as long as he was with her.

"You're all shivering," Blaze uttered between kisses, his arms tight around her.

Ayla reached for him, and once again there was no time to talk. Only when she ran out of breath did she stop. Panting, she looked into his eyes. Two bewitching emeralds, enveloping her in affection, with just a hint of concern.

No. A *lot* of concern.

Ayla startled when his gaze slipped behind her back, realising that her friends were still there. She froze in place, thoughts racing.

Blaze walked her inside and shut the door behind him.

For a long moment, nobody spoke.

"Um, congratulations on your Joining," Lyssa's voice took a higher pitch than normal.

Rowan cleared his throat. "I think we should go."

Blaze raised his hand, stopping them. "Wait. Just give me a few minutes of privacy with Ayla. I won't stay long and I'll need you by her side when I leave."

Leave?

Panic lashed at her like a whip. Everything went black, her accelerated heartbeat suddenly too loud. "No, no, you can't leave. Please, don't go, Blaze." She grabbed onto him like a lifeline, seeking comfort in his eyes.

"My work is far from done, sweetheart. The Enforcers are having a meeting now that doesn't require my presence, so I thought I'd stop by and check on you. I miss you, my sweet angel." He buried his fingers in her hair, gently massaging her head. "But I can't stay too much longer."

"Take me with you," she pleaded on the verge of crying, already knowing his answer.

"I can't. It's not safe for you out there. I'll never forgive myself if you become the next victim because I was careless. This house is the most protected place, I made sure of it. As long as you're here, nothing can get to you." His face grew dark. "Not even a blood bond."

Ayla ignored his last comment, though a small voice in her mind wondered if Blaze knew the true reason she left his side during the Slumber. "You don't understand. Every second is hell. I can't take it. Please, spare me this pain."

He pulled her closer into a hug. The smell of his aftershave, the masculine sandalwood with a hint of fresh citrus, mixed with the inevitable dustiness of a traveller was the best thing in the world. Being close enough to smell it, to feel his heartbeat next to hers, his hands on her body, was the ultimate gift. The most desired reward. Everything she needed. Why did he have to take it away?

A sudden flush drowned her senses in a rising frustration. No matter what she did, he wasn't going to budge. This moment was all she had until he came back again. Her breathing became shallow, red spots dancing behind her closed eyes. The memory of her mocking reflection stood before her.

You can't hide from yourself, Ayla. The clock is ticking and shadows are closing in. Embrace the darkness—or die.

She let out a long breath. The tingling of magic cut through the haze of the potion like a knife through warm butter. It was stronger than before, its force overwhelming. There was nothing she couldn't do. *Embrace the darkness*, she told herself.

The plate with chocolates fell off the kitchen bench, its sharp sound almost unnaturally loud. Blaze's arms let go of her, but it was too late. Panic turned into self-destructive anger that blinded her. Balling her hands into fists, she kept her eyes closed as her will threw the plates flying on the floor, each shard like a dagger to her heart.

It's all my fault. I'm cursed, tainted. He's going to abandon me, too. Just like Eric. He's just too nice to say it to my face, but I know this is what will happen. One day, he won't come back.

A soothing voice kept calling her name. Warm yet firm hands kept hold of her shoulders. "It's okay, Ayla. I'm here. Please, try to focus. You can do it, sweetheart. Clear your mind and breathe. Remember our lessons."

Panting, she opened her eyes to the destroyed room. Furniture was moved off its spots, the floor full of scattered shards of glass and ceramics. Hands trembling, she avoided Blaze's gaze. What had she done?

"I'm sorry," she whispered.

"Your power is greater than I thought," he said slowly, as if weighing every word. "You need training as soon as possible. Please, don't miss your meditation sessions. You need to learn to contain your impulses and stay calm."

Her heart stopped when another memory slapped her like a strike of another man's hand. Corbin's eyes peered at her with that hint of discontent in them. His disappointed expression as he scolded her before another punishment. That was what he would do. Physically restrain her until she learned her lesson. "Or what? Are you going to contain me? Will you force me to stop?" Angry tears ate their way down her cheeks, each a burning track. Let them.

Blaze lifted her chin and looked her in the eye. "No, sweetheart, why would you think that? I'm here to guide you and help when you need it. You are a beautiful, strong woman, and I believe with all my heart that you can make your own decisions. Right decisions. Your power is strong, but your will is stronger. You'll learn to control it yourself." He sighed, wiping her tears away with a tip of his thumb. "I'll try to organise more frequent breaks and spend more time with you, okay? It was a mistake to think you can be alone for such a long time, especially after our first Joining, without any comfort. I'm sorry."

Red shame replaced the anger. She acted like a spoiled child, and all he did was soothe her when she had to be punished. That was it, her only way to redemption.

"No, it's my fault. I need to be punished," she whispered, looking up at him again. "I have to be hurt so I remember to be more careful next time. Please, make it hurt."

The expression of pain in his eyes was unmistakable. He cupped her cheeks in his hands, shaking his head. "My sweet angel. You have to understand that things we do in the bedroom are very different from the outside world. I would never hurt you as punishment. The very fact that you think you deserve it makes my blood boil. I wish I could kill the son of a bitch who conditioned you to believe that." He wrapped her in another hug, holding her tight. "I don't have much time left. There's one thing I want you to remember, though. This is not your fault. Sometimes, even the strongest break, and this is what Corbin did to you. He broke you. The healing process will take time and I know we'll get there. In the meantime, I need you to be strong. This is not your darkness; he put it inside you on purpose. But you're better than this. You can fight it off."

Ayla grabbed onto his shirt. Tears rolled out of her eyes, but these were tears of gratitude. He believed in her. He didn't think she was cursed, just wounded.

With a shaky breath, she collected her will and forced her fingers to let go of him. If he had to leave, he had to leave. She already embarrassed herself enough. "What do I do now?"

"First, clean up this mess," he smiled. "On a serious note though, continue your meditations. Remember what I taught you—clearing your mind will help you connect with your power, which will help you control it. You can go into the Mist if it brings you solace, but please don't use magic when you're in. I'd prefer that you stay away from the Mist altogether, just for a little while, but I understand that sometimes this is not something you can resist and it's okay. I'll ask your friends to keep our secret for a little longer." He traced her cheekbone with the back of his index finger. "I have to go now, sweetheart, but I'll come back as soon as I can."

He planted a gentle kiss on her lips and in a second, he was gone. Ayla sat down on the chair amid the chaos in her living room. Being alone with her thoughts was punishment enough. Once she concluded that, it became easier to come to grips with reality. She learned a lot today and needed time to think it through.

Lyssa and Rowan rushed in, talking over each other. Neither seemed surprised at the destruction in the house. Ayla smiled. Of course, Blaze would have told them to spare her feelings from having to explain. She expected Rowan to make a joke about it or create an illusion of something like a mammoth stomping around the kitchen-ware, but he didn't. Both spoke in hushed tones as if cautious of distressing her. Lyssa showed her how to channel energy and put piece to piece together, bonding them to make sure they stayed in place. Ayla chuckled as her friends worked with her to restore order in the house. They were great people. She was lucky to have them in her life. She was lucky to have Blaze who set everything up for her originally. He was right. She just needed time to heal and she needed to learn to contain her emotions.

The only problem was whether she could believe her subconscious. *Embrace the darkness—or die*.

The phrase echoed in her head, its sinister words growing fainter. Going to the back of her mind until their time came again, awakening from a fleeting hibernation.

CHAPTER 23. AYLA

Voices cut through her sleep. Ayla rolled to the other side, throwing her arm over the bed. The rest of her blissful dream evaporated when she encountered nothing but another pillow. Her eyes snapped open. Her suspicion was correct: Blaze was gone.

Last night was the first time he stayed over. Ayla could tell right away how exhausted he was, and silently cursed herself. The work with the Enforcers was draining. It was no wonder he couldn't see her more often before her melt-down. She felt guilty about her behaviour and the effects it had on her lover. Guilty but secretly glad to have his arms around her. Even exhausted as he was, he still gave her some affection.

She stared at the ceiling, taking slow breaths in and out. There had to be a logical explanation for his absence. Despite her fear of being abandoned, she had to trust that he wouldn't do it to her. He probably got up earlier and didn't want to wake her, but he had to be around somewhere. He wouldn't have left without saying anything.

The voices were a bother. Ayla freshened up in the bathroom and grabbed the first outfit out of the wardrobe without looking. It turned out to be a plain sheath dress. Olive green to compliment her tan and brighten her eyes. She ran her fingers through her long hair and tamed the gentle waves with a quick boost of magic. Much better.

The noise of multiple people's presence washed over her the moment she stepped outside of the bedroom. The small living area couldn't keep everyone in. Peeking at the back, she realised there were visitors in her backyard, too.

Someone's hand grabbed hers.

"Good morning, sleepyhead!" Lyssa's smile shone bright as she dragged her to the kitchen.

"Um, good morning," Ayla replied cautiously. She stopped, looking over her small living area. All the people she already knew: the Healers, students from her classes, possibly some people she hadn't met. So many faces and voices at once reminded her of the first time she had this many visitors. When she just arrived at Whitestone and they wanted to welcome her. She wondered what made them all show up now.

Her appearance brought out a cheer from the crowd, and a few glasses were raised in the air. Ayla shifted her weight from one foot to another, uncomfortable with the attention.

"Good morning, sweetheart," Blaze's smooth voice purred in her ear as his arm wrapped around her waist.

Ayla turned around to face him. Before she had a chance to reply, he pulled her in and gave her a gentle kiss. His presence was soothing, yet she was concerned.

"What are you doing?" she whispered. "Weren't we supposed to keep this a secret?"

"Someone found out and told everyone. It was bound to happen, especially once I started spending nights here. I just didn't expect it so soon. This isn't the best scenario, but we'll just have to wing it."

"Congratulations on your Joining!" The glasses clinked. Ayla squinted, trying to pinpoint the source of the phrase, but now everyone picked it up. Cheers were coming from all angles. The room quickly got stuffy.

"I need some air," she squeaked.

Blaze nodded. "Of course. Let's go."

"No," Ayla raised her face to his. "I need a moment alone to collect my thoughts."

He looked into her eyes, concern carved on his face. "Are you sure you can be on your own right now?"

"Yes. I won't be long." She suppressed the urge to run out. Giving his hand a gentle squeeze, she went for the front door. Thankfully, nobody tried to stop her.

A warm summer morning was a refreshing change from the overwhelming stuffiness inside. Ayla settled on the wooden steps of her front porch, still cool after the night. Thoughts were buzzing in her head like a hive of angry bees.

"Why the long face, babe?"

"Not funny, Levi," she replied, glaring at the newcomer.

The young Mage looked as nonchalant as ever. Trendy ripped jeans and a half-undone button-up shirt with a raised collar. Ruffled hair. Sly grin. Only his eyes betrayed his true self. Another human being who had his own demons to fight behind the careless façade.

"I'm not laughing." He plopped on the step next to her. "A bit overwhelming, isn't it?"

"It is. Why is the whole town so interested in my private business? First, they shun me, then they come to congratulate me on a new relationship. What the hell?"

"Oh, you're not off the hook yet, Ayla." His expression grew serious. "Someone's building a case against you. Blaze is trying to get you out of trouble and keep your reputation clean. Going to be trickier now that the news of your union is out. Conflict of interests, you see."

"Still doesn't explain why the whole town is here. It's not a wedding or anything like that." Ayla's cheeks burned. She hadn't thought of that possibility before, but it seemed like a logical outcome.

Levi chuckled. "You don't need to get married, silly. Being destined is a much stronger bond. Having a couple accept it and Join is a big deal for the whole community."

"And why's that?"

"Well, the whole point of being united with your destined one is to produce offspring. The children of two destined Mages carry a strong magic bloodline. Our population is on a decline, with so many Mages choosing a life with humans who possess no power of their own. This dilutes the blood further. So, yes, the whole town is celebrating because you're now expected to help out the community. Don't be surprised when people start asking if you're pregnant yet." He patted her hand. "It's okay, though. A Joining would almost guarantee you get knocked up. Nothing to worry about."

"What? I hardly know him." Ayla's throat grew dry. *Blaze didn't tell me any of this.*

"It's destiny, babe! You're not even supposed to be having these thoughts. Destiny takes over your mind, especially in the beginning. Once you're settled with him, you might start looking around again." He winked, making her startle.

"Wait. Doesn't a destined couple stay together?"

"Oh, they can stay together, of course. But you're still only human. If you have feelings for someone else, destiny wouldn't destroy them. Dull them down, perhaps, but it wouldn't stop you from desiring others. Let me tell you a story."

Ayla stared at a piece of peeling paint under her feet as Levi rambled about a destined couple who were in committed relationships with others before they felt the pull. How they would only get together when the woman was ovulating, as this was when the pull would become unbearable. How she conceived and had his children whilst being married to someone else.

This was terrifying. Images of other women surrounding Blaze popped up in front of her again. So he didn't have to stay with her after all. He could do whatever he wanted, with whomever he wanted.

"We're not designed to be monogamous," Levi's voice broke through her thoughts. "The sooner you accept it, the easier it will be for you, babe. Think about your past lovers. You still have feelings for them, good or bad. Love is infinite. Why limit it to just one person, even if it's your destined one?"

"So I'm supposed to have as many children as possible while he can go and date others?" Terror gripped her heart.

The mocking voice in her mind chuckled. *I told you it was too good to be true. You won't get your heart's desire, because you don't deserve it. He never said he loves you, Ayla, because he doesn't. You are cursed, so why bother? Embrace the darkness—or die. Create your own destiny. This is the only way you can ever be happy.*

Ignorant of her inner struggle, Levi continued, "Precisely, but so can you! Now you're getting it. The Council has a Breeder lined up for him in case something happens with you. Breeders produce perfect babies that have the exact powers of their fathers. That chick, Sherice? She's had three already and proved herself."

Ayla's head spun. "I need to be alone," she mumbled, scrambling up on her feet. She grabbed onto the railing to keep herself steady. This was too much to take in. She was given this moment of happiness only to have it ripped away from her. There was no light ahead. Only darkness could save her from heartbreak.

"Hey, where are you going?" Levi's voice followed her.

She didn't care. Tears rolling down her cheeks, she ran down the path away from the cheerful crowd in her house, away from the town's neat buildings. All the way towards the forest looming in the distance. The shade of the lush trees fell onto her like a cold shower, blocking off the heat of the rising sun. There, surrounded by the refreshing smell of pines and soothing birdsong, she finally stopped. Where to now? Whitestone was surrounded by a magic wall. If she kept walking in a straight line, she was bound to find it. Then, she could test her magic to see if it would be enough to break through.

Ayla considered her options. Staying was no longer a good idea. Her fresh attachment to Blaze, the craving for his company, and the desperation for his touch turned into an angry fire. She hated him for making her feel this way. It was all his fault, and she was too naïve to believe she was finally happy. How could she? After everything she'd gone through, she should have learned it was never going to happen.

You can't run from yourself. The clock is ticking and the shadows are closing in.

I don't care, she replied to the chuckle in her head. *Let them.*

How about 'the target on your head'? You'll never make it beyond the walls of Whitestone. Pathetic, helpless, with your magic still untrained. Easy prey to whoever wants to hunt you down.

Ayla stopped, grabbing on to a thick oak tree. Everything seemed to be an effort. Every breath like a shard of glass plunged into her lungs.

You know what? I don't care. Let them come. At least if I die, I won't suffer anymore. Should have been dead long ago, and none of this would have happened.

She sank on the dead leaves, cursing her bad luck that started following her after her father's death. She wondered if it began earlier, when she was abandoned in the park as a child, with all her memories erased, or if she was already cursed when she was born. There was never an answer. No matter how hard she tried, those memories remained hidden. Others resurfaced, though.

The crack of the whip marking her body. The raised hand striking her. Corbin's face, distorted by a grimace of anger. She shivered as those images flooded her mind. Yes, her old Master abused her. But he also gave her solace. She thought about the sessions he had with her. How he soothed her and took all her fears away with just one look of his midnight eyes. The gentle touch of his mind spells that left her numb and hazy. She told him she never wanted to see him again, and he left. Would he come back if she asked? If so, how could she summon him?

Ayla looked at her arms, limp on her lap. The blood bond would alert him of anything happening to her. If she was in danger, he would know. Maybe if she hurt herself enough, he would come to stop her. Then, she could ask him to take her away. Back where she belonged, in his cold mansion, shaking with fear of his next punishment. She didn't deserve any better. It was foolish of her to believe otherwise.

"What are you doing here?"

She startled, looking up at the newcomer. "Nothing. Why are you here?"

Mace lowered himself on the leaves next to her. "I sometimes come here for my meditations. Being away from the town works much better than feeling all the presences around. Are you okay, Ayla? Does Blaze know you're here?"

She drew in a deep breath. "No. I don't want to see him."

Mace held a pause. "What happened? Did he...hurt you?"

"No." She had to calm down. Ayla focused her eyes on a tiny twig under the neighbouring tree. A little crooked fork. She wondered if it would be too heavy for one of the forest birds to carry it to the treetops and weave it into a nest. It was probably too late now to start building. Most of the birds would be sitting on eggs this time of the year. It wouldn't be too long until the eggs cracked open and tiny chicks came out to meet the world. Cute little bird babies.

Babies.

Tears rolled out of her eyes as she grabbed onto Mace's arm. He turned towards her, letting her press her face against his shoulder. His warm presence was reassuring. In just a few moments, he started patting her back, but didn't say anything. Without realising it, Ayla told him about the conversation with Levi.

"He's a moron, Ayla, you should know that already. Someone really needs to teach him when to talk and when to hold his tongue. Blaze adores you. Everyone knew it from the second he brought you here. Think about the way he treated you from the very beginning. How he respected your boundaries and never pushed for more than what you were ready to give. He would never do anything to hurt you. I'm surprised you don't feel it through your connection to him."

"I don't think I even have that connection," she whispered. "Everyone keeps telling me I should just know some things, but I don't. Something is wrong with me, Mace."

"It's overwhelming, I know," he soothed, giving her a little squeeze before he let her go. "We can stay here a little longer if you want. But Blaze will be worried sick when he notices your absence. We'll need to head back soon."

Ayla wiped her face with her sleeve and held onto his arm as he helped her get up. A tiny crack of a twig under someone's foot made her turn around.

Blaze stopped a few metres away, watching them. Ayla's heart skipped a beat.

He just saw me hugging another man, in the middle of the forest, alone. He's going to be so mad!

She shivered, thinking about Corbin and his ways when he lost his temper. What would Blaze do, especially considering how much closer she was with him?

She gulped down a knot in her throat that wasn't going away. No words passed through her lips.

Blaze looked her over as if making sure she was unharmed, then turned his gaze to Mace. "Thank you for being here for her."

"No problem." Mace glanced at her sideways. "It's okay, Ayla. Remember what we spoke about. He's not your enemy."

She averted her eyes, guilt warming her cheeks. The leaves rustled under Blaze's feet as he made a few steps forward and stopped just outside of arm's distance.

"Ayla. Please don't be afraid. I won't touch you if you don't want me to. Tell me what's wrong."

She shook her head, averting her eyes. She just wanted to feel safe and happy again. Nothing made sense anymore.

"Levi told her a few disturbing things," Mace said. "Um, I'll give you two some privacy."

Ayla followed his departing figure with her eyes, avoiding thinking about the inevitable. She failed to escape, and she still wasn't sure if she could trust Blaze again. Levi's words burned hot in her mind.

"Please, Ayla. I need you to talk to me. What did he say to upset you so much?"

"About children. And that it's normal to have polyamorous relationships here," she braved, staring at him.

Not a muscle moved on his face. He stepped closer, shaking his head. "I can tell you the full story if you want. We probably won't have much time now. People are expecting us back, and our absence is suspicious."

"I need to know," she responded, studying his face. Nothing in his expression indicated that he was lying.

Blaze sighed. "Both statements would be true, I'm afraid—if this is what I think it is. Destined couples are expected to have as many children as possible. It's not unusual to see a family of six or more. It is also not unusual to see couples have multiple lovers—this is not very common, but it does happen. Mostly in cities, though. Smaller towns and communities prefer the older system of 'one destiny—one partner'." He looked into her eyes, expression sombre. "My parents were destined, and they both remained true to each other until the end. They only had two children," he whispered.

"Only two?" Ayla blinked. "Is there a choice?"

"Not for everyone. Look, Joining pushes people into a primal state they cannot control. Remember your own urge and when I told you we have to be careful? I don't want you to get pregnant yet, not until we've spoken about everything. This is your decision as much as it is mine."

"Then how come *you* were able to control yourself?"

Blaze chuckled. "I'm a shapeshifter, remember? I've had decades of practice to control my instincts." He reached out for her, stopping mere centimetres from her face. Ayla leaned into his touch, enjoying the warmth of his hand. "Sweetheart. I know what you've been through. Our bond is still very fresh, and there is a lot for you to take in. Next time you doubt me, please think of anything I've done to make you unhappy. And talk to me about it. Only communication will help us remain strong."

He is right. I jump to conclusions when all he's ever done was being kind and thoughtful. Can't believe I was so stupid to think poorly of him.

She threw her arms around his neck. "I'm so sorry, Blaze. I don't know what happened to me."

"It's okay," he smiled, wrapping his arms around her waist. "I understand, sweetheart."

Someone cleared their throat behind her, and Ayla turned to the source of the sound. An unfamiliar Mage stood a few metres away, glaring at her.

"I really hope she wasn't trying to escape," he pronounced accusingly. "The only reason this girl is not in jail is because you vouched for her, Blaze."

Jail?

Cold sweat trickled down her spine. Blaze never mentioned anything about it. She shivered, starting to hyperventilate.

"Ayla needed some air. It was too overwhelming to stay in the house. You saw yourself, Jasper. It's not designed to accommodate so many visitors."

"I think we'll need to put her under house arrest then, once everyone's left. It's unacceptable, having her run around as she wishes. Be sure I'll be bringing this little incident to the jury's attention next time."

Ayla's body shook with dread. The thought of being locked up was terrifying. She remembered the past year that she'd spent isolated from the world behind the walls of one mansion or another when she was still with Corbin.

No, this can't happen again. Please, don't lock me up here. Not you, too.

Blaze glanced at her, his hand squeezing her a little. "Good luck with that, Jasper. I won't tolerate these accusations. The fact that you brought them here and threw them in her face is an insult. I sincerely hope you understand there will be consequences."

"There will be indeed, if I prove that she tried to run away." Jasper scoffed, throwing a disdainful look at her. "Watch yourself, girl. You better not be involved with those murders."

I'm not! she wanted to say, but words got stuck in her throat. She pressed herself close to Blaze's body, her desire for comfort stronger than ever.

"I know you're innocent," he whispered, caressing her hair. "They just need someone to blame and are feeling helpless. I'll protect you no matter what, my sweet angel. But for now, we'll need more intensive training for you. If something happens to me, I want to be sure you can defend yourself."

"Why would something happen to you?" Terror gripped her heart. He was the rock in her world. The only constant. Someone to stand by her side. There was no way she could lose him.

I was so stupid. How could I doubt him? And now I've made them more suspicious. Maybe this attempt to escape undermined all of Blaze's work to keep me out of trouble. Maybe I've put his life in danger. He can get killed because of me.

Shaking all over, she hugged him with all her might. She hardly heard his reassuring words. The only thoughts in

her mind were echoes of the mocking voice in the back of
her head.

*Fight darkness with darkness. Protect your lover. Embrace
your true power, and you'll be unstoppable.*

CHAPTER 24. AYLA

A gust of chilly evening breeze snapped at Ayla's skin. Flushed as she was after the strenuous exercise, she hardly paid it any attention as she focused on her opponent. The man slowly circled her. Instinctively, she mirrored his movement to keep him in her line of vision.

"Well, well, well," he rasped. "Let's see what this precious little thing is worth." Without another warning, he charged at her. Ayla's belated resistance didn't do much good as she landed on the ground with a sharp pain in her ribs.

"Again!" the man barked.

"I wasn't ready, Reeves," she replied in a higher pitch than normal. These training sessions were driving her crazy. Even though Blaze was still gone on another of his trips, the lessons continued. In his absence, the school's Board hired another teacher for the self-defence classes that were now mandatory for everyone.

"Your assailant won't wait for you to be ready. You have to be prepared for an attack at any moment, any time!" He followed his words with a sensitive punch on her arm that made her yelp.

"Hey! That really hurt!"

"Life hurts. Suck it up, princess!"

She was prepared this time and managed to avoid another punch on the arm. Instead, Reeves tripped her on his foot and she fell back to the ground. The darkening sky outlined the bright crescent of the moon and the shy first star nestling next to it. A chilly draft crawled under her *gi*, cooling her body. It didn't help to know she was the last in class to do a proper sparring session with him, with most students already gone to have their dinners and spend time with friends.

She got up, more cautious this time. Reeves grinned, raising the palms of his hands. He started another circle and she followed again, calculating his possible move. So far from his training with others, she noticed a pattern. He would start with lighter, predictable moves and move towards more complicated ones. Only a couple of students ended up with bloody noses, and that was for not paying attention.

Another lunge. Ayla jumped back, Reeves's fist only missing her flesh by an inch. "Not bad."

"Thanks," she hissed, keeping her breathing steady. Reeves may not have been the most pleasant person to train with, but he was good at keeping his students on their toes. It was hard to know when he deemed the lesson over; there was no time limit and the student was free to go whenever he told them so.

Ayla glanced around to see how many people stayed back and that was a costly mistake. A hit landed on her chest, followed by another one under her ribs. As she bent down holding her stomach, he tripped her again. She slumped on the floor like a bag of potatoes, without any resemblance of grace. Reeves squatted next to her and grabbed a handful of her hair.

"Giving up so easily?"

She coughed, pressing a hand to her burning stomach. "Enough, Reeves. I'm out of steam."

"Really?" A crooked smile crossed his lips as he rolled her head back. "So worthless! You're an unprepared, weak, feeble little princess who needs to be shielded from the real world." His eyes radiated danger, sharp and deadly in descending darkness.

Fighting through the pain, Ayla bit her lip and tried to push his hand away. "Let go!"

"Or what?" Reeves twisted his hand, pulling on her hair. "What are you going to do, little girl?"

Ayla made another attempt at breaking free from his grip. The situation was quickly becoming too similar to something she had experienced before, and she didn't like it.

"You'll be such an easy prey for the Dark Master," Reece whispered and the skin on her neck pulled taut. "He's going to devour your mind, rip off your power like the wings of a butterfly." His free hand shot up in the air and slapped her. The hit wasn't a strong one, but it stung. He let go of her hair, but before she had a chance to breathe in relief, he grabbed her by the throat and lifted her in the air. His steel grip had no limits; a feeling she knew so well from her life in the Sorcerers' world came back in full blow. Tears of pain rolled down her cheeks.

"Please," she pleaded, clawing at his strangling hands. Reeves laughed and threw her against the brick wall of the house. Ayla's head spun from the blow.

"Then he will torture and rape you for his amusement, and once he tires of you, he'll give you to his servants to play with until you lose your mind to the madness," he followed his words with a series of stinging slaps. "Your old Master messed you up nicely; we only need to scratch the surface and you'll be back where you started."

"Why are you doing this?" she managed through her tears.

Reeves sniggered. "Because you're a worthless little bitch that everyone puts too much hope into! There is nothing special about you. Nothing! So what's the point? Why keep fighting?" Another slap went across her face and Reeves let her go. "You're just a toy for the Master's amusement. Nothing else."

Red rage covered her vision like a blanket of steel wool. Blinking through it, Ayla focused her eyes on Reeves's triumphant back. He heeded her no more attention, considering her defeated. The white flame of magic jumped on her fingertips without prompting, as if it had always been there, watching, waiting for her command, ready to protect her. Heart pumping, she took a deep breath which did nothing to calm her down. Blaze's words about keeping a cool head when using magic were pushed back by a raging desire to serve justice to her assailant.

Thinking through the veil of anger was like walking through jelly. Ayla knew that Reeves was a Mage himself; he would have no trouble fending off her awkward attack. However...

She looked around for ideas and immediately saw what she needed. A wooden chair from the Hub's patio. A weapon that was light enough, yet suitable for a powerful hit. With a sharp breath, she lifted the chair with her mind power, throwing it as hard as she could onto Reeves's loathsome head. In the last moment, he sensed it and covered his head, though the hit still sent him to the ground. Wooden shards pierced the skin on his arms, drawing blood. Ayla's nostrils flared as she took in the picture in front of her. If this was the feeling people got when they served justice to those who hurt them, it was the sweetest thing in the world.

"You're the worthless one!" she screamed as she hit him with a wooden leg that fell off the chair during impact. "Go back to your Dark Master and tell him to fuck himself, for I am not a victim anymore! And don't ever touch me again, for I swear I'll rip you to pieces!" She paused, catching her breath, as the red veil slowly cleared up. "Or I'll find someone else who will," she finished quietly.

"Good work, little one." Reeves studied the cuts on his arms and Ayla dropped her weapon, ashamed. She couldn't believe she lost her temper like that. This was supposed to be a training session, not a confrontation. "Impressive use of telekinesis. Couldn't win a physical fight so you thought outside the box. I like that. Why didn't you go for a staff?" He pointed at the neat rows behind the chairs.

She picked up the bits of the chair off the ground. "I don't know how to use one, apart from swinging it around until I hit something."

"Fair enough." Reeves gave her a smile, genuine this time.

Ayla studied his rough features, unsure of what to believe. "So you were just provoking me?"

"I was. And it worked, didn't it?" His gaze grew serious. "I've known Blaze for years, Ayla. We worked at the Force together and have fought our share of battles. You are his destined one, and I would have never betrayed you. My training method isn't as subtle as his, though; Blaze focuses on building resilience gradually, while I aim for faster results. This can sometimes backfire, of course, but I knew you were strong. You wouldn't break, but you would find your strength. So you did."

Ayla shook her head, a smile spreading across her lips in response. "I did believe you wanted to take me to the Dark Master."

"That was the point. Only when you're threatened can you find your true strength."

"This is crazy." She shook his offered hand, still light-headed from the fall. "Thank you though."

"Any time." He studied her, chewing his lip. "I'm glad you found your magic, Ayla."

Her thoughts jumped to the disappearances of the Mage girls, and a cloud of sadness crossed her mind. "Me too, Reeves. Me too."

CHAPTER 25. AYLA

I t tickled.

Ayla giggled, rolling on her back. Blaze's lips brushed against the sensitive skin on her neck, up to her earlobe, only to tease her with a barely feasible nibble. "I could get used to this, you know," she purred, enjoying the smell of his fresh aftershave. They hardly ever got a chance to sleep in like today. Every moment together was precious.

"It's a special day," he responded.

Ayla quickly ran the calculations in her head. None of the potentially important dates fell on today. "What do you mean?"

"I don't have to go back today. The Enforcers are taking a break from the case, and the court is closed. We have a whole day to spend together."

"A whole day?" Ayla couldn't believe her ears. This was the most generous gift she could have wished for. After weeks of barely seeing him this seemed almost impossible.

"Yes, sweetheart. I'm taking you out on a date."

She shook her head in disbelief. Blaze pulled up a tray with a plateful of French toast, fresh strawberries and whipped cream on the side, complemented with fragrant coffee. A tiny vase in the middle held a single white rose. White, to show he believed she was innocent. Or maybe the choice of flower was just a coincidence. She decided not to ruin the mood by asking. This was such a beautiful morning, the beginning of a glorious day. Her lover had brought her breakfast in bed. This was something she thought only happened in romance books!

Careful not to spill anything, she sat up on the pillows. "Where are we going?" she asked, biting into the juicy fruit.

"It's a surprise," he smiled, accepting a berry from her. "Thank you."

She chuckled, deciding not to push. This would be their very first day together. Still not fully accustomed to his presence, she didn't want to make any faux pas. After the episode in the forest, she was very careful. It was clear that he was hurt by her attempt to run away, though he never mentioned it. Nothing in his attitude changed, but she felt guilty. The worst thing was her suspicion that something was wrong with her. Otherwise, why wouldn't she trust him the way he trusted her?

Eager to make every moment count, she grabbed the first outfit from the wardrobe. Smoothing the pale golden sundress over her hips, she smiled at her reflection. There was no time to do her hair and makeup. She didn't want to make him wait.

Ayla breathed out, holding the palm of her hand open in front of her. As always now, her magic came without any effort. She pictured what she wanted to achieve and ran her fingers through her hair and over her face. The result was stunning. Beautiful beach waves descended almost to her waist now, with the golden highlights sparkling in the morning sun. Her skin glowed with the gentle tan she added to her existing tone. Her eyelashes got thicker, hazel eyes a little greener. She sighed in content, studying her reflection. This was perfect for a casual day out. And if Blaze decided to take her somewhere fancy, she could easily change this. After all, now she had plenty of practice.

"You look gorgeous," he commented as she appeared out of the bathroom. He was wearing a light cotton outfit himself that was a match to hers. Ayla wondered if her own choice of clothes was driven by their connection. It could have been a pure coincidence, though. Summer was at its last peak of heat before autumn rolled in. With the hot weather they were having, light cotton was perfect.

"When did you learn to use glamour?" he asked, caressing her with the gaze of his emerald eyes.

Ayla frowned, deciphering his words. "I didn't."

His hands hovered over her face and gently touched her hair. A subtle breeze brushed against her skin, gone before she registered it. "This is not glamour. You used magic to change your looks instead of casting a simple illusion."

"I guess," she shrugged, trying to figure out what the big deal was. Why did he get all serious? She had plenty of magic to spare.

Blaze sighed. "I'm sorry, Ayla. I keep forgetting how much you still don't know. An illusion takes a fraction of your power. This is one of the first things we learn once we connect to our magic. Even the weakest Mages can work up an illusion. Glamour is one of its forms that requires more skill, as this is something you'll need to keep consistent. Transforming something is a different thing. It requires a lot more power and much more to make it stay."

"But what about yourself? When you shift, you change the whole structure of your body and can remain in your other shape for hours. You told me this helps you restore the balance, not take away your magic."

"This is similar in a way. Being a shifter, I use less power during transformations, but this has a cost. After each shift, I have a couple of days of low power while I recover."

Ayla sulked, feeling like a child caught red-handed over a cookie jar. "I have a lot of power, though. Why would I even be concerned about using a little bit to look pretty?"

Blaze chuckled as she fluttered her eyelashes at him. "You are already beautiful. Check your power now. Summon it as I taught you and see for yourself."

She closed her eyes and called to her power. The flame jumped at her command as it always happened these days. Ayla studied it with a critical eye. Did she imagine it or did it grow smaller? Were the top petals of the flame fainter than before, reducing their volume? She gasped, breaking the connection. "If I keep the transformation, is it going to keep using my magic?"

"Yes. This is why Mages should only use it sparingly. Everything we do comes at a cost. Before you start something you're not familiar with, it's best to find out the price you'll pay for it first. Best case scenario, it will drain some of your magic. This one is easy—you'll just need to have a safe place and rest until the power is fully restored. Magic never goes away forever—not unless you use it all up. This is called burnout. Once you've reached that point, the flame disappears for good."

Ayla averted her eyes. He wasn't being overprotective as she thought before. It was a tangible danger that she willingly stepped into and he only wanted to help. "I think someone told me before but I didn't realise how quickly it can go. Thank you for reminding me, Blaze."

"That's what I'm here for." He chuckled when she playfully pushed his shoulder. "You know what I mean."

Ayla called back her magic and took his hand. It felt warm and safe to have him next to her. The feeling of belonging with someone was the best experience she'd ever had. She thought about all the things they could do together. All the adventures they could have. This was only the beginning of the beautiful life that lay ahead of them. Once the murders were dealt with, she'd have nothing to worry about.

If only it was that easy.

She didn't hesitate when he led her towards the portal of light. There was nothing he would do to harm her. None of her nightmares were true, she was sure of it. He was hers as she was his. It was nothing like what Levi had told her. Blaze would never lay his eyes on another.

Worry about yourself, the voice in her head interrupted her thoughts. *You're the problem, not him. Your connection to him is not whole. Your power is dark. What will he do when he finds out about your true self? That you bear a curse that destroys everything around you?*

I'm not cursed. Shut up! she ordered the voice, pushing it back to the furthest corners of her mind. Faster than before, it obeyed. *That's better. You won't stop me from having a good life. You won't tell me what to do. I'll make my own good and I will follow his light. He will never shun me.*

Ayla covered her eyes from the blinding sun. The portal closed behind her with a gentle pop. Once her eyesight adjusted to the light, she squealed with delight.

"Oh, Blaze! This is beautiful!" she threw her arms around his neck and for a long moment, neither of them uttered a word.

"I thought you needed a little distraction." A wide smile graced his face.

Ayla took in her surroundings. A beautiful white sand beach spread as far as she could see. Gentle waves lapped at the shore. She kicked off her sandals, enjoying the grainy texture under her feet. Warm and welcoming, like the embrace of her lover. It was almost exactly like the place he'd taken her for their Joining. She cast a careful glance at him. It was impossible not to love this man. She was sure of her feelings now. Did he feel the same?

Of course he loves me. I won't ask, though, because I'm not insecure and desperate. I'm confident and safe. He'll never betray me.

Once again, his touch interrupted her thoughts. She turned to face him, chasing away the sadness. This was their first real date. She shouldn't let her insecurities ruin the mood.

"Shall we go for a swim?" he asked. He gave her hand a gentle squeeze, and she understood. He knew what she felt and wanted to reassure her without saying it out loud.

"I'd love that!" She threw her dress on the sand. It didn't matter that she only had her underwear on. Nothing mattered when she was with him. Giggling, she followed his lead into the warm water.

It was a magnificent day. Ayla's spirits were high. She enjoyed holding Blaze's hand and finally being careless and free the way she'd never been before. Free to be herself. To feel completely safe. To have his arms around her and taste his kisses, salty after their play in the water. To make love and never feel tired. To forget all about time.

The sun hung low above the horizon when she finally rolled on her back, resting her head on his chest. Gentle blues and pinks of sunsets coloured the water a pastel palette that made it look like a sheet of melted pearl. Ayla listened to Blaze's steady heartbeat, hoping it would help tame her rising anxiety. The day was gone. In just a few minutes, it would be time for them to go back to Whitestone. If she was lucky, Blaze would spend the night with her, only to leave again the next morning. She understood he only did this to protect her, but it didn't help. She knew he tried to come back as soon as he could, but there was no way of telling when it would happen. Every second without him was torture. Even busying herself with lessons, she could still feel the draining hole in her heart. And her paintings got more real each day.

He moved his hand, startling her. Ayla raised her head, looking into his emerald eyes. "Is it time to go?" She tried to sound neutral, but her voice broke, betraying her.

Blaze caressed her hair, gently untangling it. "Yes and no. We need to get out of here and have some dinner. After that, I've got another little surprise for you. We won't be spending the night at Whitestone."

Hope bloomed in her chest. "We won't? Where are we going then?"

He chuckled, pressing his finger to his lips. "You wouldn't want to ruin the surprise, would you?"

A gentle glow in the distance drew her attention. The walk towards the little beach restaurant didn't take long. Fairy lights strung throughout the place threw blurry sparks on the water. Tantalising smells of fresh cooking filled the air. Grilled meats, seafood, pastries. Everything at once, in a perfect symphony of aromas. Ayla's stomach rumbled, reminding her that she hadn't eaten anything since breakfast. It was no surprise that the place was packed. She looked around in disappointment. Every table was taken.

Blaze held her hand as he followed the courteous waiter to the waterfront. The "Reserved" sign was taken off as he pulled out a chair for her. Ayla gasped in surprise. This was the best table in the whole restaurant. Waiting for them. Blaze had organised everything for a perfect date. She couldn't stop smiling as she browsed through the menu framed by a textured leather cover. This man guessed everything she wanted even before she realised it herself. Who needed an enchanted house?

"What did I do to deserve this?" The words slipped off her tongue before she caught them.

Her companion covered her hand with his. "You don't have to do anything to deserve it. I want you to have everything you desire, and I'll do all I can to provide that. Seeing you happy is my best reward."

Tears of joy welled up in her eyes.

How do I make him happy myself? I can't figure out what he thinks, what he likes. My connection to him is damaged. Something's wrong with me.

She blinked the tears away, as his gaze became concerned. "I'm just so happy, Blaze. I've never thought anything like this would ever happen to me. Thank you for making this my reality."

A waiter appeared with a tray laden with food.

Ayla was silently grateful, too distracted to extend her thanks. She didn't want to tell Blaze about her dark thoughts, not on a night like this. She had to fight her own demons. After everything he'd already done for her, she had no right to burden him with her troubles. He deserved to be happy, too. Even if she couldn't feel him the way he felt her, she was determined to do all she could to make up for it.

Just as she thought things couldn't get any better, they did. A violinist played romantic tunes all through dinner. A flower girl gave her a beautiful white rose. Dessert was the lightest souffle she'd ever had. Holding on to Blaze with one hand and carrying her rose in the other, Ayla looked forward to his next surprise.

Another short walk, and they found themselves among cosy villas. The main building of the hotel was hidden out the back of the lush gardens. The smiling young man at reception handed a golden key to Blaze and wished them to have a nice stay.

Their villa looked out to the deserted beach and the calm sea waters, silvered by the shy crescent of the new moon. A light breeze rocked the transparent curtains back and forth. Following a tiny gesture of Blaze's hand, dozens of candles came to life, lighting up the area. An array of white rose petals covered the floor, leading up to the bedroom, with more of them scattered on the bed. Ayla placed her flower on the bedside table and turned to Blaze again.

"This is the best day of my life," she breathed into his ear. He enveloped her in a loving embrace. There was no need for words; the whole world disappeared. Nothing could get between them. She was sure of it.

CHAPTER 26. AYLA

In the murky nothingness, she walked towards the
ocean. The wind blew her hair off her face, tangling it
behind her back. Sharp and cold, it was nothing like the
playful breeze from just a few hours ago. Ayla stubbornly
moved her feet, drowning in the sand that was no longer
warm nor stable. Quickening and writhing, it made each
step a challenge. Her will was strong, though; no matter
what happened, she couldn't stop before she reached her
destination.

Once the wind abated and she could look straight without squinting, she saw him right away. Lying flat on his
stomach, waves nibbling at his snowy hair. Ayla's breath
caught up in her throat. She stopped, shaking her head. It
couldn't be. It was nothing but a nightmare.

Ignoring her racing heart, she ran towards his immobile
body and threw herself on the white sand next to him. The
grainy texture dug tiny needles into her skin everywhere
the sand touched her, but that didn't matter. Pain helped
her focus.

"Please, Blaze. Please, wake up." She pushed his body in an attempt to turn him over. It was heavy, lifeless. She managed to roll his head to the side and gasped. His emerald eyes were glassed over, their light gone forever. Ayla bit her lip, trying to make sense of this. He was asleep next to her just an hour or so ago. How did this happen?

She caressed his face, calling his name, already knowing he wouldn't answer. The perfectly straight wound across his throat drew her attention. The same one she had seen so many times before on those Mage girls who were killed for her. The visions that were too real to be dreams. And now, this happened to the person she loved. The one she considered her solid rock in the cruel world. Dead, because of her.

It's all my fault. He put his life in danger for me, and my curse killed him. I should have known, I should have stayed away! Joining with him was the biggest mistake of my life.

"Indeed," the mocking voice replied.

Ayla raised her head, tracking its source. It wasn't in her mind anymore; someone was speaking somewhere very close. "Go away," she sniffled. It wasn't the time for jokes from her imagination. She didn't need to hear any more of the terrifying things that voice whispered in her ears. She needed to be alone with Blaze.

"He died because of you. Sad, isn't it?" A blob of darkness swam into her line of vision, transforming itself into a tall man's figure. He stopped a couple of paces away and lowered himself on the sand to be on the same level as her.

She didn't respond. Whoever this was, she didn't care.

"Don't be upset, Ayla. He's just a man, nothing more. You'll find another," the figure taunted.

Ayla drew an angry breath. "Nobody asked you! He's not just a man. He's my destiny."

The figure leaned forward, eyes sparkling an eerie blue. "*Was* your destiny. What are you going to do now?"

"I don't know." Ayla caressed Blaze's hair, no longer silky soft. She had to get him out of here. Go somewhere else, maybe put him on the bed. Lie down next to him and pretend like this never happened. Wake up to his heartbeat and see his dazzling smile. She'd give anything to bring him back to life. No matter what it cost.

The man sighed. "Oh well. This was pretty boring. Let me know when you come up with something more entertaining." He made a move to get up, but his dark eyes were fixed on her.

Ayla glared at him. "What *can* I do? Nothing can cure death. This is the only thing in the world that's final."

"Is it?" he chuckled, studying her face. "Or is this something you're telling yourself to avoid the truth?"

She bit her tongue, holding back a snarl. Maybe, just maybe he had something valuable to say. A clue of any sort would help.

"Think about it," the man offered. "You have the power now...so much power. Use it. Turn it around and command. Listen to yourself and embrace what's coming from within."

"And what? I can't bring him back from the dead." Tears started rolling down her cheeks. It was useless. Here she was, having a conversation with a phantom because she couldn't accept the truth. Her beloved was dead. It was all her fault.

The tall man sighed and flicked his hand towards the beach. "Come on now. You're not stupid, baby. They will all end up here unless you get your act together. Look!"

Ayla gasped. The beach was no longer empty. Dozens of bodies covered it. Throats slit. Blood drying under them. Eyes staring into the murky night sky.

Lyssa. Saree. Mace. The Healers. The coffee shop owner. All the people she had ever met in Whitestone found a place on the cold sand. Breath caught in her throat, Ayla didn't move. This was too terrifying to be true. She squeezed her eyes shut, chasing the gruesome scene away. When she opened them again, it was still there. And the strange man with a smirk on his face.

"You!" she whispered. "You killed them, didn't you?"

He chuckled. "No, Ayla. *You* did."

"Me?" She looked at her hand squeezing a ceremonial dagger. How did she get that? Panicked, she threw it into the tide. "No. No, I couldn't have. It wasn't me."

"So sad, baby. You poor thing. There's no one left to take care of you now. Looks like you'll have to make it out on your own. Unless you do something, of course."

"Like what?" she snapped. "Who are you anyway?"

The man shook his head, his long black hair snaking down his shoulders. "You'll know exactly who I am once you've accepted who *you* are. Admit it, Ayla. You're not the good girl they all thought you were. Your curse won't feel like a curse once you've stopped lying to yourself. Embrace the darkness. It will show you the way."

Ayla's gaze stopped on her lover's face. There was nothing she could do to bring him back. Was there?

She closed her eyes, taking a deep breath. Magic jumped at her command, tingling in her fingers, its white flame waiting for her. "No," she whispered. "You can't help me. Not on your own."

The ground trembled as she absorbed the flame into her arms, directing it along her veins, all the way to her heart. Blaze would have never taught her that, but he wasn't there to stop her. The light threads tinted crimson that grew darker as she poured her pain into it. A gentle touch was a surprising distraction. Ayla opened her eyes to the swirls of grey fog peeking through the sand, caressing her skin. She stretched her arm towards it, and the Mist flowed to her. Its healing embrace brought her the comfort she was seeking. And with it, the understanding.

"Help me," she whispered as the swirls grew larger.

"Good girl," someone breathed in her ear.

Ayla turned to the detestable man's face. "You don't get to patronise me. Go away before I make you disappear!"

The man chuckled at her attempt to drown him in fog. "Ah ah! I'm the one who taught you this, and I'm the one who can take it away." He opened the palm of his hand and a ball of fog curled on it like a kitten. "You can do great things, baby. Don't be shy to use your abilities."

She glared, trying to make sense of him. This was the mocking voice taunting her all this time. This man was a complete stranger, yet she felt connected to him somehow. His ability to command the Mist was unnerving. A half-blurred memory sprinted in her mind. A Mage who did the impossible and became part of the Mist. An urban myth that was still so fresh people knocked on wood and refrained from pronouncing his name. The man who lived in her head.

The Mistwalker.

She'd never found out what happened to him. Now was her only chance.

"Wait! What's your name?"

The man grinned, his figure dissipating in the fog. "You'll know soon enough. Don't lose your chance, Ayla. If you want him back, bring him back. You can have anything you desire. All you have to do is take it. Embrace your darkness."

Ayla blinked as the last traces of the Mistwalker disappeared, then focused on the task at hand. Something in his words triggered a tingling feeling in her stomach, as if a kaleidoscope of butterflies was about to burst out of her. Anticipation filled her lungs. She knew what to do.

This time, it didn't take much effort to roll Blaze's body on his back. Ayla placed the palm of her right hand on Blaze's forehead, her left hand on his chest. She imagined the steady, soothing rhythm of his heartbeat. His relaxed breathing. His mesmerising eyes and velvety voice telling her it was going to be alright. She would explain everything later. For now, she had to do whatever it took to wake him up.

His eyelids moved. Encouraged, Ayla kept her concentration, pushing all her will to make her vision a reality. He was alive and well, just asleep. All she needed to do was to wake him up. Blaze's long eyelashes moved, and his emerald eyes focused on her face. She smiled with relief as she felt his chest rise with a breath, then another. His gaze was the most welcome sight.

Blaze's fingers wrapped around hers.

"Wake up, sweetheart." His lips didn't move, yet she heard his voice clearly as if he spoke straight into her ears. "Please wake up. We have to go."

"Go where?" she asked.

Blaze didn't answer. The beach, the fog, the bodies disappeared in a whirlwind of dull colours. Only the wind and the sound of crashing waves remained. And Blaze's mesmerising eyes.

***

"Wake up," he repeated.

Ayla blinked, focusing on his worried face. "What?"

"I'm sorry I had to wake you. We need to leave, now."

She sat up, rubbing her eyes. The peaceful villa looked the same as when they got there. Breeze rocking lightweight curtains. The view of the sea outside crystal clear windows, silver in the moonlight. Nothing changed. Ayla looked around and finally noticed it.

Rose petals on the bed and all over the floor were no longer white. Coloured a blood-red now, they were a disturbing reminder of her visions. Blaze gave her a hand to get off the bed.

"I'm sorry, sweetheart. I didn't feel the interference. Someone managed to get through the wards I've set up for this place. We have to leave before something else happens."

The walls moved, threatening to squash her. Ayla soothed herself.

It's not real. I just feel claustrophobic because someone was here and we didn't notice. Probably the same person who gave me that strange vision. Or people.

The thought made her sick. She rushed to the bathroom, ready to empty the contents of her stomach. What she saw made her hair stand on end.

A simple bouquet of wildflowers skilfully arranged in a small vase was waiting for her on the bathroom shelf. A modest pastel note sat right in front of it. Hands shaking, Ayla picked it up.

Say farewell to one more friend,
You don't need to play pretend.
Go enjoy your last embrace,
There's no way to win this race.
Just before all good is gone,
I will crush your heart and soul.

With a yelp, she threw it on the floor. The note dissipated in the air before it touched the ground. Ayla ran out, stumbling on the way. It was a trap. Her vision was a warning, and she had to suffer the circumstances. They had to get out immediately.

She stopped in her tracks as realisation hit her. The look in Blaze's eyes confirmed her suspicion.

"Your magic?" she breathed, already knowing the answer.

"I can't open a portal," he confessed, a sea of turmoil in his gaze. "We've been placed in a neutral zone. A dome. The only way out is on foot."

She grabbed onto his hand and ran out of the villa. The lights were gone. Other buildings looked abandoned. The only way out of the coveted village was through the main building. Blaze yanked the reception door open to let her through. Ayla rushed in and stopped.

The friendly receptionist rested his head on the desk as if he were asleep. Only a thin trickle of blood dripping on the floor betrayed the gruesome truth.

"He's dead," she turned to Blaze, too terrified to blink.

He nodded. "So is everyone else in the hotel. We have to brace ourselves, sweetheart. I can sense other auras outside, closing in on us. The neutral zone ends by the restaurant," he pointed towards the small dot of darkness that only a few hours ago basked in the romantic light of candles. "We'll need to hurry if we want to make it out alive."

Ayla squeezed his hand. "I'll run as fast as I can," she promised with a small smile. Blaze rushed through the reception to the opposite door right onto the beach. The waves were no longer gentle laps on the soft warm sand. Roaring, they ripped onto land, threatening to pull her under. The sand was heavy and unyielding under her bare feet. Salty wind threw her back, for the first time in her life making her regret being so lightweight. Thankfully, Blaze was strong enough for both of them. He dragged her through the storm towards their destination, which seemed to be too far. Almost on the horizon. Never getting close, no matter how fast they ran.

Ayla stumbled on a washed-up rock and made the mistake of looking back. Shadows were slithering on the sand, approaching fast like snakes. Behind them, dark figures seemed to float in the air. All hooded, yet she somehow knew what they were. Sorcerers. The ones like Kendall. The ones with blood lust in their veins. The ones sent to take her.

With a yelp, she grabbed onto Blaze's hand, determined to make it to the end of the zone. Yet another rock caught her foot, throwing her off balance. The figures grew closer. Without hesitation, Blaze threw her over his shoulder and continued on his way. Ayla raised her head, lips pursed, as she studied her enemies. There was no time to find out what they wanted. After her nightmare, she wasn't sure what to believe anymore. Was it her they were after? Or was it...Blaze?

You're not getting him. Not in your wildest dreams.

She called on to her magic but nothing came.

Of course. Blaze said magic wouldn't work here. It wasn't much help in my dream, either. But what if...

Ayla closed her eyes and imagined the soothing clouds of the Mist. The way it grew its tentacles up in the air, strangling her enemies. Stopping them from following her. Dragging them into the depths even she was afraid to explore. There was a darkness within her. If it was already in her heart, why not make it an ally? Why not...make a deal with it?

She exhaled and opened her eyes. The sound of the storm came back ripping at her ears. The shadows were still closing in, though their movements resembled a dance now rather than a chase. The beach was full of bodies, scattered on the sand as far as she could see. Dead? No. Just knocked out. She knew they would wake up and come after her again. The tiny swirls of fog were dissipating in the air under the dark cloaks.

Serves them right.

She allowed herself a small chuckle. They made it! Blaze crossed the threshold, and the colours returned. The restaurant was lit up as before. A new moon hung high in the sky, clouds running past, its reflection distorted in the roaring waves.

A quiet swoosh announced a portal opening. Blaze put her down on the ground, his eyes full of concern. "Sweetheart…"

She pressed a finger to his lips. "We made it, that's the only thing that matters now."

He nodded, turning her towards the shimmering door in the fabric of reality. Ayla stepped through it, catching her breath. Finally, this was over. They were safe.

A quiet gasp made her turn back. Just before the portal snapped shut, she caught a glimpse of Blaze's face, distorted by a grimace of pain. And a dark figure behind him with a bloodied knife in its hand.

CHAPTER 27. AYLA

Houses blurred past as she sped down the sleepy streets of Whitestone. The night was on its way out, with dark objects around her gaining shape. The stillness and beauty of the hour before dawn annoyed her. How could people be asleep when danger was looming over their heads? When their beloved hero was dying somewhere on cold sand, surrounded by foes?

Ayla bit her lip hard, praying for the pain to distract her from dark thoughts. After a few tormenting attempts to open the portal back, she knew it would be no use. Without proper knowledge of how to do it, her magic didn't work. So she did what her inner self told her. There was no magic she could use, but her darkness had worked. She saved her lover only to lose him. Her nightmare became reality. It was unfair.

Her mind briefly turned to the strange figure in that dream. *You can have anything, just take it. Embrace your darkness.* That was what he said. That was what she did. It didn't work.

Wild hope kept pushing her between shoulder blades until a modest cottage floated into her line of vision. She caught her breath, wondering where her instinct brought her.

There was nothing out of the ordinary here. A cottage like many others. Three steps to the wooden porch, front door painted a faded white. A house for one dweller, just like her own.

Ayla hammered her fists on the door until someone's sleepy head snatched it open. A pair of pale blue eyes glared at her. "What do you want, bitch?"

"We need to talk. Now," Ayla pushed Sherice out of the way and stepped over the threshold. The air held a trace of the blonde's sweet vanilla-infused perfume. Disgusting. Suffocating. Ayla ignored it, imagining the freshness of the citrus. She had to focus.

"Do you know what time it is?" Sherice yawned, not bothering to cover her mouth.

Ayla flicked her hand towards the kitchen bench, channelling her power. It was almost too easy now. The kettle boiled in an instant. A cup with coffee and sugar popped up on the bench, scorching water filling it by two-thirds, milk on top. She pushed the drink into Sherice's hands. "Have some fucking coffee and wake up."

Sherice's fingers laced over the smooth ceramic. "You're different, girl. So many changes in such a short time. But even with your new power, I can still kick your arse. Especially considering how careless you are about using it." She shook her head, taking a sniff of the coffee as if concerned it was poisoned. "Blaze needs to teach you some manners before you get yourself in trouble."

"I've been in trouble all my life, Sherice." She took a deep breath. "I know it was you who opened the portal for the Sorcerers."

Her opponent scoffed. "Seriously?"

"Yes. I'm not here to accuse you of anything," Ayla rushed. She had to plead her case before Sherice lost her patience and became uncooperative. "I just need your help. Blaze is injured. He's been taken somewhere by a horde of Sorcerers. I know they wouldn't kill him because he's not their target. I am."

Sherice's blue eyes were alert. "How do you know this?"

"Because I saw it. I walked through the portal and he stayed behind. Now I can't find my way back." Ayla exhaled, taming her racing heart. "I know that you can take me there."

"You are a disease, you know that? If it weren't for you, Blaze would have been safe and sound. He would have partnered with me and there'd be nothing to worry about. But no. You had to come along and steal him away."

"Look," Ayla lowered her voice. The blonde was taunting her, but this wasn't the time to lose patience. "I'll make you a deal. Whoever is hunting me is part of that group. I'm sure of it. They wouldn't have taken Blaze if they didn't want to lure me in, and they will keep him alive for now, or so I hope. 'I will crush your heart and soul', that's what the latest rhyme said. He is everything to me." She felt tears building up in her eyes. "You have nothing to lose. Take me to them. I'll go willingly and exchange my life for his. You'll have me out of the way and Blaze will get to live."

For a long moment, Sherice didn't respond. An ivory comb appeared in her hand and she brushed her long hair with an absent-minded expression on her face. Ayla waited patiently, fighting the urge to shake her. Every second was vital to Blaze's wellbeing, and she was wasting this precious time.

Too bad you can't use a mind spell and force her to do your bidding. Maybe I should have made you a Sorceress, the mocking voice echoed in her ears.

Bad timing. Shut up, she ordered it.

"I hope you understand that the stakes are much higher in this game." Sherice took a sip of her coffee and wrinkled her nose. "This is foul. I don't take sugar in mine." Instead of using magic to dispose of it, she placed the cup on the table by her side. "The Sorcerers' attack meant war, regardless of who led them here. The Council is delusional. They should have taken measures when the Sorcerers infiltrated Whitestone. But no. They are a bunch of softies. We need a strong hand to guide us. Someone who won't bother with the charade of democracy. This would have been Blaze's son, if raised right. If you didn't show up to ruin our plans."

"*Our* plans?" A chill crept up Ayla's spine.

An evil grin spread across Sherice's lips. "Oh, you want to know, don't you? Of course, you do. All the questions about your adoptive father's murder and the people who tried killing you last year. If it weren't for that Master of yours with his life ritual, everything would have been perfect."

"You knew about this," Ayla whispered. Her eyes widened. Despite her shock, she processed that the key to her pressing questions had been right before her, yet she never thought of the possibility.

"Well, I only have time for one thing. I can take you to the Sorcerers who allegedly have Blaze, or I can tell you the truth about your family and all the politics you're in the middle of. Choose wisely." She shrugged, heading towards a tall wardrobe which produced a range of jackets.

Ayla bit her tongue. She wasn't going to respond to provocation. As tempting as it was to finally give answers to questions—ones that tormented her since the kidnapping that threw her into the cruel world of the Sorcerers—she had more pressing things to do. No matter the cost, she was going to save Blaze's life. Everything else could wait.

"Great! Blaze it is." Sherice threw her hair over her shoulder and Ayla realised she had voiced her thoughts out loud. With a swift move over her body, Sherice replaced satin pyjamas with a pair of leather pants and a lightweight shirt. Grabbing a leather jacket out of the wardrobe, she cast a sly glance at Ayla. "Let's go then."

Ayla matched her brisk pace as the blonde walked her out of the house, through the back door and out into the streets. They walked towards the Healers' Hub as the town slowly woke up around them. There was still nobody out, but she didn't care. The residents couldn't help her. Not with the ordeal she was dragged into.

The portal was waiting in the narrow alley by the Hub. Ayla recognised it right away. This was the place where she got attacked. The little lane she couldn't find after. She wondered if it only existed because Sherice was there, but brushed off the thought. It wasn't important. She needed to focus.

"After you," her companion said, gesturing towards the darkness.

Ayla drew a sharp breath. *I'm not afraid*, she whispered to herself before stepping over the threshold.

The blonde followed suit, pushing her between her shoulder blades. "Hurry up, will you? I don't want to stay here a second longer than I have to."

The mansion loomed in front of them, its dark walls emanating danger. Something Corbin would have liked to stay in. Ayla wondered if it was one of his and whether this was all a ruse to lure her back into his clutches and get rid of her lover. A chill crept under her skin as she thought about the possibility. It wouldn't be out of character for him, even though she shunned him.

The door squeaked on the hinges. The unfriendly face of a middle-aged Sorcerer looked her up and down like a piece of meat before hammering on a grin. "Hey, little girl. Don't you look delicious."

"A gift for the Master." Sherice inserted herself between him and Ayla. "I have an offer he cannot decline."

"Very well." The Sorcerer beckoned them to follow. As they walked down the dimly lit corridors, fear crept under Ayla's skin all the way to her heart. She could have been wrong in her assumptions. Blaze could have been dead on the cold sand, and she walked into the lair of the beast for nothing.

"By the way," Sherice threw nonchalantly, casting a brief glance over her shoulder. "Your friend Lyssa was taken last night. The last of the four."

Ayla's heart drummed in her chest. Now there wasn't one but two of her dearest people locked up in this dungeon. She bargained for Blaze, but what of her best friend? There was nothing left she could offer. Before panic took over her senses, the large door opened and she walked into the room.

Nothing out of the ordinary. A small living room. Heavy curtains were drawn to block out the light of the rising sun. Mottled calfskin encyclopaedias gathered dust on a bookshelf. Cosy fire danced in the fireplace, illuminating the most detestable face in the world. The bully from her days at the Sorcerers' Academy.

"What a lovely surprise." Julian grinned at her before turning his attention to Sherice. "I didn't expect her so soon. Did she figure it out on her own?"

"Yes, Master." Sherice bowed. "She offered her own life for Blaze's."

"How interesting." Julian rubbed his chin. "Lady Tenebris has her own plans for him, you see. This was a last-minute thing. I'm sorry, Sherice, but it looks like you may not be getting your Mage after all."

"I've brought you two lives, Master," Sherice rushed. "She has Joined with him. Chances are she's already pregnant. A much better deal for you."

"What?" Ayla breathed out. This wasn't a possibility she thought about. It made sense that she rushed into danger without thinking. Hormones would do it.

A flash of green on Julian's index finger made her gasp. The graduation ring that marked him as a full Sorcerer. So he finished his studies at the Academy while she was away. She tried speaking again, but no words came out as if someone held a hand over her mouth. An invisible binding tightened around her arms, pressing them to her sides. A spark of metal in his hands showed her the most hated—and feared—object. A slave collar.

The lock clicked shut around her neck and a strange numbness subdued her senses. She watched Sherice gulp nervously. Whatever this was, it wasn't what she expected. Then again, she didn't spend any time developing a plan. *Stupid, stupid Ayla.*

"Don't worry, it will only neutralise your magic so you don't waste it on silly things like trying to break out of the spell," Julian soothed. "Shame about the baby, though. We'll need to get rid of that little inconvenience."

The binds held her in place. Terror, regret and a violent homesickness mixed then curdled in her mind. Oh, the turmoil was poison, tearing her apart from deep within her biology. Not only was she going to lose Blaze, but his child, too. How could she have been so naïve?

I deserve this. This is what I've brought upon myself and now I have to atone for it.

Julian sniffed her hair, slowly tucking stray strands behind her ears. His breath travelled down her neck all the way to the collarbone. "My sweet little bunny. I can't wait to get my hands on you. Don't worry, the ritual won't take long. Tenebris will take your magic and then I'll get to keep you all to myself. Imagine how wonderful it will be."

Sherice cleared her throat. Ayla breathed out, thankful for the intervention. Whatever her rival had to say, it was better than feeling like a helpless toy in Julian's hands.

"Forgive me, Master. We had a deal. I bring you what you want in exchange for what I want. I over-delivered by offering you two lives instead of one. I'm giving you this girl at the peak of her power as I made sure she didn't waste it on the way. Won't you honour your own word?"

Julian growled, glaring at her. "You don't get to tell me what to do. But you're right, I did give you my word. How about this. If the Mage is still alive after Tenebris is done with him, you can keep him."

"Why does she even want him? I thought her goal was the original twelve and this one to finish the cycle."

"None of your business." He snapped his fingers, summoning two guards. "Take this one to the cell with the other girl."

"What? No! This is a mistake!" Sherice protested as they grabbed her arms.

"Shut up! I can't have you going back to Whitestone and blabbering about things you've seen here. Not until this is over, at least. Once we're done with these two, I'll let you go. But not a second before then."

The door slammed shut behind them. Julian grinned, turning back to Ayla. "Finally all alone. I don't like total silence, though." He waved his hand in front of her face, the ring flashing as he uttered a quiet spell. The binds on her body loosened and the invisible gag disappeared. Ayla moved her arms, unsure of his motives. Julian chuckled, watching her. "Come on, little bunny. You have nowhere to go. No magic to protect yourself. No powerful boyfriend coming to the rescue. It's just you and me now.

Tell me how scared you are. What you'll give me for a chance to keep your will before I crush it."

He raised his hand. She whimpered, sure that his fingers, his palm, left a red mark on her face.

"Talk, damn it!"

"Please, don't hurt me," she pleaded, her mind racing. This situation was far from ideal, but it had to do. She had some freedom in her movements, but no magic to use. If he wanted her to beg, she'd beg. She just had to make sure she sounded convincing until she thought of a solution.

He rolled a moan around his mouth. "That's better. We can still have a bit of fun before Tenebris requires your presence. She'll be happy to see you so soon after the Mage's arrival."

"How does she know I'm here?" Ayla sniffled, forcing some tears out.

Julian's laughter echoed against the empty walls of the room. "Silly girl. Haven't you figured it out yet? She has a mental link to you. Not something she knew about at first, but once you started peeking at her rituals, it was a matter of time. Tenebris doesn't like unwelcome guests."

"Who is she?" Ayla thought about her bloodthirsty visions. Blaze was right. She was innocent of the murders. How cruel she was to herself to believe that she could've killed so mercilessly.

"You're a linguist, bunny. Tenebris means 'shadow'. When Blaze took you away, Corbin couldn't settle. His attachment to you was so strong he completely lost his mind. This obsession brought him on a search for an ancient artefact. The sapphire, Caerulus, holds an immense power. Much like other magic stones, though, Caerulus has a mind of its own. With its help, Corbin created a replica of you, using the objects you used and loved. The other you was named Tenebris. Your shadow. To nourish the magic keeping her alive, Corbin had to delve into a series of ritual sacrifices. Each of them made Tenebris stronger, until she was powerful enough to challenge him. The rest is history. The old Master is no longer a problem."

Ayla was quiet, processing the information. "Did she kill him?"

"Of course not, did you forget about your blood bond? You'd have been dead if this happened, and who knew if she would be, too. He was banished, that's all."

"What does she want with Blaze?" Ayla lowered her eyelids, watching his expression through her lashes. She had to tread lightly.

"You should be more concerned about your own fate, bunny." He snatched her chin, forcing her to look into his eyes. "You two look completely alike on the outside. Blaze is wounded and not in his right mind. It would be easy to mistake her for you. All she is going to do is drain his power, just like she will drain yours. After that, she won't need any more sustenance." Julian studied her with a crooked smile on his face. "Any more questions, baby?"

She shied away from his gaze, carefully checking the floor. On the verge of reality, transparent swirls hovered just above it, with more joining them from under the floorboards. The temperature dropped as the fog slowly covered the rest of the floor.

"No more questions. I think I've had enough." She pushed him back, stepping away from him. The Mist rose, following her silent command.

Julian's eyes widened. "How did you...?" He glanced at the collar on her neck.

Ayla scoffed. "I don't need my magic here. This is my realm. My rules. You are going to tell me where Tenebris is holding my lover, and I might just let you live."

It was a pleasure to watch him change his tune. The arrogant, annoying bully being held in place by tentacles of darkening grey. This was the darkest she'd ever seen the Mist, but she didn't care. She was going to do anything to save Blaze, no matter the cost.

Losing his confident posture, Julian showed her the way to the furthest end of the stone-cold corridor. The fog followed them, keeping him in check, under Ayla's watchful eye. Obeying her command, Julian removed her collar before turning to face her. "I didn't realise how much darkness you had inside you, too. Be careful with the Mist. Its voice is subtle but deceitful. Take caution before you lose yourself."

"Really, Julian? You're going to give me life lessons now? Why such a sudden change? No more bunny for the big bad wolf to play with, huh?" she taunted.

Julian shook his head. "You are just like her. I should have known."

"Shut up!" she hissed, cautious not to raise her voice. "I'm nothing like her."

I'm the good guy here. Not someone who succumbs to darkness to torture people. I give mercy to those who deserve it.

She paused before pushing the door that held the answers to all her troubles. Julian didn't reply, his eyes wide open as the tentacles of fog kept him in place. "Wait here," she snapped. Once she'd crossed the threshold, it wouldn't matter how she achieved what she wanted. Her magic might be enough to fight Tenebris. Once that threat had been dealt with, she'd explain everything to Blaze.

She was sure he would understand she had no other choice.

CHAPTER 28. AYLA

She was too late.

Through the dark veil of denial, Ayla watched her opponent slowly get off Blaze's body. Tenebris fixed up her dress—Ayla's dress!—and turned towards her. A triumphant grin spread across her face. "Good timing. I was just finishing up here."

Ayla stood rooted to the spot, barely noticing the heat in the room. There was nothing around her, just her perfect reflection and her lover who lay immobile by her opponent's feet. Her senses were numb with denial. This was nothing but another nightmare. She was going to wake up in Blaze's arms, in that beautiful villa in the woods, and none of this would have happened. He was safe next to her, his heart beating, his touch gentle. Nothing could take him away.

Tenebris snapped her fingers in front of Ayla's face. "Come on, wake up now. Look what happened to your little boyfriend. Your true love, your destiny, right? Didn't last that long, I'm afraid. What are you going to do about it?"

Ayla knew this was a provocation. Blaze was lying on the floor, his face turned away. There was no way of knowing if he was still alive. She scorned herself for the thought. Of course, he was alive, just unconscious. Tenebris was lying, she had to be!

Her opponent sighed. "Everything is so boring around here. Why won't you people cooperate?" Her grin got wider. "He was pretty good though. Lots of delightful magic! His power was a rare treat, like nothing I've tried before. Fierce, uncontrolled, raw. Such a shame I had to kill him."

"You...killed him?"

"Why don't you go check?" Tenebris watched her like a cat would watch a mouse. The sapphire gleamed on the gold chain tucked between her breasts.

Ayla shook her head to chase away the illusion. How would someone fight their exact reflection? This was supposed to be a copy of her. Not this...thing. That was it. Tenebris was no longer her copy. She was something else entirely, changed by the stone. Her power was great, but so was Ayla's. The only problem was that Tenebris had had time to train hers. Ayla hadn't.

Only the iron grip of her will stopped her from rushing towards her lover's body. Her heart beating like the drums of war, Ayla turned her gaze to her opponent. This was how she wished she looked. Lean yet curvy in all the right places. Hair shinier, eyes brighter, skin aglow. The perfect Ayla. The one without a curse above her head. The one without the mark of destiny. The one who wasn't ashamed to enjoy Corbin's forbidden pleasures and who wasn't afraid to kick him out once she'd had enough. The one who was free to do as she wished.

Nobody said you can't do the same, the voice in her head whispered.

It's too late. She's stronger than me, more cunning. She knows all my weaknesses and will strike with precision. I have no chances to win.

She might have everything you do, but she doesn't have me, the voice advised. *I didn't make you a helpless loser. Open your eyes, pull yourself together and show her your true worth.*

"Talking to yourself again, love?" Tenebris chuckled, studying her. Eyes sparkling the iridescent blue, she covered Caerulus with her hand.

It was time. Ayla didn't have a chance to think when Tenebris struck her. The phantom hand reached for her out of nowhere, a heavy slap sending her flying against the stone wall. The sharp sting on her cheek burned like the anger in her chest. She thought about Blaze who never moved since she'd arrived, and about her evil twin. She refused to believe the truth. That would be something for her to think about later. If she ever got a chance.

The second hit got her in the solar plexus. Ayla folded in half, holding her arms to her chest as if it would protect her from pain. Tenebris stepped closer, a condescending smile on her lips. A tiny flick of her raised hand pressed Ayla against the wall, immobilising her, as a thousand needles dug into her flesh.

"Does it hurt, sweetie? Or do you want more? Something to make your dirty dreams come true?" She laughed at Ayla's stunned expression. "Oh yes, I know all about it! You used to peek at my most enjoyable sessions with your old Master, didn't you? Watching every single moment, wondering if it was true, questioning your sanity. Hoping that it would be a secret you could keep from everyone, even from Blaze. You wouldn't want him to think you're nothing but a dirty slut, would you?"

Unable to move, Ayla glared as if it would help her break free. Physical pain was nothing compared to the red shame scorching her chest.

Tenebris laughed as she continued, "Pathetic. I can't believe you are my original. Helpless and weak, even with the power Blaze woke in you. Your only purpose is to obey a Master. You'll do well as a toy at Julian's dungeon. Nothing but a source of pleasure until he tires of you." Tenebris dropped her hand, releasing the pressure.

Ayla slumped on her knees, gasping for air. Harsh words burned, even though they were untrue. Were they?

Struggling to ignore the voice of self-doubt, Ayla scampered on her feet. "I can't believe you're my copy. So mean and insensitive. Do you only think about yourself?" She wriggled her fingers, silently summoning her power. The white flame danced bright and free in her mind. Gentle tingling alerted her of its presence. All she had to do was keep her opponent talking until she figured out a weak spot.

Tenebris grinned. "I'm doing you a favour. You never knew magic. Now you have it and you still have no idea what to do with it. Mindless blasts of raw power? Please! There are so many things you could do if you had the brains to go with your looks. Good thing Corbin shared his knowledge when he created me. You don't need magic, Ayla. I'll relieve you of this burden and you'll have your normal life back. Trust me, it won't be so bad."

Focusing all her will on the white flame, Ayla pushed the ball of energy at her enemy. All her focus went into it. The look of astonishment on Tenebris's face told her she did the right thing. Attacking while the opponent was busy gloating was a good tactic—until the energy ran out. Ayla preferred not to think about it.

Pressed to the wall, Tenebris covered her eyes from the blinding light of magic fire. As it intensified, she lost her ability to move. It was Ayla's turn to grin.

I shouldn't talk to her. I need to keep pushing until I destroy her, and then I can go and check on Blaze.

The thought of her lover on the cold stone floor threw her focus off. For a split second, the tension weakened, but that was enough for Tenebris to catch up. Her hand grabbed the stone on her neck. Caerulus shone a brilliant blue, cutting through the white petals of Ayla's magic. The temperature rose again. Ayla's hair stuck to her neck, air too musty to breathe. Like the still jungle in summer, but worse.

There was no strike back. Ayla stepped away, staring at her opponent. Caerulus pulsed an eerie blue through Tenebris's fingers. A triumphant smile on her face. Ayla summoned her power again and directed another wave at her opponent, aiming for the stone. It sparkled, throwing an array of lights across the walls—and absorbed her power.

"Silly girl. Did you really think your barely formed power could overcome the ancient magic of Caerulus?" Tenebris flicked her hand, sending a wave of blue light towards Ayla.

Pressed between walls of scorching magic and ice-cold stone, Ayla struggled to breathe. Panic flowed over her. The fear of being stuck, restrained and helpless, came crashing down on her senses. Anything was better than this. She was willing to give whatever it took to be free again.

Tenebris took a deliberately slow step towards her, the gem pulsing and heaving in her hand. "This is it, sweetie.

You lost. Now I'll take what's left of your magic and then send you off to Julian. Stop fighting me, you're only going to hurt yourself."

A chill crawled down Ayla's spine as she recognised Corbin's words. This was the exact phrase he used to tell her every time he tortured her. Tenebris must have chosen it on purpose, to throw her even more off balance. "Did you really kill Blaze?" Ayla managed through the iron grip of terror snatching the air from her lungs.

Tenebris chuckled. "Who cares? He's gone, Ayla. You need to think about your own survival."

The scene from her nightmare flashed before her. The man she was just getting to know, who seemed to always guess her needs. Who took care of her no matter what, never asking for anything in return. Who protected her till the end. His life, taken so ruthlessly. Ayla squeezed her eyes, chasing away the terrifying thought. The last thing he saw was her twin. He probably thought Ayla was the one who betrayed him.

She couldn't bear it.

Ayla released the resistance to the pull of Tenebris's spell. Who cared indeed. Let her have the magic. Ayla had no need for it now. She had no need for anything. Her life had no meaning without her destined one.

The tug of Tenebris's power didn't hurt once she stopped fighting. Eyes glassy, she stared at the pulsing gem. It seemed alive in Tenebris's hands. Absorbing the magic to keep for itself. She wondered if it controlled Tenebris's actions or if it left her some free will.

"We could have been friends, you know," she heard herself say. "Even with these differences, we're still so similar. You know everything about me, and I've seen a lot about you in my visions. Did you figure out a way to get back at me through our mental link? Is that how you knew where I was to send me those wildflowers?"

Tenebris scoffed, tightening the grip of her spell. "Are you just now realising that? We would have never been friends. The only reason I'm letting you live is because I owe this little favour to Julian who helped me gain power once Corbin was gone. You'll be harmless under his thumb and without magic."

Without magic. But magic wasn't the only thing she had.

Ayla imagined the gentle tentacles of the Mist making their way through the floor. Rising higher in innocent swirls until they reached her foe. Immobilising her in place. She thought about Tenebris's eyes open wide in astonishment as she watched her disappear in the soft fog. Never to be seen again.

"Interesting," Tenebris commented.

Ayla opened her eyes and gulped. The fog covered the floor in a soft cloudy carpet, but it didn't seem to bother her opponent.

Tenebris raised her hand, and the fog followed. She dropped it and the fog abated. "So this is your other power?"

"How did you..?"

"Everything you have is what I have, too. Remember?" Tenebris chuckled, watching the greyness around her. "I wonder if I can harness this gift, too. After all, you won't have any use for it."

Ayla tensed up, her mind racing. So Tenebris could control the Mist, just like her. That didn't leave her any other weapons to fight. She tried to get the fog to grab her opponent one more time, but it stayed soft and obedient under Tenebris's feet.

Tenebris stretched her arm forward, inviting a slither of the fog to curl around it. The greyness obeyed, enveloping it in a soft cocoon. She laughed and shook it off. "It tickles! How curious. Thank you for showing me this opportunity, Ayla. I'll make use of this. Might very well become my next project. With this beautiful fog and Caerulus by my side, I'll be truly unstoppable."

Ayla closed her eyes. Resistance was futile. Her alter ego was right. There was no room for her in this world. Her best friend was taken and probably already dead. Her lover was dead. So was her father. Everyone she loved was taken away from her. Killed or shunned forever by her curse. There was no point in fighting.

"You're right," she mumbled. "Do what you want, I don't care anymore."

"Is that all you've got? No more fighting?" Tenebris taunted, stepping closer.

"No more fighting," Ayla echoed. Hazel eyes were so close now, changing their colour to blue and then back again. Golden highlights in her hair a cold azure in the light of the sapphire gleaming on her neck. Mesmerising, drawing her in like a mind spell. Her own eyes, corrupted by the ancient artefact. Her own strengths, amplified by dark magic.

Her own weaknesses, too.

"I'll tell you everything about the Mist." Ayla looked straight into her opponent's eyes. "If you promise to release me. Take my magic and let me go. That's all I'm asking."

Tenebris arched an eyebrow. "Convince me."

"It's going to take you forever to learn about its powers. I'm offering you the whole knowledge right now. It's not much to ask, especially if this is the last thing I'll ever ask anyone."

This was it. Tenebris hesitated, her face a clash of doubts. Ayla waited, hiding her impatience.

"Fine." Tenebris grinned. "Show me what you've got and I might just grant your wish."

Ayla raised her hands to meet her alter ego's. It felt bizarre to have the same sensation as if she touched her own skin, yet somewhat different. She looked into Tenebris's ever-changing eyes. "Take it all," she breathed and let Tenebris into her mind.

Flashes of light swirled in front of her. All the painful memories about her old life that came back to her after the Joining. Tortures and mind spells. Sweet words and wounds. Pain and reward. She filled her mind with all the emotions she kept locked away. Fear of confined spaces. Gaps in her memory. Strange visions. Shame of her darkest desires she never wanted anyone to know about. And above all, her overpowering love for Blaze and the deep grief over losing him.

"Stop it!" Tenebris ordered.

Ayla held onto her hands, maintaining eye contact. Now she knew better than ever how Corbin used his mind spells. She understood how detrimental this could be for both parties, but she didn't care. Only one of them was going to make it.

I came to this world with nothing. No family. No friends. Adopted by a lonely Sorcerer who dreamed about having children of his own. Then, abducted and forced into slavery. Bullied at the Sorcerers' Academy. I was of no use to my Master except to serve and obey. But I couldn't even get that right. I'm a failure. I got a second chance at Whitestone, but failed that, too. The curse I bear destroys everything around me. Everyone I love either disappears or meets a gruesome death. What's my point here? Why am I even alive?

Tenebris tried to rip her hands out of her grip. Ayla kept holding on, filling her opponent's mind with images of her own. All her insecurities and dark thoughts poured out in an endless flow, gushing from her traumas.

I was never good enough for anything. Yes, I had success in my earlier years. But why were my childhood memories wiped? Why did my biological parents never try to look for me?

Yes, I liked being punished. I believed this was what I deserved, and truth be told, it felt good. You know this, Tenebris. You are me. Why did you like it yourself? Did you feel useless and deserving punishment, too?

Tenebris pushed her against the wall. "Don't you dare do this to me. I'm nothing like you!"

This is it. I did my best, but it didn't work. She's going to kill me now. Maybe this is for the best.

Ayla squeezed her eyes shut. Blaze's image popped in front of her, his emerald eyes mesmerising, his smile reassuring. "Don't be afraid," he whispered. "We'll be together again soon." Tears flowed down her cheeks as she braced herself for the inevitable impact—which didn't happen.

Her vision blurry, she didn't register the change in front of her. Tenebris's hands were grasping onto her neck where the gold necklace had been seconds ago. Without a doubt, Ayla pushed her away. The stone barely glowed as it rocked back and forth on its gold chain. Held by the hand of her most precious person. Blaze.

He wavered on his feet, eyes dim as if he'd been drugged. His skin lost a lot of colour, almost blurring with his snow white hair. But he was alive. Helping her with all the strength he had left.

Ayla switched her focus to her twin. This was a temporary distraction. Even without the sapphire, Tenebris was dangerous. With all the magic she'd already absorbed from the offerings and the ability to use the Mist, Ayla wasn't sure if it was possible to do any more damage to her. No matter what, she needed to make sure this creature was destroyed.

Tenebris stumbled and nearly lost her balance. Her eyes burned with anger. "Give it back!" she yelled, trying to snatch the necklace.

Blaze met Ayla's gaze and in an instant, she understood. With an immense effort, she opened a small whirlpool in fog just under Blaze's hand. He threw the pendant into it, and Ayla forced it shut.

"No! Give it back!" Tenebris dove after it, but the soft grey had consumed the gem without a trace. Raking through the swirls, she growled, "Stupid bitch! Do you even know what you've done?"

"I don't care," Ayla ordered the Mist to rise. *This is not me. It's nothing but a copy. A fake*.

The fog obeyed her command this time. The greyness enveloped Tenebris from all sides, but she didn't say a word. Instead, her eyes lingered on Ayla's. "You'll regret this. I could have lived your life, happy and free. Now you'll just keep hurting everyone. The curse on your head will bring misery to everyone you love."

"You would never be happy," Ayla whispered. She felt sad. This was what she must have looked like herself. Scared and desperate, eyes wide with fear and anger. Knowing what was to come, yet not giving up hope.

Blaze watched her, holding on to the wall with one hand. Ayla lowered her eyes to Tenebris again. It wasn't his battle. It was up to her to fight her own demons. To go her own way. He helped her where he could. But she was the one to finish this.

The Mist bulged to the ceiling, darkening in its core as it engulfed the slender silhouette. Then, everything went quiet.

She turned to her lover, but couldn't utter a word. An overwhelming gratitude washed over her. The reassuring smile on his face was the best sight in the world.

"I knew it wasn't you," he uttered. His composure was as strong as ever, though it was clear he didn't have much energy left. His gaze was still full of affection, his arms warm around her.

Ayla allowed herself to relax against him. Listening to his steady heartbeat, she drew a deep breath in. "We're safe now. Everything is going to be fine," she whispered.

He held her tight, fingers gliding through her hair. "Yes, sweetheart. It's all over. We can finally go home."

CHAPTER 29. AYLA

I ron bars surrounded her from every side. The ceiling, a thick metal plate. A perfect reflection of its counterpart that served as the floor. The room was bare, except for an old wooden chair by the opposite wall.

Ayla breathed in the stale air. Arms around her knees, she sat still, trying to keep warm. It wasn't cold in the room; the chill was coming from her own body. Her magic depleted after the confrontation with Tenebris and couldn't penetrate this cage that blocked her power. The cold was her punishment.

It was all wrong. She didn't save the world from the evil of Tenebris to end up in jail herself. All she wanted was to go home with Blaze and have a good life with him. Settle down, have a family. One of the first things that happened after the events at the mansion was the Healers checking if she was pregnant. She wasn't. Ayla recalled an expression of pity across Rhonda's face as she advised that if she was an expecting mother, the trial would have been suspended until she had the baby. Without it, she had no way out.

Lyssa sat by the cage, staring at her. The bars carried an electric charge that shocked anyone who tried to touch them, as Ayla found out in the first moments of her captivity. She didn't expect to be snatched from Blaze when he was still vulnerable and couldn't protect her. She didn't realise she was still a suspect. *Silly, silly Ayla*.

"Sherice testified against you," Lyssa whispered. "She offered to go through a mind-read, and they saw what they thought was proof enough to convict you."

Ayla turned her focus to her friend. "I didn't do it, I've told them before. Tenebris looked exactly like me. I have an alibi for the last kidnappings."

"You were with Blaze," her friend uttered. "The Enforcers won't let him testify, as he's involved with you now. It's a conflict of interests. They know he'd protect you at all costs." She held an awkward pause. "They never found any traces of Tenebris, though there was a thorough sweep of the mansion. No one was able to get in touch with Corbin, either. The Sorcerers lodged a demand to get you executed for murdering one of their own."

"I didn't mean to." Ayla thought about Julian's face, distorted by a grimace of fear when she let the Mist take him. "He stayed behind and I thought he'd come back out eventually. I didn't know he wouldn't."

Lyssa sighed, her expression sad. "I know, Ayla. The Mage Council wouldn't let them dictate their rules. However, considering all the things you've been accused of and the absence of proof...plus, finding out that you can summon the Mist into the real world. That scares people. The judge ruled for lifetime imprisonment in Ravenscliffe."

"The prison for the most dangerous criminals in the Mage world?" Ayla felt a shiver snake down her spine. She'd heard terrifying stories of people who ended up there. The prison walls allowed no one to escape. The convicted lived a life of tortures to atone for their crimes. A very long life, without visitors, without sunlight, without access to their powers. Alone in their cells, left to go insane.

Without a chance to appeal.

"Yes," Lyssa mumbled. "I'm so sorry, Ayla. I wish I knew how to help."

"Why hasn't Blaze come to visit me?" Her voice shook as she felt the familiar longing. Things would have been much more tolerable if she could see him, even for a few minutes. To hear his voice, reassuring her that everything would be okay, that she could handle it. Without him, her existence in this ridiculous cage was unbearable.

Lyssa averted her eyes. "They wouldn't let him near you for the fear that he'd try to help you escape. He's been trying everything under the sun to get a visit, but no luck."

A racket in the hallway startled her. Ayla scrambled to the furthest corner of her cage, careful not to touch the bars. Whoever was making this noise meant serious business.

Two guards in heavy protection suits walked in. "Chat time is over," one of them barked to Lyssa. "She's coming with us."

"Where are we going?" Ayla protested as he grabbed her by the arm and manhandled her out of the cage. The familiar sting of a metal collar dug into her neck.

"Don't try anything stupid," the guard warned, raising a rod with tiny electric sparks dancing on its top. "One attempt to escape, and back into the cage you go."

The guards pushed Lyssa out of the way, half-dragging Ayla out of the room. "You're only out to hear the sentence. If you behave, you'll have a chance to say goodbye to him," the other guard uttered.

"No trial? Just like that they'll sentence me to the worst punishment there is?" There was no answer. Unable to believe it, Ayla hardly noticed when the dark cold corridor was replaced by a dimly lit courtroom. There weren't many people there. None of them mattered, though. Ayla's eyes could only see one.

Blaze looked defeated. He raised his eyes to hers, regaining his confidence. His composure changed when she was pushed onto the pedestal in the middle of the room. The guards chained her hands to the sides of the stand and stepped back.

The judge with a cloaked face read off a long piece of paper that curled in his hands. "Ayla Summerfield. You've been found guilty of eleven Mage murders and one of a Sorcerer who was well-known in their community. We have managed to satisfy the Sorcerers' demand for a death penalty with lifetime imprisonment at Ravenscliffe. This decision shall not be appealed. You may say goodbye to your loved one before going to the facility. You have two minutes."

The guards uncuffed her hands. Immobile with terror, she stood on the spot. Only two minutes with Blaze, and she couldn't move. Wasting precious time.

Thankfully, he was the one to rush to her. Pressing her to his chest, he caressed her hair. "I know you're innocent," he whispered, holding her tight.

"Will you help me?" she asked, desperate.

He drew in a sharp breath and shook his head. "There is no way out of Ravenscliffe. I'm sorry, Ayla. I can't let you go there."

His eyes changed from defeated to determined. Ayla's heartbeat accelerated as she tried to read the change. Something was different; he seemed to have made a decision she couldn't decipher. Just as she opened her mouth to ask, she knew it.

The push of the blade was gentle like a lover's kiss. She kept looking into his eyes, clinging to him, unable to believe what he had done. Blaze turned the dagger just under her ribs and pulled it out. Only when the hot blood rushed out of the wound did she realise this was reality.

"What have you done?"

"I'm so sorry," his voice crooned on the verge of her hearing. "I hope you can forgive me."

His emerald eyes were the last thing she saw before darkness engulfed her.

CHAPTER 30. AYLA

"It's going to work."

"You have no idea, Blaze. You should have thought this through a little better. I do hope it works, for your own sake."

"Well, sorry about the late notice, Corbin. I didn't exactly have much time."

Ayla opened her eyes, drifting out of oblivion. Strange ragged memories of darkness in the Mist pulling her in blurred her thoughts. It was peaceful and freeing—until a demanding tug commanded her to return.

She slowly turned her head towards the voices. The smell of beeswax mixed with the sweetness of dried herbs filled her nostrils. Candles were burning all around her. She threw a sideways glance to her left, then to her right. A pentagram. She was lying on a hard bed in the middle of a pentagram like some demon.

"Thank goodness you're awake," she heard Blaze's relieved voice. His emerald eyes appeared before her, a kind smile on his lips. "How are you feeling, Ayla?"

"Should have asked if she remembered her name first," another voice commented.

"Shut up, Corbin," Blaze threw over his shoulder. When he turned back to her, his tone changed. "I'm so glad you're back, sweetheart."

A memory came to the surface of her mind. His eyes, sweet and loving. His traitor's hand, delivering a deadly blow under her ribs. "Son of a bitch," she exhaled, raising her hand to slap him across the face. There was no strength in the hit; she was too low on energy.

Blaze didn't flinch or try to stop her. He waited until she dropped her hand before continuing, "I'm sorry, Ayla. You have every right to be upset, but if you got to Ravenscliffe, you'd be as good as dead. I had no other way to save you."

"So you tried to kill me?" She struggled to sit up, pushing away his offered hand. Anger boiled in her veins, making her head spin.

"He actually did kill you," Corbin interfered, stepping into her line of vision. "An inch off and he would have caused irreparable damage that even I wouldn't be able to fix."

"It was the only way I could get you out of the sentence." Blaze threw a burning look at Corbin. "I was sure you'd make it, though."

"You weren't sure of anything. You just tried your luck and hoped it would work." Corbin gently squeezed Ayla's hand, his voice smooth as he addressed her. "See what he's done to you? None of this would have happened if you stayed under my protection."

"Yes, 'cause she would have been dead months ago," Blaze retorted.

"Can you both please stop with the bickering?" Ayla's winced at the splitting headache. Blaze pressed a cold, folded towel into her hand and she gratefully put it on her forehead. Holding on to it, she studied their faces. Both with the same worried expressions. Corbin's dark eyes, soft and alluring. Blaze's emerald gaze, loving and kind. She felt her connection to both of them more than ever before. So different yet somehow similar. "Tell me what's going on."

"You were convicted without trial," Blaze began. "I was planning to testify in your defence but nothing went to plan. The Council was terrified once they learned about your powers and they got it in their heads that you were too dangerous. I tried all other ways to get you out, but none of them worked. What I did was the last resort. I'm so sorry, Ayla. We ran out of time and I wasn't sure I'd be able to raise a blade to you. It's true, if I made even a small mistake, the damage would have been irreparable."

"Too many things at stake." Corbin handed her a glass of cool water, and she gratefully took a few sips. "He didn't know for sure if I'd come when I sensed you were dying. He didn't know if I had the tools and knowledge to bring you back. You could have been beyond the Threshold for all I knew. A human can only linger on the living side of the Mist for an hour. I don't know how you managed to stay for almost a whole day."

"Because she's the Mistwalker's daughter." Blaze's expression was sombre. "This is why you are so comfortable with the Mist, Ayla. I figured it out when I saw you summon it into the world. This is a power that's unheard of, and very dangerous in the wrong hands."

"I don't understand." Ayla's gaze went from one face to the other. "What does it mean?"

"In short? It's not as easy to kill you as a regular person. I took the chance to check if I was right in my assumption, and it worked. You have at least some of the Mistwalker's power. A unique gift, unlike any other."

"The Mistwalker is long gone. He died at Ravenscliffe after years of imprisonment for the crimes he committed against both Sorcerers and Mages," Corbin added. "Nobody thought he had any children. Looks like they were all wrong."

"What happens now?" Ayla squeezed Blaze's hand. Longing for his embrace awoke in her chest. Of course she forgave him. Why wouldn't she? He did what he did for a good cause. With the stories she'd heard about Ravenscliffe, she understood his motive. Even if he did kill her, he would have done her a favour. She squeezed her eyes shut to explain the sudden change in her attitude, but nothing came to mind. Perhaps, she could figure it out later. When she was alone with her destined one. The very thought made her lips curl up.

Blaze sighed. "I have to send you away, sweetheart. The Council checked that you were dead and returned your body to me, but I can't keep hiding you. Someone is bound to find out. I'll play the part of a grieving partner and eventually move away from people to lead a hermit life. Once everyone believes it, I'll come find you and we'll be together again."

"You won't come with me?" A giant lump stuck in Ayla's throat. She let go of Corbin's hand to reach for Blaze's embrace. He wrapped her in his arms, his fingers gliding through her hair.

"I can't. It would be too suspicious if I disappeared so soon after your 'death'. We need to be careful and keep you safe. But I'll join you as soon as I can." His warm breath tickled the sensitive skin on her neck.

Ayla grabbed onto his shirt like she'd done many times before. It was never easy to let go. Knowing that this would be a long break without him burned worse than hellfire.

Corbin cleared his throat. "My work here is done. I've packed some things for you." He caught her gaze and pointed at a large bag on the floor. "Some clothes and a fair bit of local cash to help you settle at the new place. Just letting you know that the longer you stay here, the more chances someone will learn you're still alive." He sighed, looking at her hand gripping Blaze's shirt. "Goodbye, Ayla. I wish you well."

Before she had a chance to say anything, he was gone.

Blaze pulled away, studying Ayla's face. "It's okay, sweetheart. It won't be easy, but I'm always with you." He touched the silver tiger pendant on her chest. "The amulet will lead you back to me. We'll still see each other and talk in our dreams and visions as our bond grows stronger. This inconvenience is only temporary."

He helped her off the bed. Ayla realised this was Blaze's living room, transformed into an unusually dark space. Not something she ever expected to see in his house. Blaze led her to the back door, carrying the bag. On the threshold, a brilliant white portal was waiting. Ayla paused, hesitating.

Blaze handed her the bag and hugged her again. "We'll see each other soon. I promise. Be careful, sweetheart. Please, take care of yourself."

She picked up the bag which was heavier than she thought. Someone's voice in the street startled her.

"It's time," Blaze whispered, gently pushing her forward.

One last look into his eyes, one last touch of his hand cupping her cheek. Leaving him was heartbreaking, but staying would be worse. Ayla gulped down the tears and forced a smile. "I'll see you soon, Blaze."

The brilliant white of Blaze's portal felt like a cold shower gliding over her skin. Bright light, blinding her senses. Yet, darkness loomed at the corners—the influence of another, something familiar and eerie, tainting.

Corbin's spell.

Ayla gasped as the portal snapped shut behind her back. This wasn't the time to ponder what the darkness meant. Another world lay before her. A world where she would have to build her life from scratch. Again.

EPILOGUE

Tenebris caught her breath and looked around. As far as she could see, there was nothing but the everlasting waves in the sea of fog. A world of grey, soothing and calm. The peace of the dead.

She raised her hand, and the fog rose with it. She tested her theory with circular motions of her fingers, then twists of her wrists and gestures. Whatever she did, the fog followed. Each movement mirrored her. A smile spread across her face. Things weren't as bad as they could have been.

"I didn't expect to see anyone else here," a smooth baritone touched her ears.

Tenebris turned around to the tall man's figure that hadn't been there before. "That makes two of us." She held a pause, copying Corbin's manner of dragging the information out of the opponent. As always, it worked. At least there was something useful the Sorcerer gave her.

The man smiled. "Ayla's copy, are you?"

"Originally, yes. But not anymore," she suppressed a snarky remark. How dare he compare her to that useless girl?

"How curious. And you have somehow obtained her power to *journey* through the Mist. Physical form, I assume?"

"I believe so," she replied cautiously. Perhaps, this man who seemed to know about Ayla's abilities would be helpful. She frowned as her hand met nothing but her own flesh where the necklace should have been. Caerulus was gone, and she had to find a way to live without his power.

"Well, you are both tainted with Corbin's filth." The corners of the man's lips lowered in disgust. "Even so, at least you don't have her curse of that abominable bond and the price he ripped out of her to pay for it. You inherited her power to control the Mist, and I can work with that."

Her eyes narrowed. "Who exactly are you and why should I trust a word you say?"

The man grinned. "Call me Cadoc. I'll teach you how to use the Mist to its full potential, but in return, you'll give me a legacy that Ayla will never be able to. My bloodline has to continue. Are you in?"

Tenebris cast a glance around the sea of living fog. The sea of opportunity that would feed her the power she so desperately needed. And a mentor who was happy to guide her through it under a vague promise. She was sure she'd find a loophole. After all, she was the smart one.

"I'm in."

The grasp of his handshake was firm and soft at the same time, as if he was only partially there. Before she had a chance to wonder about its meaning, Cadoc let go.

"Good. Let's start with the basics."

TO BE CONTINUED

Acknowledgements

This novel was the first story I have written after a burn-out that lasted for over a decade. The passion for writing came back to me during the COVID lockdowns of 2020 when everyone was stuck at home with not much to do. During this time, I found comfort in escaping reality and diving deep into a fantasy world. Simple at first, the plot grew and developed, and so did the characters. I would like to thank my supportive family who were there for me. Big thanks to my friends who each made an impact on the story arcs and character developments—you know who you are!

I would like to thank Shane for being my inspiration to go back to writing. Thank you, Rhett, for the kitchen conversations when I was exploring plot holes. Thank you, Sarek, for cheering me on and holding my hand when I needed it most. Thank you, my darling Edward, for being the forever motivation for me to keep going. Everything I do is for you—and a little bit for me.

A round of heartfelt thanks goes to Nicole W who is the most valued friend anyone could wish for; to Demi G who brainstormed and dreamed with me in those early days; to Gareth who braved reading a novel outside of his genre and came back with great feedback; to my awesome critique partners at Vision who helped me build confidence; to Harrie B for inviting me and organising a reading of my novel at my first-ever author event; to Raelene who showed me the world of successful authors; to Craig aka Maximus, and Cody for organising writing events that help me connect with my tribe of wonderful writers; to Dasha K who made me her role model so now I have to maintain the image; to Jane N for her admiration of my work that helps me fight the imposter's syndrome; to Tina who was one of the first people to support my work and who is exceptional at keeping my mind at ease; and to Kimmy for being the first one to believe in Blaze.

A separate thanks goes to Geri D and Kez A for being the biggest supporters of my cause. You both are an integral part of my life and I am proud to call you my friends.

A big shout-out goes to my beautiful editor, Krystal Nichol, for doing a fantastic job on this novel—you never cease to amaze me! Huge thanks to the fantastic team of talented artists at MiblArt for the stunning cover design. My gratitude goes to all the reviewers and valued members of my street team who help me with early promotion of my novels. Last but not least, a huge thanks to my readers and the shop owners who took a leap of faith and gave a chance to a new author.

To anyone I might have missed—thank you all for dreaming with me. Your support means the world.

ALSO BY ALENA JAMES

The Sorcerer's Protégée – book 1 of the Mistwalker Series

Check out the latest updates on www.alenajames.com